SINS OF THE SUFFRAGETTE

A Sam Klein Mystery

ALLAN LEVINE

GREAT PLAINS
PUBLICATIONS

Great Plains Fiction
An imprint of Great Plains Publications
3-161 Stafford Street
Winnipeg, MB R3M 2X9
www.greatplains.mb.ca

Great Plains Publications gratefully acknowledges the financial support
provided for its publishing program by the Government of Canada
through the Book Publishing Industry Development Program
(BPIDP); the Canada Council for the Arts; the Manitoba Department
of Culture, Heritage and Tourism; and the Manitoba Arts Council.

Design & Typography by Suzanne Gallant
Printed in Canada by Kromar Printing

CANADIAN CATALOGUING IN PUBLICATION DATA

Levine, Allan
Sins of the suffragette

  ISBN 1-894283-16-3

I.   Title.

PS8573.E96448 S56   2000   C813' .54 C00-920189-0
PR9199.3.L4674 S56   2000

In memory of my father Marvin Levine (1928-1993)

A child of Winnipeg's North End and a 'character' in every sense of the word. He always liked a good story…

Author's Note

TO REPEAT WHAT I WROTE in the first Sam Klein mystery, *The Blood Libel*, this is a work of fiction. The key events described in this book did not happen, nor were the major characters real people. I have, however, put real figures like Nellie McClung, the prominent women rights advocate, and John Dafoe, the editor of the *Manitoba Free Press*, among others, into the novel to give it a historical reality I believe is essential. And while, these characters did not always speak the words I have put in their mouths, I have tried to keep their attitudes and actions as historically accurate as possible. I believe that even Nellie McClung, a serious and devoted woman, but who also had a good sense of humour, would have found this tale rather entertaining.

Again, in reconstructing life in 1914, I relied on the newspapers of the day, archival material on the history of the women's movement in Manitoba as well as a wide range of books. These included: Alan Artibise, *Winnipeg: A Social History of Urban Growth 1874-1914 (1975);* Carol Lee Bacchi, *Liberation Deferred?: The Ideas of English-Canadian Suffragists 1877-1918 (1983);* Catherine Cleverdon, *The Woman Suffrage Movement in Canada (1950);* Rich Cohen, *Tough Jews (1998);* Christopher Dafoe, *Winnipeg: Heart of the Continent (1998);* James Gray, *The Boy From Winnipeg (1970);* Harry Gutkin, *Journey into Our Heritage (1980); and* Irving Howe, *World of Our Fathers (1976).*

Acknowledgements

I HAVE TO THANK A LONG LIST of friends and associates for allowing my detective Sam Klein to experience more adventures. For continuing to support my foray into fiction, my gratitude goes to Gregg Shilliday of Great Plains Publications and his friendly and helpful staff, marketing director Charmagne de Veer and office manager Jewls Dengl. Gregg and his company have become an important player in Manitoba's literary community and deservedly so.

Thanks also to Jack Templeman, curator of the Winnipeg Police Service's museum for answering more questions about the history of police work, and Winnipeg lawyer Saul Simmonds for advising me on legal issues.

For their advice and insightful comments on early versions of the manuscript, I owe much to mystery aficionados Henrietta Wilde and Gaylene Chestnut, the owners of Winnipeg's Whodunit Bookstore. My literary agent Jennifer Barclay patiently read and commented on the first draft as well as endured my daily barrage of e-mails. I am most appreciative for this work and for everything she has done to support my writing career during the past four years. Unfortunately for writers across Canada, Jennifer has decided to leave the book business. She will be missed more than she ever will know.

My heartfelt thanks, too, goes to Mark Morton for his masterful editing and suggestions. I regard his literary skills and talents as an immeasurable plus in the manuscript's ultimate transformation.

Finally, to my family, my wife Angie and our children, Alexander and Mia, I am grateful beyond words for their love and support; for their faith and conviction that "good things always come to those who wait," and for enduring the various ups and downs — usually cheerfully — that go with writing a book. Angie's advice about the flow of the story were the right ones, her ideas for the plot sound, and her instincts correct — as always, of course.

A.L.
Winnipeg, July 2000

"The wages of sin is death."
Romans, 7:23

1

Winnipeg, Canada
January 28, 1914

Winnipeg Tribune, Monday, January 26, 1914

OF INTEREST TO WOMEN

Mrs. Nellie McClung will lead a delegation of five — two women and three men — to the provincial legislature tomorrow afternoon to address Premier Roblin. Supporters of Mrs. McClung and her group include the Icelandic Women's Suffrage Association, the Grain Growers' Association, the W.C.T.U., the Trades and Labour Council, the Canadian Women's Press Club, and the Y.W.C.A. In her presentation, Mrs. McClung will urge the government to support women's suffrage.

THERE WAS NO MISTAKING the voices.

It was the sweetheart lovers.

Peering from the shadows of the alley, hidden from their view by a small shed used for trash, they stood clasping their grimy hands and pulling each other tight. At that moment they were oblivious to everyone but themselves. Did they know what people said about them? Did they care? So selfish. Through the drifting snowflakes, their voices carried far into the watching shadows.

"Antonio," she said. "Please not here. I must go into the theatre. Wasn't I clear? This has to stop."

He ignored her protests — he knew her better than that. Standing in the snow, sheltered from the cold January wind by the trash shed, his lips found hers and they kissed. She did not resist. He stroked her long blonde hair and then moved his hand lower.

"Not…"

Another kiss stifled her protests again. She tried to push him away, but he refused to budge.

"You know how I feel about you," he mumbled, releasing his grip slightly.

"I know," she said softly. "But there are things, so many things, you have no idea." She smiled and brushed her right hand over his cheek. He moved his lips close to hers and they kissed once again, longer. He attempted to run his hand through her hair, but as he did so his fingers caught her gold locket. The slender chain snapped and it fell to the ground.

"Can we meet after the show?" he asked. "At the hotel. You owe me that at least."

She nodded, then buried her face against his neck, pulling him nearer.

The snow muffled the footsteps that suddenly approached from the shadows. The figure stepped closer, then paused for a moment as if to study their silent embrace. They did not hear the anguished whisper — "Oh, Emily, why do you hurt me so?"

"Where is that woman?" Lila Mackenzie snapped to no one in particular. "She promised she'd be here an hour ago. Who's going to play the Leader of the Opposition? Not me, that's for certain. I knew she was unreliable. Didn't I tell you ladies, that woman is not really one of us. I'd say, to quote Nellie, that she has the 'mental calibre of a butterfly.' Her appearance is the only thing that matters. That and her inheritance…"

"That's quite enough, Lila," said Nellie McClung, an uncharacteristic harshness in her voice. A handsome dark-haired woman with deep, pene-trating eyes and a creamy-white complexion, Nellie at forty-one possessed an aura difficult to define. When she spoke, those around her listened. "Emily promised she would be here for the performance. It's only six o'clock. Let's give her another thirty minutes, shall we, before we panic. Name calling is quite beneath us, Lila."

At that reprimand, Lila Mackenzie pursed her lips while her face red-dened. "You know full well," Nellie continued, "that Emily is hardly the type of woman I was thinking of when I referred to silly young girls with minds of butterflies. She is eccentric, I will grant you that, but very intelligent."

"I meant no harm," said Lila.

"I realize you did not. We're all just a little nervous about tonight's performance. Have no fear, it will be sensational. What can go wrong? The Walker is sold out. I told the Premier yesterday that I would get him. I don't intend to let this marvellous opportunity go to waste."

"Yes, wonderful, Nellie," several of the women cheered.

"But we must always remember that as suffragists we have opted for a more moderate course than the one taken by our more militant suffragette sisters in Britain and the United States. There will be no shouting or marching tonight. We won't be docile or submissive, but we will be ladylike."

McClung paused to let the full meaning of her message sink in. "As for Emily," she continued, "I am quite sure that she will arrive in due course. Has anyone seen Grace Ellis yet? She must know where Emily is."

"She's late as well," called Francis Beynon from the back of the theatre's main dressing room.

"No, she told me she had an errand to run for her father and would be here precisely at 6:20 p.m.," offered Francis's older sister, Lillian Thomas.

The Walker's dressing room in the basement of the theatre was a dimly lit room with a row of mirrors, narrow green tables and chairs. It was used nearly every night except Sunday by singers, dancers, acrobats, musicians, comedy actors and actresses, even animals on occasion. But tonight, Winnipeg's premier vaudeville theatre, an Edwardian palace with rosetted lights, crystal chandeliers and crimson plush seats, was to feature the city's suffragists singing and acting.

The highlight of that evening's full programme was to be two delicious and witty satires. "How They Won the Vote" was a skit originally performed by suffragettes in London, but adapted by the women for a local audience. That was to be followed by the *piece de resistance*, a "Mock Parliament" in which roles and situations were reversed. The concept, Nellie had assured them, was brilliant: stage a parliamentary debate about men's demands for the franchise and use the male politicians' own words to make them look like fools. Not surprisingly, Nellie McClung had been the unanimous choice to play the part of the Premier — more than loosely modelled after the Manitoba Premier Sir Rodmond Roblin — while Emily Powers was to play the Liberal opposition leader, Tobias Norris.

The women hadn't rehearsed much. It was just the day before that Nellie and her delegation had delivered a pro-suffragist presentation to the Premier, only to be patronized with his usual bluster. Upon leaving the meeting, Nellie had warned, "I believe we'll get you soon, Sir Rodmond!" and she intended to fulfil her promise.

The conversation in the dressing room turned back to Emily and the weather. "There's a lot of snow on the ground. Perhaps the street car became stuck," said Nellie reassuringly. "Why just last week, it took me more than a hour to get home. There was so much snow that the Electric Company's revolving brushes couldn't move."

"That happened to me as well," said Jane Hample.

"Me too," added Gertrude Simpson. "My husband had to hire a horse and sleigh."

A knock on the door ended the discussion. Jane Hample ran to open it. Grace Ellis, tall, with broad shoulders, long legs and a slim but full figure, stood in the doorway. Her jet-black hair was done up in a tight bun, as it usually was. She was slightly dishevelled but clearly delighted to see everyone. Grace had a sensuous, though entirely natural, appeal about her.

At twenty-four, she had been a suffragist for about two years. She helped her father manage his Grosvenor Street apartment, but Nellie had been encouraging her to attend university.

"You have a sharp mind, Grace, and would make a wonderful lawyer," McClung had told her only a week before. "In order to practice you'd have to move to Ontario or New Brunswick. Still, you should definitely consider this option. And the Manitoba Bar will eventually relent, so remaining in Winnipeg is not entirely out of the question."

Grace appreciated the support, though the time wasn't right for her to leave her father alone. Her mother Mary had recently died and she had been taking care of her father.

"Grace, wonderful," said Jane. "We were all growing concerned."

"Ladies, I apologize for being so late. My father insisted I pick up this package for him at Ashdown's before they closed," she said holding up a small box wrapped in brown paper. "And then the street car on Main was stuck." Several women nodded their heads. "I had to walk from Portage Avenue," Grace continued. "The snow is awful tonight. I hope this won't deter the crowd."

"We're sold out," declared Nellie. "They'll all be here, have no fear. Now what of Emily?"

"I don't know," replied Grace. "We spoke earlier in the day. She said she had to do some shopping at Carsley's and Eaton's, and then was planning to be here by 5:30 or so. I'm sure she just lost track of time."

"Perhaps she's with *him*," sneered Lila Mackenzie.

"Oh, Lila, you shouldn't listen to such gossip," sighed Jane Hample.

"It's true, all of it, isn't it Grace?" insisted Lila. "You're her friend, you should know."

"Lila Mackenzie, you are a silly fool," Grace declared.

"But I know someone who's seen her with that Italian. They were going into the Clarendon Hotel together at two in the afternoon."

"That is very unfair," Nellie stated, rather annoyed. "Unless you've seen her with another man with your own two eyes, I'd suggest you hush up. Have you seen her with any man but her husband?"

Lila shook her head.

"Very well," added Nellie. "Then we'll have no more of this gossip. For now let's concentrate on beating the men who oppose us, not each other."

Accustomed to McClung's wisdom, the other women, including Lila Mackenzie, nodded with approval.

By show time, Emily still hadn't appeared. It was decided — actually Nellie McClung commanded — that Francis Beynon would act as the Leader of the Opposition, and Grace Ellis, who was to have only a minor role as a backbencher, would play in Beynon's role as Deputy-Leader of the Opposition. Grace was upset about Emily's continued absence but agreed with McClung's request.

"I'm sure she just lost track of the time as you said," Nellie reassured her.

"I suppose, but I'm getting worried. As soon as we're done here, I'm going to go look for her."

"And I will help you. But first, we have to think of the audience."

As Nellie had predicted, the Walker was overflowing with people. For about forty-five minutes, a steady stream of horse-drawn sleighs had rundled by, the jingling bells on the steeds heard for blocks in every direction. It was mainly a middle-class crowd that evening, supportive women from River Heights and the nearby city of Tuxedo, with their reluctant husbands in tow. Noticeably absent were women from the North End.

"Let us hope that someday they will make good Canadians," McClung was fond of saying. "But for now, we cannot concern ourselves with the concerns of Galician and Hebrew women. There is more important work to be done."

Among the handful of North Enders who did attend the show were Sam and Sarah Klein. While she looked radiant in an ivory gown, Sarah was hardly pleased to be at the Walker that night. Not that she didn't love vaudeville. A life time ago, or so it seemed now, when she had worked for Madam Melinda at the house on Rachel Street, she had spent many happy evenings at the theatre. Then Sarah revelled in being the city's most expensive whore — and in the shocked stares and gasps she provoked whenever she visited a public place.

But tonight, now that she was "Mrs. Sam Klein," the middle-class moralists who packed the hall — and who were even now engaged in earnest discussions about the evils of alcohol, immigrants, and brothels — were definitely not her cup of tea.

"I don't know how you can even consider not going," Klein had declared earlier in the day. "Emily expects you to be there. What kind of friend are you?"

"Please don't lecture me on friendship, Sam. Emily understands how I feel about her. You know my reasons…."

"Frankly, your arguments are getting stale. How do you expect the world to accept the new Sarah Klein, if you can't accept her yourself?"

Sarah had only shrugged in reply. She knew she had made efforts to fit in to her new world. Three months before, Emily had invited her to a suffragist meeting and she had reluctantly attended. It was a disaster. Nowhere had she felt so unwelcome as at that gathering. The stares, whispers, slurs against Jews. Emily could only apologize for her friends' behaviour.

Eventually, Sarah had caved in to Klein's relentless arguments and they hopped a streetcar heading downtown to the Walker. Once she was inside the theatre, Sarah couldn't help but glance up at the first row in the balcony, traditionally the section in the theatre reserved for Winnipeg's ladies of the evening. She smiled to herself. Klein noticed her lingering stare, but said nothing.

"Come, our seats are in row 15. This way."

Klein, too, at thirty-one, with his sharp face and tall angular body, had a certain dignified presence, albeit a bit rough and ready. Despite his best efforts to adopt the more sophisticated appearance of an accomplished professional detective — he now wore a black bowler hat — he hadn't quite lost the hard edges that had made him so effective as a whorehouse bouncer and trouble-shooter.

Unlike his wife, Klein hardly minded being seen in public since his latest escapade. Two weeks before, his army of young informants — gangs of teenage boys who idolized him — had provided him with a tip that had led to the recapture of murderer and bank robber Jack Krafchenko at the Burriss block at 686 Toronto Street.

Not the most brilliant of criminal minds, Krafchenko, a Ukrainian immigrant who had grown up in the small town of Plum Coulee, Manitoba, had robbed the town bank in late November of 1913, killing the bank's manager in the process. With $4700 stuffed into a grain sack, Krafchenko had fled to Winnipeg where he passed himself off as a lecturer from St. John's College. Eventually, on December 10, the police caught up with him — after one of his friends had informed on him — and he was arrested and held for trial. But Krafchenko had other plans. With the assistance of a guard at the Rupert Station jail, who provided him with a gun and rope, Krafchenko was set to lower himself from the station wall. Yet typical of his usual bumbling, the frayed rope broke as he climbed out the window and he fell forty-five feet to the ground, twisting his knee. His lawyer, Percy Hagel, was waiting below with a get-away car and drove his injured client to a hiding place.

Angry at the police for allowing this murderer to escape, town officials at Plum Coulee hired Sam Klein to find him, much to the dissatisfaction of the new Winnipeg police chief Donald MacPherson.

"Stay out of our way," MacPherson had told Klein, "or I'll have you arrested."

"Chief, you're just angry because the man you hired as a special adviser turned out to be a crook," Klein had retorted.

"Sure, it was a bad decision. We thought we could trust Jack. We were wrong. That still doesn't give you the freedom to hinder our investigation."

In Klein's view, hiring Jack Krafchenko as a "robbery consultant" upon his release from Stony Mountain ranked as one of the more foolish acts in the history of the Winnipeg police force. In any event, he wasn't about to be deterred by MacPherson's threats. Besides, he needed the work and the publicity this case could conceivably bring him.

The sensational "Blood Libel" murder case — in which Klein had proved the innocence of Rabbi Aaron Davidovitch but exposed his family friend Isaac Hirsch as the real killer of young Anna Rudnicki — had wrapped up nearly three years ago. Since then, Klein had spent months tracking down his clients' long lost relatives or spying on their suspected cheating spouses. It was hardly the glamorous detective work he had hoped for. Not to mention that most of the time he was barely making a living.

There were days when Klein contemplated giving it up for another line of work. Yet the thought of being a clerk in a store on Selkirk Avenue or hawking merchandise on the street like some common peddler did not appeal to him in the least. Typically, he kept these thoughts to himself, not even sharing them with his wife. Most of the time Sarah told him that he was being too cocky. She was right, but that was the way his clients preferred him. For some reason, it reassured them.

In any event, he relished the excitement of the Krafchenko case.

Thanks to information supplied to him by the teenage boys as well as by a bartender at the Brunswick — who had heard one of Krafchenko's pals talking too loudly — it took Klein only about a week to track down the elusive fugitive. By then, Krafchenko had holed up in a room in a west-end apartment block. Although Krafchenko had a gun, Klein was able to subdue him with little trouble. He had also shrewdly informed the *Tribune's* John Maloney of the impending capture, so the reporter was there to record the event.

The day after Krafchenkco was arrested, two photographs appeared in the *Tribune* of a smiling Klein handing over Krafchenko to the Winnipeg police. "This time," Klein was quoted as saying, "let's try to keep him locked up." Klein had surprised himself with his smug tone, but he also knew that if he did not promote his various talents, no one was going to do it for him.

Weeks later, Klein was still a celebrity. When he and Sarah entered the Walker that evening, he was greeted by cheers and friendly waves. There was even talk that Plum Coulee was going to declare January 18, the day Krafchenko was captured, "Sam Klein Day."

"Way to go, Sam!" one female admirer yelled. The detective waved and smiled.

"Excuse me, sir, " a boy of about thirteen asked Klein as he and Sarah sat down. "Could you sign my program?" He handed Klein a pencil and a single piece of paper.

Sarah shook her head in disbelief. Klein signed his name as the women walked on to the stage.

Even without Emily, the show went off without a hitch. The Assiniboine Quartet opened the festivities with several catchy suffragette songs and then the curtain rose for "How They Won the Vote." The premise of the skit was for a group of women, all related to a clerk named Horace Cole, to convert Horace to a rabid suffragist. For thirty hilarious minutes, his wife, sister and cousin bombard Horace with slogans and arguments until he is ready to enlist in the movement.

An intermission followed before the curtain opened again and Nellie and her cadre appeared on stage decorated like a legislative assembly. The lady members of the House wore simple black robes that reached their knees, though they did not quite conceal their lovely gowns.

"Remember," Nellie told the audience as the show got underway, "life on the stage is reversed. Women have the vote while men do not."

Petitions were the first order of House business, and one by the "Society for the Prevention of Ugliness" entreated "that men wearing scarlet neckties, six-inch collars and squeaky shoes be not allowed to enter any public building." Other discussions revolved around why women leave men. "Because they do not keep the house attractive," was one answer given, prompting the crowd to roar with laughter.

The climax of the festivities was a delegation of men led by Robert Skinner arriving at the legislature with a petition for male suffrage. Their slogan was "We have the brains. Why not let us vote?" In the same way that Premier Roblin had addressed the women a day earlier, "Premier" McClung now addressed the gaggle of men in a voice dripping with sarcasm.

"We like delegations," McClung began. "We have seen a great many and we pride ourselves on treating these delegations with the greatest courtesy and candour. We wish to compliment this delegation on their splendid gentlemanly appearance." The audience snickered loudly. "If, without exercising the vote, such splendid specimens of manhood can be produced, such a system of affairs should not be questioned. Any system of civilization that can produce such paragons of manhood as Mr. Skinner is good enough for me, and if it is good enough for me, it is good enough for anybody."

Nellie was hardly done, but she had to wait until the laughter subsided before she could continue. She played the crowd like a seasoned vaudevillian. As the debate swung back and forth between the government and the male delegation, McClung finally added to the utter delight of the audience: "Another trouble is that if men start to vote they will vote too much. Politics unsettles men and unsettled men mean unsettled bills, broken furniture, broken vows and divorce…"

Lying in the alley behind the Walker, she could hear the roars of laughter tumble from the theatre. But try as she might, she couldn't move her legs or arms. Her body was in agony, more pain than she had ever felt. She attempted to cry out, but her mouth was full of blood. In fact, her clothes were soaked through with it. She rolled her head to one side, and saw him lying face down in clumps of red snow. "Oh Antonio," she cried to herself. "What have I done to you?" He did not move.

All she could remember was a terrible confrontation. Then there was a knife. Slashing at her, slashing at Antonio, over and over. She had watched him die. Images of Antonio, and then Alfred, swirled in her head.

A cold wind blew across her pale face. Her breath became short and rapid. The pain was excruciating, searing, and then suddenly gone. Emily Munro Powers lay dead in the snowy streets, taking her secrets with her.

"I don't know, Sam," said Sarah as they braced themselves for the cold air outside the theatre.

"You don't know what?" Klein asked, attempting to light a cigarette in the winter wind.

"I don't know if these women will ever understand just how false and insincere they are. I haven't been in this country long, and I do appreciate what they are trying to achieve, but still it seems to me…"

Klein inhaled deeply on his cigarette.

Sarah sensed the sudden tension, but ignored it. "…that if they want real success, they'll have to open up their little club to everyone, including women like me, an ex-lady of the street — as terrible as that might be. All that ranting about liquor, whores, and immigrants won't achieve a thing. I don't want our daughter — "

"Our daughter? And what if we have a son? Come to think of it, when are we having children?"

"May I finish?"

He shrugged.

"I don't want our daughter growing up feeling like she's beneath those uppity middle class women."

"You done?"

Sarah smiled sweetly and took hold of Klein's arm. "I am."

"First of all you don't have to worry about our daughter."

"And why's that?"

"Because, my lovely wife, our daughter will be Sam Klein's daughter and that will make her feel special from the day she is born."

Sarah laughed. "How about a coffee at the Child's?"

"Sounds like a good idea to me. Maybe we can talk more about when this family of ours is going to come along."

No one served a better cup of coffee in Winnipeg than the cafe in the Child's Building, a block from the corner of Portage and Main.

Sarah knew that Klein wasn't eager to have children just yet, and she herself worried about being able to become pregnant. Her past, she feared, was going to catch up to her. "Where do you suppose Emily's been all this time?" she asked, changing the subject.

Klein shrugged. "Who knows? Missing the show — it's not like her at all."

Sarah was about to respond when a scream suddenly pierced the cold night air.

Instantly, Klein took hold of Sarah's hand and ran with her towards the sound of the scream. A crowd of people had already gathered in a nearby alley to stare at a grisly sight.

"Let me through," Klein demanded.

He manoeuvred his way to the front and gasped in shock when he saw two bodies lying there, a light skiff of snow frosting their faces.

"Maybe 'Bloody Jack' did this!" shouted one younger man.

Klein turned and glared at him, but the man was oblivious to the poor taste of his remark.

"Sam, what is it?" asked Sarah, behind him. "What do you see?"

Klein turned, his face grim. "It's Emily."

"Emily?"

"And that young Italian."

"What are you talking about?"

Sarah pushed herself forward and then covered her mouth with her hands. "Oh my God! Sam, my God…Emily."

Antonio Rossi lay on his side. Emily was beside him on her back, her skirt hiked around her hips. Klein watched as an elderly bystander kneeled to drape his coat over the bodies.

"Hold on," Klein said, stepping closer and pulling the man back. "You'll disturb the evidence."

The commotion had already attracted the attention of a police constable out on his evening patrol.

"What seems to be the problem?" asked Constable John O'Shea, tall and broad-shouldered. He appeared even larger in his Cossack fur police hat and huge knee-length brown buffalo coat, a trademark of the Winnipeg force since its earliest days. It was the only way to stay warm during the winter. His moustache was stiff with frost.

"Two people. They've been killed. There's blood all over the snow," said one woman.

O'Shea moved to the scene of the crime where he saw Klein standing beside the bodies.

"Klein, get away from there," ordered O'Shea. "What are you doing here?"

Klein stared at the constable. His relations with the Winnipeg Police Department had never been great. For a few weeks after the "Blood Libel" case, Klein had been a welcome visitor around the Rupert Avenue station. Then Chief MacRae had retired and was replaced by Donald MacPherson, the former Deputy Chief and a man suspicious of Klein's attempt to become a private detective. In MacPherson's view, Klein was a troublemaker — a Hebrew one at that — a nuisance and a hindrance to the pursuit of justice. Despite the objections of Detective Bill McCreary and retired Detective Michael Stark, the new Chief ordered that Klein be severely reprimanded, even arrested, if he got in the way of his constables' work. Klein's recent role in recapturing Jack Krafchenko merely made MacPherson angrier.

Klein glared at O'Shea, but for the moment remained silent.

"I'm talking to you Klein, what do you know about this?" O'Shea repeated.

"There's two dead people over there," Klein said, opening his silver cigarette case. "I'd say they've been stabbed. What do you think?"

"I think you know who these dead people are. And if you don't start talking straight, you'll find yourself down at the station."

"Tell him, Sam," urged Sarah.

While Klein debated whether or not to co-operate, O'Shea turned to a young man wearing spectacles and asked him to run down to Smith Street to place a call with the police signal box. The young man's eyes lit up, and he trotted off. Citizens of the Winnipeg were impressed by the unique communication system now at the disposal of their police officers. More than 200,000 feet of underground and overhead cable instantly connected patrolling constables to headquarters. Mayor Tom Deacon liked to boast that Winnipeg was the first city in North America to install such a progressive communications network and only the third in the world to use it. "We are in the same league as Berlin and Rio de Janeiro," claimed Deacon.

"So, Klein," said O'Shea, turning back to the detective.

Klein inhaled deeply on his cigarette and blew out a white puff of smoke that lingered in the cold. "The woman," he began slowly, "you should know. Her name is Emily Powers. She's the wife of Alfred Powers."

O'Shea nodded, "Of course. I knew I recognized her. She's much younger than her husband."

"Good observation."

"And the man?"

"Antonio Rossi. I believe he's connected to an Italian storekeeper near Bannatyne and Main. I didn't know him that well."

"A wop Casanova, that figures. Something going on between the two of them?"

Klein didn't respond.

"You know something about this, ma'am?" O'Shea asked Sarah with feigned civility. Everyone on the force knew about Sarah Klein — or at least who she used to be.

"Say nothing," advised Klein.

"Honestly, Constable, I'm not certain."

"Do either of you know the whereabouts of Mr. Powers?"

"No," replied Klein. "Why don't you wait for the real detectives to get here, before you start casting aspersions like that," Klein said.

"And I think you and the missus better stay right where you are. I'm certain the Chief will want to have a word with you. He'll probably want to send John Jordan along as well. I think we got a case for our morality inspector. But you're an expert on that too, aren't you Klein?"

Klein ignored the taunt, though he too wondered what had gone on here. But surely Alfred Powers could not be involved in the bloody mess that now caked the boots of everyone in sight.

2

Manitoba Free Press, Monday, January 26, 1914

MANITOBA CLUB NEWS

At the annual meeting of the Manitoba Club held last Thursday evening, Mr. Alfred Powers was elected the club's new president. This will be the second time Mr. Powers, a prominent city lawyer, will serve as the organization's chief executive. Well-known to the Winnipeg business and legal community, Mr. Powers is also on the board of the Great West Life Assurance Corporation, the Bank of Montreal and the St. Charles Country Club. He and his wife Emily are planning to host this year's spring ball at the Royal Alexandra Hotel.

IT TOOK ABOUT thirty minutes for the official entourage to arrive at the murder scene in a large horse-drawn sleigh-carriage belonging to the department. As always, they exited the rig according to rank. First off was Chief MacPherson, a no-nonsense Scot with a thick black moustache speckled with white. With his winter hat pulled low over his forehead, he did not look particularly happy. MacPherson had joined the Winnipeg force in 1903 when he emigrated from Kilmarnock, Scotland, just south of Glasgow. He started as a beat constable, but thanks to his prior experience as a police officer in Scotland, he rapidly advanced through the ranks. Chief McRae had appointed him his deputy in 1911, and there had never been any doubt that the Board of Police Commissioners would promote MacPherson to chief when McRae retired.

Two detectives, also wrapped in buffalo coats, followed MacPherson. There was Bill McCreary, an intimidating veteran who angered easily, played favourites, and sometimes used physical force to obtain a confession, but was regarded by his fellow officers as the best detective in the department. He had a natural gift for understanding how criminals think and possessed a keen insight into their behaviour. His key role in solving the "Blood Libel" case hadn't gone unnoticed by city officials — including the fact that he had almost been killed in the line of duty — nor by Sam Klein, who had reluctantly learned to trust McCreary's instincts. The two men would never be good friends, though they had a tacit agreement to share information. No one on the force, including Chief MacPherson, knew anything about McCreary's working relationship with Klein, and McCreary intended to keep it that way.

As he arrived at the crime scene, McCreary immediately saw Klein and his wife standing to the side. The two men glanced at each other, but that was all. No words were exchanged.

Behind McCreary was his new partner, Alex Taber. At thirty-four, Taber was tall and well groomed, from the top of his bowler hat to the tip of his shiny black boots. He was a striking figure in a three-piece suit and popular with the ladies. More remarkable, however, was that Alex Taber was actually Aleksei Taburov, a Russian immigrant. He had come to New York with his parents when he was still a young boy, added English to the five European languages he already spoke — and eventually become a police officer in the Lower East Side.

He owed his rank and presence in Winnipeg to Chief MacPherson. Dissatisfied with the department's dealings with the burgeoning North End population, MacPherson reasoned that a detective who understood "those people" — as he called the Russians, Ukrainians, Lithuanians, Jews, Germans, and Galicians — might have success in lowering the North End's high crime rate. It wasn't just public drunkenness, the most common infraction, that concerned the chief. Recently in the North End there had been far too much theft, gaming, opium use, assault and even murder. Not to mention there was the daily debauchery in the Point Douglas brothels. MacPherson knew why and how his predecessor, Chief McRae, had made a deal with the local Madams to control the problem — he was just not happy about it.

One of the first things MacPherson did after he had assumed command was to find a recruit talented enough to deal with Winnipeg's "alien problem." Through a police contact in Chicago, he learned about the unique qualifications of Officer Taber of the New York Police Department and courted him with a promotion to the rank of detective and a salary of $120 per month — $40 more than he was making walking the beat in the Lower East Side.

For Taber, there wasn't much to think about. His parents had both died and there was no special woman in his life tying him down. His "collection," as he referred to them — a group of about seven women, both single and married, along with a few Jewish prostitutes that he regularly visited — would have to survive without him. And the bitter winters for which Canada was famous wasn't an issue. He remembered the cold Russian weather and welcomed a return to it.

"Such temperatures build character," Taber maintained when questioned about his decision by his skeptical New York superiors. "It makes a man feel like he is alive."

It wasn't only Taber's willingness to adapt that made him an attractive candidate for MacPherson, but also his approach to controlling the foreign population.

"You must ensure by whatever means that they always know who is in control of their miserable lives," he had told the Chief. "Only then will they respect law and order and life will be tolerable. And the Jews, you must watch them the closest. They are conniving and manipulative. Personally, I wouldn't trust any of them. There's no doubt in my mind that Jews are responsible for the urban blight that cities like New York and Winnipeg face each day, as well as the anarchy and revolution now threatening the world. Know this, that if there is a war in Europe between the great powers, as many predict, it will be the fault of a Jew somewhere. I guarantee it. Capitalists, whoremongers and revolutionaries, that's what they are."

From Chief MacPherson's point of view, pairing someone like Taber with Bill McCreary made perfect sense. McCreary's long-time partner, Michael Stark, had retired, and finding another detective who could put up with McCreary's brash temperament wasn't easy. The Chief was certain that the two men, who shared similar opinions about immigration problems, would work well together. The past few months had proved him right. Though it took a bit of time for McCreary to accept that his new partner was neither Canadian-born, nor of British or Scottish stock, he had to admit that Taber was his match when it came to intimidation tactics.

The fourth and last member of the investigating team was the burly John Jordan, the city's Morality Inspector. Jordan, a big-framed balding man, had the appearance of a kindly uncle or preacher. Nevertheless, he took his work seriously. A beat constable and a good one, he had been plucked off the streets by former Chief McRae in late 1911 to head the restructured Morality Division. His assignment was to police and clamp down on serious violations in the Point Douglas "red light" district. That meant no ladies being rowdy outdoors and ensuring that blinds and drapes were pulled tight at each and every brothel.

As Klein heard it from Madam Melinda, however, Jordan had a weak spot for a young brunette named Katie whom he visited now and again.

"He's in and out quickly, if you know what I mean," Melinda had told Klein with smirk. "But he looks the other way at our gambling tables. Never seen a more satisfied client than Jordan. I'd love to let his wife in on the secret."

Jordan may have looked the other way when it came to gambling in Melinda's back room, but not elsewhere. He had established a reputation for being a fervent anti-gaming crusader. At any hour of the day or night, he and his men would appear unannounced at various hotels in order to break up a game of poker and arrest the perpetrators.

Only one game in the city was off-limits to Jordan by a special order of the Police Commission. That was the high-stakes poker game regularly convened at an apartment on fashionable Roslyn Road and attended by civic politicians, business executives, grain brokers and some of the wealthiest gentlemen in the city. It wasn't uncommon for $500 to be wagered on a single hand.

Jordan's official motto was "Uplift." As he put it, "Whenever a person, previously of good character, is seen in bad company, he or she is notified of the undesirableness of the companionship which they are keeping, and are assisted in every way possible to lead a better life and become a useful member of society." The hypocrisy of his own words eluded him.

As Constable O'Shea briefed the chief and his detectives about the murder, Jordan nodded his head knowingly.

"What is it, John?" asked MacPherson.

"Can't say I'm surprised to find the two of them lying here like this. I've been keeping my eye on Mrs. Powers for some time. My informants on the street told me she had been seen with the Italian. I tried talking to her about it just last week. I told her I was going to go to her husband. But she ignored me. As for Rossi, he was a hot-blooded troublemaker, maybe a pimp as well. Anything to make a few dollars. More than once, I heard he was causing problems down at the CPR yards, telling the other wops to stand up for their rights, start a union. The 'prentice' boys weren't happy with his meddling."

"You think a machinist could have done this to a big Italian?" asked the Chief.

"Not one by himself, but a gang of them. Maybe they caught up with him here in the alley. It's possible."

"What about Mr. Powers?" interrupted O'Shea.

MacPherson ignored his constable's comment and turned to McCreary and Taber. "You got any preliminary thoughts?"

"I don't think any gang of CPR boys did this," said McCreary with a tone of authority. "Look at the snow around the body. Even with the light snowfall, it's still too clean. I'd say this was a one-person crime, probably someone they both knew. Maybe the husband."

O'Shea nodded his head.

"And what about you, Alex?" MacPherson asked the other detective.

Taber reached inside his bulky coat and drew out a cigarette, though his eyes did not leave the two murder victims.

"Taber, did you hear me?" the Chief asked again. "What do you make of this?"

"Yeah, I hear you. I was trying to piece something together." He casually lit his cigarette and looked toward Klein and Sarah. "Maybe the husband. It makes sense. He found out about his young wife playing with the wop and decided to take matters into his own hands."

"Exactly," said McCreary. "O'Shea, you find any weapon, yet?"

"No, sir."

"You are looking for a knife about this big," said McCreary drawing his hands apart. "Like a knife to carve a turkey at Christmas."

"I was going to add," continued Taber, "that we could save ourselves some work by questioning our Hebrew friend, the eminent detective."

By this time, Sarah was shivering and Klein had stood in the snow long enough. "You got a question for me, Taber, ask. Because in about two minutes, I'm taking my wife home. That woman lying there was her friend."

"Doesn't surprise me," said Taber.

"Pardon?"

"You heard what I said. Your wife was a friend of the slut. It makes sense."

"Don't, Sam," said Sarah. "He's not worth it."

"If I were you, Alex, I wouldn't provoke him," added McCreary.

"He doesn't scare me."

"Have it your way."

"Am I your partner? Or is Klein? I know you two have worked together."

"In the past, once. That's it."

"Enough of this," said MacPherson. "Klein, what do you know about the murder?"

Klein shrugged. "Nothing. Like I told your constable, my wife and I were at the women's show at the Walker tonight. When we came out, this is what I found," he said pointing at the bodies. "It's true that my wife and I were friends of the Powers, but I don't know anything more. If I do, you'll be the first person I'll tell. Now, if there's nothing else, you know where to find me."

Constable O'Shea moved closer to the Kleins, as if he intended to block their path.

"Leave them," ordered MacPherson. "Klein, I've told you this before. Stay out of our way or you'll find yourself in trouble. Leave the detective work to professionals."

Klein took Sarah's arm and began to walk in the direction of Portage Avenue. Then he abruptly stopped, left Sarah, and walked back towards Taber. He whispered something to him in Russian. Taber's fists clenched, then he turned his head and spit. Klein smiled and strolled back to Sarah.

"What was all that about?" asked McCreary.

"It was a threat, imagine that. The Jew threatened me!"

"Yeah, imagine that," repeated McCreary.

"I hate to interrupt your conversation, gentlemen, but I want answers. O'Shea, get these bodies over to Dr. Macdonald at the McIntyre Block."

"Right away, sir. An ambulance is on the way."

"Good. Bill, you and Alex see if you can make any headway with the murder weapon. John, you and I are going to pay a visit to the Powers household." He turned to the constable. "O'Shea."

"Yes, Sir."

"Once you have dealt with this mess, round up another five men and meet us at Alfred Power's home on Wellington Crescent. I think we might need some assistance with a search of the premises."

Sarah and Klein sat in silence on the streetcar ride home. It was already eleven o'clock and both were tired.

"Poor Emily," Sarah finally said, as the streetcar plodded its way down Main Street toward the North End. "I just can't believe it."

"Well, believe it. It happened."

"You sound like those damn detectives."

At that, two women at the front of the car turned and stared in Sarah's direction.

"You keep using that language in public," Klein admonished his wife, "and…"

"And what?"

"And you'll keep getting stares like that. I told you, you're not at Melinda's any more."

"Sam, stop the lecture. Please not tonight."

"What do you know about her and the Italian?"

"His name is Antonio."

"Okay, what do you know about Antonio?"

Sarah hesitated for a moment. "As much as you. I knew she was seeing him. She told me…she told me he was willing to do anything she desired. That, as she put it, he was a wonderful *paramour.* "

"What the hell does that mean?"

"It's French for lover."

"And?"

Before Sarah could respond, the streetcar had reached the corner of Burrows and Main Street. For the North End, Burrows Avenue, with its row of side-by-side wooden frame houses, was a slightly better neighbourhood than most of the surrounding streets. Some of the residents actually owned the houses they lived in and that meant fences were standing upright and paths were cleared of snow. In the backyards, there were stables for horses and occasionally an attached shop. The most popular of these small enterprises was Frankie Fontana's fix-it shop at 452 Burrows, where it was possible to get anything and everything repaired — from a broken wagon wheel to a pair of pants. The Lees, a few doors down, who operated the only laundry service on the street, also had a steady stream of customers, no matter what the season. In the winter, the billowing steam from the tubs could be seen for blocks.

At this late hour, Burrows was relatively quiet. White smoke drifted from brick chimneys and hovered overhead before dissipating into the cold night air.

Occasionally, as Klein and Sarah trekked the five blocks to their apartment on McGregor, they could hear muffled fragments of conversations, Ukrainian from one house, Polish from another, and Yiddish from a third. They barely noticed this Babel of languages, a cacophony heard ten hours a day on the streets and playgrounds of the North End.

At Strathcona School on McGregor and Alfred, where the neighbourhood children attended, there were many days near the beginning of each school year when the teacher was the only one in the class who could speak English. For weeks she would speak to her students very slowly, using hand gestures and drawing on the chalkboard, until her class of young immigrants understood the rudiments of the language. How to make them into good Canadian citizens was the real challenge for such educators, though there were no easy answers.

Sarah clutched Klein's arm as they headed up the icy path to the Lady Angela apartment block. The unique name had been the idea of owner Sidney Vineberg, a second-generation Jewish Winnipegger. In the late 1870s, his father, Hiram, had emigrated from a small town in Russia to Portage la Prairie, just west of the city. A brilliant man, Hiram Vineberg was one of the first Jewish physicians on the prairies.

Sidney, on the other hand, had caused an uproar in his family several years before when he married his childhood sweetheart, the very Catholic Katherine Taylor, and then named their daughter — who arrived only seven months after the wedding ceremony — Angela. Sidney owned about six houses spread all over the North End, but the Lady Angela, like his young curly-haired daughter, was his pride and joy. He and Klein got along well — that is, as long as Klein paid his rent on time. Sidney loved to be regaled with details about Klein's detective work, and Sam did not mind humouring him from time to time.

"I wonder if Emily had any relatives who need to be notified," said Sarah. "She never talked about her family, even with me. And the poor Rossi family. Antonio's death is going to hurt them so much."

"Come, Sarah, inside."

Just as Klein turned the key in the door, Sarah fell back into him, a look of horror on her face.

"What is it?" demanded Klein. Then Sam saw for himself. There in the corner of the foyer stood his old friend Alfred Powers, dazed and in an obvious stupor. There was blood all over his torn coat and pants. Even the left side of his face was smeared. And in his right hand, with a black handle and stained steel blade, was a large knife, the kind of knife, Klein thought to himself, that you'd use to carve a turkey.

3

Winnipeg Tribune, Monday, June 10, 1912

THE SOCIAL WHIRL

A large wedding took place at Holy Trinity Church, Saturday evening at 7 o'clock when Miss Emily Munro of Chicago became the bride of Mr. Alfred Powers. Archdeacon Octave Fortin performed the ceremony.

The bride was a picture of beauty as she walked down the aisle on the arm of her good friend, Sam Klein, Winnipeg's own dashing private detective, as Mr. P.R. MacLagen played the wedding march. Her wedding gown was of white ivory satin and was caught up at the sides; a wreath of orange blossoms held her veil in place, and she carried a beautiful shower bouquet of brides' roses.

The bridesmaid was Miss Grace Ellis, a suffragist sister of the bride. She wore a lovely gown of shell pink charmeuse trimmed with gold and shadow lace, and carried a bouquet of pink roses. Graham Powers, the bridegroom's son, acted as best man. Miss Elizabeth Powers, daughter of the bridegroom, sang "Beloved it is Morn," during the signing of the register.

After the ceremony, a large number of guests attended the reception at the magnificent crystal ballroom of the Royal Alexandra Hotel.

Mr and Mrs. Alfred Powers left on the 10:30 p.m. Golden State Train for a three-week holiday in San Francisco.

IT WAS AS IF she had appeared from nowhere. "Just dropped from the heavens," was how Grace Ellis, Mabel Johnson, Francis Beynon, and other fine, hard-working middle-class suffragists usually put it. Then again, few people in Winnipeg — or rather, the people that counted — could remember when Emily Munro was not an integral part of their lives. From the moment she had stepped off the train from Chicago on a cold day in November of 1911, Emily had been a force to be reckoned with.

She was everywhere or so it seemed. During the past several months, few names turned up as much in the *Tribune's* "Social Whirl" column as Miss Emily Munro. If she wasn't raising money for the General Hospital as a member of the Ladies Auxiliary or one of the other half-dozen charities she supported, then she was campaigning for women's rights or participating at the Winnipeg Literary Club commenting on new works by D.H. Lawrence, F.M. Mayor or Edith Wharton.

Mayor's new book, *The Third Miss Symons*, especially appealed to Emily with its realistic portrayals of marriage and single life. There were pitfalls to both options. Single life as a middle-class woman in the United States or Canada was far from perfect. But Emily had seen far too many women enslaved and miserable in unhappy marriages. She wasn't going to make the same mistake. Long before she had met Alfred Powers, she decided that marriage, if it happened at all, would be on her terms. No man was going to dictate how she lived her life — tell her who friends could be, where she could work, or what she could read. She wasn't going to wake up one day wondering why the man lying next to her in bed had absolute control over her life.

Arriving in Winnipeg, she had rented a tastefully-furnished two-bedroom suite at the Grosvenor Court at the corner of Grosvenor and Stafford for only $35 a month, a real bargain. The landlord, Grace Ellis's father Frank, had wanted to charge $45, and in fact the suite, with its large opulent fireplace and beautiful oak trim and French windows, could have fetched a rent as high as $50 a month. But it only took one glance from Emily, one sensuous smile, for Frank Ellis, as burley as men come, to go weak in the knees.

"Thirty-five dollars a month would be fine, my dear," he said, uncertain how he was going to explain the cut-rate charge to his wife.

In truth, Frank Ellis never had a chance. Emily's power over men was something to behold. Without so much as a word, she could bend them to her will. It merely required a brush of one of her long fingers against theirs, a pout or a smile, and they became compliant to her every whim.

At a time when lust was regarded as a contemptible sin, and when upstanding middle-class ladies were advised to dress modestly to ward off men's natural and uncontrollable "animal desires," Emily Munro was an enigma. She was her own woman, following her own path, doing what she wanted when she wanted to do it. Most women of her class wore their hair short or gathered at the back by a bow or tie, yet Emily's long blond hair swooped over her shoulders suggestively. Occasionally, she tied it at the side in a mane, but the effect remained the same. When asked about it, she claimed that since it was her fortune to have been born with such beautiful hair, why would she want to cut it? True, every so often, the dark reddish roots started to creep into view. Still, no men seemed to pay much attention to whether she had dyed her hair or not. Given her charm, it hardly seemed to matter.

Of late, she also was using cosmetics more often. She carried a small compact of white face powder in her handbag, along with a special cream that made her skin soft and silky. She paid scant attention to the taunts and criticisms from Lila Mackenzie, Gertrude Simpson and other members of the Women's Christian Temperance Union who claimed that such embellishments made her look like a North End harlot.

"Not that this is any of your business," she would tell them impatiently, "but I have read that cosmetics are very popular among women in Paris and other European capitals." Then she would add for good measure, "And frankly, I can handle any man who thinks I belong in a brothel." Her remarks naturally shocked some members of the W.C.T.U. right down to their knickers. Many of the "White Ribboners" — named after the snowy ribbons they wore as their badge — would have expelled Emily from their little group, yet Nellie McClung, Alice Kelly and other members of the executive wouldn't hear of it.

"For better or worse," McClung, among others, would maintain, "Emily Munro stays. She may not be perfect, far from it. But she is a superb fundraiser and few of our members have given the fight against alcohol as much publicity as Emily."

And that generally ended the discussion until the next time Emily said or did something to offend one of her W.C.T.U. sisters. Several of the women frowned on her taste in clothes. Before she met Alfred Powers, Emily favoured $15 navy or black silk dresses from Eaton's Department Store. Now Powers insisted she spend no less than $25 on any garment, silk, satin or otherwise. Emily willingly complied. In anticipation of the cold Winnipeg winter, Powers had already purchased for her a lustrous $400 black Persian lamb coat. With her blond hair flowing, the effect was stunning. Powers had wanted to buy her a matching hat, but he knew better.

Unlike nearly all other women in the city — for that matter, in the entire country — Emily did not wear a hat, not ever. No other lady left home without one. Recently, the popular wide-brimmed hats adorned with flowers and bouquets had been replaced by the new styles from Paris. Smaller rounder hats decorated with a large feather that curved down past the cheek were all the rage. Emily did not care. Wearing a hat, she said, made her feel matronly and much older than her twenty-two years. No arguments from her friends or fellow suffragists about proper attire could convince her otherwise.

"No one," declared Emily, each time her taste in clothes was questioned, "runs my life. I have seen too much, done too many things against my will, given in to what other people want far too often."

And that was that. She rarely elaborated about her past experiences when pressed for more details.

"Trust no man. Be responsible for your actions," was her reply. With the exception of Nellie McClung and Francis Beynon, few of her female companions understood precisely what she meant. Their fathers, husbands and brothers might be stubborn and demanding, perhaps even physically abusive from time-to-time, but that was to be expected. It was, as the saying went, "a man's world."

According to accepted wisdom, each sex had their proper sphere. A "true" woman was pure, pious, and obedient to her husband's will. A "true" man worked hard, provided for his family, and dominated his wife in all respects (including in the bedroom) as a benevolent authoritarian.

That was the way it was. And until recently, there seemed to be little chance of things changing, little chance of the two spheres engaging in any give and take. But in fact you only had to pick up a newspaper or glance around the house to see how rapidly the world was being transformed. There were stories about airplane flights, x-ray machines, electric lights in New York City's Time Square, and Thomas Edison's latest invention — talking pictures. In some upper and middle class homes, women even had power washing machines, vacuum cleaners, gas stoves, electric toasters and coffee percolators.

Some people, including many middle-class women in Winnipeg and throughout North America, feared this modern revolution that was seizing their lives. They saw only the squalor and poverty of the growing city, how prostitution, alcohol abuse, crime, and massive immigration threatened their comfortable world. A few like Emily, however, saw the situation differently.

When it was her turn to speak at the founding meeting of the Winnipeg Political Equality League held at Jane Hample's house on Wolseley Avenue about a month before her wedding, Emily addressed this issue of fear. "Why be afraid of change?" she asked the fifteen other suffragists present. "You must first embrace it, either accept or reject it, and if the latter, then do something about it." The ladies politely applauded.

"We can make a difference," she continued. "This League we are establishing today can take an active role in improving the lives of working women forced to toil in sweatshops eight and nine hours a day. And I'm not speaking about factories in New York or Chicago, but right here in Winnipeg, only a ten-minute street car ride away."

"The other day, I accompanied Mrs. McClung and the Premier on a brief tour of such a factory. Mrs. McClung can tell you more about this, but it was shocking for all of us. The room in which these women toiled lacked both heat and ventilation. I will not mention the state of the toilet facilities. One of the girls at the sewing machines was coughing so severely that I wouldn't be surprised if she had consumption. The worst of it, however, was that both the factory manager whom we met and Premier Roblin didn't seem to care one way or the other. The factory manager informed us that any girl was free to quit. When we suggested to the Premier that he appoint a female factory inspector, his response was, and I quote, 'I tell you it's no job for a woman. I have too much respect for women to give any of them a job like this.' Too much respect, ladies. The question we must ask ourselves this evening is whether or not we are prepared to sit back and permit these young girls to suffer while the Premier and other male politicians consider their options. What is your answer?"

The small house overlooking the Assiniboine River erupted in sustained applause as Emily sat down in her chair.

"That was lovely," gushed Grace Ellis.

"A fine speech," added Nellie McClung, much more reserved. "You are an excellent public speaker. Very impressive."

"Thank you. That's very kind of you, Nellie."

"You may be a little different Emily, perhaps even slightly eccentric. We can ignore that, for I predict great things for you here in Winnipeg as we carry our fight for the vote forward."

Emily smiled. Eccentric? There was no doubt about it, she had thought, she was different from the rest of them. Oh, how she would have liked to tell them the whole tale, the truth and nothing but the truth. That would have shocked them right out of their skins. None of them, of course, suspected anything. And that was the way she planned to keep it. Alfred was a fine catch, a fine respectable catch with a large fortune.

As he stood at the front of the church, looking elegant and debonair in his black tuxedo, crisp white shirt and black bow tie, Alfred Powers was oblivious to the crowd before him. His eyes were transfixed on the back of the sanctuary where his young bride was about to emerge. Quite uncharacteristically, his mind and his body churned with emotions and a passion he hadn't felt for many years. Though at fifty-eight years old he was a well-respected lawyer, a former mayor of the city, a member of all the right clubs and societies, and had travelled throughout Europe many times, at that moment he was as giddy and excited as a school boy.

Never in all his years, even before his first marriage to Margaret, had he been around a woman like Emily. Her intelligence, insight, and wit were remarkable. And in the bedroom — there were few words to describe it. Powers considered himself an experienced man for his times — as a bachelor he had courted several beautiful women. There was one lovely debutante he had met on a trip to London. Irene was her name, as he recalled. She was the daughter of an American businessman. They had attended the theatre and then found themselves back at Powers's hotel room. He was certain that he had been the first man she had been with and he always relished that recollection.

With Margaret too, before she became ill with cancer, sexual relations had been satisfying, though by the time their children, Graham and Elizabeth, had entered their teens, it had become a tad predictable. Margaret had been a devoted mother and wife, and a proud society lady. She had enjoyed nothing more than dressing in one of her numerous satin gowns (always accentuated by gold or white lace) and attending the various balls and banquets of the Winnipeg season. She had been as keen as her husband when it came to the city's annual Horse Show. Margaret had always shown a good eye for horse flesh, especially jumpers. She had insisted Elizabeth enrol in riding lessons and had watched proudly as their daughter had taken first prize in a jumping competition with a jet black gelding named Rajah that Powers once owned.

What more could any successful man have wanted? Powers was deeply committed to his wife and children, as he was to his flourishing law practice. Few lawyers in Winnipeg had a better track record in court. Even on those rare occasions when Powers lost a case, he still won. This had happened only last year when he had defended Rabbi Aaron Davidovitch, accused of killing a young Polish girl as part of some twisted Hebrew ritual. Despite only circumstantial evidence, the jury had found his client guilty. But thanks to the efforts of a brash young detective, Sam Klein, justice had been eventually served. The rabbi was subsequently acquitted and the real murderer, hardware merchant Isaac Hirsch, had been exposed and killed — a turn of events that had astonished and stunned the entire city, Alfred Powers included.

One good development from that case, however, was that Powers had acquired a trusted friend in Sam Klein and a competent detective for his legal investigations. If he had stopped to think about it, Powers would have been the first to admit that he and Klein were unlikely companions. Not only were they separated by an age difference of nearly two decades, but they also — literally — came from the opposite sides of the tracks.

Powers was the product of White Anglo-Saxon Canada that he now epitomized, while Sam Klein, the young Russian-Jewish immigrant, was the product of poverty, congestion, booze and brothels. That he had managed to become something more than a peddler — or in Klein's case, more than a handyman and bouncer for a local whorehouse — was notable.

From the moment Powers had met his young Hebrew friend, Klein's resourcefulness, toughness, sense of purpose, and honesty had impressed him. The two men had a natural affinity that defied class and ethnicity. True, Powers was a rich and powerful *goy*, as Klein was fond of pointing out to the lawyer, but at least he didn't want to change anything about the detective or any other immigrant for that matter. He accepted Klein's view that he could be both a good Canadian and a Jew at the same time.

That had been his message only a few months before, when he addressed the members of the Winnipeg Development and Industrial Bureau.

"Assimilation is not the answer for the country's race and immigrant problems," declared Powers. "Let the Hebrews, Galicians, Negroes, whomever, adapt at their own pace. Let them find out for themselves where they fit into the vast scheme of things and I promise you, gentlemen, that life in this city will flourish and prosper without any backlash or agitation. It is my opinion that we would be wise to forget about any 'white man's burden' that we feel we possess. Such a policy might have been necessary for the British in Africa, but not in the proud Canadian West."

For that speech, Powers received nervous and half-hearted applause. Most of the audience, businessmen optimistic about the city's future despite the urban problems caused by immigrants and their slums, left the hall shaking their heads. Even his friend, *Free Press* editor John Wesley Dafoe, thought Powers was seriously mistaken. "Lawyer Advocates Chaos" — that was the headline on the following day's *Free Press* editorial about Powers's speech. It embodied Dafoe's more cautious view of such sentiments and echoed the opinion of most members of Winnipeg's elite.

Soon, however, it was more than Powers's radical ideas about immigration that were raising eyebrows, but his love life. In this, too, Sam Klein played a role.

Powers had been born and raised in Collingwood, Ontario and educated at the University of Toronto's Faculty of Law before deciding to move west to Manitoba in search of his fame and fortune. He quickly found both. He integrated himself into the Winnipeg establishment, joined the city's Board of Trade and become a member of the best clubs — including the eminent Manitoba Club and the St. Charles Country Club where he favoured golf and cricket. Year by year, Powers's law practice grew. He specialized in criminal law and was as dynamic in a courtroom as any practitioner of his day. A gifted orator, he could and often did reduce a jury to tears with his impassioned pleas for justice. Beyond that, he understood, more than most lawyers, the importance and value of trial preparation. Investigating the scene of the crime was mandatory, as was ensuring that witnesses were going to give him the answers he wanted to hear. Powers had an equally well-deserved reputation for manipulating the police.

Once, many years before, one of his clients was accused of murdering a rural storekeeper. The man charged admitted that he had been in the victim's store on the morning in question. He had purchased a tin of molasses and then, as part of his health training, he had run the five miles back to his farm. The man claimed to have arrived at his farm within twenty-five minutes of leaving the store and that he was back working in the field when the murder occurred.

Before the trial, the Crown lawyer disputed the man's story, claiming that no one could run that fast, and suggested the man was a liar. When the issue was brought up at the trial, Powers was ready. Unknown to the Crown prosecutor, Powers had arranged for his client, a lean and tall man, to run the five miles from the store to his farm, but this time followed by a police constable on a motorcycle. Sure enough, the man reached the steps of his farmhouse in twenty-two minutes. At the trial, Powers's first witness was the police constable, who confirmed the man's alibi. After this convincing testimony, a verdict of "not guilty" was never in doubt.

Although successful as a lawyer, Powers had made his fortune investing and speculating in Western Canadian real estate, along with his financial associates Bill Alloway and Henry Champion. The previous year, when Alloway and Champion had sold a huge parcel of land in Alberta to the Canadian Northern Railway, Powers, like several key investors, reaped a windfall.

Unlike many members of the city's powerful and influential commercial elite, Powers rarely boasted about his wealth or accomplishments, though he did enjoy a few of the finer things money could buy. No one had a more exquisite carriage in Winnipeg than Powers, or two more magnificent black shire geldings to pull it. At the family's mansion on tree-lined Wellington Crescent, Powers kept a ready stock of fine French brandy and wine that a Parisian dealer shipped to him regularly, as well as a supply of gold-tipped Egyptian cigars.

Life had been good to Alfred Powers. His two adult children, Graham and Elizabeth, were both settled and on the road to success. Graham, thirty-one, had followed in his father's footsteps and had received a legal education at the University of Toronto. He had returned to Winnipeg intent on making it on his own. Powers had offered him a partnership in his firm, but Graham had, for the time being, opted for a job with Tupper, Phippen and Tupper. The offer remained on the table and was often raised at family dinners.

Elizabeth Powers, three years younger than her brother, also possessed a keen mind. Upon graduation from high school, she won a prestigious scholarship to Lady Margaret Hall, the women's college associated with Oxford University. She was the first Winnipegger to win such an award. At Oxford, Elizabeth obtained her bachelor's degree with a program comprising Literature, Ancient History, Latin, Religion and Moral Philosophy. When she returned from Britain three years later, she was imbued with the spirit of social reform. She had seen first-hand the slums and poverty of London's East End and returned to Canada intent on saving the world's poor, starting in the city's North End immigrant quarter.

Powers did not always agree with his daughter, but he and Margaret were terribly proud of her commitment — even if she was becoming more Methodist by the minute. Still, Powers knew that it troubled his wife to watch Elizabeth leave for work each day at J.S. Woodsworth's All People's Mission wearing "North End" garments as she called them, purchased at a dingy shop on Selkirk Avenue. Woodsworth used to joke that Elizabeth was his only worker who resided on Wellington Crescent, but he appreciated her help with young immigrant children in the Mission's kindergarten.

Despite her daughter's unusual career choice, Margaret Powers tried to ensure that Elizabeth had a proper social life. She pushed her to join curling and skating clubs, to resume her interest in horse riding or attend the Manitoba Club's annual society ball. "When do you think you'll find the time for a husband and family?" Margaret would ask her. "Do you honestly believe you are going to find the man of your dreams among those foreigners?"

But such pleadings were to no avail. Elizabeth ignored her mother's protestations and began to spend more and more time with her suffragist friends. Many of them, too, were devoted to curing the world's ills. Obtaining the vote for women was important as well, though making the city a better place to live was clearly a priority.

The world of the Powers family collapsed one miserable day in early October 1911. It was only about a month following Sam Klein's marriage to Sarah Bloomberg. Powers later remembered how he had arrived home from the office commenting that he must wish Sam and Sarah a happy one-month anniversary. Yet before the words were completely out of his mouth, the grim look on Margaret's face stopped him cold.

"Out with it Maggie," he admonished his wife. "I've known you far too long and besides, you've never hid your feelings very well. Typical of a woman…"

"Cancer," she said, looking out the window nearest the fireplace.

"What?"

"You heard me, Alfred. I saw Dr. Thomas today. Those dizzy spells I've been complaining about."

"Head ailments, you mean?"

"No, Alfred, there's something wrong with my blood. It's cancer. That was what the doctor said."

"And, what type of treatment did he recommend?" asked Powers, moving closer to his wife, his left hand trembling as it settled on her shoulder.

Margaret looked into her husband's eyes and Powers knew there was nothing more to say.

Within weeks, Margaret was confined to bed. The disease spread faster than the city's top medical experts had anticipated. Alfred Powers, a man who prided himself on taking control of a situation, found himself in a helpless predicament. No man should have to watch his wife die a painful death in her own bed. Selfishly, perhaps, he withdrew into a deep depression. Work seemed the only way to avoid the tragedy unfolding at his home. He began to stay at his office until late in the evening, often eating alone at the Manitoba Club and returning to his house well after midnight. His wife said nothing.

One day, about two months after he first received the bad news, Powers had reluctantly accepted a dinner invitation from the Kleins. It had been his daughter Elizabeth's idea, and Sam and Sarah had agreed to try to distract Powers, if only for a few hours.

The Kleins lived in a small one-bedroom apartment near the corner of McGregor and Burrows. It wasn't much, about the size of the Powers dining room, Klein liked to joke. But for a rent of $30 a month it was a place where Sam and Sarah could begin their life together. It also doubled as Klein's office. Klein's mother Freda and her cousin Clara Hirsch had helped them buy the furniture, a table and a few chairs. Madam Melinda, "Queen of the Harlots" as she was referred to by the city's press, and Sarah and Sam's former employer, had graciously provided the couple with a brand new brass bed. Sarah would have been happy to take her old bed with her, but she could appreciate Klein's refusal on this matter.

"Too much history," he mumbled when the issue was raised. "I don't need to be reminded each night how many…"

"Your point is taken, *Shailek*," Sarah interrupted, using Klein's Yiddish name. She wrapped her lean fingers around his neck and lightly kissed his cheek. "Such history is best forgotten."

He would nod his head in agreement, then light a cigarette and Sarah knew that the discussion was over.

When Powers arrived that night, he quickly discovered that he wasn't the Kleins' only guest. Sarah had taken the liberty of inviting one of the few friends that she had met since leaving Melinda's, Emily Munro.

Sarah had finally found someone she could talk to about her most intimate problems, a woman who would listen and then offer sound advice. There was a real connection between Sarah and Emily, even Klein sensed that. It was as if Emily understood perfectly where Sarah was coming from and how difficult it had been to start her life over yet again. Klein, of course, was delighted that Sarah had at last found a female companion, though on occasion as he watched Sarah and Emily talk by the fire late into the night, he wondered about the bond between them.

It had been Klein, in fact, who had brought them together. He had been hired by Emily's landlord Frank Ellis to track down a long lost relative, a dying uncle who was supposed to have some money. During the investigation, as Klein came and went from the Grosvenor Avenue apartments, he encountered Emily. And like all men who met Emily, he was struck by her beauty and charm. As he learned more about her, that she was a newcomer to the city from Chicago, he thought that she would be someone Sarah could befriend.

That night, Alfred Powers, too, was overwhelmed by Emily's vivaciousness, wit, and irresistible charm.

As Sarah served the brandy Powers had brought with him and Klein supplied cigarettes for Sarah and his guests, Emily had turned to the distinguished lawyer.

"Tell me, Mr. Powers," she had asked him coyly, "do you believe that the suffragists' campaign will succeed? That women in Canada will get the vote?"

"I believe that is inevitable, yes," he replied taking a deep drag on his cigarette. "It will happen sooner than later."

"And this is a good thing?"

Powers hesitated for a moment. "You mean do I think that woman suffrage is revolutionary and that it will be the ruin of the family?"

"Yes, exactly," said Emily with a smile.

"As to the first point. The campaign presently being waged by Mrs. McClung — and I presume women like yourself — hardly constitutes a revolution. More an evolution, I think. All intelligent human beings deserve the right to vote and we both know that most women are more intelligent than most men."

Both Sarah and Emily laughed, while a smile crossed Klein's faced. He watched in silence, smoking, as Powers rose from his chair, his brandy in one hand, as if he were addressing a jury. "Now, Miss, as to the issue of the family, this is a more delicate matter. Perhaps I am showing my age, but I believe it's fair to suggest there could be in some instances cases when the unity of a family could be disrupted by politics. On the other hand, the average male voter is a fool who doesn't know a Grit from a Tory, so bringing women into the picture will only help. Does that answer your question?"

Emily nodded.

"I now have a query for you. I cannot help but notice, Emily, the white ribbon of the W.C.T.U. on your lovely dress and the snifter of brandy in your hand," said Powers, his voice rising slightly. "Is this not somewhat of a contradiction?"

"There is indeed, sir," she replied. "There is indeed."

"I believe, Alfred," said Klein, "that the verdict has been delivered."

"Yes it has," the lawyer laughed. "Emily, I trust this will not embarrass you, but you are a remarkable woman."

"And you, sir, are a remarkable gentleman."

An awkward moment of silence passed, as Powers and Emily stared at each other.

"Anyone care for more brandy?" asked Klein.

By the time the dinner party had finished, Powers had been won over. Emily's youth and beauty had intoxicated him, and her sensuous style — the smell of her perfume, the way she brushed the hair from her face, the manner in which she smoked a cigarette — aroused in him long dormant passions.

They met for a discreet luncheon about a week later at an out-of-the-way diner in St. Boniface. Again, Powers had been amazed and amused as Emily ordered for them in French.

"I pick up languages quickly," she had explained. "One of my many natural talents."

"And the others?" Powers had asked.

"Are you certain you want to know?" she responded, slowly wiping a droplet of wine from her lips.

"I believe I do."

When Powers later reflected on that luncheon and subsequent events, he wasn't sure what had come over him. It was if he had taken leave of his senses. Certainly, he cherished his dying wife and valued his family life. But the thought of undressing this young beautiful woman, of taking her to his bed, was more overwhelming than any vision that had penetrated his mind for some time. For weeks, day and night, it was all he could think about. Even Margaret suspected something wasn't right.

"Alfred, what is wrong with you?" she inquired from her bed. "I've never before seen you this distracted, not even during a murder trial."

He kissed his wife lightly on her forehead. "Nothing, my dear. Nothing at all. Please rest easily."

On at least one occasion, Powers had been seen with Emily by a family friend and neighbour, Katherine Dixon, the wife of the grain merchant Charles W. Dixon, attending a vaudeville show at the Walker Theatre. It hadn't been a pleasant moment. At first he had resisted the idea of going to the theatre, but one pout from Emily and he changed his mind. Besides, he wanted to see William Brady's new comedy, "Over Night" which had been the talk of the New York vaudeville season during 1911. He had, however, insisted they enter the theatre when the lights were down and sit in the first balcony.

In the midst of a particularly funny scene in the play, in which two husbands mistakenly find themselves with each other's wives, Powers noticed Mrs. Dixon out of the corner of his eye. She wasn't amused. Worse, it was clear, even in the dark that he was holding Emily's hand. Katherine Dixon glared at him for a long moment, then turned her head in disgust.

Of course, Katherine did not say anything to Margaret about this episode, nor to Powers himself, when she next stopped by the house to visit his wife. He thought about explaining his actions, but what was the point? By then, he had resolved in his own mind to end his brief affair with Emily. He had planned to break the news to her at their next reendezvous at a small hotel on Provencher Street in St. Boniface — close to Chef Simone's, the French restaurant where they had first dined.

Emily, sensing what was coming, was prepared. Powers arrived at the hotel after a full day in court. He entered the room to find Emily standing before him in a black lace corset, cut low in the front, and black patent pumps. Her blonde hair dangled on her shoulders. The smell of her perfume filled the air of the small room, making Powers dizzy. He tried to speak, but no words would come from his dry mouth.

"You like it, Alfred?" she asked, stroking her corset. "It belongs to Sarah. She said I could keep it for as long as I like."

The lawyer nodded.

She moved closer to him, but did not touch him. "Take off your hat and coat, Alfred." Powers complied. His breath was short, and his blood was churning. He was totally transfixed by this woman who stood before him. Nothing else mattered to him. Not his family, his children or his work. The image of his wife lying on her death-bed vanished like a sinking stone.

Suddenly, after what seemed like an unbearable width of time, he lunged for Emily, caressing her with kisses, deep and passionate. That day, he experienced carnal delights he hadn't thought possible. From then on,

Alfred Powers was a man no longer in control of his own destiny. He was under the sexual spell of a twenty-two year old woman, a woman he craved night and day.

Margaret Powers died on January 3, 1912, a bitterly cold Monday. She went to her grave never suspecting that her devoted husband of thirty-two years was bedding a younger woman. To honour Margaret, and no doubt to relieve some of his guilt, Powers donated $10,000 to the Winnipeg Equestrian Society, organizers of the city's Horse Show. Starting the next season, the Margaret Powers Memorial Cup would be given to the best female rider in the show jumping competition.

Less than six months later, and presumably with his conscious clear, Alfred Powers took Emily Munro to be his wife. Their engagement, announced in the spring, had caused an uproar among Winnipeg high society. It was the best gossip to hit the growing prairie metropolis in years. While Margaret Powers's female friends denounced Alfred's scandalous behaviour, their husbands quietly joked about the affair over drinks at the Manitoba Club, then grew flushed and silent as they slipped into fantasies of Emily's full breasts, her slender waist, her bare shoulders.

While Graham Powers more or less accepted his father's decision, Elizabeth was both devastated and embarrassed.

"You know what they're saying behind your back," she declared in one heated discussion with her father. "That the great lawyer, Alfred Powers, has either gone mad or succumbed to the temptations of the devil. My Lord, father, she's six years younger than me. What were you thinking?"

"Elizabeth, I love you dearly," Powers began slowly, putting down his cigar. "But I don't owe you, Graham, or anyone else for that matter, an explanation. Your mother, God rest her soul, would have understood. She would want me to be happy."

"Happy? Is that what you call this. I'm not deaf, father, I've heard the rumours. You were with her while mother was dying in bed. Weren't you?"

Unlike many parents of his day who subscribed to the notion of "spare the rod and spoil the child," Powers did not believe in hitting his children, no matter the infraction. And as Graham and Elizabeth grew from childhood to active young adults, he and Margaret never wavered from this position — not even when Graham at age twelve threw a baseball through the glass door of his mother's china cabinet. Yet at that moment, his initial impulse was to strike his daughter for her disrespect.

"I will say this once and only once Elizabeth. You are never to speak to me like this again. Ever. And I expect, no I demand, that whatever your feelings might be, you show Emily respect and common courtesy. Is that understood?"

Without another word, Elizabeth stormed out of the parlour and out the front door of the house.

By June, things had settled down. While they would never be close friends, Emily and Elizabeth were at least civil with each other, sharing their views on women suffrage and other matters. Of course for Elizabeth social reform came first — saving the urban poor, ridding society of alcohol, establishing the "Kingdom of God on Earth" — and the vote for women was secondary. Emily, on the other hand, placed a priority on achieving the vote. Curing the other ills of the world would naturally follow.

Though she did not comment on it, not even to her W.C.T.U. sisters, Elizabeth's worst fears about Emily's sincerity were confirmed the Friday night before the ceremony. It was then that she witnessed her father's future wife sip champagne in a pre-wedding toast. Despite her brother's urging, she herself refused to drink anything that evening but water. For her, Emily's hypocrisy was nothing less than shocking.

June 10, a Saturday, was a lovely day in the city. A clear blue prairie sky greeted Powers and Emily's guests as they made their way to the majestic Holy Trinity Church on Donald Street. With its turrets and spires, the white bricked Anglican Church, nearly as old as the city, resembled a fairy tale castle. Dressed in their finest gowns and tuxedos, Winnipeg's elite arrived, including the Lieutenant-Governor, Sir Daniel McMillan, and Lady McMillan, in a magnificent procession of horse-drawn carriages and shiny and polished automobiles. The McMillans were followed by Mayor and Mrs. Richard Waugh, along with the other members of the establishment: the Nantons, Ashdowns, Bawlfs, Drewerys, Sutherlands, Brydges, and Chief Justice Mathers and his wife, dressed "in a lovely gown of flame-coloured chiffon velour, the bodice of silver lace with diamante embroidery and finished with a butterfly bow of black tulle," as the *Tribune* later reported. Premier Rodmond Roblin, Hon. Robert Rodgers, his chief minister, and Thomas Kelly, the contractor vying for the new Legislative Buildings project, estimated to be worth close to $3 million, arrived at the church together with their wives in an exquisite black rig.

Behind them, and feeling slightly out of place, were Emily's suffragist sisters and their husbands: Wes and Nellie McClung, journalists Vern and Lillian Thomas, her sister Francis Beynon — who only days before had been appointed the editor of the new women's page in the *Grain Growers' Guide* — and the indomitable Miss E. Cora Hind, famous across the prairies for her uncanny crop predictions and the only woman allowed on the floor of the Grain Exchange. Lillian and Francis had intended to send their regrets, upset as they were with the gossip and innuendo around Emily's liaison with Powers. But Nellie McClung, who found Emily a stimulating companion and shunned all gossip until it was proven accurate, convinced them otherwise. Besides, Nellie reasoned, it would give her another opportunity to pester the Premier about women's suffrage.

Still, Nellie in her black Henrietta cloth dress and black stockings felt a bit awkward among the expensive satin gowns worn by the other ladies. When Roblin saw McClung enter the church with her husband and noticed the white ribbon of the W.C.T.U. pinned to her dress, he turned to Rogers and Kelly and remarked loudly enough for Nellie to hear, "You know, gentlemen, that W.C.T.U. doesn't really stand for Women's Christian Temperance Union, but rather for Women Continually Torment Us!"

"Excellent," said Rogers, with a loud bellow.

"Yes, Premier," added Kelly, "I do like that."

"Ignore them," said Wes McClung, sensing his wife's anger.

"I know we are in a place of worship, Wes, but…"

As Nellie moved toward the Premier, Archdeacon Fortin emerged from his vestry resplendent in a white robe. If you didn't know better, members of the congregation were fond of saying, you would swear that the Archdeacon, with his distinguished grey hair and beard, bore a striking resemblance to recently departed King Edward VII. Of late, Holy Trinity's aging rector — he had held that position since 1875 — seemed to be spending more and more time in his vestry, accessible only by a twisting private staircase. Gossip in the church had it that he sat up there with a bottle of scotch whisky, reading the New Testament and contemplating life.

As he climbed the few steps to the dais to the left of the raised stage, the guests took their seats on the oak pews in the grand hall. Just to the right and behind the Archdeacon was a huge stained glass window, at least twenty feet high. The majestic window had been donated to the church in 1896 by the family of the late Sir John Christian Schultz, once the much maligned leader of the Canadian faction that had opposed Louis

Riel, and later Manitoba's Lieutenant-Governor. In the window's centre stood Jesus in a robe of golden yellow, surrounded by disciples garbed in deep blue and red.

The other eight stained glass windows that ran down both sides of the sanctuary were equally impressive. Between them were memorial plaques of white marble with names of departed congregants. The largest and saddest read, "For Ethel, Myrtle, Ernest, and May White, who drowned in the Red River while trying to save one another, August 11, 1906."

At least two hundred people filled the pews that evening. Peter MacLagen began to play the organ as Alfred Powers walked down the aisle with his handsome son, Graham, followed by the Maid of Honour, Miss Grace Ellis, in her shell pink charmeuse trimmed with gold and shadow lace.

In a small anteroom at the back of the church Emily patiently waited, looking splendid in her white ivory satin wedding gown. Beside her, in a black tuxedo with tails, and feeling more out of place than the suffragists, was Sam Klein, his body tight with tension.

Desperate for a cigarette, Klein wondered what in the name of Moses he was doing there. Several weeks before, he had received a late night visit from Emily who asked him if he would march her down the aisle. His first instinct, of course, had been to refuse. But Emily wore him down. She had no other relatives — her family members had all been killed in some sort of Illinois train wreck. The details had never been clear to Klein, but he didn't press her about it. Other than Alfred and Grace Ellis, he and Sarah were her only real friends. In fact, Emily had wanted Sarah to be her bridesmaid, but she had steadfastly refused.

"I love you, Emily," she had finally said after an hour of debate. "You make me laugh and see life the way it really is. But I cannot do this thing you ask. It would be far too uncomfortable for both of us. Please don't make me do this."

"It would be a sensation, Sarah. You know that?"

"My point, exactly."

And so, after more heated discussion and futile argument, Emily had settled on Grace Ellis. Klein was to be the consolation prize and Sarah wouldn't let him refuse. He could only shake his head.

"These rules you set and live by make me crazy. You know that, don't you?" he had said to his wife later that night in bed. "Marching down the aisle of that church is no good for you, but for me it's okay? Can you help me understand this?"

"It is the right thing to do," said Sarah with a smirk. She cuddled next to him, positioning herself so that Klein's left leg pressed against a wet, warm spot between hers.

"The right thing to do? Now don't take this the wrong way, *Shayndele*, but I believe that if women like you and Emily ever get the right to vote, the world will be turned upside down. One day there will be a war, the next day it will be over. And who knows what will happen the day after that. For now you only make men *mishigina* at home. But soon it'll be all the time. Can you imagine a woman as president of the United States?"

Sarah stopped his tirade by moving on top of him. "Thanks, Sam," she said, as she took his hands and place them around her waist.

"Is this a payoff?" Klein asked with a chuckle.

"Something like that."

Klein's thoughts of the past few weeks were interrupted by the playing of the wedding march. The music echoed and reverberated throughout the church. The door of the anteroom swung open, and Emily in all her glory stepped into the sanctuary with Klein on her left arm. A hundred heads turned to stare at them, as they slowly moved towards the front of the church. Ignoring the glances and whispers, Klein focused on the large stained glass picture of Jesus on the wall ahead. As he stepped forward, he wondered what this Christian saviour was thinking.

"Hebrew sinner! Why do you desecrate this place of worship? Go back to your own people who have forsaken me." The words rang in Klein's head.

"Almost there," said Emily softly.

The next few moments passed in a haze.

"Dearly beloved, we are gathered here in the sight of God, and in the face of this congregation, to join together this man and this woman in holy matrimony…" Archdeacon Fortin's booming voice brought Klein back to reality. "…Therefore if any man can show any just cause, why they may not lawfully be joined together, let him now speak, or else hereafter forever hold his peace." Klein looked to his left and met the eyes of Elizabeth Powers, standing by the organ and waiting to sing. For a brief moment, she looked as if she were about to speak, then her lips closed tightly.

After Emily and Powers exchanged vows of love, the Archdeacon glared at Klein. "Who giveth this Woman to be married to this Man?"

"I do," replied Klein.

"Yes, of course," declared the Archdeacon, barely masking his tone of disdain. Or perhaps it was just Klein's imagination.

The remainder of the ceremony proceeded quickly. Elizabeth sang "Beloved is Morn," as her father and Emily signed the register. But it was clear to Klein that Elizabeth's heart wasn't really in it.

Following the conclusion of the ceremony, a cavalcade of carriages, horses, and automobiles — Packards, Fords, Stanley Steamers, and McLaughlins — made the short journey to the stately Royal Alexandra Hotel on Main and Higgins for a magnificent reception in the crystal ballroom — so called because the room was brilliantly lit by several glittering chandeliers hanging from the high ceilings. The walls and pillars resembled canestone, tastefully accentuated by the hotel's famous Challenger murals that had been moved, for this evening only, from their permanent home in the nearby dining room.

Powers, not known for his public extravagance, spared no expense on the food, music or floral decorations. Sumptuously prepared by the Canadian Pacific Railway hotel's own French chef, Georges St. Pierre, the menu included roast duck and creamed sweet potatoes. For dessert there was Chef St. Pierre's house speciality, mousseline au chocolat. And on each table, there were Egyptian cigars for the men, as well as Wrigley's spearmint pepsin gum for the ladies. The latter had been Emily's idea.

Following dinner, Powers and Emily held court in the Royal Alex's splendid rotunda, a favourite spot for Emily each Saturday afternoon where — during a lunch of tea, sandwiches and cakes — you could listen to presentations by local musicians and singers, and all for forty cents. Just last week, as part of a promotion by the Winnipeg Oratorio Society, a twelve-piece contingent from the visiting Minneapolis symphony orchestra performed. Their selection was an excerpt from Handel's Messiah that Emily found especially poignant.

"Ah, Dr. Parker," said Emily as she extended her hand toward a distinguished looking young gentleman. He looked about thirty years old, clean shaven, wire-framed glasses, and a full head of dark hair combed back.

"Alfred, this is Dr. Oliver Parker. I've told you about him. Not only is he the finest surgeon in Winnipeg, but he is also the city's most famous and accomplished psychic spiritualist."

Powers nodded and shook Parker's hand. "I know Emily is a believer in the 'other world,' Dr. Parker, but I remain skeptical. Maybe it's my legal training. But certainly I mean no offence. I, too, have heard some rather amazing tales of your levitations and table rappings."

"No offence taken, Mr. Powers," said the doctor. "Why not come with Emily, the next time she visits our meetings, and then decide for yourself."

"I will consider it."

"I'm sorry my wife Erica couldn't attend. Little Ollie was ill this morning."

"I hope he is feeling better," said Emily. "We appreciate you attending."

Next in the long reception line behind Dr. Parker was an elderly couple accompanied by a tall, olive-skinned man, perhaps twenty-five years old.

"Ernesto, thank you for coming," said Powers warmly. "This is my new wife."

The elderly gentleman extended his hand. He was wearing a dark brown suit, slightly large on his aged frame. His wife wore a long black dress and looked more out of place than Sam and Sarah Klein. The young man with them seemed uncomfortable in his black suit, as if the tight collar chafed his neck. Emily immediately noticed that instead of the oxfords that usually complimented a man's formal attire, he was wearing dusty high-laced boots. Clearly, she mused, this man belongs outdoors, laying track or hauling freight under the hot noon sun.

Powers continued speaking, making the introductions. "Emily, this is my friend Ernesto Rossi, his wife Rosa, and…"

"Our nephew Antonio," interrupted Ernesto. "Only here a few weeks from Sicily. Already can speak beautiful English. He is a good student."

"And their nephew Antonio," Powers repeated. "I have been shopping at Ernesto and Rosa's fruit store on Bannatyne for at least ten years. Isn't that right, Ernesto?"

"Ten years, at least."

"They have the sweetest oranges in Winnipeg."

Ernesto beamed proudly. "We opened the store on April 7, 1901. Now Antonio has come from our Sicilian home to help. We are getting tired and old, I'm afraid."

"Nonsense," said Powers. "You look as young as ever. Don't you agree, Emily? Emily?"

"Yes, of course, I was day dreaming for a moment."

"Are you feeling sick, my dear?" asked Mrs. Rossi. "Your face is so red."

"No. Just all the excitement, I suppose."

Antonio Rossi smiled broadly at the blushing bride. Taking Emily's hand in his, he looked directly into her eyes, "May you and Mr. Powers have a long life together," he murmured in a musical accent. He bent and kissed her hand.

"You come and buy fruit anytime, Mrs. Powers," announced Ernesto, as they began to step away.

Emily nodded in Antonio's direction, her eyes holding his own for a charged moment. He smiled back at her.

The highlight of the evening's festivities was a twenty-minute vaudeville comedy performance by Ned Nestor and Bess Delberg, in town for a week of performances at the Empress Theatre. To everyone's amusement, they offered an appropriate musical comedy number entitled, "In Love," in which they fell all over each other in a hilarious "love waltz."

Then, it was time for waltzes of a different kind, along with lancers and "money musks" danced to the music of a twelve-piece orchestra brought in by Powers from Chicago. It was the best music the city had had in years. The bride was spectacular. Few women in the city could match Emily's expertise or style on a dance floor.

On the other hand, the entire event — the wine, the music, the revelry — was all too much for the ladies of the W.C.T.U. They left as soon as the comedy act — which they collectively deemed inane at best — was completed. Only Nellie McClung and her husband Wes remained, dancing a few numbers before departing at nine o'clock.

About an hour later, Emily had changed from her wedding gown into a light blue blouse and matching skirt, travelling clothes for her trip to San Francisco. As she and Powers were saying farewell to her guests, a hotel waiter handed her a note. She opened it and read it quickly. Her face went white.

Klein, standing near her, noticed the change in her demeanour. "Emily, what's happened? You look like you saw a ghost."

"Oh, it's nothing." She crumpled the note in her right hand.

"You're certain, we can't do anything for you?" Sarah asked with concern.

Emily kissed both of them on the cheek. "Really, it's nothing."

She turned for a moment to face the wall, so that no one could see her. She unfolded the piece of paper in her hand and reread the brief message, poring over each word. She was stunned to think that someone knew her secret, but more astonished at the offer the note contained. Once its contents had sunk in, she turned back to her guests and scanned the crowd before her. A pair of eyes met hers. She looked at her correspondent and lifted an eyebrow, seeking confirmation. She received a slow nod in response.

4

Winnipeg, Canada
January 29, 1914

Winnipeg Tribune, Thursday, January 29, 1914

WOMAN FOUND BEATEN

Miss Katie Johnson was discovered early yesterday morning in an alley near the Royal Alexandra Hotel. She was unconscious and badly beaten. Miss Johnson lives and works at 118 Anabella Street, a notorious house of ill-fame. She was immediately taken to Winnipeg General Hospital where she is presently recovering. Miss Johnson's employer, Madam Melinda Hawkins, refused to comment on the incident. Miss Hawkins, known widely as "Queen of the Harlots," has operated her bawdy-house for many years.

In an interview with the Tribune, *Winnipeg Morality Inspector John Jordan observed that such attacks on these ladies of ill-repute have been more common in recent months. "In such situations, there is little my constables can do," says Inspector Jordan. "We have made an effort to police the Point Douglas neighbourhood more frequently. Nevertheless, given the immoral trade conducted by women like Miss Johnson, I am afraid that these attacks will continue."*

"YOU CAN'T KEEP HIM here indefinitely," Sarah argued. "It's only a matter of time before the police come here and then they'll arrest the both of you." Her voice echoed through the chilly apartment.

Klein walked to the wood burning stove in the middle of the small kitchen, reached for the metal pot and poured himself a mug of coffee. He broke off a piece of brown rock sugar kept on the nearby counter, placed it between his teeth, and sipped.

"*Shailek*, did you hear what I said?" asked Sarah, speaking louder and growing more agitated. "You're going to find yourself in jail. MacPherson is just waiting to get you on something like this. My God, the murder weapon is lying in our bathtub. What is wrong with you?"

Klein set down his steaming mug. "You don't have to shout, I've heard every word you've said. And I do know that Alfred can't remain here much longer. But before I turn him over to MacPherson, I need to speak with him further. I'm still not satisfied with the bits and pieces he's managed to tell me."

"You believe he's innocent, then?" Sarah said. "You believe his *mishigina* story about how he found Emily and Antonio already dead? That he picked up the knife…"

"I do. All of it," said Klein. "I'm prepared to give him the benefit of the doubt."

"That's very big of you. You'll be in jail and then what will happen to us? Think about your family. Graham Powers has telephoned here twice now, once last night and again early this morning asking about his father. I have had to lie to him twice. I won't do it again."

"Don't worry, Sarah, you won't have to. I'm sorry you had to lie for me at all," said Alfred Powers.

The famous lawyer stood at the entrance to the kitchen, still wearing the clothes Sarah had given him after they found him at the doorway of their apartment building. Klein had rolled Powers's own tattered and bloodstained suit in an old bed sheet, and placed it out of sight in a hallway closet.

At first, Klein had intended to burn Powers's clothes and destroy the weapon. That way, he reasoned, there would be no evidence linking his friend to the murder scene. But as he was about to throw the clothes into the coal furnace in the basement of the apartment, he had second thoughts. What if his instincts about Power were wrong? What if, as Sarah suggested, the lawyer had stumbled upon his wife making love to Antonio and attacked them both in a jealous rage? Though such a scenario seemed unlikely to Klein, he knew full well from his past experience with the late Isaac Hirsch that anything was possible. He knew that when irrepressible emotions and deep passions were involved, nothing could be taken for granted.

"I'm sorry, too, Alfred," said Sarah. "I didn't mean for you to hear that. It's just that I'm worried Sam will get into trouble with the police."

"You don't have to apologize, Sarah. You're quite right, I should call my son. And my story does sound…what was the Yiddish word you used?"

"*Mishigina*. It means crazy, absurd."

"Yes, mi-shi-gi-na. The whole sorry mess sounds that way to me too. I just can't remember it all. I was supposed to meet Emily at the theatre. I recall arriving late. The women's show had already started. I was about to enter the building when I heard a scream coming from the alley. I ran to see what was going on. And she was lying there…My God, how could this have happened? What was she doing with Antonio? I thought she loved me. And do you know the worst of it?"

Neither Sarah nor Klein said anything.

"The worst of it," continued Powers, his voice breaking up, "is that I forgive her. She cheated on me. She deceived me and if she were still here, I'd take her back in a minute. Have you ever heard of anything so ridiculous?"

"Alfred," said Sarah, touching his shoulder. "I'm sorry, I believe you. We believe you. You couldn't have done this terrible deed. Here sit down."

"No, I'm fine," said Powers, regaining his composure. "But thank you for your faith. I hope it isn't misplaced." He turned to face Klein. "Sam, I've made a decision."

"I'm listening."

"I want you to call Graham and Elizabeth and let them know where I am. I can't imagine what they've been through. I'm sure the police have been to the house. Next, tell Graham that I'm going to turn myself in to the police."

"Alfred, are you certain you want to do that? I wouldn't trust MacPherson or his henchman Taber. At least let me speak with McCreary. I'll find out where they are in the investigation."

"No. I want Graham to meet me at the Rupert Station at three o'clock. I'm not about to start hiding from the police — not at my age, not with my reputation. And, I want you to give me my suit and the knife I picked up."

"Alfred, you'll be committing suicide. Why not leave the box where it is. We'll give it to them in due course. Let's see what Graham has to say. Mark my words, if you arrive with that knife, they'll crucify you."

"Sorry, Sam. I'm not going to be a party to obstructing justice. I'll have to take my chances. My son is a damn good lawyer. He'll have to convince a jury that I'm no murderer. But I think he's going to need some help. And that's where you fit in."

"You want me to investigate this?"

"I want you to find out everything you can about Emily. I'll tell you all I know, although it's not much. We didn't dwell too much on her past. But you are to leave no stone unturned. Are we clear?"

"You're certain about this? Once I start, there's no going back."

"I want to know how long she was seeing Antonio, how often they met, and where. I know Emily came from Chicago, at least that's what she told me. Maybe a trip there will turn up something useful. Money isn't an issue. Whatever you need. I'll tell Graham to advance you $500 to start."

"That's not necessary, Alfred."

"No, it is. Let's do this right. Also, it would probably be a good idea to speak with Dafoe at the *Free Press*. We go back a long way. He might be able to provide you with information. He has contacts all over North America."

Klein nodded. He rarely wrote things down. After becoming a full-time investigator, he discovered that he possessed a good memory for details. He would file away facts, figures, and faces in different parts of his head and then draw on them as he needed.

"I don't know how much, if anything, Emily would have revealed about her affair to her suffragette friends," continued Powers, speaking quickly, his tone more desperate, "but I have always found Nellie McClung to be a forthright and honest person. She could be of some assistance, as could Grace Ellis. Yes, you must speak with Grace, a lovely and lively woman. She and Emily were close friends. I suspect she must know most of Emily's secrets, perhaps even the dark ones."

Finished with his preliminary assessment of how Klein's investigation should proceed, Powers walked to the window above the kitchen sink and stared into the alley opposite the Klein's first-floor apartment. "I know in my heart that I couldn't have killed her," he said in low voice. "Nor do I think this was a simple robbery gone wrong. There's something deeper. I can feel it. "

"Yeah, well, I'd keep those feelings to yourself for the moment," interjected Klein. "And, don't count on any sympathy from the cops or the province. They're going to go out of their way to make sure you're treated like any other alleged murderer. Maybe worse."

"I can handle myself. Don't worry. Besides, I have faith in the Manitoba courts. The truth will come out."

That's what I'm afraid of, thought Klein as he struck a match against the iron front of the kitchen stove.

The grand home on Wellington Crescent was strangely silent. Only the flickering of an upstairs lamp in the master bedroom indicated that anyone was at home. Though this house, like most in Winnipeg, had electricity, Elizabeth Powers preferred an old kerosene lamp that had once belonged to her grandmother. It had also been one of her mother's favourite household items. Many evenings, she had sat next to her mother in the main floor parlour while both of them read. The lamp between them provided a bright flickering light.

The front door opened and then closed with a slam.

"Graham is that you?" Elizabeth cried out from the upstairs bedroom.

"It's me," replied her brother. "I see you have yet to clean up this mess. Those damn police. What did they expect to find? What did they think? That the murder weapon would be hidden inside one of mother's vases?"

At thirty-three, Graham Powers, of medium height with a stocky build and clean-shaven, already epitomized the Winnipeg business establishment. He was rarely dressed in anything but the attire of the commercial elite: a black three-piece suit with a crisp white shirt and a silk necktie. His brown hair was neatly trimmed and combed to the side — he visited Joe, the barber at the Empire Hotel, every Tuesday at one o'clock — and his round wire glasses gave him a fitting air of intelligence.

Most days, the younger Powers was in his downtown office by eight o'clock in the morning and remained there until well after seven in the evening, servicing the needs of his law firm's commercial clients. He was most adept at negotiating high-priced land deals and had earned a reputation among the business community for being worthy of trust.

Following in his father's footsteps, he was a member of the Manitoba Club, the St. Charles Country Club and had recently been appointed the newest director of the Dominion Bank. Though he occasionally escorted Helen Smythe, the lovely and charming daughter of banker Thomas Smythe, to society balls and affairs, Graham was too busy and ambitious to become involved in a serious relationship.

He stood at the bottom of the wide staircase surveying the damage done by the police in their exhaustive search. Expensive paintings had been ripped off the walls and lay scattered on the hardwood floor. Beside them were ornaments, vases, and his mother's gold candlesticks that had been toppled from the fireplace mantle. Books from the large oak shelves on the far side of the room also had been thrown about, including Graham's collection of the works of Alexander Dumas, favourites as an adolescent. To add further insult, the police had helped themselves to his father's expensive box of Egyptian cigars, kept in a special glass container by the window.

"Have you seen this?" Graham shouted again to his sister. "My God, why did they cut open the love seat in the parlour? I'm going to send the city a bill. I don't know why but I expected father's property to be treated with a little more dignity."

Still there was no response.

"Elizabeth, are you there?"

A young woman, wearing a simple blue patterned dress with a frilly white collar, her long auburn hair pulled back tightly in a bun, appeared at the top of the stairs. "Graham, I'm sorry, I was upstairs in father's bedroom. I couldn't hear you."

"I thought you were going to clean up this mess."

"I'll get to it. And if I don't, Ethel will be here in an hour. Now do you have any news?"

"Nothing. No one has seen father anywhere. I've spoken to all of his friends, including Klein. I've been to his office. It's as if he has vanished from the city. I don't know about you, but I'm worried. I can't believe he hasn't contacted us. And to make matters worse, it sounds as if the police have already convicted him."

"This is a living nightmare," said Elizabeth, collapsing on the top stair. "And you know whose fault it is?" She didn't wait for her brother to respond. "That woman. Forgive me for saying this, but I'm not sorry she's dead. Nor will I shed one tear for her."

"That's not very Christian of you, Elizabeth."

"No, it isn't. But Emily was an evil woman, deserving no Christian charity from me or anyone else. There was nothing sincere about her. I don't care what Nellie McClung or anyone else says, she was not a loyal champion of the suffrage cause or any other cause for that matter. She was interested in one thing and one thing only — Father's money. Carrying on with that Italian labourer, in public. Drinking liquor one night and preaching against it the next. Did she have no shame? To be honest, I wouldn't blame father if he did do it. She and that foreigner both deserve what they got."

Graham shook his head. "Let me give you some advice, Elizabeth. Keep such views to yourself. All you'll do is make Father's problems worse. Whatever Emily's sins, and I will grant you there were many, she didn't deserve to die the way she did. No one does."

"I disagree. Now if you'll excuse me," she said rising, "I'm going to pack up all of her belongings so there'll be no trace left of her in this house. Then I'm going to take her clothes down to the mission and give them to people who really need them."

"You'll do no such thing. Have you lost all sense of judgement? Don't you think father should be the one to do that? Whatever happened between them, she was still his wife. Not to mention, you could be destroying relevant evidence."

The ringing of the telephone interrupted the conversation. Powers picked up the receiver. "Thank God. Is he all right? Please let me speak with him. Yes, I understand. I will be there as soon as I can. My God, are you certain? I don't believe it. That's impossible, impossible."

He placed the receiver back in its place and turned to his sister. "That was Sam Klein. He's with father. I'm meeting them at the police station at three o'clock. And Elizabeth, I should warn you, Klein has the knife that murdered Emily and her friend. It was in father's possession when Klein found him."

As she crossed Main Street and walked briskly through the snowy sidewalk down Euclid Avenue, Sarah couldn't help but notice the stares from the people she passed. In the past few weeks, she had made it a point to stay away from Point Douglas and Melinda's. That was what Sam had wanted. And she had abided his wishes. At least until today, that is.

"Sarah, nice to see you," shouted a woman from across the street. "You coming back to work? Or just here for a visit?"

"Just a visit, Henrietta."

"Well, dear, you know you have a standing offer to come work at my house. I'll even only take fifty percent. That's a lot less than Melinda took from you. Am I right?"

Madam Henrietta Scarth was a Winnipeg institution. She had been operating a brothel in the city at least as long as Melinda had. Her house on McFarlane Street was popular with an assortment of male clients, especially railway men. Supposedly Henrietta had come west from St. Louis where she had learned the tricks of the trade. But who knew for certain?

"Thanks for the offer," said Sarah, "but as I said I'm out of the business. Besides...."

"Besides, you're loyal to Melinda," added Henrietta.

"It was nice seeing you, Henrietta, but I do have an appointment to keep."

"Say hello to Melinda for me, will you my dear? She and I haven't seen much of each other recently."

Sarah smiled and continued on her way. Inside, however, her she was churning with emotion. The past twenty-four hours had been difficult to believe. Emily killed, murdered in the street. Then Alfred turning up at their door last night with a knife in his hand. Walking faster against the blustery wind, she was determined to put these terrible thoughts out of her head.

The odd thing was, Sarah thought, that despite everything, returning to the streets of Point Douglas where she had once reigned did make her feel good. These were foolish thoughts and dangerous ones, she knew that. Still, there was something to be said for status, money and position. She was glad Sam had left early with Alfred. That way, there would be no explaining to do.

Melinda had suggested that they meet at ten o'clock at Miller's diner. This was a small out-of-the-way eatery located in a two-storey house on Mead Street popular with the neighbourhood girls. Mrs. Bernice Miller lived on the second floor of the house with three of her daughters. Sarah had eaten there many times in the past. The food wasn't especially good, but Mrs. Miller ran a discreet establishment and knew the value of not asking questions.

Sarah gently opened the door of the house, stamped her boots on a mat in the veranda and entered. There were about a dozen patrons, a few women Sarah recognized and an assortment of men, mostly elderly ones, who lived in the area. The murmuring and whispers started at once. Sarah nodded in the direction of the other women, who waved at her. The men merely smiled. She knew what was on their minds.

"Sarah, it's been far too long," said a middle-aged woman, slightly round and wearing a blue polka dot dress with a white apron.

"Hello, Bernice, how have you been?" said Sarah.

"Fine, my dear. Quite fine. As you can see, we're as busy as ever. Shirley is engaged to be married, a boy from Carman. Comes from a good family. The wedding is going to take place in the spring."

"I'm happy for you, Bernice. You haven't seen Melinda anywhere? I was supposed to…."

"Right behind you, Sarah." The voice was strong, distinct and confident. Melinda Hawkins, somewhere in her forties, with her trademark ruby red lips and her eyes thick with blue liner, entered the diner like royalty. Removing her fur coat, the famous Madam revealed a flowing and frilly peach dress, naturally cut low in the front. Among the men of the city, her buxom figure was legendary.

Sarah gave her a peck on the cheek as Bernice Miller showed them to a table in a small private room on the other side of the house. The eyes of every man in the diner followed the two women as they crossed the room.

"You two get comfortable and I'll be by with coffee in a few moments," said Bernice.

Melinda pulled out a gold cigarette case and offered one to her friend.

"Sarah, I heard about Emily. I'm sorry."

"Thanks, I appreciate that."

"How's Sam doing?"

"He's okay. We had a bit of surprise last night. But what's this about that girl of yours — Katie? Is it true?"

"They found her behind the Royal Alex. Now the cops will be all over the place. God knows what she was up to. See, this is what I have to deal with."

"Will she be okay?"

"I spoke with the doctors. They say she's pretty beaten up, but she'll make it. They're may be some other complications, however."

"Such as?"

"Let's talk about that later."

"Here it is, ladies," said Bernice placing two steaming cups of coffee on the small table. "Anything else for you? I just made some cinnamon buns."

"Nothing right now," said Melinda.

"It is nice to see the two of you together again," said Bernice with a grin as she left the room.

"Okay, now down to business. Tell me, is the house still for sale?" asked Sarah.

"It is. I spoke with Lynette yesterday like you asked me. She's ready to retire. Says I can have the entire place, girls included, for twelve thousand."

"Sounds like a lot of money to me."

"It's a little high. The property itself is probably only worth about six. But she's agreed to let us pay it off over ten years and the deal does come with a good group of girls, at least for the first year. From what I can figure, the payments are easily affordable if the place is properly managed."

"Which is where I come in."

"You sure you're up to this Sarah? You've spoken to Sam about it?"

There was a brief silence.

"You haven't, have you?"

"I was going to. But I just couldn't find the right moment."

"You've got to speak with him about this, dear, if you're serious. You know I'm not forcing you into anything."

"I know that. After all, this whole thing was my idea," said Sarah, smiling slightly. "But give me a few more days. Wait until Sam has had a chance to deal with a few other problems and then I'll speak to him. But promise me, until then not a word."

"Well, I was planning to ask him for some detective help with Katie. I got a call from my man at the police station. They found opium on her."

"You think it was hers? She never struck me as a user."

"I agree. That's why I need Sam's help. I have some ideas."

"Tonight, Melinda. I promise I'll speak to him tonight," said Sarah as she stirred a piece of sugar into her coffee.

The small office on the second floor of the Rupert Avenue station reserved for the "plain clothes men," as the detectives were often called, had been quiet all morning. That was surprising given the improvement in the winter weather. Any cop worth his salt in this prairie city understood the correlation between cool temperatures and crime. Simply put, the colder and more miserable it became, the less opportunity there was for breaking the law. In January, constables on the night beat spent most of their time on the look out for harmless drunks in danger of freezing to death. As temperatures improved, the thugs returned to the streets.

Yet this morning, there was an eerie calm, a stunned tranquillity. The bloody double murder of Emily Powers and Antonio Rossi, as well as the brutal beating of a young prostitute in the red light district, had thrown Winnipeg's citizens into a collective daze. This included the petty thieves, pickpockets and riffraff who plied the hotels, saloons and nickelodeons along the Main Street strip from the CPR station on Higgins to Portage Avenue. Even the old timers, who could still recall the day back in 1869 when Louis Riel and his gang had seized the upper fort, were shocked by the gruesome "Powers affair," as it was being called in the *Tribune*.

As the morning progressed, a constable or clerk occasionally came in to the office with a report to be checked or to search for a case file in the black bound books that were kept on a large shelf to one side of the room. At that moment, however, Bill McCreary and Alex Taber, whose desks faced each other, were alone.

"You don't seem too concerned," said Taber, flipping through a pile of papers. "We've been out for two hours going door to door. We've been all over the murder scene and we still have nothing. No murder weapon or murderer. I've never seen anything like this. The trail is dry as a bone."

McCreary leaned back in his chair, put his big boots on top of his cluttered desk, and lit a Roxboro cigar.

"You still smoking those cheap things?"

"The best money can buy," McCreary said with an uncharacteristic grin. "The Bay store keeps them in stock just for me."

"What do they run you, Bill? Two dollars a box?"

"Something like that."

"Here, try one of these," said Taber as he threw his partner a cigar with a gold paper label around it.

"What's so special about these?"

"Right from Cairo." Taber bit off the end, spit it out on to the floor, popped the cigar in to his mouth and reached for his box of wooden matches. "Nothing finer than a good cigar...especially when you don't pay for them."

"Powers's collection?"

"Of course. A present from O'Shea. He found them during his search of the premises, which, I might add, turned up nothing that's going to help us convict this high and mighty lawyer."

"I wouldn't get too excited, Taber. My experience is that if you let things unfold as they will, matters fall into place all by themselves." McCreary blew a whiff of smoke up towards the low hanging lights. "Besides, you keep forgetting we got this," he said, waving a single sheet of paper in the air.

"I know all about Jordan's report. I probably have most of it memorized. You forget what a fantastic memory I have for details?" Taber didn't wait for a reply. "It's my Russian heritage."

At that, he began to recite the police surveillance report verbatim. "February 10, 1913. Mrs. Emily Powers is seen in the lobby of the Leland Hotel at 3 p.m. in the company of a dark haired man, not her husband. April 7, 1913, 7:30 p.m. Plain-clothes men on Selkirk Avenue witness Mrs. Powers walk in an alleyway near Selkirk and Salter. She is with the same man. They emerge fifteen minutes later. Mrs. Powers is fixing her hair and straightening her dress. April 28, 1913, 5 p.m. A woman working for Jordan at the Leland Hotel rents a room to one Luigi Zucchi, obviously an alias. Twenty minutes later, Mrs. Powers appears at the hotel desk asking for Mr. Zucchi's room number. May 5, 1913…"

"Enough, Taber. I get the point, very impressive. I see they fancied the Leland, a classy hotel. I'm sure they weren't too happy about the fire in December which shut it down."

"They moved over to the Royal Albert."

"Yeah. Well, as I said we got a motive: One cheating and dead wife, one dead Italian boyfriend, and one jealous husband. It shouldn't be too much trouble to tie it all together. Funny, though, in all my dealings with Powers, he never struck me as the murdering type. Rich, successful, you know what I mean?"

"But let's not forget that seeing your twenty-four-year-old wife screwing a wop in the street could make even the upstanding citizen go a little crazy."

"Agreed. But I'd feel better if we had at least one witness before we string him up."

"You sound like you're going soft, McCreary."

The detective laughed. "Hardly, Taber. But when you've worked on as many cases as I have…"

Taber groaned.

"That's right," McCreary continued, "When you have as much experience as me, you know when things don't smell right. Not that I don't think Powers is capable of such a crime — after the way Isaac Hirsch strangled that young Polack a couple years back, nothing surprises me anymore. And I've seen husbands beat up their wives for a lot less than screwing a dago. Only last month, you'll recall we had to arrest that damn fool Ferguson over on Arlington Street for nearly killing his wife. Here's an accountant, lives in a nice house, has a few kids. Doesn't matter. He comes home from work after a few drinks at the Brunswick and his dinner isn't on the table. I hear his wife is still spitting out teeth."

As he listened, Taber leaned back in his chair and lifted his feet onto his desk.

"So, don't get me wrong," McCreary continued. "Maybe Powers has a temper like anyone else. But before I make up my mind, I want to talk to him. He at least deserves that. And besides, he's got a lot of powerful friends in this city. Remember that Taber."

"I know all about Powers's influential friends at city hall. They don't scare me. But to make you happy, we'll do this by the book."

A sly grin crossed McCreary's face. His young partner's cocksure attitude reminded McCreary of himself, back when he was fresh new detective and didn't let anything or anyone get in his way. He had learned since that one must sometimes be patient, shrewd and calm. Taber was in too much of a rush. In time, he'll learn better, McCreary thought.

"You know, Taber, we may be overlooking another angle."

"That's already occurred to me. So what do you want to do about it?"

"I got an idea. I'll fill you in later."

"You hear about the young hooker at Melinda's?" asked Taber.

"Katie Johnson? One high-priced and good looking whore. A real shame, but I hear she'll recover."

"Yeah, she's lucky to be alive. But that's not the end of it."

"No?" He knew full well what Taber was about to reveal, but played along.

"Jordan, our saintly inspector, was one of her gentlemen callers."

"That's yesterday's news, Taber. I'm surprised at you. I thought you kept up with the gossip around here. Can't you name all the cops who get favours on Anabella Street?"

"I know a few names. I even hear there was one woman at Melinda's that you once fancied."

"That was a long time ago," McCreary sneered, "a very long time ago. Now, I'm a reformed man, don't you know that? I'm as clean as the Reverend Woodsworth. No more booze, no more whoring. That woman you're talking about got married and left the business."

"Let me guess? The lovely Sarah Bloomberg, now otherwise known as Mrs. Sam Klein?"

A nostalgic smile crossed McCreary's face.

"Yeah, a real shame she's not available anymore," Taber continued. "She's one pretty woman. Whatever faults they have, Hebrew women enjoy being with a man. They love to please. They'll do anything you want. I knew these two girls in the Lower East Side, Hannah and Rebecca. I'll leave it to your imagination."

"Please do. As for Sarah Klein, let me set you straight, Taber. If you know what's good for you, you'll stay away from her. She's out of that work and her husband has a mean temper."

"Let me tell you something, McCreary. There's no such thing as a retired whore. It's in their blood. Once they have six or seven men a day, they crave it all the time."

McCreary took a deep drag on his cigar and said nothing.

"As for Klein," Taber continued, "he doesn't scare me. Not one bit. I've seen his kind before in New York. Tough Jews who think they own the world. But once they're challenged, they run like scared rabbits."

"You think so? Don't say I didn't warn you. Anyways, what do you know about who laid the beating on that whore?"

"Not much so far. Probably a client with too much to drink. Hardly unusual for that area of the city. But they did find a pouch of opium in her purse. Jordan's so angry about somebody messing up his whore that he's decided to handle the investigation himself. And I hear he's going to try and shut down Melinda. Says she's to blame."

"That'll be easier said than done. That woman has more markers at city hall than anyone I know. She knows too many secrets. Jordan's not stupid enough to get into a fight with her. He'll lose for sure."

Shouting from down the hall interrupted the detectives' conversation. As Taber rose from his chair to investigate, a constable, out of breath, dashed into the office. "It's Powers," he said. "Klein is downstairs and he's got Alfred Powers with him. He wants to turn himself in."

It only took McCreary and Taber moments to scramble down the stairs and push through the crowd of constables swarming around Powers. It wasn't every day in this frontier city that a former mayor was likely to be charged with murdering his cheating wife and her boyfriend.

Powers stood erect beside the sergeant's desk, his dark brown eyes gazing ahead, oblivious to the commotion around him. Sam Klein leaned against the wall near the window, smoking a cigarette. Under one arm he held a large brown bag. Powers was determined to face the police by himself.

For a brief moment, no one said anything, then McCreary moved forward. "Mr. Powers, we've been looking for you."

"So I've heard. Well, I'm here now." There wasn't the least trace of tension in his voice.

"I'm sorry about your wife's death," said McCreary with all the civility he could muster, "but we have some questions to ask you."

"Quit beating around the bush," said Taber. "Let's get this guy upstairs."

"I'm handling this. Don't forget who the senior detective is."

From the other side of the room, Klein chuckled.

"What the hell are you doing here?" Taber said, looking in Klein's direction. "I knew you were involved in this."

Klein ignored him. He walked towards McCreary. "Here, these are for you," he said handing the detective the package he was holding.

"What's this?" asked McCreary.

"They are, detective," interjected Powers, "the knife that killed my wife and the suit I was wearing the night of the murder. It's covered in blood."

A knowing smile crossed Taber's face. McCreary remained stone-faced.

"He didn't do it," announced Klein. "I hope you have the good sense to figure that out."

"And what makes you such an authority?" asked Taber. "Where did you find Powers?"

Klein remained silent.

"You ought to be charged with obstructing justice. I'd like to get you in an interrogation room for a few moments."

Klein murmured a few choice words in Russian.

Taber's face reddened. "No one talks to me like that." He charged towards Klein and tried to grab his left arm. But Klein was too fast for him. He brought his right arm up and caught Taber lightly on the chin with his elbow. The detective stumbled backwards. Suddenly, four or five constables had their hands around Klein's arms and neck.

"Leave him be," said McCreary. The constables held their ground. "That's an order."

Reluctantly, they released their grasp. "Taber, I warned you not to mess with him." McCreary handed his dishevelled partner the two wrapped packages. "Take these to Hicks upstairs in the laboratory. Tell him we need them examined for fingerprints. Then I'll meet you in the office with Mr. Powers and the three of us will have a chat. And Taber, remember what we talked about."

"You think I'm an idiot?" Taber spat, glaring at Klein. "This isn't over between us."

"Yeah, I think it is," said Klein.

"What's going on here?" a voice boomed from behind the crowd. "Is this a circus or a police station?" Chief MacPherson made his way to the desk as a path opened before him. "McCreary, fill me in."

"Nothing to report, yet. As you can see, Mr. Powers has come in for questioning and he brought the murder weapon with him."

"I see," said the Chief. "Anything else I should know about?" he asked looking in Taber's direction.

McCreary shook his head. "Just a difference of opinion, but it's been resolved. Isn't that correct, Alex?"

Taber ignored the question. "If you'll excuse me, Chief, I've got work to do upstairs."

"Very well, then get at it." He turned in Klein's direction. "Why do I have a feeling you're mixed up in this?"

Klein shrugged. "Just here supporting a friend."

The Chief waved his hand. "McCreary, get this troublemaker out of my station house and then deal with Powers. But before you formally charge him, call me."

McCreary nodded as MacPherson headed to his office on the second floor.

"Don't you all have work to do?" shouted McCreary.

"You heard the detective," said Sgt. Mac Thomson, the burly officer behind the station's main desk.

Slowly, the remaining crowd dispersed. Several constables dressed in their buffalo coats moved towards the front entrance and left the building, while others reluctantly sauntered back to their work areas.

"Mac, do me a favour," said McCreary to the desk sergeant. "Take Mr. Powers to the second floor interrogation room and keep him away from Taber until I get there."

Without another word, the policeman lifted his big frame out of his chair and took Powers by the arm. The lawyer glanced back at Klein.

"Graham will be here soon, Alfred," said Klein reassuringly. "He'll get you out of here, don't worry."

Powers smiled sadly. "I have confidence in both of you."

McCreary and Klein now stood alone eyeing each other from across the hallway.

"If you expect me to apologize," said Klein flicking his cigarette into a nearby spittoon, "I don't plan to. Taber deserved what he got."

"No arguments from me," conceded McCreary, "but his personality aside, he's not a bad detective."

"That's what I say about you when your name comes up."

McCreary laughed. "He's definitely as obnoxious as I used to be — when I drank, that is."

"Worse, if you ask me."

"You should have brought Powers in earlier. I'll try to keep your name out of it. If the Chief finds out you were withholding the murder weapon…"

"Then I could have bigger problems than an angry Russian out to get me."

"Something like that."

"Thanks for the advice. But I won't be stepping aside just yet."

"Let me guess. You don't believe Powers did it."

"I know it looks bad."

"To say the least. We have him in possession of the knife, his clothes are covered in blood, and he clearly had a motive — jealousy. It won't take much of a lawyer to paint him as the vengeful husband. He'll swing, without a doubt."

"What if I can provide you with another possibility, McCreary? Will you consider it?"

The detective drew a small cigar from his inside coat pocket and lit it. "Sure, go ahead and knock yourself out, Klein. That way you'll stay out of trouble." He paused. "You serious?"

"I've never been more serious. I'm not saying it doesn't look bad for Powers, but it just doesn't add up. I've never seen him lose his temper, not once. In court, no matter what the situation, he's calm and collected. Sure, he may get emotional from time to time, I'll grant you that. But a murderer? He's just not the kind of person to lose control. Not ever."

"Okay, Klein humour me. If not the husband, then who?"

"Listen, Emily Powers was deeply involved in the woman's rights movement. Maybe someone took offence to the suffragists' campaign."

McCreary leaned back and blew a puff of smoke toward the ceiling.

"Or what if," Klein continued, "Rossi was the real target, not Emily."

In fact, that thought had occurred to McCreary as well, but for the moment he decided to keep it to himself. He had his reasons. He shook his head and chuckled. "Yeah, and I'm running for prime minister. I think you've been at this private detective job too long. You're not making sense. Powers did it, face facts. Now, if you'll excuse me, I've got one fancy lawyer to charge with a double homicide."

Klein moved closer to the detective. "Will you at least keep me informed about what's going on?" he asked quietly.

"Same arrangement. We'll use 'One-Arm' Eddie at the Brunswick for messages."

Klein was almost through the door, when McCreary abruptly called after him. "I forgot to tell you something else."

"Let's have it."

"Your former employer is in a bit of trouble. You heard about that young whore, Katie, getting beat up last night? Well, Jordan's on the warpath. He aims to close Melinda down."

"That hypocritical son-of-a bitch. Have you any idea how many times in the past month Jordan has visited Melinda's looking for Katie?" Klein didn't wait for McCreary to answer. "I'd say about a dozen. Maybe Maloney ought to get this story. The headlines would be sensational."

"I think you got enough problems keeping your lawyer friend from being strung up. Don't tangle with Jordan. He can be mean, believe me."

"I'll keep that in mind."

It was four o'clock by the time Klein stepped out of the police station into the cold winter air. He looked left towards Main Street hoping to see Graham Powers, but there was no sign of him. It was odd, he thought, that the young lawyer hadn't yet arrived. Though Alfred Powers had nearly convinced Klein that he would be able to handle himself in a police interrogation, Klein knew full well that Taber could be rough. He wished Alfred had waited till Graham had arrived before turning himself in.

Still, at that moment there wasn't much more he could do for Powers, and Melinda undoubtedly needed some assistance dealing with Jordan's threat to close her down. As he buttoned up his coat and raised the collar around his neck so that it almost reached the brim of his bowler, he figured the wisest plan would be to start his murder investigation the next morning. His first stop would be at the Rossi family, something he wasn't looking forward to.

From today's reports in Winnipeg's three dailies, the *Tribune, Free Press* and *Telegram*, it was clear to Klein that the city's close-knit Italian community was not only horrified by the news of Antonio's death, but also terribly shamed by the revelations of his association with Emily Powers. The Italian immigrants Klein knew were proud, passionate people, determined to build new lives for themselves in Canada. The last thing they needed was this type of bad publicity. "They're nothing but criminals and thieves," is what the good citizens of Winnipeg would be saying next, Klein thought. "They have no respect for the law, no respect for another man's wife."

But Klein needed to know as much as possible about Emily's handsome Sicilian. If Ernesto Rossi could get beyond the embarrassment and tragedy, perhaps there might be a clue in Antonio's background to explain what had transpired in the alley behind the Walker.

From his study of the crime scene last night, Klein had arrived at the same conclusion as McCreary and Taber: that this wasn't a robbery gone wrong. There was no indication of a protracted struggle. Emily and Antonio had apparently been taken by surprise, probably by someone they knew. The killer must have had a score to settle with one, or perhaps both, of the victims. His instinct told him that this tragedy had more to do with Antonio than Emily — or at least, that's what he wanted to believe. But he would still have to speak frankly with Powers about his young wife, and who knew where that might lead?

Klein was well aware of the powerful opposition in the city against the causes Emily had propounded, especially temperance and the women's vote. Yet it was hard to imagine that any of the anti-suffragettes could have resorted to such violence. Sure, they ranted and raved that giving women the vote would destroy the family and produce an army of unnatural "female men." But cold-blooded murder? It seemed unlikely. And for that matter, why target someone like Emily? Why not go after the really influential leaders like Nellie McClung or Francis Beynon?

The so-called "liquor interests" were another matter. Klein did believe there were those who would resort to almost anything to protect their lucrative businesses. "Stop prohibition at any cost" — that was their motto. The city's hotel owners and liquor salesmen despised the "Banish-the-Bar" movement. Emily had been a prominent member of that cause, even if she herself hadn't always practised the temperance movement's dictates.

Not long before, Klein had witnessed an ugly altercation in front of the Bell Hotel between some thirsty farm workers passing through the city and a small group of prohibitionists, men and women, led by Rev. Donald Hargraves of the Moral and Social Reform Society. Had it not been for intervention of Sam Bronfman, the Bell's young owner, matters might have got really out of hand. As it was, the Reverend Hargraves merely slunk away with a bloody nose.

Money. That was what was really at stake, Klein thought. Owning a hotel bar or wholesale liquor store in Winnipeg or any other city in Canada was a license to print money. The profits flowed as fast as the beer. From the moment they opened in the morning, the bars and stores along Main Street from the CPR station at Higgins Avenue south toward McDermot Avenue could barely keep up. Most hotels also provided a free lunch so no one had to go home for dinner. At the Brunswick, where Klein regularly stopped for a shot of whisky, there were always large bowls of pickles, ham, cheese, and pretzels to feast on. As long as you had a mug of beer or a glass of booze in front of you, the food was on the house. There were also pool tables to while away an afternoon and rooms reserved for poker, safe from the prying eyes of John Jordan's morality inspectors. For customers who disdained the public nature of the Point Douglas brothels, some hotel managers would even arrange a private room and a female companion.

From the perspective of the W.C.T.U. and other temperance support-ers, the bars were to blame for every problem. Divorce, stealing, cheating husbands — all caused by drink. Even Klein, whose view was that a man should be able to have a beer whenever he wanted, had conceded in one of his last discussions with Emily, that booze and wife beating did go hand-in-hand. He had heard the violent arguments in his own apartment building.

Stephan Piotrowski, his wife Mary, and their two young children, a Ruthenian family, lived one floor above the Kleins. Piotrowski was a pleasant enough when employed and sober, which lately wasn't often. Winter was always the worst for him since job opportunities at lumber yards or on road gangs were limited. During those long, cold months, Mary supported her husband and his drinking habit by working ten hours a day as a maid for a wealthy German family in the south part of the city known as Armstrong's Point.

Arriving back at her apartment, she would be usually greeted by her husband, drunk and angry that supper wasn't on the table. Inevitably, he would reach for the thin strip of birch behind the kitchen door, and, Mary, who had long before concluded that resistance only made it worse, stood there and took the beating. There was no point calling the police, for even if Piotrowski had wound up before the magistrate he would have been released with a stern warning, or at most one day in jail. As Nellie McClung constantly pointed out, "In this province, you get in far more trouble with the law for stealing a cow, then for beating your wife half to death."

About a month before, during one particularly bitter fight upstairs, Sarah had insisted that Klein intervene. Usually Mary didn't cry out during the attack. But this time her husband had also struck one of their children, a nine-year-old boy, who had come to his mother's defence. Mary's screams were too much for Sarah to bear. And though it was Klein's opinion that what went on between a man and his wife was a private affair, he, too, couldn't ignore Mary Piotrowski's pleas for help.

When he entered their apartment and saw Piotrowski whipping his wife with the birch strip, he lost his temper. Without uttering a word, he grabbed the birch from the drunken man's hand, threw him down to the ground, and slapped him across the face a few times.

"Get the hell out of here, Jew," Piotrowski had screamed.

At that, Klein hit his enraged neighbour several times with his own whip.

"Stop, please, Sam," Mary had pleaded.

Klein had then thrown the rod on the floor and leaned close to Piotrowski. "If you so much as scratch your wife again, I'll be back to give you far worse. You understand?"

Piotrowski had meekly nodded. And after that, a calm descended upon the household up above. Klein wasn't sure if his threats had done the trick, but Stephan did lay off the booze. No one in the apartment building, though, figured the peace would last long.

At any other time of the year, Klein would have walked the mile and a half to Melinda's house on Anabella Street, but the deep snowdrifts made such a trek difficult. He decided to wait for the streetcar. In January, the days were short — by four o'clock in the afternoon, the sun was beginning to set. Soon, darkness and even colder temperatures would push the people off the streets until morning.

For a good six months of the year, the average citizen of Winnipeg spent much of their time indoors. True, there were hardy winter enthusiasts who enjoyed skating and sledding at Assiniboine Park, though Sam and Sarah

Klein weren't part of that group. For them, like so many other residents of the North End, winter was a season to be survived. It meant bulky clothes, cold floors, drafty ice-frozen windows, and hoarding wood for the stove.

Occasionally, about mid-January when winter was at its most bitter, with high snowdrifts and howling Arctic winds, Sarah would raise the issue of leaving Winnipeg for a warmer climate. She'd notice ads in the papers about sunny Florida.

"Imagine, Sam, a place with no snow. Year-round summer. No more cold mornings, no more winter coats and boots. And the money! The newspaper say that in cities like Miami and Jacksonville, someone with a little ambition can become wealthy beyond their dreams."

Klein would nod, smile, but offer nothing more in the way of a real response. What was there to say? It wasn't that he found the idea of moving to the United States any less tantalizing than Sarah did. It was just that he couldn't abandon his mother, Freda, especially since she'd been having dizzy spells the past few months. There was also his sister Rivka, who was probably going to marry Solomon Volkon. Solomon was a decent man, trained as a schoolteacher, but he was unemployed most of the time and spent his days drinking coffee and philosophizing about improving the lives of Jewish factory workers rather than actually earning a living. Klein was certain that Rivka would have to support this man for the rest of her life. For these reasons, he needed to remain in Winnipeg.

Besides, he had his so-called reputation to consider. In this city, in some quarters at least, he was a "somebody" — a man who commanded respect. He would be the first to admit that the public's perception of him as a dashing detective was highly exaggerated. Still, why would he want to start over somewhere else?

The streetcar ride down Main Street was uneventful as it made its way past small crowds of men gathering in front of hotels in anticipation of a night of revelry. Deep in thought, Klein hardly paid attention to the chatter around him, mainly heated discussions by North End women about bargains won or lost during an afternoon of shopping at downtown stores. At one point, Klein thought he sensed someone watching him, but before he could take a casual look at the collection of riders behind him, the car reached his stop at the corner of Main and Sutherland.

He walked briskly down Sutherland to Anabella Street and turned left. There was hardly a soul to be seen. January and February were always slow months for Melinda and the other city madams in the neighbourhood. At any other time of the year, the brothels would be packed with hordes of single men on Winnipeg stopovers, farm labourers and immigrants looking for work. They would arrive at the nearby CPR station, have a few drinks at a hotel bar, and eventually stumble to Melinda's doorstep in search of female company. Despite their poor wages, money never seemed to be a problem. There were few who couldn't find — or borrow or steal — the four dollars required for a half-hour of satisfaction.

It was more than three years since Klein had quit his job as the bouncer at Melinda's, a position he sometimes recalled with nostalgia. Or maybe it was that he sometimes yearned to be single again and answerable to no one but himself. But he wouldn't trade his life with Sarah for anything. She was his *basherte,* his perfect match, as even his mother, Freda, grudgingly conceded. Walking up the path to the brothel at 118 Anabella Street, he struggled not to imagine Sarah on the stairs heading to her room with other men. Long ago, Melinda had warned Klein that Sarah's past life wouldn't be easy to erase from his mind or that of the public.

"People are funny. Once they see you as a whore, honey," she had told him, "it's a difficult thing to change. That's why I stay put. Could you see me selling dresses at Eaton's?"

Then, Klein had chuckled, certain he would be able to ignore the stares and whispers that Sarah would provoke every time she appeared in public. And indeed, when they were first married, Sarah's transition from queen of the whores to wife of Sam Klein had been the talk of the town. Klein knew that local gamblers had bet as much as $150 that his marriage would never last. Even McCreary was said to have got in on the wagering down at the police station.

While the gossip and sneers hardly bothered him, the rude comments troubled Sarah. On such occasions, he would try to placate her, dismissing her critics as inconsequential. What disturbed him more was a nagging feeling that Sarah preferred her old life to her new one. Of late, even before Emily's murder, this feeling had intensified. Though Klein couldn't put his finger on it, he believed that his wife — as odd as this seemed to him — missed the security, friendship and family-like environment Melinda had provided.

Shaking his mind free of these thoughts, he turned the knob of Melinda's front door and entered.

"What can we do for you, sir?" an unfamiliar voice asked. The accent was British. "Looking for a lady. Perhaps I could suggest someone?"

Klein unbuttoned his coat, pushed his bowler hat back on his forehead, and peered into the face of a young man, perhaps nineteen years old. He had a day's stubble on his face. He wore a white long sleeved shirt and brown trousers held up by suspenders, but his muscular build was clearly evident through his clothes.

"And you are?"

The man smiled blandly. "Name is Shepherd, Edward Shepherd, but everyone just calls me Teddie."

"You new around here, Teddie?"

"About a month or so. I was planning to head farther west when I first arrived. I was looking for a job in the machine trades. That's why I left Liverpool. But once I got to Winnipeg, I lucked into this work. Pays good and you can't beat the company, if you know what I mean."

"I do."

"So what'll it be, blonde, redhead, brunette. We have all kinds."

"I'm here to see Melinda."

"Do you have an appointment? I got strict orders that she's not to be bothered. We had a bit of trouble around here and…"

"Don't think I need an appointment. You just go tell her that Sam Klein is here."

A warmer smile lit up Teddie's face. "I've heard about you."

"That so?"

"You're a bit of a legend around here. Girls still talk about Sam doing this and Sam doing that. I was hoping we'd meet."

Klein grinned. "Melinda. You go tell her I'm waiting."

"Yeah, right away. Why not go into the parlour and I'll fetch her. I guess you know the way."

As Klein made his way through the narrow hallway leading to the parlour, he noticed that Melinda had made some much-needed improvements. There was a fresh coat of dark red paint on the walls, in the parlour a new lavender sofa and matching love seat. On the walls, however, hung the same gaudy tapestries that Klein remembered. Melinda had her own peculiar tastes — European, she called them — and it definitely gave the house a unique character.

Except for a young man waiting nervously beside the mottled player piano in the corner of the room, the parlour was empty. Klein reached into his jacket pocket for his silver cigarette case, took a cigarette out, lit it, and sat down on the sofa. Only a few minutes passed before a woman Klein didn't recognize entered the room. He figured she was twenty at most. She wasn't especially striking. She was wearing a black silk chemise with matching pumps and not much else. Her long dark hair hung over her shoulders and her body was curvaceous and taut. The most noticeable thing about her was the dark bruise under her left eye.

"It's your turn, now," she said coyly to the young man. She reached for his hand, but he sat frozen in his chair. "Come on, now, honey, I haven't got all day. This your first time or something?"

"Today's my eighteenth birthday," he stammered. "My friends took a collection so I could come here." At that, he dug into his pocket and produced a handful of coins.

Across the room, Klein watched this encounter with a grin. He already knew how it would end.

The woman smiled. "What's your name?"

"George…George Parks. I live in Stonewall," he said softly. "You know where that is?"

"I've heard of it. We have a few regulars from there," she said with a smile. "They usually come for a visit when they're in the city to buy supplies, have a drink."

He nodded cautiously, never taking his eyes off of her. "Did someone hit you?" he asked pointing to the mark under her eye.

She shook her head. "I fell…I fell down the stairs the other day." Her tone was hardly convincing. "But you don't worry about that. You're here for a birthday. Isn't that right, George?"

The young man inhaled sharply. He stood up slowly and took the woman's hand. His hand was shaking. "Don't get too excited, dear," she cooed. "Your birthday present is only beginning."

As she led George up the stairs to one of the rooms on the second floor, the woman turned and blew a kiss in Klein's direction. "Give me fifteen or twenty minutes and I'll be back for you."

"Any other day, I'd oblige you," he said, "but I got some business to —"

"Sam, I'm so glad you're here," said Melinda, suddenly striding into the parlour.

Klein stood. "You look lovely," he smiled, "as always."

"And you're a gentleman as always," she said giving him a peck on the cheek. Melinda turned to face the young prostitute still standing on the stairs with her nervous client. "What are you standing there for girl? Get up those stairs. The boy can't wait forever. And I don't want a mess down here."

"Yes, Ma'am. I thought you might want to introduce me to your handsome friend."

"He's off limits. Now go on, don't dawdle, you got work to do."

The woman peered into Klein's eyes, shrugged, then grabbed George's limp hand and led him up the stairs.

"What's her name? I suspect she's awfully good."

"Oh, Molly? She is. A little rough around the edges. Needs a bit of discipline. But I do have high hopes for her."

"I noticed the bruise on her eye."

Melinda waved her hand. "Oh, it was nothing. We had a disagreement about money. Naturally, I set her straight."

"Naturally."

Klein knew that Melinda was a fair employer, though, like most madams and pimps in the city, she did have an authoritarian streak. There were certain rules to be obeyed and her girls soon came to understand that. The first rule was that Melinda's share amounted to about three-quarters of their nightly earnings. The second was that Melinda's opinions were not to be questioned. Klein suspected that the young woman's black eye was the result of an ill-conceived attempt to discuss financial matters. He also knew there would be no point trying to get Melinda to ease up on her girls. Such were the realities of life in a Winnipeg brothel.

"Molly has been here maybe six months," added Melinda. "Right off a farm somewhere south of the city. I'm still training her, but on a good night she can handle ten or fifteen men. I expect she'll soon be as good as…"

"Sarah?"

"Sorry, Sam. Wasn't thinking."

"Forget about it. Now, tell me what kind of trouble you're in. I hear Jordan is coming after you."

"Yet again," said Melinda, wrinkling her forehead. "That man is intolerable. He's even worse than those moral reformers who used to parade in front of the house."

"So what happened? How's Katie?"

"Katie will recover. The doctor says that she had a concussion and must stay in the hospital for a few days. She's complaining of headaches, but I think she'll be back on her feet soon. The girl is tough. As to what happened, there's not much to tell. A few days before, she received an envelope with twenty dollars and a note with instructions: if she wanted another twenty, she should be at Room 204 at the Royal Alex at seven o'clock. Now, you know my rules about the girls working in hotels. But for that kind of money, I decided to make an exception, especially since she told me about the offer. I mean she could have just gone without telling me."

"And risk the back of your hand?"

Melinda chuckled and paused to light the cigarette Klein handed her. "I run a clean and orderly house. You of all people should understand that."

"I do, of course. Go on."

Melinda blew a whiff of smoke upwards. "When the time came for Katie to walk over to the hotel, who do you think she's with?"

"Jordan?"

"The good inspector showed up at about six o'clock that evening. He said that he was here because some cattle buyer who was in the week before claimed that one of the new girls stole his pocket watch. He asked me a few questions about it, and then of course he added that he'd have to have a little chat with the girls, starting with Katie. He can't keep his hands off her. She says he's a slobberer and has some peculiar tastes."

"Such as?"

Melinda moved closer to Klein. "He likes to pretend that Katie's his teacher and he's a naughty student."

"You're not serious?"

"Oh, yeah, I am. When he was done playing games with Katie, he offered to escort her to the Royal Alex in his sled. Said he had to go there anyway to check on their liquor licensing. An hour later, the cops arrive, telling me they found Katie badly beaten in an alleyway behind the hotel. They said she had a pouch of opium in her pocket. But as far as I know, she was never a smoker. Later, when Jordan returned to bother me again, I asked him what had happened. He said that after they got to the Royal Alex, she went to the front desk, and he went to the see the barkeep, and that's the last he saw of her."

"But you don't believe him?"

"As far as I'm concerned his word isn't worth a plugged nickel."

"What did he say about the opium?"

"His usual rant about how I'm corrupting young women and turning them into addicts. It's all hogwash. Sam, you know that I don't allow opium smoking in the house."

Klein nodded.

"That drug is a curse, plain and simple," continued Melinda, growing angry. "No girl who lives for her next smoke is useful to me. Do you know what Lee calls the addicts? Opium ghosts. White-faced, hollow cheeks, blank eyes. Who'd pay for that kind of company? Besides, you've seen Katie, she hardly looks like an addict."

"Maybe she wasn't using it, but she could have been peddling it. Opium isn't hard to find in the North End. There's that house over on Logan run by that Chinaman Wong. There's a lot of money to be made."

"I would find that hard to believe. It just doesn't seem like something she would do."

"Either way, I hear that Jordan has already made up his mind. He plans to come down hard. Says he's going to shut you down."

"What a two faced son-of-a-bitch. Can you believe his nerve? He screws one of my girls like a goat and then goes home to his family all saintly. He should know I've got friends at city hall that'll be more than willing to help me."

"Well, I'll try to lend a hand too. If I have a chance, I'll make some inquiries. I'll pay a visit to the hospital and see what Katie has to say. But I have some other work to do first."

"I'm sorry, Sam. I'm so wrapped up in my own problems I forgot to ask you about Powers. My God, your friend Emily was murdered. You don't think Powers killed her, do you?"

"It doesn't look good. He showed up at my apartment with the murder weapon. But still…"

"You think he's innocent, don't you? Well, I don't blame you. I've always thought he was a gentle man. On the other hand, as for Emily, there was something odd about her. I only met her once or twice when Sarah brought her by a while ago now. Certainly not you're typical suffragist. I don't think any of her "sisters" would condescend to be friends with the likes of Sarah."

"How do you mean she was odd? In what way?"

"I don't know. Just a feeling, that's all. Now, I've got some work to do and I'm sure you do too."

"What's with the big rush? You seem awful nervous all of a sudden."

"I am. With Jordan on the warpath, twenty cops could come crashing through my door at any moment. So go on," said Melinda pushing Klein lightly on the shoulder. "But keep me informed if you find out who attacked Katie."

Klein smiled at two scantily-clad prostitutes who entered the parlour as he was departing. They were wearing black satin-laced corsets and sheer robes. "Darlene, Heather, always a pleasure. I like the outfits. But be careful in this weather that you don't get a chill."

They giggled like schoolgirls. "You still married, Sam?" Darlene asked playfully.

"Come back and visit us again," Heather added.

Klein buttoned up his coat and headed outside into the cold. He glanced across the street and noticed a figure lurking near a neighbouring brothel. Maybe the guy's getting cold feet, thought Klein. It was odd, though — there was something about the person that seemed familiar.

"That was too close," declared Melinda "What if he would have seen you here? Then what? I'm not happy about this at all. I don't like lying to people at the best of times, and certainly not to Sam."

A lean, dark-haired woman emerged from Melinda's back office. "I don't enjoy lying to him either," said Sarah Klein. "I promise to tell him soon. As soon as you and I work out all the arrangements and settle the money issues, I'm going to tell him."

"Honey, I don't think I would want to be there for that."

"Sam's a very understanding man. I'm sure he'll see this is something I have to do. That it's for the best."

"And if he doesn't?"

"Then I have a problem, don't I?"

Emotionally exhausted, Sarah sat on parlour sofa and peered out the dark window. Despite Melinda's doubts, in her heart she knew that Sam would see it her way. She just knew he would.

5

Manitoba Free Press, Thursday, January 29, 1914

POLICE MORALITY INSPECTOR ISSUES REPORT ON OPIUM USE

The year 1913 saw an increase in the number of people in Winnipeg convicted of offences related to the use of opium. According to City Police statistics, 25 individuals were charged as inmates of opium dens and 10 of keeping opium dens.

Morality Inspector Jordan blamed the increased use on the activities of Chinese drug merchants who operate their sordid activities from dilapidated rooming houses. In fact, all the opium joints were located in the area of the city west of Main Street known as Chinatown. The 1911 census recorded approximately 750 Chinese in Winnipeg.

"They introduce their drug on unsuspecting young women who then often become inmates of bawdy-houses as the only way to satisfy their addiction," Inspector Jordan writes in his annual report. "They are extremely dangerous and devious, these Chinamen. They cannot be trusted. Opium is a social evil of immense proportions. It will continue to spread if left unchecked. In my view, the only way to stamp out opium use is to halt Oriental immigration. Not all Chinamen are addicts or users, but far too many have been corrupted by this devil narcotic."

THERE WAS NO PEACE to be had. Not even a bottle of whisky could dull the terrible pain. No one had wanted matters to come to this. But Emily couldn't be shared, especially with that dirty Italian. What she saw in him was anyone's guess. They had argued about her relationship with him only days earlier. She had promised to end it. Yet when it came right down to it, Emily was too weak. She couldn't refuse her appetite for pleasure. She had once read out loud a passage from Oscar Wilde, one of her favourite writers — "We are each our own devil, and we make this world our hell." She had certainly accomplished that.

But regret was beside the point now. The deed was done, and nothing could bring Emily back. Self-preservation was the issue at hand. The authorities would never understand the passion of the moment. They would demand punishment in the extreme. There was no choice but to lie, dissemble, and obscure the truth. In this, Klein might prove to be an unwitting ally.

On McCreary's orders, they had isolated Alfred Powers in a hot stuffy room on the second floor of the station and had left him there for two hours. It was an old police trick McCreary had used many times. "You let them sit there thinking." he'd explain to new recruits. "And even the tough guys get scared. It's all part of wearing them down. Eventually, they'll tell you exactly what you want to hear."

Admittedly, Alfred Powers was not your average perpetrator nor was the crime itself routine. Petty thieves, drunks, robberies and assaults — these were the staples of the Winnipeg police department. If there were murders, they usually occurred during brawls or a robbery gone wrong. That had happened just a month before when a local tough named Jake Tyson had murdered Thomas Murray, a Winnipeg Street Railway employee, in a botched hold-up.

Similarly, a few years back, Jim Ferguson, a respectable Main Street merchant, had been robbed and beaten badly by a trio of American thugs on a rampage. Ferguson eventually died from the vicious beating he received. After a few weeks, his three assailants were captured, convicted, and hanged. Occasionally, murders, like the one involving young Anna Rudnicki, had a bizarre twist to them. But besides that 1911 case, McCreary figured he would have to go way back in the police files to 1895 and William Farr to find anything rivalling the Emily Powers-Antonio Rossi killings.

William Farr was a CPR railway engineer who decided to kill his wife and four children by setting his house on fire. If not for the heroic efforts of the fire department, the family would have burned to death. Shortly after his arrest, Farr managed to escape from jail and disappear without a trace. A few weeks later, the police in Vancouver apprehended him while he was boarding a ship headed to Hawaii. He was returned to Winnipeg where he finally stood trial and was sentenced to ten years at Stony Mountain. Throughout the trial, his wife refused to accept his guilt, despite a handwritten confession from the man himself. The confession revealed his original plan to flee the city with a younger woman, one whom authorities could never locate or apprehend.

Although Taber scoffed that leaving Powers alone in a room for an hour would hardly wear him down, he agreed to abide by his partner's tactics. Taber wanted to treat Powers like a common criminal and deal with him as quickly and as roughly as possible. But for now, they would do it McCreary's way.

Once the interrogation got underway, it failed to satisfy either detective. The lawyer remained stoic and in control. He steadfastly maintained that his recollection of the night of the murder was hazy. He claimed that he had arrived at the theatre expecting to meet his wife, had heard a scream, and then saw the bodies in the alleyway. He didn't know how he came to be at the Kleins' apartment with a knife in his hand.

"I really have nothing more to say, detectives, until I speak with my son. I don't understand where he could be." About an hour had passed.

"We aren't getting anywhere with this," said McCreary. "I'll check whether Hicks found any fingerprints on the knife. Let's give him a rest, Alex."

After McCreary left the room, Taber sat for five minutes staring icily at the silent lawyer. Finally, as if he could no longer contain himself, he growled, "You don't need your son to tell us the truth." He moved closer to Powers who remained seated on a small wooden stool.

"Can you explain how your wife's blood got all over your suit?"

"I cannot recall."

"Well, then, how about telling me what it felt like to see your wife in the streets with another man?"

"Pardon?"

"Don't play this game with me, Powers. Just admit that you killed both of them and I can go home for dinner."

"I told you I can't remember what happened."

"And I think you're a goddamn liar. Who could blame your wife for wanting someone else to satisfy her."

Powers flinched.

"She was a slut, admit it."

"Go to hell. I demand to see my son. Do you know who I…"

Suddenly, without warning, Taber wheeled and hit Powers across the face, catching him in the nose. The blow knocked Powers off the stool and on to the cold floor. Blood trickled from his nose.

"Now, Mr. Powers, do you want to tell me how you killed your wife and her boyfriend with a knife? What you did when you saw them — how shall I put this — enjoying each other's company in that alleyway? You attacked them. Correct?"

Powers attempted to stand up, but Taber pushed him back down on the stool. "First the truth, then you can get up."

"You're a real son-of-a-bitch, detective. Has anyone ever told you that?"

"Many times."

"When the Chief and Mayor find out what's gone on here…"

Looming over him, Taber delivered another blow to the side of Powers's head.

Powers blinked rapidly. "I want to see my son," he said in a firm voice.

As Taber was contemplating his next move, there was a knock on the door of the interrogation room. "Everything okay in here Detective Taber?"

"Oh, it's you, O'Shea. Yeah I was just having a little chat with Mr. Powers."

O'Shea noticed the blood on Powers's face, but ignored it. "McCreary told me to take Mr. Powers back to the holding cell for now. That okay with you?"

"Sure."

"This way, Mr. Powers," he said, taking the lawyer by the arm.

Powers stood up and wiped the blood from his nose with his handkerchief. "It's cops like you, Taber, who give the police a bad name."

Taber smirked. "Not when we get a conviction."

Taber closed the door as O'Shea departed with Powers. He took out a fat cigar from his vest pocket, another one from Powers's private stock, and sat down on the stool. This wasn't precisely what he had planned. He had hoped wringing a confession out of Powers would have been easier.

Instead, he had got a little carried away and now had some explaining to do. McCreary wasn't going to be happy about a bruised and swollen accused.

Rossi's death, he mused, had also been unexpected, but he had adapted as necessary. Such situations were bound to happen. He prided himself on his ability to quickly alter course if circumstances warranted. It was the reason he enjoyed the game of chess and why he was so good at it. Move and countermove. He craved the challenge — though sometimes it was himself he had to keep in check.

Rossi was such a poor unlucky bastard, Taber thought, and just when a payoff looked imminent. He had warned him to stay away from the woman, but Rossi hadn't listened. Then he had tried to double-cross him. That was serious error in judgement. Yet at least with Rossi out of the way there would be no more squabbling about who got what. Rossi's share was up for grabs. At the same time, a confession from Powers would make life easier and the fewer the complications the better. This operation, in his opinion, was dragging on far too long.

Only the Ashdowns had a finer sleigh than the Powers family. Built in London, Ontario and shipped to Winnipeg at a considerable cost more than a decade before, the Powers's sleigh was a handcrafted gem, made of pure-grained maple and painted a deep black. Its thick India rubber roof could be raised or lowered and provided ample protection against the winter winds. The interior had fur-lined cushion for extra warmth. Driven by Alfred Powers's loyal man, Elspeth, and pulled by two huge black shire geldings, it was the envy of most Winnipeggers, forced to use open cutters in the freezing prairie weather.

Bundled beneath a colourful Hudson's Bay blanket, Graham Powers told Elspeth to get him to the police station as quickly as possible. Nodding, the tall, silent Scot urged the large horses on, guiding them down Wellington Crescent and over the Maryland Street Bridge north towards Portage Avenue.

Staring out into the late afternoon winter haze, young Powers still couldn't fathom all that had taken place: Emily murdered while with another man, his father the prime suspect. It seemed like a terrible nightmare and yet he knew that he would have draw upon every ounce of his legal training to prove his father's innocence. Yes innocence, he had confirmed that much in his own mind.

Even with the love triangle aspect, he had decided that his father couldn't have committed this horrible act. He knew that other lesser men might have reacted in a jealous rage, but not his father. He possessed an even temperament and rarely got angry. It was the reason he was such a successful lawyer. No matter what Emily's sins were — and now clearly there were too many to count — he would never have raised a finger to her, never mind stabbing her to death.

Soon after his father had introduced Emily to him and his sister, Elizabeth had remarked that no good would ever come from a relationship based on a one-sided infatuation. How prophetic she had been.

As Elspeth turned the sleigh left on to Portage Avenue past the Winnipeg skating rink crowded with children, Graham suddenly remembered that weeks ago he had made plans for this evening. Those obviously would have to go by the wayside. Courtesy of a grateful client, he and a few of his lawyer friends had been presented with tickets for the welterweight wrestling championship slated for the Coliseum that night. There was no love lost between the two combatants, Walter Miller from St. Paul and Cleveland's Otto Suter, and Graham Powers had looked forward to the match with great anticipation.

As a young boy, he had been introduced to wrestling and boxing by his father, also an avid fan, and it had remained a passion they had shared. Usually, it was an elegant dinner at the Manitoba Club and then a night at the ring. They would talk about the law, politics, sports and business. Graham had always looked forward to this time with his father.

"We're nearly at Colony, Sir," announced Elspeth his bearded face covered in a tartan scarf. "Shouldn't be much longer."

With the horses trudging through the snowy street at a steady pace, Elspeth took little notice of the two lone figures standing on the corner of Colony and Portage. The two men, dressed in long overcoats with flat caps pulled low over their heads appeared to be waiting for Elspeth to pass them by so that they could cross the wide avenue. Elspeth glanced in their direction, noticed they were Oriental, and nodded. He wondered what they were doing in this neighbourhood. It wasn't like them to stray from Chinatown. But before Elspeth could imagine an answer, one of the men drew a revolver from his coat pocket and fired it twice in the air.

Startled, the two geldings abruptly reared, forcing Elspeth to pull back hard on the reins. Inside the carriage, Graham Powers toppled onto the wooden floor.

"What the hell was that?" Graham shouted. There was no response from his driver. "Elspeth did you hear me? I thought I heard a gun shot."

"Certainly you did," said an unknown voice. The accent was distinctly Chinese.

"Who is that? Elspeth what's happened?"

"I'm fine Mr. Powers, just a little shaken up," said the driver as he steadied the horses. "But I surmise that these two Oriental gentlemen are offering to relieve us of our wallets."

"What?" Powers eased himself up and out of the sleigh. The two men stood beside the carriage. Neither looked large, but they exuded a cocksure air. One, with a thin black moustache, was pointing the revolver directly at Powers. The other, with a slightly darker complexion and a glazed look in his eyes, was holding what appeared to be a wooden club against Elspeth's neck.

"Let's move off the street," said the man holding the gun. For a Chinaman, thought Graham, his English is good. Powers and Elspeth stood in their tracks. "I said now." He waved the revolver at both of them. "You," he told Elspeth, "bring the team."

The driver grabbed the reins and tugged as the sled lurched forward. The group moved off Portage to an alleyway behind Colony Street. It was deserted.

"We don't want anyone to get hurt, so why don't you lower that," Powers said to the man with the gun, "and tell me what it is you want from me." He lifted his right hand and was about to reach inside his coat.

"Stop right there, you son-of-a-bitch," said the man with the revolver. "Put your hand down, unless you want my friend to crush your driver's throat." His tone was firm and his dark eyes piercing. He gripped the revolver tightly and aimed it directly at Graham's chest.

Powers did as he was told and his arm dropped to his side. Alfred Powers had always told his son there were some men who couldn't be reasoned with — that a violent streak was part of a man's basic personality. It seemed to Powers, as well as many other wealthier Winnipeggers, that such savage traits were more common among the foreign-born than "true" Canadians. And there was something especially unsettling about an Oriental with a gun. Someone of Graham Powers's class didn't venture very often into Chinatown — the tenement neighbourhood around King Street between Logan and Pacific — other than perhaps to fetch some laundry from a Chinese shop. While Graham had occasionally opposed more stringent immigration laws, he decided at this moment that a $500 head tax on Chinese newcomers wasn't such a bad policy after all.

"Slowly put your hands up in the air," ordered the man. Again Graham did as he was instructed. His assailant moved closer, keeping the gun ahead of him. Graham could smell the stench of cheap whisky and tobacco on his breath. He reached into the young lawyer's inside coat pocket and found his gold pocket watch. He yanked it hard and the chain and clasp broke. Then he put his hand a second time to retrieve a black leather billfold.

As he stepped back, the other man watching Elspeth eased the wooden club away from the driver's neck. "You got all, now, Yew?" he asked, turning his head toward his partner. As he did so, Elspeth — who became the Powers's driver after retiring from the wresting ring — decided to take matters into his own hands. Moving swiftly, he lunged for the club, grabbed it and shoved it backward into the man's stomach sending him reeling.

"Elspeth, no!"

It was too late. The man with the gun turned and fired, hitting the driver in the shoulder. Elspeth collapsed on to the snow beside the agitated horses. A pool of blood formed quickly beneath his overcoat. "I ought to kill you both for that," the man said. He cocked the hammer of his pistol and pointed it at Powers. His fingers wrapped gently around the trigger as if he was preparing to fire his weapon.

"Yew, stop!" his partner cried, getting to his feet. "There's to be no murder. You heard the orders. He'll kill us both if we disobey."

The man walked toward Powers. "Give me your billfold and we'll let you go to your driver."

Graham pulled his money out of his inside coat pocket and handed it to the man.

"Thank you," said the man picking up his club. "A pleasure doing business with you Mr. Powers."

The man holding the gun spat at Powers. "Next time you might not be so lucky. You think you own the world, don't you? All of that money. But that money won't help your crazy father." He threw his hands to his neck as if trying to loosen a non-existent noose. He laughed, then turned and ran off, his friend close behind. Within moments, the two thugs were out of sight.

"No question about the prints on the knife," declared George P. Hicks. "They definitely belong to Alfred Powers." The diminutive Hicks, prematurely bald with a neatly trimmed black moustache and round wire-framed glasses, was the Winnipeg police department's fingerprint expert. In fact, Hicks, who had spent a summer in London training with Scotland Yard, was one of the foremost identification authorities in the country. In court, his reputation preceded him and most local jury members had come to accept his testimony without reservation. This was despite the best efforts of defence lawyers to denigrate the entire process as scientific voodoo.

"Great work, Hicks, as usual," said McCreary. "The prints on the knife, together with Powers's bloody suit and the obvious motive, should be enough for the Crown to do its job."

"I suppose so."

"What's wrong Hicks? You sound skeptical."

"No, the evidence strikes me as quite complete. But you know me, McCreary, I'm a perfectionist. Drives the missus crazy. I've rebuilt our fence five times in the past few years…."

"Hicks, your point?"

"Yes, of course. You see that?" He pointed to a small spot at the bottom of the knife handle.

"What? I don't see anything."

"Trust me, there's a partial stain which I can't account for. It might belong to Powers, but my professional opinion is that it doesn't. Look at the way the ridges form. I'd say, there's a slight chance that someone else might've touched the murder weapon."

"It might also be nothing, correct? Or perhaps one of the constables accidentally left a print."

"I thought of that. But I've already checked with O'Shea. He claims he was wearing his gloves at the murder scene. Let me work on it for a few days and I'll see if I can isolate it."

"You haven't told anyone else about this yet?" McCreary asked.

"No one, but you."

"Do me a favour, let's keep it that way until you've arrived at your final conclusions."

Hicks hesitated for a moment. "You'll deal with the Chief?"

"Leave him to me."

"Then, I'll agree. But, McCreary, if I should find strong evidence of another finger print I won't leave it out of my testimony in court."

"I wouldn't ask you to."

Alone in his cell, Alfred Powers sank into a deep depression. It wasn't the treatment he had received from Taber that troubled him so much. No, even before he had arrived at the station, he couldn't stop thinking about Emily. He couldn't get that terrible image of her from his head. She had betrayed him, and yet he still cherished her.

In the decades he had worked as a lawyer, he had counselled many distraught clients with words of encouragement. He had told them there was always hope. But now, he had none for himself. What was the point of going on, he wondered? Without Emily, what was there left to live for? He shut his eyes for a moment and once again he was in the alley behind the theatre. He was standing over the body of his wife, her bloody body, the knife in his hand....

It took McCreary only a minute or two to return to his office. Despite Hicks's doubts, he was confident that the evidence against Powers would be convincing. What did the average middle-class Winnipegger know about real police work? McCreary's experience had taught him that if a lawyer put an "expert" on the witness stand, whether a physician or a scientist, jurors were usually impressed enough to heed their words like the Bible. The world was changing too fast for most of these common people — salesmen, teachers, farmers, and factory workers — to keep up. Society's experts provided certainty for them.

As McCreary rounded the corner, he bumped into Taber.

"What's going on?"

"Come, on. Powers says he wants to speak with you. Says he wants to confess."

"What are you talking about?"

"I just heard from O'Shea. He told me that Powers has changed his mind."

"Peculiar, don't you think? You didn't have anything to do with this, did you Taber?"

The detective was silent.

"What happened?"

"I got a little carried away, that's all."

"Carried away?"

"Mr. Powers has a slight nose-bleed."

"I thought I warned you. This could ruin everything."

Taber was silent.

"The Chief is going to have your hide for this, Taber. I can't protect you on this one."

"Easy does it McCreary. It's a nosebleed, not a cracked skull. I didn't do anything that I haven't seen you do a hundred times."

The two detectives moved down the stairs toward the holding cell area. They found Constable O'Shea with Powers.

"You okay, Mr. Powers?" McCreary asked.

"I want to confess to the murder of my wife," declared Powers, staring straight ahead.

"You sure about this, sir?"

"I am, detective. It's true, I murdered my wife and the man she was with. Write something up and I'll sign it. I'll sign whatever the hell you want."

"I thought you wanted to speak with your son first. We could wait."

"No! I did it. That's all I have to say for now."

"And you weren't coerced or harmed by Detective Taber?"

"No, the detective didn't touch me. I fell on the corner of the table."

"Here," said O'Shea, "I've already taken the liberty of writing this up. All Mr. Powers has to do is sign it."

He dipped a pen in a bottle of ink and handed it to Powers with a piece of paper. The lawyer grabbed it and scribbled his signature. "Now, leave me alone."

Pleased, though astonished, at this unexpected development, McCreary didn't know what to say.

"You heard him," Taber finally said. "McCreary, you awake?"

"Yeah, I heard you. Let's go."

Quickly word of the confession got around the station. In a matter of minutes, Chief MacPherson rushed into the detectives' office, but he wasn't smiling.

"McCreary, Taber, I thought I warned you about getting rough with Mr. Powers. Are you trying to get us fired? You think a confession obtained after a beating will hold up under cross-examination?" His tone was firm and his Scottish accent thick.

"McCreary didn't have anything to do with it," said Taber. "I'll take full responsibility. It was an accident. But that doesn't discount the confession. He freely offered that. There was no coercion."

"That right, Bill?" asked the Chief.

"It's like Taber says. No one forced Mr. Powers to confess. It was his idea. I don't think Taber's shenanigans had anything to do with it."

MacPherson said nothing for a moment. "All right, then, proceed with the charges."

McCreary and Taber eagerly strutted back to the interrogation room. McCreary approached the disconsolate lawyer. "Alfred Powers, you are hereby charged with the murders of Emily Powers and Antonio Rossi. You will be confined to a jail cell here and appear before a magistrate in Police Court at the earliest possible date. Do you have any questions?"

The lawyer said nothing.

"Taber, take Mr. Powers to a cell on the lower level where he'll be more comfortable. And if he as so much as stubs his toe, I will hold you personally responsible. Is that understood?"

"Understood."

As Taber and Powers receded down the hallway, MacPherson reappeared and took McCreary to the side. Together, they leaned against a warm and hissing radiator.

"Okay, Bill," said MacPherson. "What do you really think?"

"We have a confession, Chief. What is there to worry about? You think Powers is innocent?"

"No, I'm quite certain he did it, but let's see what comes out in court. I'm concerned about Taber. He's a dangerous combination of mean and smart. And it's not just that he roughed up Powers a little. It happens. There's something else. I can sense it."

"You're imagining things, Chief. Taber just has his own way of getting the job done."

MacPherson smiled. "I'm sure you're right. Must be his Siberian blood. I hear those people can be unpredictable."

"Exactly. But if you like, I'll keep an eye on him."

"Good, then, I'll leave this with you. And I suggest that if Powers sticks to his story about Taber's interrogation, we should too. No sense making matters worse. Now I have to make a full report about this to Deacon, before he reads about it in the newspaper. There's nothing worse than a cranky mayor."

The Chief departed and McCreary returned to his office to write up his report on the arrest of Alfred Powers. It had to be perfect. He knew the Attorney-General would probably bring in a special prosecutor, maybe someone like Timothy Jarvis or Bryan Black, to deal with this quickly but prudently. He also knew that Powers and his son were likely to be left high and dry — that Deacon, Fowler, Macdonald, Shore, Wallace and the rest of city council would wash their hands clean of the entire sordid mess. He could just hear their conversations around the dining tables at the Manitoba Club between cigars and brandy, how they were not about to let the Powers tragedy get in the way of their professional careers or civic progress. The personal problems of one of a fellow club members, even though he was Alfred Powers, could not hinder Winnipeg's glorious future as the "Chicago of the North."

Those pompous blatherskites, thought McCreary — they would sacrifice their own mothers in pursuit of economic greatness. And to his mind, the vision of progress propelling Winnipeg into the next decade sometimes left much to be desired.

McCreary knew he was playing a dangerous game — like walking on rotten planks. Sooner or later, he was going to have to let MacPherson in on his plans. But not yet. The confession by Powers was a gift from the heavens. Who could have asked for a more perfect turn of events? It fit the plan better than he could have imagined. Yet he, too, was bothered by Taber's latest actions — even if Powers had confessed of his own free will. His instincts told him that his partner was too unpredictable. More and more, he doubted whether he could trust Taber to watch his back.

"Sarah, you home?" Klein called out as he entered his apartment. There was no answer. It was seven o'clock by the time Klein arrived back at the Lady Angela in the North End. Sarah had told him she would be back by six. He threw a few pieces of wood into the kitchen stove and put on the pot of *borscht* his mother had brought over earlier in the week. Soon the pot of stewed meat and beets was bubbling. He scooped out a large bowlful, and gulped it down with a hunk of fresh rye bread as he glanced through the evening edition of the *Tribune*.

There was yet another article on the never-ending debate over provincial education. Sooner or later, Klein thought, the powers that be would ensure that all school instruction took place in the English language. It was inevitable. Long live the British Empire. The other story that caught Klein's eye was that Robert Reid, the police constable who had helped Jack Krafchenko make his daring escape, had been sentenced to seven years in the penitentiary.

Reid was a fool for becoming involved with "Bloody Jack" and all for promises of more money. But Klein also understood that most police officers in the city barely made ends meet. You couldn't go far on $85, the salary paid for working twelve hour shifts six days a week. It was only two years ago that former Chief McRae managed to arrange one day off a week for his men, as was the custom in Britain. The money Krafchenko offered Reid was too tempting to pass up. And he wasn't the only cop in Winnipeg who was on the take.

After visiting Melinda's, Klein had stopped for a shot of whisky at the Brunswick and to find out if McCreary had left any messages with 'One-Arm' Eddie, the hotel's bartender. He had sat by himself nursing his drink at a table in the corner of the dark and musty saloon, away from the pool hustlers and pimps that usually congregated around the long oak bar that stretched from one end of the room to the other. It was payday and the crowd of railway workers and labourers swarming the Brunswick wanted their cheques cashed right away. They had few other options. Winnipeg banks closed at three o'clock and other retail establishments a few hours later. Hotel bars provided a much-needed service by cashing their patrons' cheques. That some of the men drank away half their salary before they went home for dinner and lost a bit more playing cards was clearly of no concern to the hotel owners.

Klein was eventually coaxed into sitting in on a poker game while one of the players, Spicer Doyle, a local pool shark Klein was friendly with, took a bathroom break. In fact, he was gone from the table for more than an hour, fleecing down a few young rubes who thought they could beat him at snooker. Meanwhile, with a full house of kings and tens, followed by a straight flush with jack of spades high, Klein was up twenty dollars from what he began with.

Naturally, the conversation around the table had turned to the Powers-Rossi murders. Most of the men wanted to hear Klein's opinions. But one of the other poker players, a popular Italian street vendor known around Main Street as Frankie, prattled on about what he knew about Antonio Rossi.

"Sure he was always trying to stir up problems at the CPR shops, telling his *paesani* to stand up to the bosses and English men in the machine shops. But that's not all. He called himself a *padrone*, a man who could find work for other men. But he was a liar and a cheat, carrying on with a married woman. Everyone knew it, including his own family. I hear he even stole money from his uncle. But worse — "

"Go on," everyone around the table had urged him.

"Nothing. I talk too much, like a fish wife."

Eventually, Spicer Doyle had returned and Klein had given him back his chair. By the time he left the Brunswick for home, there was still no news from McCreary. He told 'One-Arm' Eddie, he'd telephone him in an hour. As he was leaving the hotel, Frankie had called out to him. He asked Klein to follow him outside to a secluded spot in the alley.

"There's one more thing, I must tell you about Rossi," said the street vendor in a whisper.

"Let me guess — he had a wife and child back in the old country."

"No, nothing like that." He stopped and glanced around.

"Frankie, I've had long day. My wife is waiting for me. So out with it."

"I've heard that Rossi was mixed up with a high-ranking policeman."

"I see," said Klein, a little more interested. "You got a name."

Frankie hesitated for a moment. "A detective, and a nasty one."

"You mean Taber, Detective Alex Taber?"

"I don't know what was going on between them, but people have seen them together. That's what I've heard."

Taber and Rossi, mused Klein as he finished off his *borscht* — was there ever a more mismatched pair? But now that he thought about it, Taber had been more ornery than ever last night. Maybe Rossi's death wasn't part of his plan. McCreary might know something, although if Taber was crooked he would surely try to keep it from his partner. Wouldn't that be ironic, Klein smiled as he lit a cigarette: Taber investigating a double homicide that he might be responsible for. If so, Klein knew that Taber would go to any length to convict Powers, innocent or not.

He glanced at his pocket watch again, 7:45 p.m. and still Sarah hadn't arrived. He was becoming more concerned. It wasn't like her. He knew she was terribly upset by Emily's death. Perhaps she needed time alone.

It was time to check again with 'One-Arm' Eddie. He walked into the hallway where the telephone sat on a small mahogany table. Not everyone in the North End had a phone, but Sid Vineberg was a decent landlord and had arranged the connection with the Manitoba Government Telephones. It made Sid feel like a *macher*. "My tenants have phones," he would brag to his friends.

"Operator, please get me Main 6487."

"The Brunswick?" the female voice asked.

"That's right."

"One moment, sir."

A few clicks followed and then a short ring. "Brunswick Hotel."

"Eddie, it's Klein."

"McCreary was here, maybe half an hour after you left."

"And?"

"And, his message is this: the lawyer's confessed and been charged."

"What? Jesus Christ, what's going on over there? How could he have confessed?"

"You got a message for McCreary?"

"Yeah, if he comes back tonight, tell him to be at Dolly's for coffee tomorrow morning at 10."

Klein pushed the receiver holder down several times. "Hello, operator…operator."

"Don't get excited Sam, I'm here."

"Fanny, you working late tonight?"

Fanny Katz, a close friend of his sister Rivka, was one of the few Jewish telephone operators hired by the provincially-owned utility. But Fanny was planning to get married in the spring and that meant she would have to leave her job — company policy, single women only.

"Fanny, I need Whitehall 3492 and quickly."

"Right away, Sam. Say hello to Rivka for me when you see her tomorrow night."

"I will." Tomorrow was Friday night and *Shabbas* dinner was always held at his mother's. Fanny knew that Rivka would be there with her boyfriend, Solomon. With everything going on, Klein wouldn't have minded missing the family get-together, especially since Freda and Sarah had been bickering lately. But he knew that his mother and Clara Hirsch expected them to attend and would accept no excuse. Klein could live with many things, but not his mother's disappointment.

Fanny made the connection and a woman answered the phone at the other end.

"Elizabeth, this is Sam Klein."

"Yes Sam, I'm thankful you've telephoned. I've just spoken with Graham."

"From the police station, I hope."

"No. I'm afraid he's run into some trouble."

"Serious?"

"Yes. On his way to see father, he was robbed…"

"Robbed? You must be joking?"

"I'm not. They were held-up by two Chinese men, and Elspeth, our driver, was shot in the arm. Graham has taken him to the hospital. He's still there."

For a moment, Klein didn't say anything. Was it coincidence that Graham Powers was robbed on his way to the station? Robberies were a fact of life in Winnipeg, as in most large North American cities, but in this case the timing was suspicious. But why would someone want to prevent Graham Powers from contacting his father? To get an answer, he would have to track down the two thugs.

"Sam are you there?" asked Elizabeth.

"Yeah. Listen to me. If Graham calls you again, tell him that he must get to the Rupert Street station as soon as possible."

"Why? What's happened? Why haven't they let father come home yet?"

"I'm sorry Elizabeth but I just heard some unsettling news. They've charged him with the murders of Emily and Rossi. I expected that. But…"

"But what, Sam?"

"Apparently he confessed to killing them both."

"Oh My God, that can't be. Father couldn't have done it, Sam. I'm going down to the station myself. Maybe they'll let me speak with father."

"Hold on, Elizabeth, I'm going to need your help. I want to speak with Emily's friends."

"That'll be a short list."

"All right then, the women in her suffragist and temperance groups. They might have some useful information."

"I doubt if they'll tell you much, Sam. The ones who were fooled by her are too embarrassed."

"I take it that doesn't include you."

"No. I never trusted her. Not for a moment. She was…"

"Go on."

"I've said enough. I'm a good Christian woman, but she brought out the worst in me. Call me tomorrow. I'm certain I can arrange a meeting. I do know that Nellie McClung thought highly of Emily. The Lord only knows why. And of course there's Grace Ellis — they were inseparable. She might be helpful."

Klein hung up the receiver as the door to his apartment swung open. It was Sarah.

"They've charged Alfred with the double murder," he said grimly.

"You're not surprised, are you?" she asked, removing her scarf and coat.

"No, but that's not the worst of it. Alfred signed a confession."

Sarah showed no emotion as she hung her coat on a hook in the hallway.

"Nothing to say?"

"I'm sorry, Sam," she said rubbing the back of her neck, "I'm a little preoccupied. Talk with Alfred. I'm certain you'll get to the bottom of this. But, *Shailek*, I also think you'd better prepare yourself for the fact that he might be confessing to something he really did."

"And what makes you such an authority?"

Sarah shrugged. She kissed Klein on the cheek. "Come, look what I got today."

"Not right now."

"Come, on, *Shailek*."

Reluctantly, Klein followed his wife into their small bedroom. He sat on the edge of the bed while Sarah unwrapped her parcel. "Look, isn't it beautiful. And you won't believe the sale the Hudson's Bay was having."

Klein smiled. He knew that Sarah usually justified her numerous purchases by claiming that a particular item was "on sale."

"I know what you're thinking, but see for yourself." She opened the brown cardboard box and took out a navy wool v-neck sweater. "Regular $3.50, I paid only one dollar," she said proudly.

Klein reached around her waist and pulled her down towards the bed. He gently pushed her dark hair away from her face and kissed her.

"What was that for?" she asked.

"Does a man need a reason to show affection to his wife? Now tell me why you're so late. You couldn't have been shopping all this time?"

"Oh, I was doing this and that. I was at Eaton's for a little while and stopped at the cafeteria for a snack."

"That's it?"

"That's it. And since when do I have to report my every movement to you?"

"I'm your husband. I have a right to know these things."

"Enough talk." She stood up and unbuttoned her blouse and skirt. In a matter of seconds, she stood naked before him.

Klein gazed at her, not uttering another word. He was still moved by her lithe body, with her high firm breasts and swelling hips. She took him by the hand and led him to their bed. She smiled as she crouched on top of him and deftly undid his belt buckle. His hands moved all over her body, stroking and arousing her, searching for spots that he knew gave her pleasure. He stopped for a moment and reached for a rubber sheath he kept in a small box by the bed.

"You don't need that, Sam. It's the right time of the month."

Klein didn't argue. He had no love for prophylactics at the best of time — "It's like a wearing a wet sock," he'd complain. Besides, even when they had forgotten to use protection, nothing happened. Sarah didn't become pregnant. In fact, even when she worked at Melinda's it had never been a problem. Still, he never doubted that when the time was right, she would conceive a child for them.

They never left the bedroom the rest of the night, holding each other and making love as many times as Klein was able. In between, they sipped on a shared glass of whisky and smoked a handful of cigarettes. Every so often, Sarah attempted to start a conversation, but would stop herself.

Klein hardly noticed. As he lay beside her, content and relaxed, his mind was already working out the details of his investigation. He couldn't stop thinking about what had happened to Graham Powers. There had to be some connection, but nothing he came up with made any sense. The one thing that kept gnawing at him was that somehow Taber was involved. He could feel it in his bones. And nothing was going to give him more pleasure than nailing that crooked cop.

"Do you think the police will release the bodies soon?"

"What's that?" Klein mumbled half asleep.

"I want both of us to go to Emily's funeral. I doubt many will show up, and no one should be buried alone."

"I'm sure it'll only take a few more days. Probably by Monday."

"I wonder if they'll allow Alfred to attend? Sam, did you hear me?" She nudged him lightly. He was sleeping. She stroked his face as a worried frown furrowed her brow.

How am I going to tell him, she thought. She was kidding herself — he wasn't going to understand, not ever. The money wasn't going to make a difference to him. But as much as she loved him, she also had to think of herself, of her sanity. Another year of doing nothing was unacceptable. What other options did she have? A clerk? A stenographer? Face it, she was only good at one thing. The arrangements with Melinda for Lynette's house were already worked out. They would be equal partners. Melinda would work out the financing, and Sarah would run it. Sarah didn't have to live there, she didn't have to do any actual whoring, and Darlene would be in charge after closing time. She could pay back Melinda in a few months. What businesswoman could ask for a better deal?

Sarah got out of bed and put on her cloth night gown and kimono. She walked quietly out of the bedroom and into the kitchen. She poured herself half a glass of whisky, lit one of Sam's cigarettes, and sat at a chair in the darkened room. Moments passed before she stood up again and opened the cupboard next to the sink. She pushed aside a few large bowls and a silver tray, a wedding present still not used. Finally her hands found the object she was searching for, a small black leather-bound book.

She sat back down at the table, lit a kerosene lamp — no point turning on the lights at this late hour — and stared at the book with the initials "E. M." engraved on the cover. Despite her promise, she knew that she would have to show this to Sam. She suspected that he wouldn't understand her loyalty to her friend. Her fingers gingerly leafed through the pages until the book opened near the middle. In the flickering light, her eyes stared at the delicate handwriting.

September 5, 1912

The demon has got hold of me again. I am too weak to fight it. The feelings, the urges too strong. I don't know what is wrong with me. But the enjoyment and pleasure too wonderful for words. Lunch with Antonio yesterday. We had dessert in a hotel room. Dangerous to be seen in public. I'm sure Elizabeth suspects something. I hate her. Do I not satisfy Alfred as well? I'm not denying him. Has there ever been a man more satisfied in Winnipeg? But these feelings are overwhelming. Even now as I write this, my body tingles with anticipation. Masquerade cannot last forever.

6

Winnipeg Telegram, Friday, January 30, 1914

CHURCH NEWS

Grace Church is proud to announce a public lecture by Rev. J.S. Woodsworth, entitled, "The seamy side of social pathology." The former superintendent of the All People's Mission, Rev. Woodsworth is also the author of two highly acclaimed books, "Strangers Within Our Gates" and "My Neighbour," a well-received study of the modern city published in 1911. His lecture will be based on research he conducted for the latter work. Currently, Rev. Woodsworth is continuing his surveys of several Canadian cities in conjunction with the Methodist and Presbyterian Church councils. This important discussion on the vices and immorality of city life will be held on Monday, February 2 at 7:00 p.m. All are welcome.

JOHN JORDAN KNEW THAT this wasn't a good idea. He had left the house in the middle of the night with a note by his wife's night table, a lie. Yet another one. Cursed was the day he had entered that house of sin and saw that young creature, her ruby lips beckoning him. He was ashamed but hadn't been able to stop himself. He would see her just one more time, he told himself as he walked down the white hospital corridor. She would answer his questions and that would be the end of it.

He had heard the whispering and jokes around the station and ignored them. So far the Chief had ignored them too. That was fortunate. Yet this latest incident had reminded him of just how dangerous a game he was playing. Fornication was one thing, drug trafficking quite another. The world was sinking deeper into a mire of sin and depravity. His mission was to curtail it and he had, at least in his opinion, done a reasonable job. Yet there was much more work to do. The fight against liquor and temptation could never be won without him. Yes, he was an invaluable warrior.

Except for a lone nurse in a long white dress and cap working at the front entrance, everyone else on the ward was asleep. The smell of antiseptic hung in the hallway. Because Katie had been involved in a crime, she was given the luxury of a private room. The city footed the bill for the extra costs. Normally, someone of her ilk would have been allotted a bed in the larger dormitory where the physicians and nurses attended when they had a free moment.

"Excuse me, sir, where do you think you are going?" the nurse asked Jordan.

"Police business," he said, waving his badge.

"It's the middle of the night. Can't this wait until morning? I won't have my patients disturbed…"

"Ma'am, please. Do you know who I am?"

"I do."

"Well, then, you'll stay out of my way and let me conduct my business as I see fit."

Sensing that further argument was futile, the nurse returned to her post. Katie's room was the last one on the right. Jordan nudged the door open and looked inside. A finger of early dawn shone through a the seam in the curtains, providing enough light for Jordan to find Katie's bed.

For a few moments, he stared at her. It appeared as if she had recovered quickly: only a small bruise above her right eye was evidence of the attack she had suffered in the alley behind the Royal Alex. Katie was typical of the girls who found their way to Melinda's. Disowned by her family at a young age, she had become independent, stubborn and hard-nosed. Melinda had worked diligently on softening her demeanour as well as her working-class appearance. She had succeeded fairly well. With her short brown hair, long legs, and sly smile, it was understandable why Jordan had been smitten by Katie. She wasn't the kind of woman he would bump into at his children's annual school picnic — and that fact excited him more than he cared to admit.

Jordan noticed the way the blanket clung to her body and his mind began to wander. Immediately, he caught himself, trying to wipe such filthy thoughts from his head. But oh, how the sight of her made his skin tingle.

Sensing his presence, Katie awoke with a start. She sat up quickly and moved to the far side of her narrow bed. She wiped her eyes and focused on her unannounced visitor. "Jordan. What are you doing here?"

"I need some answers. You have no idea how much trouble you're in, do you?" He didn't wait for her to respond. "I have not submitted my final report yet, but I suspect it will include something about your involvement in the city's opium trade."

"Opium! You know that's a damn lie. I'm not a user. Melinda doesn't allow it."

"When we found you lying in the snow and mud behind the hotel, there was a pouch of opium in your handbag. That's a fact."

"Someone set me up. Find out who left that twenty for me. Find out who was waiting for me at the Royal Alex and you'll have the bastard who did this to me."

"Sorry, Katie. I've checked that out already. The room you were heading for, number 204, was empty. Hadn't been rented in three days."

"Then, I guess you'll have to arrest me. Go ahead, I'll take my chances in court. I don't know what happened that night. I left you just inside the hotel and then — I can't remember." She gingerly reached for her handbag on the small dresser beside her bed and found a cigarette.

"Didn't the doctors tell you that that smoking tobacco is not wise while you're recovering? It certainly isn't ladylike..."

"Jordan, we're not far from the Arlington Street Bridge."

"Yeah, what of it?"

"Why don't you go jump the hell off. Now leave me alone. It's too early in the morning for the likes of you. Go home to your adoring wife and kids."

"I'm sorry you feel like that. I do believe we can help each other."

"Here it comes," Katie murmured to herself.

"I have no desire to drive you or your employer out of business."

"Melinda? She's got nothing to do with this."

"Perhaps. But where there is one opium user, there is likely another."

Katie shook her head in disbelief. Jordan moved closer and sat down beside her. Her sweet smell instantly excited him. Though it made her sick to her stomach, Katie understood how the game was to be played out. She edged her hand closer to his thigh and then moved it slowly between his legs. She undid the buttons on his fly and reached inside. He was already stiff.

"Now, I have an idea," she whispered as she fondled him. "I think you and I should become partners. The first thing I want is for you to lose that opium."

"I don't think I can do that," he said weakly. "Too many people…"

Her hand moved faster and faster. Then abruptly she stopped.

Jordan grimaced. "I'll see what I can do. Yes, I'm sure I can accommodate you."

Katie smiled. "Well then, I'm sure I can accommodate you as well."

In moments, he exploded onto the white hospital sheets. "Now look what you've done, John. I'm going to have call the nurse."

Without another word, he stood up, wiped himself off with his handkerchief and departed. Katie lay back on the bed. She found Jordan a repulsive but useful ally. Such a simple, weak man.

She knew, too, that Winnipeg's esteemed morality inspector was the least of her worries. The assault in the alley troubled her greatly. It was no accident — she was certain of that. She had a pretty good idea who was behind it and why. She would have to be more careful in the future. But the money was owed her, and she had no intention of forgoing it.

No one served better homemade strawberry jam in the city than Dolly. A piece of fresh rye bread topped with the jam and accompanied by a mug of hot coffee. For fifteen cents — only a dime on Tuesdays — there wasn't a tastier breakfast on the Prairies.

By the time Klein arrived at Dolly's cafe on Hargrave Street a little after ten o'clock, McCreary was into his second helping of bread. There was an empty stool at the end of the counter beside him and Klein settled on to it.

"Morning," he mumbled.

The police detective nodded as he sipped his coffee and scanned the front page of the *Tribune*'s second edition. An ad for a 1913 Rambler sedan with an electric self-starter and priced at only $1,500 immediately caught his eye.

A full-figured woman with greying hair and round wire-framed glasses approached. "What'll it be today, Sam?" asked Dolly. Klein had been eating at Dolly's for years but the lovely proprietress never seemed to age.

"I'll have what he's having," said Klein pointing in McCreary's direction, "along with an egg, hard-boiled."

"Coming right up." Dolly poured Klein a cup of coffee and the steam from the mug drifted up into the cloud of kitchen and cigarette smoke hovering in the restaurant. He broke off a piece of sugar from the stick in front of him, placed a small piece between his teeth and his cheek, and took a gulp of his drink.

"On your salary, you'll never afford that," said Klein looking at the automobile advertisement. "You'd better stick with something a little less expensive, like a horse and buggy."

Still McCreary didn't speak or raise his head. A minute passed before he responded, still keeping his eyes on the newspaper. "Not that I don't like you Klein, but meeting in a public place makes me edgy. You aren't the most popular guy around the department."

"Relax, McCreary, there's no one in here that matters. I've already checked."

"Me too, but that's beside the point, isn't it?"

"Anything more in the paper about Powers?"

"If you mean does the press know that we have a confession, the answer is no. MacPherson insisted we keep that quiet. He wants to go nice and easy with this one, everything by the book. Honestly, I think he's afraid of Powers's friends at city hall."

"Come on, McCreary, 'by the book'? How in the hell did you get a confession out of him? We both know that he came upon the murder scene after it had happened."

"The confession? That was Taber's doing, sort of."

"I'm not surprised. Did he beat it out of him?"

"Take it easy, Klein. He might have shoved him around a bit, but nothing serious. The lawyer actually caved all by himself. I think he just wanted to get it off his chest."

"That's a load of baloney. It'll never stand up in court, not after Graham Powers gets done. The kid is even sharper than his old man. Speaking of which, what do you know about this robbery?"

McCreary shrugged. "It's nothing unusual, happens all the time.

"You heard it was two Chinamen?"

"Yeah, what of it? Orientals are crooks, always scheming."

Klein frowned.

"Listen, Klein, you've seen the crime statistics in the newspapers. Twenty-five percent of the city's population, foreign-born one and all, committed forty percent of the crimes. What's more to say?"

"That's pretty fancy figuring, McCreary. Winnipeg has a population that's sixty percent English, Scottish and Irish. Right?"

"Yeah. so what of it?"

"Just this. I read that those fine descendants of the British Empire were responsible for more than fifty percent of the crimes. So what do you make of that?"

McCreary waved his right hand in the air. "You don't know what you're talking about. As for young Powers, he and his driver were held-up around Colony and Portage. That's all I know. I'll nose around Chinatown later to see what I can find out. The kid did telephone the sergeant's desk from the hospital. Said he'd be at the station around now. His daughter's been waiting there all night to see him."

"You couldn't let her in?"

"Chief's orders. No one can see him until he's spoken to his lawyer. You know Sergeant Sykes, he's as obedient as a Prussian."

"That family has been through hell and you're making it worse."

Dolly interrupted with more hot coffee. Klein waited until she had finished pouring before he continued the discussion. "What do you have on Emily and Rossi?"

"Why? Do you think it'll make a difference?"

"Humour me."

"Well, according to Jordan's reports, they've been sneaking around with each other for at least a year, maybe more."

Klein shook his head. "Christ, she only married Powers in June of 1912."

"From what I can gather she and her Romeo liked the Leland."

"Maybe I'll pay Sid Rochon a visit, see what I can find out. I hear he's got plans to rebuild the hotel."

"Mm. Anything else, Klein? I have work to do."

"Yeah, one more thing. It's about Taber. I've been hearing some strange things about who his friends are."

"That so? Anyone I know?"

"Yeah, you know him, though it might be tough to bring him in for questioning."

"Why's that?"

"Because at the moment he's on a slab at Doc Macdonald's office."

"Rossi?"

"That's what I hear."

"Is it reliable?"

"I think so. I'm going to dig around a little, see what turns up. I'm hoping it's true. Nothing would give more pleasure than to see that son-of-a-bitch locked up."

McCreary took a last sip of his coffee, put a few coins beside his cup and stood up. "You probably got it wrong," he said moving towards the door. "On the other hand, go ahead and poke around. Just let me know first if you find out anything serious."

"I'll think about it," said Klein lighting a cigarette. McCreary hadn't been gone a minute or two before a woman in a long black overcoat sat down beside him. Immediately, Klein noticed the scent of her perfume. The lilac smell was familiar, but from where? The woman removed her coat and hat. Her jet-black hair was done up in a tight bun and she was wearing a long grey skirt and red wool sweater, the kind he had seen Sarah with yesterday. He glanced more closely at her.

"Grace Ellis, right?" he asked her with a polite smile.

"Yes. Mr. Klein, isn't it?"

He nodded. "You're…"

"Emily's friend. That's right."

"I'm sorry. This must be a terrible time for you."

"I've had better days, that's a fact. It's an awful tragedy. She was so young." Tears welled in Grace's eyes. Then just as quickly, she regained her composure.

"Coffee, Miss?" Dolly asked.

"Yes, please, and two slices of toast."

"Can I top yours up, Sam?"

He pushed his mug forward. "To be honest, Miss Ellis…"

"Grace, please."

"Yes. Well, Grace, I'm glad I ran into to you. I spoke with Elizabeth Powers only last evening about making appointments to speak with Emily's friends."

"You don't think Mr. Powers murdered her, then?"

"Not for a minute. Whatever Emily was doing, it wouldn't have provoked a man like Powers to kill."

"I hope you're right. I haven't heard anything from Elizabeth yet, but if I can be of any assistance, I shall. I was fond of both Emily and Alfred.

There must be some other explanation. Perhaps it had something to do with Antonio Rossi?"

"Perhaps. Did Emily speak about him?"

"We were the best of friends, Mr. Klein. She shared many confidences with me, or so I thought. I do know that Emily was fond of your wife, Sarah."

"Sarah enjoyed her company also."

"As for why she took up with Antonio, I'm not quite sure. We talked a little about it, but Emily was confused. I don't know many details of their liaisons — that was something she didn't share with me. But she did confide, perhaps about a month ago, that she planned to end it. Emily could be rather compulsive and she…well, oh dear, how shall I put this." She moved her head next to Klein's left ear. Her perfume scent was stronger still. She paused, then spoke softly.

"You see, Mr. Klein, there are people who enjoy giving and receiving nothing but pleasure."

Now it was Klein's turn to look uncomfortable. "And Emily was one of these people?"

Grace nodded. "It wasn't that she didn't care for Alfred. I know she did. But, sometimes she couldn't stop herself from exploring other…adventures, let's say," Her face reddened. "I believe I've said enough for one morning. I trust I haven't shocked you, Mr. Klein." She took a sip of her black coffee and glanced toward the door.

Klein wasn't sure if he was shocked by this new revelation or merely amused. While employed at Melinda's he had thought he had seen and heard just about everything — men who enjoyed being slapped, others who were rough and abusive, and one wealthy gentleman who offered Darlene and eighteen-year-old Hildy two hundred dollars if he could watch them fondle each other. Yet even Melinda, who coveted money like any one else in the red light district, drew the line at such "perversion," as she called it.

"In my kind of work, I have met many different types of people," Klein finally said as he inhaled his cigarette. "I guess I'm not all that surprised. Still, it sounds like Emily was quite different from any suffragette I've ever come across."

A fond smile crossed Grace's face. "Yes that's very true. But let me assure you, Emily was as dedicated to our cause as any of our members, perhaps more so. She wasn't afraid of speaking out and deplored injustice of any kind. I do believe that's why Mrs. McClung befriended her. She could see beyond Emily's flaws. We are meeting tomorrow evening on Wolseley Avenue, number 223. Actually, it's supposed to be a W.C.T.U. gathering but with the election coming soon, I'm certain there'll be more pressing matters to discuss as well. Nevertheless, I'm sure it would be acceptable if you paid us a visit. Mrs. McClung would be happy to speak with you about Emily. She and her husband are acquainted with Mr. Powers as well."

Klein pulled a small note pad from his vest pocket and jotted down the address. "Very well then, Grace, I'll see you Saturday evening. Oh, one more question."

She stared at him attentively.

"I've heard that Emily and Antonio favoured the Leland Hotel — before the fire, that is. You know anything about that? And I was told this past month they moved over to the Royal Albert."

"No, I know nothing about that. As I said, Emily didn't share intimate details with me."

"If anything else comes to mind, please contact me immediately."

Klein paid Dolly for breakfast, put on his bowler hat, and bid Grace goodbye. He hadn't quite reached Portage Avenue when he suddenly remembered. Of course, he thought — Grace's perfume. It was exactly the kind Emily wore the night she came to dinner at his apartment, the night she had met Alfred Powers.

The trek through the snow from Hargrave Street to the southwest corner of Bannatyne and Main took Klein about fifteen minutes. A large "Closed" sign written in black block letters was what he found tacked to the door of the Rossis' confectionery and fruit store. They hadn't opened their shop since news of the tragedy had reached them late Wednesday night. Klein peered through the frosted window, but could see nothing more than several boxes of rotting bananas.

He walked around to Bannatyne where the entrance to the Rossis' upstairs apartment was located. Directly across Main Street was the imposing Ashdown's Hardware Store, three floors crammed with any item a man could want. In the distance was Market Square, quiet this time of the year but a main centre of business for Italian fruit sellers and Jewish peddlers from April to October.

As far as Klein knew, the Rossis were good people. In fact, most of the Italians he had met in the city were hard working immigrants who would do anything for their families. The majority of Winnipeg's Italians, about two thousand in number, had emigrated like the Rossis from backwater towns in Sicily. They were simple, illiterate peasants, unprepared for life in the big city. Yet people with more drive and physical endurance he hadn't met. Even the ambitious members of the Jewish community were often no match for Italian industriousness.

Still every national group had its dark side and Klein had read the stories in the papers about the mafia underworld — the Black Hand — in New York and Chicago. Maybe the late Antonio Rossi was a liar, woman-chaser, and a cheat just as Klein imagined. Hell, there were Jewish gangsters as well. He doubted if the Rossis would be able to shed any light on their nephew's after-hours activities, but it was a start.

He knocked several times until Ernesto Rossi shuffled to the door and opened it the width of a hand. He was wearing a pair of dark pants and a white long-sleeved shirt. "Yes, what do you want? I talk to no more news-papermen. Go away, you've bothered us enough."

He was about to shut the door but Klein managed to get his boot in the way.

"Mr. Rossi, I'm with no newspaper. You might remember me, Sam Klein. We met at...we met at the wedding of Emily and Alfred Powers two years ago."

"Mr. Klein, yes, of course, I apologize. You are a friend to Mr. Powers." He dropped his head.

"That's right, I'm trying to help him. May I speak to you and your wife for a moment?"

"Yes, please come in out of the cold. Rosa is up in the kitchen. I should say, Mr. Klein, that both of us loved Antonio like our own son. This is a terrible nightmare. I had to send a telegram back to the old country to inform his parents, my older brother and his wife, as to what has happened. But I could not tell them the truth. I wrote that Antonio was killed in a railway accident. I hope they never find out. I don't know what that boy was thinking...such a young fool."

He led Klein up a narrow flight of stairs. The aroma of garlic, onions, stewed tomatoes and simmering red wine wafted throughout the corridor. "We are hoping the police will let us have Antonio some time today so we can say our good-byes to him properly. Jesus taught us forgiveness and that is what we must do with Antonio."

He didn't sound convincing to Klein.

"He was a good boy, you must believe us." The voice belonged to Rosa Rossi. Dressed in black with a white apron, her eyes were puffy from crying. "Please come in, Mr...."

"Klein, Sam Klein," said Ernesto. "He's a friend of Mr. Powers."

"Come in Mr. Klein. I'll pour you a cup of a coffee." She returned to the stove where there were several bubbling pots. "Our people will come by after the funeral. There are many Termitani in the city…" Her voice cracked as she placed a small cup of coffee on the table. "Please sit down."

Klein did as she requested and took a chair next to Ernesto. On the wall beside him was a map of Italy. "We come from here," said Ernesto proudly, pointing to a tiny spot on the northwest part of Sicily, "Termini Imerese. It's a small village of *contadini*, peasants I think the word is in English." Rosa nodded approvingly. "Who would have thought that some day we could run such a profitable business? There are so many more opportunities in Canada. Antonio came here only a few years ago with such hopes and dreams…Oh, what's the use." He slammed his hand on the kitchen table, an act that immediately brought a stern Italian reprimand from his wife. "Rosa is right, Mr. Klein — please accept my apologies. The truth is that we are terribly ashamed of Antonio's wicked actions. Some would say that he came to a fitting end."

"Mr. Powers is a friend of yours," Klein began, adopting a more business-like tone, "and of mine, but I'll need to ask you some questions, personal questions, about Antonio."

"We'll do whatever we can for Alfred Powers. Please go ahead," urged Ernesto.

"Did you know about the…friendship between Antonio and Mrs. Powers?"

"Nothing," said Ernesto. "He told me he had met a young English girl. I was a little concerned since I suspected she wasn't Catholic. But I never thought for a moment that the woman was married, never mind married to Mr. Powers. We were training Antonio to run the store, though to be honest I don't think he enjoyed it. He was a young man in a rush. He wanted to be rich. He wanted to wear a fine suit, live in a big house. Such nonsense."

Rosa parted her lips to speak, then stopped herself.

"You wish to add something, Mrs. Rossi?"

She hesitated for a moment. "What is it?" Ernesto demanded.

"I knew," she finally blurted out.

"Knew what? About Antonio and Mrs. Powers?" asked Klein.

She nodded meekly.

"Rosa! You knew and didn't say anything?" said Ernesto. "Why didn't you tell me?"

"And upset you? What was the point? He promised me that he was going to end it. I believed him." She covered her face with her hands.

"Please Mrs. Rossi, tell me what you know?"

"It was maybe five or six months ago. I saw them holding hands. They were walking out of the Leland Hotel. Later, I talked with Antonio about it. At first, he denied it was him who I'd seen. But after I threatened to tell Father Deposi, our priest, he eventually admitted it all. We had a terrible argument, but he said he was going to stop. I never spoke to him about it again."

"I've heard that Antonio often caused problems at the CPR yards..."

"A lie," said Ernesto. "Let me tell you that a few years ago, soon after Antonio had arrived in the city, some Italian boys were beaten up badly by a group of English workers. They yelled that the boys were taking their jobs, all sorts of foolishness. The boys were scared to go back. Antonio decided to do something about it. He talked to the boys, organized them and tried to speak with their boss. For this, he was respected."

"Then, he wasn't acting as a labour contractor — a *pa-dronee*, is that how you say it?"

Ernesto laughed. "A *padrone*, Antonio? Who told you such nonsense? More lies."

Klein paused. "One last question. Did you ever hear Antonio speak about a man named Taber? He's a police detective."

"Taber? Never. The only acquaintance of Antonio that he ever introduced us to, only a few weeks ago, was a very respectable Chinese gentleman. Dressed in a suit, not like most Chinamen. He came into the store, bought a bag full of fruit and vegetables. Rosa what was his name?"

"Kwong, I think. Yes, Antonio called him Kam. Why do you ask?"

Klein waved his hand. "It's nothing," he said, standing up to retrieve his coat from a hook near the door. "It may be necessary for you to testify in court on behalf of Mr. Powers," he added.

"I don't know," mumbled Rosa.

"What don't you know Rosa?" said Ernesto. "Mr. Klein, you tell Mr. Powers that we'll do whatever we can for him. We owe him that, if not more, much more."

Klein buttoned up his coat, stepped out on to Bannatyne Avenue and walked back to Main Street. Dodging the noontime crowds, he had one more stop before paying a visit to Alfred at the police station. His conversation with the Rossis had convinced him that Antonio had been up to something crooked. Kam Kwong, the "respectable" Chinese man Antonio had introduced to his uncle and aunt, was trouble, plain and simple. He ran a brothel in Chinatown that also doubled as an opium den. He treated his women like slaves and had a reputation for beating them unconscious, and still having customers come in to make use of them. Klein knew that Kwong had been arrested several times, but thus far had managed to stay out of jail.

Klein had run into Kwong only once before, back when he was still working as Melinda's bouncer. Kwong had accused her of stealing one of his blonde women, as he called the white prostitutes in his keeping. There had been a heated argument, but eventually a financial arrangement had been worked out which settled the matter. Klein had advised Melinda not to pay Kwong one cent, but she had insisted on a token amount. Clearly, she didn't want to stay on Kwong's bad side.

If Antonio was mixed-up in some illicit deal with Kwong, then Klein figured opium had to be involved. It made sense considering Rossi's ambition to get rich, fast and easy.

The more intriguing question for Klein was how all this still connected to Taber. Was it possible that the detective was in on an opium sale? That he was associated with the likes of Kam Kwong? If the three were in cahoots, maybe Rossi had welched on his part of the bargain, and paid for it with his life. And Klein would lay pretty good odds that it had been Kwong's men who had held-up Graham Powers. A visit to Kwong's establishment would soon be in order.

It was a short walk over to the Royal Albert Arms Hotel. Not in the same class as the Mariaggi or the new Fort Garry Hotel, the Royal Albert, with its red-tile roof and iron lights and balconies, looked like a villa in an Italian postcard. Klein sauntered through the hotel's double-arched doorway. The carpets were a blue tint, very plush, and paintings and Roman sculptures emphasized the continental ambience. Crowds of businessmen, mostly brokers and bankers with commercial interests in the grain trade, were milling around the lobby. Klein walked up to the front desk.

"May I help you, sir?" asked the clerk, sizing Klein up and down. He was dressed impeccably in a black suit and black bow tie. Everything about him was neat and not one hair on his head or in his thick moustache was out of place.

"Yes, I'm looking for someone."

"And you think he might be here?"

"I know he's here."

"Well, then, perhaps you could give me a name and I will check the register."

In Klein's opinion, Winnipeg had too many of these pompous and arrogant would-be gentlemen. They thought — mainly because their grandparents once met Lord so-and-so or because they had an uncle who still lived in Bath — that they were better than other people, especially dark and swarthy foreigners. In reality they were on the fringe of the middle-class, smugly servicing the whims of the wealthy merchants and businessmen they envied. Sometimes, if he was in the right mood, Klein enjoyed toying with them. But the conversation with the clerk had gone on long enough.

"You won't find the name in the register."

"Then perhaps he's a guest at another…"

"Sid Rochon."

"Pardon?"

"Mr. Rochon. That's who I've come to see."

"Are you a friend of his?"

"You sound like you don't believe me."

"Not at all, sir, but Mr. Rochon is a busy man. Mr. McGuire, the owner of this hotel and a good friend to Mr. Rochon, is allowing him to reside here while he sorts out his problems at the Leland."

"What's your name?"

"My name?"

"That's right. You have a name, don't you?"

"Simon Masters."

"Mr. Masters, I've known Sid Rochon for several years. We were playing billiards together when you were still in grade school." It was a slight exaggeration, but Klein hardly cared. "Now, will you tell me where I can find him?"

The clerk pulled his gold stopwatch from this vest pocket. "At this hour I believe he is in the barbershop across the street."

"Thank you."

The Albert Street barbershop was a few doors down. As he entered the establishment, Klein grimaced as he was assaulted by a confusion of sickly-sweet colognes and after-shaves. The shop was noisy with a garble of conversation and laughter, along with the clipping of metal scissors. E.J. "Sid" Rochon, formerly of Fort William and the Leland's 58-year-old owner, was easy to spot. He was just getting out of the third of five black leather barber chairs lined up on the left side of the shop. Manned by a team of Italian barbers under the supervision of Vincenzo Donato, the shop's waiting area near the front was full.

"Sam, what are you doing here?" asked Rochon as he brushed himself off. "It's been far too long."

Klein walked toward Rochon and offered him his hand. He was a large man and still in good shape despite his elder years. He had a well-deserved reputation for being an avid sportsman. Whether it was curling or horses, Rochon usually excelled. He grasped Klein's hand and shook it firmly. "How's that lovely young wife of yours?"

"She's doing very well."

"Good. You here to let Vincenzo cut your hair?"

The barber, dressed in a white coat with a tie underneath, immediately brushed off his chair and offered Klein a seat. "Come, you could use a trim."

"Yeah, I probably could," said Klein removing his bowler hat and brushing his hair to the side. "But maybe later."

"Any time," said the barber. "A friend of Sid has to wait no more than five minutes."

"Thanks, I'll keep that in mind." He turned to Rochon. "Is there somewhere we can chat for a minute in private?"

"Of course, follow me."

He led Klein out of the barbershop and back into the Royal Albert.

"Any one in the billiard parlour, Masters?" Rochon cried out.

The hotel clerk shook his head.

"Good. I don't want to be disturbed."

The two men entered the parlour and Rochon shut the large oak door and latched it.

"I think I ought to buy this hotel instead of rebuilding the Leland. I wonder if McGuire will sell it?"

"Everything is for sale in this city, you told me that."

Rochon laughed. "What a mess. You know, I thought about tearing the whole place down. That damn fire. The police still have no idea how it started."

"I thought it was from the third-floor kitchen?"

"That's what they told me, too. I just don't believe them. I was there that night. The kitchen wasn't being used. Once the police make up their mind about something, it's hard to change it. Didn't you tell me that? Anyway, until the weather gets warmer, there isn't much I can do. Enough about that — maybe you'd like to shoot a game of billiards while we talk."

"If you're up to it."

"When was the last time you were able to beat me? Come on, Sam, rack 'em up and tell me what's on your mind, as if I can't guess. You're on the Powers case, correct?"

Klein reached for the wooden triangle and arranged the brightly coloured billiard balls inside it. The table was trimmed with rich mahogany and covered with the finest green felt money could buy.

Klein's friendship with Rochon had been established about two and half years before. He had helped the hotelier track down a notorious grifter named James Duke, who had bilked several elderly Leland customers. Klein had played a hunch and sent a few inquiring telegrams to contacts in Chicago. The contacts put him in touch with a young tough in Detroit named Freddie Silverstein, who cabled Klein that the matter would be taken care of. Within two weeks, Rochon received a package with three thousand dollars, more than enough to compensate his customers. James Duke was never heard from again. Klein decided it was better not to ask Silverstein too many questions and the matter was dropped. Ever since, Rochon had felt obligated to Klein.

Once the balls were ready, Klein grabbed a cue from the side, gently placed the white ball in the middle of the semi-circle imprinted on the felt at the other end of the table and shot. The balls scattered, but none dropped into a pocket.

"So how can I help you, Sam?" asked Rochon as he leaned forward for a shot.

"Tell me about Emily Powers and Rossi. I hear they used to meet in one of your rooms."

"It's true, I did see them here on many occasions. Discretion, you understand, is the mark of a good hotel manager. I make no moral judgements about my clients, unless they are disruptive or bothersome to other guests."

"I wasn't judging you, Sid."

"I know you weren't. It's a terrible tragedy what happened. Emily was such a lovely woman." Rochon drew his cue back and popped in a ball. "You know who you should talk to," he said lifting his head up, "the young woman who looked after the reservations and the bills."

"What young woman? You mean somebody other than Emily?"

"On most occasions there was another woman. I don't know her name. She was always nicely dressed, tall and slim. Oh yes, she wore her dark hair in a bun at the back of her head."

"Interesting," mused Klein. "That sounds like Grace Ellis."

"Grace who?"

"Grace Ellis, one of Emily's close friends. You're positive about this?"

"I am. Is it a problem?"

"No, it's odd that's all."

"Now let's finish the game. Loser buys lunch."

"The way you're playing we should be eating soon. Just no steak dinners."

Although he tried to suppress his consternation, Klein was troubled by what he had just learned. Less than an hour before, Grace Ellis had told him that she didn't know much about Emily's affair with Rossi. That seemed to be a lie. The question was: Why?

7

Winnipeg Tribune, Friday, January 30, 1914

CLUB NOTES

Parker House

A meeting tonight at Parker House, 15 Kennedy Street at 8:30 p.m. Dr. Oliver Parker, esteemed surgeon and psychic investigator, will be delivering a lecture on teleplasm and other psychic phenomena. Members and guests are cordially invited.

"**I**'M SORRY, SON, I guess this isn't going to do much for your budding political career," said Alfred Powers, gingerly sipping a cup of coffee through his cracked lips. The night in jail hadn't been pleasant. He hadn't slept well and the worn and sagging mattress had left him with an aching back.

"That's the least of my problems right now," replied Graham Powers, who had finally made it to the station house. "Besides, Roblin is too arrogant. And even though I respect Norris, he wants to make too many changes too quickly. I could fight for women's suffrage and compulsory education, but I can't say I would find it very easy supporting direct legislation. I mean how can you bring every issue back to the voters for their approval or rejection. Nothing would ever get done and…" Graham stopped himself. "You've done it again, father."

Alfred Powers smiled.

"You always manage to steer me away from the matter at hand."

"You'd make a fine politician, Graham. You shouldn't be so quick to dismiss the idea. Either party would jump at the opportunity to have you as a candidate. Personally, I'd go with Norris and the Liberals as well. I think Roblin and the Tories may be in trouble. I've heard some unsettling rumours about construction kickbacks involving the Legislative Buildings contract."

"Father, please. I'm not in the mood for political speculations. I've just come from the hospital."

"I'm sure Elspeth will recover. Robbed in the middle of Portage Avenue — now that's frightening."

Graham sat down in a small wooden chair that the police had brought for him. The cell was cool and damp. "Father, why did you sign that confession and how did you get that gash on your nose and lips? Who hit you? Was it McCreary? I've heard about him."

"Graham, one question at a time. I want you to listen to me," he began. His tone was calm and his demeanour relaxed. "There isn't going to be any trial."

"Father, what do you mean?"

"Please let me finish. I will not have Emily's reputation dragged through the mud. I know what you must be thinking. She cheated on me and that I owe her nothing. I just don't see things that way. The confession will stand and the courts can do with me as they see fit."

"Are you finished?"

Powers nodded.

"Now let me tell you the way I see things. First, you're not going to hang for a crime you didn't commit. And don't tell me that the confession is real. Both of us know that that isn't true. Emily was no saint, but you're no murderer. That's not to say I didn't like Emily — she was a vivacious woman and she made you happy. But why punish yourself for her transgressions? Whatever happened, she brought this on herself. If nothing else, think of Elizabeth and me, and your future grandchildren."

"I don't know…."

"Father, look around this cell. Is this where a man of your standing belongs…for a crime you didn't commit? And why? To protect a dead woman."

"A woman that I cared deeply about," said the elder Powers, his voice strained.

"No, a woman who betrayed you. That's what this is truly about — betrayal. Please, I beg you — don't lose sight of that fact."

Powers covered his eyes with his hands and then reached up and put his hand on his son's shoulder. "I need your help, Graham. Tell me what to do. I'm afraid my judgement is faltering. But…" He hesitated for a moment.

"Go on."

"In my heart I know that I didn't kill her. I have reviewed that fateful night a hundred times in my mind."

"And?"

"And she was already lying in the snow when I arrived. She was barely alive when I found her. I cradled her in my arms. There was blood everywhere. She tried to whisper something. I think she said she was sorry. Or perhaps that's what I would like to think she said. Then she shut her eyes and it was over. I must have picked up the knife and somehow made my way to the Kleins' apartment."

"Whose responsible for your bloody nose?"

"It was Detective Taber. Forget about him, he's a nobody. He had nothing to do with the confession. Yesterday I just didn't see any point to going on. Graham, I gave up. It's as simple as that. I'm sorry. You know what you have to do now?"

"Try to schedule a *voir dire* and have the confession quashed. And Father, if I have to I'll use the police beating as just cause."

"Agreed."

"Elizabeth has been waiting all night to visit you. I'll see if I can arrange for you to see her downstairs."

"Take your time. I don't have any plans for the day."

Graham Powers called out to the police guard on duty. The officer arrived a minute later and opened the cell door. He walked directly to the detective's office and found McCreary at his desk.

"McCreary, I'd like you to permit my sister, Elizabeth, to speak with my father for a few moments, but not in that cell. Can you bring him down into one of the interrogation rooms?"

"A confessed murderer, not likely," said Taber from the other side of the room.

McCreary ignored his partner. "Yeah, I suppose we could do that. Give me about ten minutes."

"Bad decision," said Taber.

"I don't think we've been properly introduced," said Graham. He extended his hand to Taber.

"Alex Taber," he said, refusing the offered hand.

Graham leaned forward, his eyes hard. "Yes, Detective Taber. I've heard many things about you — none of it good. From what I can gather you are a son-of-a-bitch who won't hesitate to break every rule in the book."

"Is that so?"

"That is so. I'll tell you something else. I'm going to see a magistrate this afternoon to schedule a hearing about my father's so-called confession. And while he's decided not to pursue your outrageous conduct, I will have it on the front page of the *Tribune* if it happens again. Touch my father once more, detective, and I swear to you I'll do everything in my power to put you behind bars."

Powers didn't wait for Taber to respond. He turned and walked past McCreary. "I'll bring my sister upstairs. Why don't you have my father brought here?"

"I'll do it right now," said McCreary.

"One more thing," said Powers as he walked towards the doorway. "I've already talked to the Chief. Sam Klein can speak to my father whenever he wants."

"How did you manage that?"

"Let's just say it helps to have friends."

McCreary watched Powers leave the office before turning to Taber. "That was plain enough, Taber. You going to toe the line?"

"Go to hell, McCreary. Just go to hell. The confession will stand, mark my words."

"I wouldn't count on it just yet. Not only do you have two competent lawyers on the case, but you also got Klein nosing around. Lord knows what he'll turn up."

Taber reached for a cigarette, lit it, and walked toward the far window. *No one is going to cost me this job*, he thought. *Certainly not Graham Powers or that Hebrew pain in the ass, Klein.* It was time to pay a discreet visit to a friend. He would have some ideas how to handle this situation.

Even in the middle of winter, the start of *Shabbas* on Friday evening was a special time in the North End. Jewish men, dressed in their best suits under their bulky overcoats, scurried to and from nearby neighbourhood *shuls* or synagogues. Despite the harsh weather, some wore their prized *tsilinders* or top hats. Others preferred black bowler hats and varying sizes and shapes of *yarmulkes*. Once they had given thanks to God for the good health of their families, for the roof over their heads, and for the freedom they enjoyed in this new land, they hurried home for the *Shabbas* dinner.

Most Jews in the North End of Winnipeg were, like the Klein family, not that devout. Yet old world habits didn't die easily and so the *shul* remained an integral focus of day-to-day life. It didn't matter if their annual synagogue dues were late or even if they attended services regularly. What counted, as Freda Klein was fond of reminding her children, was what was in your heart. Life was about how you treated others and how others thought of you.

"Respect" and "*tsdaka*," or charity, were two of Freda's favourite words and around the dinner table she worked them into the conversation, no matter what the context. "No one makes a better pastrami sandwich in the city than Sam Magid," Freda would announce, "and you know why? Because he's a man of *tsdaka*. God watches over him and his sandwich shop."

"Do you think God watches over his hot mustard and sauerkraut?" Klein would ask irreverently, sending his mother into the kitchen for a cup of tea.

"As if you don't have enough *tsouris* already. Living in that house for so long, marrying that woman." The funny thing was she referred to Sarah as "that woman" whether she was in the room or not. Usually, Sarah ignored the slight, but sometimes heated words were exchanged. On good nights, everyone calmed down by the time dessert was served — Clara Hirsch's honey cake nine-out-of-ten times — and life went on.

This particular Friday night, Sarah wasn't feeling well. She had felt nauseated most of the day. She wasn't sure whether it was caused by something she had eaten or what she had just read in the diary. She did know, however, that she had to read further before she confided in Sam. Her discussion with Melinda might also have upset her, or rather the fact that she had yet to broach the subject with her husband.

Undoubtedly it was a little of everything. Whatever, she would have much preferred to sit by her own warm stove with a mug of tea mixed with a few drops of whisky. But Sarah knew how Sam insisted on being at his mother's, every Friday, rain or shine, sleet or snow.

In truth, Klein, too, would've been more than happy to stay home that evening. His early investigation had turned up more questions than answers. He still wanted to figure out the connection between Rossi and Taber and between Rossi and Kam Kwong. Were all three partners? Would Taber even allow himself to collaborate with a Chinaman?

A visit to Chinatown earlier in the day had turned up nothing substantial — Kwong was nowhere to be found. No one had answered the door at his brothel, a small dingy house on Pacific Avenue not far from King Street, its windows covered with newspapers. He also knew that the women who inhabited the brothel, mostly opium addicts, rarely got out of bed before four in the afternoon. After pounding on the door for fifteen minutes, he had left and decided to return later in the evening or the next day.

The smell of roast chicken, potato *kugel, tsmiss,* and chicken soup filled Flora Avenue as it did many streets in the area. As members of the Jewish community were fond of saying, the North End wasn't called "New Jerusalem" for nothing.

"Sam, Sarah, come in," said Rivka Klein. "Mama, it's Sam and Sarah. Sam has just come from *shul.*"

Sarah laughed, despite her discomfort. "That'll be the day."

"Didn't you know you married Rabbi Klein?" Rivka asked with a large grin.

Klein unbuttoned his coat and handed it to his sister. "Here, make yourself useful and tell me how's life in the factory."

Instantly, Rivka's brow furrowed. "Actually worse, if that's possible. We work like dogs for a few dollars a week. They are now allowing sub-contracting right on the floor. You know what that means?"

"I'm sure you'll explain it to me."

"Some of the men, the boss's favourites, are given extra piece work to perform at a specified price. Then the men offer the work to girls at a lower rate, slave wages really. The girls have to work day and night until the job is done. If they refuse, Swartz fires them without a second thought."

"Chaim Swartz is a good man," said Freda Klein from the next room. "He is well-respected and always gives his fair share to *tsdaka.* Is the man not entitled to make a living?"

"That's record time Mama," remarked Klein to no one in particular.

"The man is a crook," Rivka insisted. "If he could make me work eighty hours a week he would. The only thing that may stop him is a trade union."

"Oh, oh, here it comes," said Klein under his breath.

"Please *Shailek,* don't start," said Sarah, walking into the small parlour.

Few issues stirred the twenty-eight-year-old soul of Rivka Klein more than workers' rights. An avid Bundist, Rivka was committed to the future of the Jewish masses. The utopia she envisioned was one in which Jews in the needle trade were respected, had tolerable working conditions, and were paid a decent wage. She wasn't prepared to forfeit her Jewish heritage to become part of the larger Canadian labour movement, nor did she support the Zionists' idea of a homeland in Palestine. "Absurd and backward," she would argue on this point. "We must become part of the societies in which we live, but still maintain a certain detachment," she'd declare in Yiddish. Always Yiddish, a language she was proud of.

"It's *Shabbas*, children," said Clara Hirsch, emerging from the kitchen. "No arguing tonight — for your mother's sake, please."

A handsome and gentle woman, Freda's cousin Clara was a font of received wisdom. She provided a much needed calming influence on the household. Though no one ever dared mention it, Clara was a much happier person, more at ease with her life, since the death of her husband Isaac three years before.

Klein took his sister by the arm. "I don't know about you, but I'm starved." They walked together to the dining room, just off the parlour where Sarah and Rivka's boyfriend, Solomon Volkon, were already sitting.

On cue, Freda Klein, wearing a black dress covered by a multi-coloured apron, her gray hair up in a bun, made her grand entrance. Seeing her children together for Friday night dinner always warmed her heart. She even gave Sarah a peck on the cheek.

"What's the occasion?"

"Sarah, please, not now," said Klein.

"What, a mother-in-law can't welcome her daughter-in-law on *Shabbas?*" asked Freda.

"Of course you can, Mama," added Rivka, "Sarah was just joking. Weren't you Sarah?"

Sarah rolled her eyes upward. Despite Freda Klein's lukewarm feelings toward her, she was fond of Sam's mother. The one thing she couldn't bear, however, was the way Rivka and Sam catered to her.

"So what did the doctor say today, Mama?" asked Rivka.

"I'm fine," insisted Freda. "There's nothing wrong."

"You're certain, he didn't say you had to take any medicine or pills? What about those pains you've been having in your chest?"

"Rivka, please. Sarah, you'd like to *bench* the *licht?*"

"Me, light the candles? I couldn't. Rivka, you do it."

"Come on, Sarah," said Klein, "go ahead. You remember how don't you?"

Sarah reluctantly stood up from her chair and approached the two candles standing in the golden candelabrum. It had been a long time since she had last done this. She lit the candles, made a circular motion over the flame with her hands and then placed them over her face. "*Baruch atah adoni eloheinu melech haolam,*" she began, looking at Rivka for help. "*Asher kidishanu,*" interjected Rivka. "*B'mitzvotav v'tzyvanu,*" continued Sarah, "*l'hadlik ner shel shabbas.*"

"Lovely," said Freda. "Now *Shailek,* the wine."

Klein reached for the glass decanter his mother kept on the small shelf beside the dining table and poured a glass of red wine. He stood up, raised the wine and recited the blessing.

"*Gut Shabbas,*" Freda announced when he was finished. "*Gut Shabbas,*" everyone at the table replied in unison.

Rivka, Sarah, and Clara assisted Freda in bringing the soup to the table, while Klein and Solomon Volkon remained in their seats as was customary.

"Working on any big cases?" asked Volkon.

"I keep busy."

"You know the Powers family, don't you?"

Klein nodded.

"You think the husband killed his wife?"

"Don't know."

"Sure seems like it. I read she was killed with her Italian boyfriend."

"I didn't think you concerned yourself with such matters, Solomon?"

"I've been trying to improve my English. Don't tell Rivka, but it's my opinion that no Jew will go very far in this country without good English. We're going to have to learn to communicate with our Gentile neighbours, including the ones on the other side of the tracks."

"Solomon, I'm surprised at your clear-headed thinking. I believe we actually agree on something."

Volkon laughed as he took another sip of wine.

Klein more or less liked Volkon, though he found the thirty-year-old a bit too much of an intellectual. Worse was the fact that Solomon couldn't seem to make up his mind where he stood. One week, he was a Revolutionary-Marxist, the next a Socialist Zionist, the week after that he was calling himself an Anarchist. But his sister seemed to love the man, so who was Sam Klein — married to the former Sarah Bloomberg of Madam Melinda's — to judge her. If she was happy, he was happy. And who knows, he thought, given the right opportunity, Volkon might turn out to be a capitalist like everyone else.

"Did you hear, Sam?" Rivka said, ladling some steaming chicken soup into Klein's bowl, "Solomon will have a new job in a few months."

"Yes?"

"There's to be a new night school, the Jewish Radical School, and Solomon has been hired to be a teacher."

"I owe the job to my friend Boris Ginsburg. He recommended me. But there's already thirty children registered. We will be using a classroom at Aberdeen School."

"Wonderful," added Freda. "And what does it pay?"

"Mama," pleaded Rivka. "What does it matter? Solomon will be instructing young children about Yiddish literature. I.L. Peretz, Abraham Resin, Sholem Asch. What could be more important?"

"A man has to make a living. He has to feed his children and family?"

"You'll never understand there's more to life than material goods. That raising the consciousness of the Jewish masses is what ultimately counts."

Freda turned to her son with a look of exasperation. "*Shailek*, you know what she's talking about?"

Klein shrugged. "Why don't we finish dinner and leave the troubles of the world outside for a few moments."

"Well said, Sam," Clara Hirsch added. "Rivka and Solomon will make of their lives what they will. We can only wish that they have lots of health and happiness…and lots of children."

"Oh, Clara," said Rivka, giving her a hug.

"And when are the two of you having children?" Freda said, looking in Sarah's direction. "I can't wait forever to be a *Boba*."

"Mama, can we not have *Shabbas* dinner in peace?" asked Klein. "I have had a very long day. I have a friend in jail…" He closed his eyes and sighed, then suddenly stood up from the table. "If you'll excuse me, I need a cigarette."

By the time Klein and Sarah had left his mother's house, it was nine o'clock. The remainder of the evening had passed without any major incidents or controversies, except for a minor argument between Rivka and Solomon about whether or not war would break out in Europe any time soon. Solomon believed that the Kaiser would be more than willing to goad Russia into a fight, while Rivka took the contrary position.

As for Klein, he didn't care. He had more immediate problems to solve, such as keeping Alfred Powers from the hangman. European leaders would have to solve their political difficulties without his input.

"Sam," Sarah finally said once the two of them had reached Salter Street. "I want to talk with you about something."

"What is it?"

"This is important and I've given it a lot of thought. I know that you and I are not like Rivka and Solomon — that we do care about where we live and how much money we have."

"Yeah, I could live on Wellington Crescent one day."

"Please be serious. I want…."

Before she could say another word, four men stepped from behind a hedge and encircled them. As soon as Klein looked into their faces and saw that they were Chinese, he knew what was happening.

"Kwong," he shouted. "Where are you? What do you want? Or are you too much of a coward to show yourself."

From behind the same hedge stepped Kam Kwong, dressed impeccably in a long fur-lined coat and a black bowler hat. A thin cigar was stuck in his mouth. His hands were covered in white gloves. "I hear you've been looking for me, Klein."

"News travels fast."

"In Chinatown it does. We're a small community. I've come to deliver a message to you."

"And what would that be?"

Before he could say another word, one of Kwong's thugs abruptly kicked Klein in the stomach. He doubled over. "Sam," Sarah shouted. Another man grabbed Sarah and flung her to ground. "Stay put, slut, or you'll be sorry."

The other three men moved to Klein and took turns kicking him. Sam rolled over in the snow, leaped to his feet and rammed his fist into one man, then another. Before he could turn around, the third was able to take hold of his arms from behind.

"Stand him up," ordered Kwong. "Okay, Klein, enough of this. Stay out of my way and out of Chinatown. Let Rossi's family bury his secrets with him. Do you understand?"

"Go to hell."

Kwong laughed, turned and walked closer to Sarah.

"Leave her alone, Kwong or so help me I'll kill you."

"I think you have your hands full at the moment." He motioned to one of his men. The thug took a pistol from his pocket and with one quick gesture struck Klein hard across the head. He dropped to the ground unconscious.

"Sam, no!" yelled Sarah, struggling to her knees.

Kwong clapped his hands and his men vanished into the dark. Then he took a step towards Sarah. He removed a glove and stroked her face as she kneeled in front of him. "You could come work for me anytime. I've heard many good things about you."

"That's enough, Kwong," said a voice from the darkness. "Leave the woman alone. She's mine."

Sarah knew that rough voice.

The figure approached and stepped into the moonlight. "Hello Sarah, I think I like you in that position." He chuckled. "I told your husband that someday I was going to have my way with you. Maybe now's the time?"

Sarah got to her feet and sneered. "You wouldn't know what to do."

"I'd watch myself if I were you," said Taber. "Next time, your stupid husband won't be so fortunate. Come on Kwong, our business is finished for now." Seconds later, the two men had disappeared down the dark street, and Sarah ran to help Klein.

The tall grandfather clock in the parlour struck midnight as the lights in the house on Kennedy Street were dimmed. Not one of the eight people sitting in wooden upright chairs around the table made a sound. The three men and five women held hands, adding to the heightened tension. Another man wearing a white shirt and dark vest, stood in the corner of the room beside a box camera mounted on a tripod. In his right hand, he held his flash box, filled with powder ready to ignite.

Finally, after what seemed like hours, Dr. Oliver Parker, dressed in a black three-piece suit, emerged from a closet at the back of the gloomy room on the second floor of the grand home. Mrs. Flood was at his side. She, too, was dressed in black, her grey hair covered with a shawl. Had the circumstances been different, this matronly-looking woman, only in her mid-forties, might have passed for a grandmother.

Mrs. Flood and the doctor sat down at the two empty chairs at the front of the table. The doctor signalled that the seance was to begin, and his wife, Erica, dimmed the lights. Earlier in the day, the room's two windows had been covered with oiled tarpaulins so that no light penetrated. In the darkness, Mrs. Flood closed her eyes tightly and in a matter of minutes had gone into a deep trance.

Suddenly, the table shifted upward ever so slightly. Startled, one of the girls, a petite stenographer named Rosie, gave a short scream.

"Calm yourself," ordered Dr. Parker.

"Please forgive me," pleaded Rosie. Dr. Parker nodded as if to signal that the spell hadn't been broken.

Mrs. Flood's hands slowly raised over her head and then crashed down on the table. Dr. Parker instructed the two people on either side of her to grab them, which they did, trembling. Mrs. Flood stared straight ahead. Suddenly, from behind her right shoulder, a moan was heard, then a series of words: "*Nayn*, Abe, *nayn. Loz meer.*" The voice was throaty, but clearly female. The phrase was repeated three times.

"Who speaks to us?" asked Dr. Parker.

There was no response.

"*Nayn*, Abe, *nayn. Loz meer*" the voice declared a fourth time.

"It sounds like German," whispered one of the women.

Mrs. Flood raised her head and the doctor sensed it was time. "Now, John, do it now," he ordered.

The man standing with the camera readied himself and snapped three pictures. Each flash illuminated the room like a bolt of lightening.

"I have it," said the photographer.

Just as he finished speaking, Mrs. Flood collapsed on the table.

With Dr. Parker supervising, John Duffin, one of the city's most talented photographers, retired to the small dark room that the doctor kept across the hall. It was less than an hour before Dr. Parker and Duffin returned to the seance room with the prints. The lights had been turned on and all eight people remained seated around the table, eagerly awaiting the opportunity to examine the pictures. Mrs. Flood, who stated she was exhausted, had left the room to lie down in one of the bedrooms.

As the photographs were laid out on the table, there was a collective gasp. Even Dr. Parker appeared to be taken aback by what he saw.

Each picture clearly showed what seemed to be a white foamy cloud — or a teleplasmic phenomena, as Dr. Parker explained — emanating from Mrs. Flood's mouth. In the middle of the cloud was a hazy image of a woman's face.

"I know...I know that face," sputtered Rosie.

The other men and women stared at her, waiting for her revelation.

"That's Mrs. Powers, Emily Powers, I'd swear on the Bible."

Dr. Parker, too, recognized Emily's face but said nothing.

8

Manitoba Free Press, Saturday, January 31, 1914

VISITING PROFESSOR TO SPEAK ON OPIUM WAR

Professor James Mackinnon of the University of Edinburgh will deliver a lecture this afternoon at 3:30 p.m. in the Great Hall in Wesley College. The subject of Dr. Mackinnon's talk will be his new book British Trade Policies in China, 1729-1842 *including a discussion on the Opium War of 1839-1842. Professor Mackinnon has also lectured in Hong Kong and will be teaching a history seminar at Wesley College during the winter semester. He promises that his lecture will be stimulating and informative.*

Mr. John Dafoe, editor of the Manitoba Free Press *and President of the Literary Society, will be introducing Professor Mackinnon and Mr. Charles N. Bell, Secretary of the Winnipeg Grain Exchange. The Society's Vice-President will act as moderator. A small admission fee will be charged to non-members.*

"HERE *SHAILEK*, REST EASY," said Sarah as she wiped her husband's forehead with a warm wet compress. "The doctor says that you weren't hurt too badly."

Still groggy, Klein could barely muster a smile as he stared up into Sarah's eyes.

"What is it?" she asked.

"Nothing."

"I know that look. You love me and have never been happier," she whispered with a smile.

"I didn't say that."

"No, but it's what you're thinking."

Klein remained silent. No one could accuse him of being sentimental.

"Have it your way, you stubborn man," She gently kissed him on the cheek.

"I need a cigarette," he muttered.

She found his silver case in his jacket pocket, lit one, and placed it between his lips.

He inhaled sharply. "I feel like I've been kicked in the head by a horse."

"It was one of Kwong's men. He hit you with a revolver."

"That I remember. What else happened?"

"Sam, Taber was with him. They're working together."

"He didn't hurt you did he?" Sam cried, struggling to get up.

"No, please don't get excited. He didn't do anything to me."

"First Kwong, then Taber. They were somehow involved with Rossi. I knew it." He paused and looked around. "How did you get me here?"

"I didn't know what to do so I ran into a house on Salter and telephoned Melinda's. She sent Teddie Shepherd and Lyle Korsen with a sled and team. They brought you here. By then, it was nearly eleven o'clock."

"Remind me to thank them," he said touching his forehead. "Christ that hurts."

"Here, take a few of these." She handed him a small square tin box.

"Milburn's Heart and Nerve Pills? No thanks. Where do you get this stuff, Sarah? Last week weren't you taking something called Apiol and Stell Pills?"

"That was for female problems, but Milburn's, well, I've told you they calm me down when I get anxious. Dr. Frankel says they work."

"Jack Frankel is an old quack."

"Well, he came to look at you as soon as I called his apartment."

"I'm forever grateful. Now, please, dear, just a glass of whisky."

"It's six in the morning, *Shailek*."

"I'm well aware of the time."

"Have it your way." Sarah took a bottle of Seagram's "83," Klein's favourite, poured a half glass and handed it to her husband. Klein swigged it down in one gulp. "Feel better?"

"I'm starting to. I've got a busy day today. You think it's too early to call Graham Powers?"

"Kind of. *Shailek*, there's something I need to talk to you about. I tried last night, but then the trouble started. And I wouldn't bother you about this now, given everything…There's just no way around it."

"Sarah, what is it? There's nothing wrong with you?"

"No, no. My stomach is still a little queasy, but Dr. Frankel said it would go away with some syrup medicine."

"So what is it then?"

"It has to do with a business proposition I'm considering."

"A business proposition?"

"Please, Sam, before you say anything else, I want you to hear me out. Will you do me that for me?"

"Go on."

"You know I haven't been especially happy lately. You have your work, you're busy. You're starting to make enough money to pay most of our bills, at least most months. But it's not enough. I know you think I purchase too many clothes and other goods, but really I don't. Not compared to some women in this city." She shook her head. "That's not really the point. What I'm trying to say is this: that I'd like more, maybe our own house, some day. I'm not blaming you, it's just the way things are."

"And?"

"And I think I have an answer."

"Why do I get the feeling I'm not going to like this?"

"May I finish, please."

Klein lit another cigarette. Business, he thought, it's not going to be a dress shop.

"For the past few weeks, I have been speaking with Melinda."

"Shit, Sarah, you've got to be joking."

"Yes, Melinda. She's interested in opening another house down the street. She's prepared to buy the property if I'm prepared to manage it. I don't have to live there. We'll split the profits 65-35 for the first few years unless I use my option to buy anywhere up to 60 percent of the house. Melinda thinks she can buy the house for under $5,000, even though Lila Anderson paid more than double that six years ago."

Klein sat upright and threw the damp cloth on his forehead to the ground. He then poured himself a full glass of whisky. He cast his eyes down, unable to look at Sarah directly. "I'm going to make this easy for you," he finally said, "I will give you a choice, me or a job as madam. But you can't have both. It's bad enough you were once a…"

"A whore?"

"You said it, I didn't. Let's just say I've learned to live with your past, but I'll be damned if I'm going to permit this to be part of our future." He threw his cigarette down into an ashtray. "I can't believe this, Sarah. I also can't believe, Melinda said nothing to me. I was just there…"

"It's not her fault. I made her lie to you."

"Is that supposed to make me feel better? It doesn't. My mother, and everyone else for that matter, warned me before we were married. Said you'd never change. Once you've had a dozen men in one day…"

Tears welled in Sarah's eyes. She strode close to Klein and slapped at the glass of whisky he was holding. It went flying across the room, hit the wall and shattered. "You go to hell," she cried. "Is that what you think of me? What's so wrong with what I want to do? It's running a business. I'm not going to be working there."

"Okay, one night, a rich banker comes in, offers the madam of the house a hundred for a good time. What are you going to do? You'll be up the stairs so fast…Oh what's the use."

"That'll never happen. I promise you."

"Never?" Though his head was still throbbing from the attack, he stood up and grabbed his coat.

"Where are you going at this hour? Nothing is open yet. *Shailek*, please you're shaking."

She reached for him, but he pushed her arm away. "I need to get away from here, away from you for a while. If you're not here when I return tonight, I guess I'll know the choice you made."

Sarah's face turned white. "That's it?"

"It's up to you. I'm not forcing you like most men would. No, it's your life, you decide. But remember, if you leave, there's no coming back. I will not be made the butt of more Main Street humour. Do you understand?"

Sarah remained silent. Without another word, Klein walked to the door of the apartment and left, slamming the door behind him. For a good two minutes, Sarah stood in the middle of the room, unable to move. Then, exhausted, she collapsed on a chair, covered her face with her hands and cried. With a deep sorrow in her heart, she knew what she had to do. Damn him, she detested ultimatums. Who was he to tell her how to live her life? If he wanted her to choose, well then, she would choose. She stood up, went into her bedroom and took out a grey valise. It was the same one she had used to carry her clothes from Melinda's.

Klein wandered. Up and down the streets of the North End, past Jewish families on their way to neighbourhood synagogues for Sabbath day prayers, past merchants on Selkirk Avenue clearing the snow from in front of their shops, past peddlers with their horses and sleighs about to embark on another day's work. His head was still spinning, but he kept reviewing again and again his argument with Sarah and each time he arrived at the same simple conclusion: he was right and she was wrong. He knew what people said behind his back — "There's Klein and his high-priced wife" — and it didn't bother him. But this, the idea of Sarah as a madam, was too much. As he trudged down Main Street, he became more confident that Sarah, too, would eventually see it his way.

After a quick stop at the Brunswick Hotel for a few cups of One-Arm Eddie's strong coffee, Klein felt a bit better. He telephoned the apartment, but Sarah didn't answer. Maybe she was sleeping. He had a full day ahead of him on the Powers case as well as paying an unannounced visit on Kam Kwong. He decided to let matters with Sarah subside and try to talk some sense into her later.

Perhaps a nice dinner at Emma Pannaro's would cheer her up. The Italian restaurant near the corner of Main and McDermot served the best spaghetti and meatballs in the city. After that, he and Sarah could go to the nickelodeon picture theatre across the street. It wasn't quite as good as a live vaudeville show at the Walker or Orpheum, but for only a nickel a piece — as compared to twenty-five cents a ticket for vaudeville shows — it was thoroughly enjoyable. Maybe there would be a new film by that young British comedian Klein liked so much, Charlie Chaplin.

Klein also knew that Sarah was looking forward to the opening bill at the new Pantages Theatre on Market Avenue on February 9. He had been lucky to obtain tickets through one of his many contacts downtown — *"schlep"* was how Jews in the city referred to such connections. The inaugural show at the Pantages, featuring Mademoiselle Adgie and her lions in a "Dance of Death," was advertised as the most sensational vaudeville to play in Winnipeg since the Ben-Hur production at the Walker several years ago. There was no way Sarah would make any rash decisions before then. Her appetite for vaudeville was too great — at least that was what Klein hoped.

Or maybe at that moment he wasn't thinking straight. Would she really listen to reason? Could he convince her to change her mind with an evening of entertainment? She could be so stubborn. He paused for a moment to tie one of his bootlaces dragging in the snow. Damn, he thought, that woman makes me crazy.

His first stop was at the police station. It was a few minutes before nine when he walked through the door. Other than the heavy-built sergeant behind the desk, the station was empty.

By way he shifted in his chair, it was obvious that Sergeant Holland wasn't delighted to see Klein approaching. "Too early in the morning for you," he scowled. "Don't you know the Chief doesn't want you loitering around the station."

"I'm here to see Alfred Powers," said Klein, ignoring the officer's surly tone. "And all the paper work has been done."

"Yeah, I'm well-aware of what's going on, Klein. You got some friends at City Hall. You're pretty important for a…"

"For a what?"

"Never mind. Down the stairs to the right. I think you know the way. His son and daughter are there with him now."

Klein knew exactly what the sergeant had intended to say: "Pretty important for a *Jew*." That was the trouble with the city. Everyone was supposed to stay in their place. The English talked a lot about the immigrants becoming "good Canadian citizens," as J.S. Woodsworth put it, but try to better yourself in your own way and you only met with resistance and hostility.

The officer on duty at the cellblock led Klein through the damp and musty narrow hall. He found Alfred Powers sitting on his bunk sipping his daily ration of tea and munching on a piece of stale bread. As far as Powers was concerned, the worst part about being in jail was that he wasn't permitted to smoke. Graham and Elizabeth sat on chairs beside him. There was hardly room for another person inside.

"Sam, I'm glad you're here," said Alfred. "You look worse than me."

"I had a run-in last night with a few toughs."

"Anyone hurt?"

"No, just my pride. I think you've already made the acquaintance of these gentlemen."

"You mean they were the Chinese thugs who held me up?"

"Quite possibly."

"Those sons-of-bitches."

"Graham, please," said Elizabeth Powers.

"My apologies. But you know what they did to poor Elspeth. He's still in the hospital."

"Listen, Graham, give me another day or so and I'll be able to tell you who they are," Klein said.

"Good enough."

"Have you come up with anything else that will help me?" asked Alfred.

"Nothing definite yet, but I have a few leads. Rossi was up to no good, I'm certain of that. Let me nose around a little more before I reach any grand conclusions. I'm sure Graham has already told you," said Klein, looking at the young lawyer, "that your confession hasn't helped much."

"We've been through that already," Graham said standing up. "First thing Monday morning, I have a hearing scheduled before Magistrate Findly to deal with bail and father's confession."

"I wish it were someone else, Graham," said Alfred. "I've had too many arguments with George Findly over the years."

"It'll work out for the best," said Graham reassuringly. "I have everything under control. You know, father, I did have a good teacher."

Powers smiled.

"I don't see what you find so amusing," said Elizabeth Powers. "I can't bear to see you in here, father. It's so degrading. It's all the fault of that…" She stopped herself.

"Emily. You can say her name, Elizabeth."

"All of this makes me so angry. I'm sorry, father, but from the moment you brought her into our lives, she was nothing but trouble. I hated her when she was alive and hate her more now that she's dead."

"Elizabeth, how could you?" Graham cried.

Alfred Powers stared at the cold cement floor. "I'm sorry you feel so bitter Elizabeth. I loved her very much, no matter what she did. No matter what."

"I need to speak with your father alone, if you don't mind," said Klein, breaking the tension.

"Of course," said Graham, "Elizabeth and I were just leaving. Father, I'll be back later today. Try to get some rest and don't worry."

Powers nodded. "You're a fine lawyer, Graham. I'm not at all concerned."

"Good-bye father," Elizabeth said, kissing Powers lightly on the cheek.

He was about to reply, yet he wasn't sure what more he could say to his daughter. She would never understand just how much he had cared for Emily.

"Let's talk later in the day, Sam," said Graham.

Klein called out for the police officer, who sauntered down the hallway and opened the cell door. He watched Graham and Elizabeth depart before turning to Powers. He took his silver cigarette case from his jacket pocket and offered the lawyer one. He eagerly took it, then glanced nervously through the bars to see if they were being watched.

"Don't worry Alfred, I'll tell them they're both mine." Klein struck a wooden match, lit both cigarettes and sat down on one of the chairs facing the bunk.

"Alfred, I have to ask you some questions…some personal questions."

"About what?"

Klein hesitated for a moment. "Emily. More specifically, about you and Emily."

"I thought you said earlier that you were investigating Rossi."

"I am. But I also have to make certain that Emily wasn't directly involved in what happened to her. My initial feeling is that she was a bystander, maybe not an entirely innocent one, but a bystander all the same, someone caught in the wrong place at the wrong time in…"

"…in the company of someone like Rossi," interrupted Powers.

"Yeah. I didn't want to say anything in front of Graham yet, but I'm quite sure Rossi was involved with Kam Kwong. You know the name?"

"The Chinatown hood?"

"It wouldn't surprise me if it was Kwong's thugs who robbed Graham and blind-sided me last night. I'm planning to pay Kwong a visit later this evening." He paused for a moment, took a deep drag on his cigarette, then threw it to the floor and stamped it out with his boot. "There's one more thing." Klein stood up and peered out of the cell to ensure that the police officer on duty was nowhere to be seen. "I don't have any hard evidence yet," he said more quietly, "but I believe that Taber might be connected with Kwong and Rossi in a three-way partnership."

"Taber!"

"Easy, Alfred. Let's keep this strictly between ourselves for the moment. I don't want you saying anything to Graham yet. Okay?"

"Agreed."

"Did Taber force you to sign that confession?"

"No. I don't know what came over me, Sam. I really don't. For a few desperate moments, I just didn't see the point of going on without Emily."

"And now?"

"Talking with Graham and Elizabeth has convinced me that I was a little premature in my decision."

"I'm glad you've come to your senses."

"Do you really think there's a connection between Taber and Kwong and Rossi?" asked Powers.

"I do."

"Taber was more than pleased when I confessed. Told me it made life a lot easier for him. That sometimes sacrifices had to be made. I wonder?"

"What are you thinking, Alfred?" asked Klein

"This sounds a little crazy but what if Taber and Kwong had Rossi killed because of a business deal that went sour? What better way to make the whole matter disappear than to pin the murder on the jealous husband."

"It sounds possible. I don't know, although it might explain the robbery on Graham. Maybe Taber and Kwong wanted to keep Graham from contacting you until he was able to secure your confession?

"If so, then Taber may not be finished with me yet." said Powers.

"I wouldn't worry too much about that. Still, I'll have a word with McCreary to keep an eye on Taber. Kwong I can deal with myself. His kind are easy to figure out. But Taber has the potential to be a lot more dangerous. He has a reputation to protect — Kwong doesn't have to worry about that."

"I'm sure I'll be safe in here, Sam. He wouldn't dare try anything while I'm locked up. Maybe I should ask Graham to forget getting bail," Powers said half-jokingly. "Now what about those personal questions about Emily."

Klein hesitated. "Yeah. This is kind of awkward, Alfred."

"Please go ahead."

"I need to know what type of woman Emily was."

"She was a kind soul, dedicated to causes she believed in. Admittedly, as for alcohol, she supported moderation more than abstinence, as you well know. And…"

"That's not quite what I had in mind," interrupted Klein.

"No? Then what precisely?"

"Alfred, you're one of the most intelligent men I've ever met. You were once the mayor of the city. I'm proud to call you a friend. But, with all due respect, you allowed a woman to take over your life. I need to know why? What power did she have over you?"

The lawyer laughed. "She was beautiful," he mused. "But also — Sam, how can I put this? No woman ever satisfied me as much as Emily. She enjoyed…"

"Pleasure?"

"Where did you hear that?"

"That's how her friend Grace Ellis described her."

"She ought to know, the two shared many secrets. But yes, Emily did derive great satisfaction from pleasing me. She introduced me to acts…well, frankly, I didn't know that a man and woman could do such things together."

Klein hesitated. "Such as?"

"Well," Powers coughed. "Is this necessary, Sam?"

"It may be. What if we're wrong about Rossi? What if it was Emily who was the real target and Rossi the one killed by chance?"

"Preposterous. I thought you said that Rossi was mixed up with Kwong. And what about Taber?"

"I know all that, Alfred. I'm sure that it was Rossi who caused the killing. But I have to discount all the other possibilities. I need to know as much as I can about her. Please, go on."

"This will remain between us."

"Of course."

"With Margaret, our married life was pleasant, though sexual relations, when it happened at all, was what she called a 'necessary evil.' Margaret, bless her soul, believed that bedroom activity was for having children. But Emily, dear Emily, truly enjoyed sexual acts for their own sake. Her desire was, let us say, unquenchable. And, she particularly liked a variety of positions."

A frown crossed Klein's brow.

"She liked it when," Powers continued, "I entered her from behind, the way dogs do it."

"I see," muttered Klein. "Is that it?"

"No, there's more, if you're up to it." Powers seemed both hesitant and excited, his face flushed.

Klein nodded, wondering if Powers had ever visited Melinda's.

"You and I have both been taught that self-touching is not healthy. You can be committed into asylum for that. But Emily showed me how ludicrous such notions were. Nothing gave her greater pleasure than fondling me and herself at the same time. She liked to talk about what she was going to do to me. She also liked it when I…" Powers hesitated. "She also liked it when I watched her."

"When you watched her touch herself?"

"Exactly."

Klein said nothing. Even though he had worked in a whorehouse for several years, he was surprised by his friend's words. Most whores' clients preferred quick and straightforward sex and, needless to say, most whores preferred it that way too — much more economical. A woman as experienced as Sarah certainly enjoyed sexual pleasure, but nothing as exotic as Emily's activities.

"Does any of this help you, Sam?"

Klein didn't answer.

"Sam," Powers repeated, "Does this help?"

"Sorry, Alfred, I'll have to think it through."

"A little difficult to believe?"

"I suppose so. What about Emily's liaison with Rossi?"

"I know she loved me Sam, but I also know she couldn't stop herself. I've been thinking a lot about that side of her character since I've been in here. And I've decided that Emily was like a man who drinks too much, spends every last nickel on booze. With Emily it wasn't drink, but physical pleasures. I think that's the best way I can explain it."

Katie had finally made the telephone call. It hadn't been a pleasant conversation. Her friend was rather despicable, but at least she had dealt with the issue. With Jordan breathing down her neck, she had to do something. Who knows what he would find out? The opium had been planted, that much she was certain of. She could take no more chances. She wanted her money and she wanted it now. If the price was to leave the city and head down to San Francisco, so be it. With some cash in her pocket, she could make a fresh start, get out of the business. There had to be a better way to make a living, especially with people like Jordan to contend with.

As she shut her eyes for a mid-day nap, she fell asleep feeling almost content. By ten o'clock tomorrow evening, her problems would be no more.

"With all due respect, Professor Mackinnon," the grey-haired gentleman enunciated slowly as if to emphasize each word, "your implication that the British government is largely to blame for the increase in the opium trade in China is rather offensive." There was polite applause from the audience. "From the facts as you have presented them in your lecture, I would argue the contrary: that the British authorities and merchants were only pursuing a natural course justified by Imperial fortitude. Simply put, if the Chinese had a problem with opium, it was their problem, not that of the Empire." As the elderly man took his seat, he received more applause.

Klein had arrived only moments before Professor Mackinnon had offered his concluding remarks about how the British government from Pitt to Palmerston had sacrificed moral considerations to commercial interests in its trade policies with China. For the Empire, balancing the import of tea from China to Britain with the export of opium from India to China was paramount. That the use of opium was illegal in China was irrelevant to English merchants such as the British East India Company.

"At every step of the way," declared Mackinnon, "British merchants ignored official Chinese wishes, promoting the opium market to the detriment of themselves and the Chinese. As F.S. Turner wrote more than twenty-five years ago in his important book, *British Opium Policy*, British administrations 'became addicted to their revenue like a Chinaman became addicted to the drug.' This was followed by a total dependence and an anxious demand for a constant supply of the product. The supplier, the British, and the user, the Chinese, couldn't stop themselves. So let us, gentlemen, not pretend that the British had no idea what they were doing. That men like Palmerston claimed that they 'had no knowledge of the existence of any but the legal trade,' to quote Gladstone, was 'a miserable equivocation.' Thank you."

Dressed in a black gown, his long dark hair flowing to his shoulders, Mackinnon was an imposing figure on the dais and an impressive speaker. He appeared to be quite comfortable amidst the other scholars and guests seated in Wesley College's grand lecture hall. Among those attending the afternoon's lecture were Rev. Salem Bland, a leading advocate of the "social gospel" and a professor of Church History;

Professor Leon Fredericks, a biblical and medieval history expert who had testified at Rabbi Davidovitch's murder trial a few years before; and millionaire hardware store owner James Ashdown, the "Merchant Prince" of Western Canada, a former mayor of Winnipeg, and a founding member of the College.

Behind Mackinnon, sat two distinguished men that Klein quickly recognized. Charles Bell was wearing a brown three-piece suit and a matching bow tie. His salt and pepper beard was perfectly trimmed as befitted the esteemed Secretary of the Board of Trade and Grain Exchange. Bell, who had lived in Winnipeg since arriving with the Wolseley expedition to save the Red River Settlement from the hands of Louis Riel, was one of the charter members of Winnipeg's commercial elite.

To Bell's right was John Wesley Dafoe, the editor of the *Manitoba Free Press*. Dafoe was a small man with a mop of red hair and a thick bushy moustache. Before moving to Winnipeg in 1901 at the invitation of the *Free Press*'s owner, Clifford Sifton, Dafoe had already edited several eastern newspapers, even though he had not yet turned thirty-five.

What Klein knew of him was that he was a man with strong opinions, especially on matters concerning the progress and well-being of the Canadian nation. And like most members of the Anglo establishment, he expressed dismay at the foreigners who were threatening the English majority's vision of the country. Last year, Dafoe had run dozens of articles in the *Free Press* critical of Manitoba's bilingual education system which, as a result of the Laurier-Greenway compromise of 1897, had allowed Germans, Ukrainians, Slavs, as well as the French in St. Boniface, to operate their own public schools. The consequences, according to Dafoe, were "disastrous." If Dafoe had his way, and he usually did, the state of Manitoba schools was going to be a key issue in the upcoming provincial election. It was Dafoe that Klein wanted to see, a meeting arranged by the editor's secretary.

Klein felt more than a little uncomfortable among these learned and wealthy men. They were part of a Gentile society that would never welcome him as a member — true, they would shake his hand if introduced, but not heartily, and not for long. The hall he sat in, adorned in fine oak panelling, was decorated with three large paintings which hung directly behind the platform. They were of John and Charles Wesley and George Whitefield, founders of the Methodist Church with which the modest Winnipeg College was affiliated.

"I'm sorry, sir," the professor said in response to his pesky questioner, "but I believe that it is you who are mistaken. Let me assure you that I do not stand alone on this issue. Both James Rowntree in his 1906 work, *The Imperial Drug Trade*, and James B. Eames in *The English in China*, published only a few years ago, reached the same conclusions. The notion that British responsibility stopped when the opium auction was over is preposterous. Allow me to provide you with an analogy. Let us say that a young lad goes into a gun store. The manager of the store, having a slow month, sells the boy a gun. Two days later, the boy accidentally shoots his younger brother. Whose fault is it?"

"Why the boy's parents, of course," retorted the elderly gentleman.

"You mean to suggest that the gun store owner bears no responsibility?" asked Mackinnon.

"In this case, no. The boy's parents had a responsibility to monitor his behaviour. The store owner was merely making a living."

Both Bell and Dafoe laughed in unison, as did several other members of the audience at the stubbornness of the questioner. Klein figured that Mackinnon could have talked until he was blue in the face and he wouldn't have convinced this gentleman, or half the people in attendance, that British officials were guilty of any wrong doing. It was widely held that Chinese "heathens" were to blame for the world's opium problems by "pushing" the drug on unsuspecting white victims. That had been verified in Canada six years ago by Mackenzie King's investigation into the opium trade in Vancouver. King's subsequent report, which Klein and other Winnipeggers had read about in the newspapers, was entitled "The Need for the Suppression of the Opium Traffic in Canada."

"To be indifferent to the growth of such an evil in Canada," King, then the Labour Minister in the Laurier Cabinet, had written, "would be inconsistent with those principles of morality which ought to govern the conduct of a Christian nation." The federal government agreed and passed the Opium Act which "prohibited the importation, manufacture, and sale of the drug for other than medicinal purposes." When that failed to halt the smuggling and dealing, the government strengthened the legislation with another act in 1911, making it a criminal offence to smoke or possess opium. Cocaine, morphine, and eucaine were also prohibited.

As far as Klein could determine, the dealers in Winnipeg were not deterred by the legislation. Every once in a while, John Jordan's morality troops would sweep through Chinatown and the nearby red light district in search of opium dens and "dope fiends," as the *Telegram* put it, but that hardly curtailed the problem. Klein knew that once you were addicted to the drug, there was no going back.

Following a few more questions from the audience and a general discussion about the role of government in regulating the free flow of goods between countries, Charles Bell thanked Mackinnon for his stimulating lecture. As the men filed out of the hall for tea and cakes in the adjoining room, Klein approached John Dafoe.

"Mr. Dafoe, Sam Klein, we spoke on the telephone earlier today," said Klein extending his hand which Dafoe grasped limply.

"Yes, of course, Mr. Klein," he said peering at Klein over top of his round wire-framed glasses. "I've been following your exploits. Most impressive, especially your work cracking the Krafchenko case. Not a lot of Hebrews in your line of work."

"No, I'm the only one," said Klein, "probably the only one in Canada for all I know."

"Most assuredly. We ran a story just last year I think about the number of Hebrew teachers, pharmacists, accountants and lawyers. Most of you make a fine addition to the community."

Klein ignored the backhanded compliment. "You wanted to speak with me about Alfred Powers, I believe?"

"Yes. Needless to say, I was most upset when I heard what had happened. I've known Powers for more than ten years. He sponsored my membership at the Manitoba Club. He's a fine man, a real gentleman. I find it appalling that the police could have charged him with murdering his wife, for goodness sakes."

"And her boyfriend," added Klein.

"Yes, her boyfriend, an Italian," said Dafoe, shaking his head. "Quite unbelievable, the entire sordid mess. Who does he have for a lawyer?"

"His son, Graham."

"Do you think that's wise? I know young Powers has an excellent reputation, but when one's own father is involved…"

"I think Graham has everything under control. He goes to court on Monday."

"Yes, I'm sure he'll be more than adequate. And I trust you will offer your investigative support?"

"For what it's worth, I'm already hard at work."

"Excellent. I'm glad to hear Alfred is in such fine hands. Now the reason I contacted you was to assure you that the newspaper and I are at your service. If there's anything I can do, any information you need. I insist that you contact me directly. I have told my secretary to put all your telephone calls through. I hope you'll take advantage of our resources."

"Thank you, I will. Actually, there are one or two matters you could help me with right away. But they have to remain confidential. Your word this won't appear in the newspaper?"

"Mr. Klein, I regularly speak with many eminent politicians, including Mr. Laurier, on a confidential basis. You may trust my discretion."

"I'm sure you have contacts in New York?"

"I do, many."

"I need information on a Detective Alex Taber. You've heard of him?"

"I have. Do you think he has done something wrong?"

"I'm not certain."

"I could send a cable to New York later today to an old friend at the *Times*."

"That would be a good idea."

"Anything else?"

"Yes, but to be perfectly honest this has nothing to do with Mr. Powers. A friend of mine is having some difficulties with John Jordan."

"A meddler of the worst kind. While I concur with many of his views, his methods leave much to be desired."

"My feelings, too. So, if you could tell one of your reporters that Jordan has been seen a lot at a house on Anabella Street…Well, I'm sure I don't have to spell it out for you."

"The Morality Inspector on Anabella Street? How will this city ever survive into the next century?"

"Don't worry, neither of us will be around to care."

"I suppose so, but Winnipeg has such potential. I pray that future leaders have the vision to build on what we are accomplishing now. I promise you, Mr. Klein, if we can corroborate your allegation, I will put it on the front page. In fact, I have the perfect man for the job. You've heard of John Maloney?"

"Maloney's left the *Tribune*?"

"I made him an offer difficult to ignore."

"Yeah, Maloney will be perfect," said Klein with a grin.

From an office he sometimes used at the Brunswick Hotel, Klein had tried several more times to reach Sarah on the telephone, but still he had no luck. A call to Melinda's also had been fruitless. "Sorry Sam," she had told him, "Haven't seen her." Klein contemplated confronting Melinda about her proposed venture with his wife, but decided that the telephone was hardly suited to such a sensitive conversation. The Manitoba Government Telephone girls were notorious eavesdroppers and gossips.

"We have more to discuss," Klein hinted to Melinda.

"Sam, I…I don't know what to say? I was only trying to help her."

"Let's talk about this later."

Klein hung up the receiver. He was tired and hungry. It was around five o'clock in the afternoon and his day was far from over. "One-Arm" Eddie's generally reliable information was that Kam Kwong could be found around the dinner hour at a small house on Dorothy Street, one block west of Logan Avenue and Arlington Street, not far from the Stock Yards. There, Klein was told, lived Kwong's latest conquest, Lilly Steeves: petite, pretty, and as white as cream. Undoubtedly, Klein thought, Kwong had already introduced the twenty-year-old waitress to the pleasures of opium. The Chinese hood rarely smoked the drug himself — he was much too clever for that — but he derived a peculiar pleasure from getting someone else to "hit the pipe," as they said in the street.

The streetcar ride down Logan Avenue took about thirty minutes. Klein disembarked with the horde of other passengers catching either the Arlington streetcar going either south towards Portage or the one heading up across the new bridge into the North End. As everyone in the city knew, the impressive steel structure that had been erected over the CPR yards three years back had been intended to span the Nile River in Egypt. When the Egyptians couldn't pay their bill, the city of Winnipeg bought the bridge from the Cleveland Iron Works. It was then shipped to Canada, piece by piece.

Klein observed that another group of riders, men only, left the streetcar and headed towards the popular Stock Exchange Hotel, probably for some after-work revelry. Given its location at Arlington and Logan and the fact that it was accessible to labourers at the CPR shops, the Stock Exchange was probably the liveliest hotel this side of the Main Street strip.

As Klein walked the block to Dorothy Street, a south wind blew the pungent odour from the nearby Stock Yards in his direction. The stench was so powerful that Klein had to cover his face with his scarf. Given the amount of manure on city streets from horses, every Winnipegger lived each day with such putrid smells. Many public health crusaders had already declared their support for automobiles over horses since cars didn't litter the streets with droppings, rife with diseases.

Klein had only walked a short distance down Dorothy when he encountered another strong smell hanging in the evening air. It was emanating from the second house on the street, number 7. The fumes from an opium pipe were distinct, a sweet and sickly odour. Kwong was getting careless, thought Klein as he glanced around. Most opium smokers took precautions to ensure the smoke didn't attract a police officer walking his beat. Usually, wet cloths were packed into cracks of windows and doors. Yet someone had left the front window open, and there were no thugs standing guard outside the house.

Carefully, Klein opened the gate leading to the house and stepped lightly through the snow, ducking his head low as he approached the window. He slowly lifted his head and peered in. Another whiff of opium smoke hit him in the face. He could see a young woman, Lilly Steeves no doubt, lying on a mattress in the middle of the house's small decrepit parlour. Beside her on the floor were all the tools of a seasoned opium user: a glass lamp filled with oil, a long steel pin called by the Chinese a *yenkok*, and of course the bamboo pipe with a small bowl where the heated opium was placed.

Kwong was nowhere to be seen. As Klein watched, young Lilly lit the lamp and held the pin in the flame. She appeared exhausted, and yet still her eyes spoke of craving and desperation. When the pin was sufficiently heated, she dipped it into a small round chunk of opium, about the size of a fifty-cent piece, that had been stuck to the back of a playing card. Next, she thrust the dab of opium on the pin into the flame until it began to bubble, and then gently placed the black mud or *pen yang* into the bowl on the pipe. Quickly she lay back on the mattress and inhaled deeply five or six times, the life of one opium pill. Satisfied, at least temporarily, she placed the pipe down on the floor.

"Kwong, come here," she yelled out.

Seconds passed before Klein saw Kwong enter the room with his sneering smile and greased-back hair. "Have you had enough for now, my dear?" he asked. "Soon some friends will arrive. I owe them some money. They've agreed that I can pay them off by offering them you instead."

If Lilly understood, it wasn't clear, for she remained silent. She reached upwards for Kwong's arms, but he pushed her away.

Listening to their conversation, Klein had an idea. He stood up, walked to the front door and knocked loudly.

"See, my dear, they've arrived," said Kwong. "Lim, Chow, is that you?"

Klein grunted.

"You're early, but she's ready for you."

As Kwong unlatched the door, Klein pushed it back hard. Kwong tumbled to the floor. When he tried to get up, Klein kicked him in the face. Not too hard, but hard enough so that he would remember it. Then he planted his boot in the middle of Kwong's chest.

"Sorry to get your suit dirty, Kwong."

"Go to hell, Jew boy. You don't know who you're dealing with."

Klein pressed his boot down harder. "On the contrary, I think it's you who don't know who you're dealing with. You're not so brave by yourself are you?"

"What do you want?"

"A bit of revenge for the other night and some answers."

"Answers to what?" He squirmed beneath Klein's boot. As he did so, he discreetly tried to reach into his pants pocket for his switchblade. Klein was ready for him. As he withdrew his hand from his pocket, Klein stomped on his fingers with his other boot. The knife spun across the floor towards Lilly.

"Don't do that again, Kwong. You and I are going to have a little chat. I want to know about your connection with Antonio Rossi." He lit a cigarette and threw the match onto Kwong's face.

"A stupid dago who couldn't keep his pants up. What else is there to tell? He got himself killed. I heard her husband slashed him and his slut."

"You and him have business?"

"None."

"Don't lie to me, Kwong. His family has already told me that you were with him. Was he selling for you?"

"Maybe."

"Maybe?"

Considering how the day had gone thus far, Klein was in no mood for games. He stooped and grabbed the collar of Kwong's suit. He yanked him up hard and slammed him against the wall. "I'm through fooling around. Was Rossi selling drugs for you?"

"He might've been," Kwong gasped, "You're choking me."

Klein released his grip, but only slightly. "Talk."

"Rossi was always coming around, visiting my women and pretending he was a real big shot. He said he had this connection in Montreal. Guaranteed delivery of a hundred pounds of opium."

"What's that worth? Twenty-five thousand? Thirty?"

"About that. Except there was a problem. Rossi needed five thousand up front to pay off a customs official."

"So how did you solve that problem?"

"We solved it."

"How?" Klein tightened his grip on Kwong's neck.

"I can't say."

"This wouldn't have anything to do with Detective Alex Taber, would it?"

Kwong's eyes widened. "I don't know what you're talking about."

"Did Taber provide the money? Maybe Rossi took the money and the deal went sour? Maybe you and Taber killed Rossi and Emily Powers? Is that what happened?"

Just then, there was a loud banging on the front door. "Kwong," a male voice said loudly. "It's Lim. Chow and a few others are here too. All friends. Open the door."

Soon to be outnumbered, Klein figured it was time to depart. He released his hold on Kwong's neck, but in a quick motion threw a right hook that landed squarely on Kwong's jaw. His adversary's knees buckled and he dropped to the floor, not far from where his dazed and doped girl friend was still lying. "That's for the other night," muttered Klein as he climbed out the back window of the house. You tell your boyfriend," he said in Lilly's direction, "that our discussion is far from over."

The woman smiled and nodded as she prepared another batch of opium to smoke. "You handsome."

"Operator, I want Main 1285 right now."

"Yes, sir. Just one moment."

"Hello," said Melinda.

"Where is she?" asked Klein.

"Sam is that you? You'll have to speak up. The house is crowded tonight."

"Where's Sarah? I got back to the apartment and she's gone. She even took her clothes with her."

"I'm sorry, Sam. Really, I am."

"Yeah, I heard you're sorry. That's why you offered her a job, a partnership for Christ's sake. What the hell were you thinking?"

"I thought...I thought I was helping her."

"Well, you weren't. Is she there? I want to talk with her."

"She's not here. I haven't seen her all day. Honestly, Sam, I don't know where she is, but if I hear anything, I promise I'll call you."

Klein hung up the receiver and looked around his empty apartment. Damn that woman, he thought, doesn't she know how much I care about her. At that moment, the various details and intrigues of the Powers case hardly seemed relevant. As he poured himself a glass of whisky and lit a cigarette, the phone rang. He grabbed the receiver. "Sarah, is that you?"

"No, is this Mr. Klein?"

"It is. Who's this?"

"Mr. Klein, I don't know if you'll remember me. My name is Parker, Oliver Parker."

"Yes, Dr. Parker, I read about you from time to time. What can I do for you?"

"Actually, I believe it is what I can do for you. I know it's late, but would it be possible for you to come to my house. I'm at 15 Kennedy Street." Klein didn't respond. "Truly, Mr. Klein, I think you would find what I have to say very interesting."

"You can't tell me on the telephone."

"No, it must be in person."

"Okay. Give me a half-hour and I'll be there."

"Would you like another cup of tea, Sarah?" asked Madame Gauthier.

"No, I think I've had enough. My stomach feels much better, thank you."

"Please if you need anything, you just call. Since Henri died, the house has been much too quiet. Not a lot of business these days."

Sarah smiled warmly. She had spent most of the day sitting by herself in the lobby of the Fort Garry Hotel, pretending she was waiting for someone. Periodically, the hotel's porter stared at her, but for the most part he left her alone. Maybe it was the sultry manner in which Sarah returned his glances. She still had a way with men. At one point during the day, she nearly picked up her bags and returned home. But then something, a feeling she couldn't explain, stopped her. Why, she thought, did it always have to be Sam's way? Did she not have a say in her own life?

Deciding that she needed more time to work this out, she went to the one place where she knew she could rest: Madam Gauthier's boarding house on Rue St. Joseph in St. Boniface. Once before, some years earlier during her ordeal with Peter Tooley, she had found refuge at the Gauthiers. Since then, she had visited Madam Gauthier from time to time.

"If you don't mind, I'm going to rest. I think I can nap now."

Sarah dozed for a few hours, yet was too troubled to fall into a deep sleep. It was well past midnight when she arose from her bed and lit the candle by her night table, along with a cigarette. She reached for one of her bags and undid the button on the inside pocket. She pulled out the small leather bound book and opened it.

January 4, 1913
A wonderful afternoon at the Leland. My body shakes when I think of Antonio. He's willing to do anything I ask. I am deceiving Alfred, but I can't help myself. Met the caller again. Strangely, money is not the issue. I cannot allow the photographs to be published, though my effort seems half-hearted at best. God damn, Abe. Why did he make me do that? Worse, why did I permit it to go on? Trying to figure out answers is driving me mad. Still, I have an idea that will alter the relationship for good and will appeal to both of us.

What photographs was Emily referring to, Sarah wondered. She glanced over the next dozen pages, but there was no other mention of them. She flipped further back, read several more entries, then returned the book to her bag. Feeling ill again, she lay down on the bed. Sooner or later, she was going to have to give Sam the diary — no matter what she had sworn to Alfred. Though she hadn't found it yet among the hundreds of entries, she sensed that somewhere in the diary were the answers Sam was searching for. Perhaps the photographs were the key?

If it could help save Alfred's life, how could she not break her vow to him? Emily would have understood — she wouldn't have wished Alfred harmed in any way.

9

Winnipeg Telegram, Saturday, January 31, 1914

WINNIPEG POLICE STATISTICS, 1913
Assault:18
Attempted Rape:5
Bigamy:2
Drunk and Disorderly:527
Gross Indecency:15
Inmate of Opium Joint:25
Unlawfully Selling Cocaine:5

Attempted Murder:10
Attempted Carnal Knowledge:3
Carnal Knowledge With a Girl Under 14:25
Exhibiting Immoral Play:7
Indecent Act:12
Seduction:18
Using Profanity On the Street:24

SLEEP WAS IMPOSSIBLE as long as she was alive. The money wasn't the issue — it could be paid, and she might even leave the city as agreed. But what if she didn't? Could the woman be trusted? There was doubt about that, a great deal of doubt.

It was too great a risk. She couldn't be allowed to live, not even for another hour. The hospital wasn't far away. But how to do the deed? That was the question. A half-empty whisky bottle was emptied into the sink, then smashed against the edge of the counter. The bottom shard was wrapped in a large rag and placed carefully into a brown cloth sack. Then, a piece of paper was taken from the desk drawer, and a note scrawled. It was folded twice and placed in the sack.

Once outside, the trek to the hospital was quick. The streets were quiet: not even the bread and milk cutters were on the road yet. It took no time at all to reach the corner of Bannatyne Avenue and Olivia Street.

The lone clerk at the front door was face down on his desk, snoring. "Room 156 — Miss K. Johnson," was written in the register book. Quietly down the hall. No nurses on duty. There, room 156 at the end. Katie was sleeping soundly, probably dreaming about spending all of that money. The gall she had, demanding an additional $5,000. The original bargain had been satisfied. She had been paid her $1,000. The subsequent blackmail had been a surprise.

Swiftly and before Katie knew what was going on, her pillow was pulled from under her head and pushed hard onto her face. She struggled, kicking and thrashing, but her assailant was too strong. Two minutes passed, then three. Finally, Katie stopped moving, though she wasn't dead yet.

Wearing black gloves, the assailant removed the broken whisky bottle from the sack and unwrapped it. The sleeves of her night gown were pulled to her elbows — one slash, then another, and the blood streamed from her wrists, dripping onto the white sheets. The attacker took out the note and placed it on the nightstand beside Katie's bed.

Dear friends,
The craving for the drug will not stop. And I cannot live my life as an addict.
I have seen the poor fools in Chinatown, spending all of their waking hours in
desperation. I fear I will go insane. Pray for me. Katie.

Now, the secret was truly safe. There was still Klein to be concerned about, but there too it seemed that his investigations were leading him to the desired conclusions — false ones.

What could Parker want with him at this hour, Klein wondered, as he gently nudged the horse forward with a snap of the reins. He had borrowed the cutter and horse, a brown nag named Liza, from his neighbour Mr. Sikorski, who lived across the street. A Polish immigrant from Rovno, not far from the village of Mezherich in the province of Volhynia where Klein had grown up, Igor Sikorski was a decent fellow. Two years before, soon after he had arrived in Winnipeg with his wife Anna and their two children, Klein had found him a job delivering goods from Marmel's Hardware Store on Selkirk Avenue. Since then, Sikorski insisted that Klein use his cutter in the winter and wagon in the summer, whenever he wanted.

Liza trudged down Kennedy and across Broadway. The wide and grand avenue with the large homes and apartment buildings was serene. Dr. Parker's home was third from the corner, directly across from Government House, an exquisite white mansion set back from the street where the Lieutenant Governor resided. In the moonlight, Klein could make out the Union Jack hoisted high on the house's flagpole and fluttering in the wind. Glancing further down Kennedy Street, he could also see the large home of millionaire grain broker Nicholas Bawlf. He was, Klein knew from what he had read in the newspaper, an upstanding citizen, a community leader, and a pioneer of the Winnipeg grain trade.

Klein left Liza and the cutter in front of the house. There was no need to tie the horse down — Liza was too well trained to wander off. He walked up the path to the two-storey house and knocked on the broad door. In a moment it swung open.

"Mr. Klein, I'm so glad you came," said Dr. Parker. "Please come in. Let me take your coat."

Parker led Klein into the main parlour. An enormous stone fireplace, nearly covering one whole side of the room, crackled with burning logs. A wall of medical texts, novels, and piles of magazines were stacked on shelves opposite, between two large windows.

"Could I get you a sherry or perhaps some whisky?" asked Parker.

"Whisky." Klein noticed an open book on the wide table in front of him: *Studies in Hysteria* by J. Breuer and S. Freud.

The doctor poured a glass of whisky from a tall decanter kept on a small wooden table near the fireplace and handed it to Klein. As soon as Parker sat down, his wife, a middle-aged woman dressed in a navy skirt and matching jacket, set down a plate of salted crackers and cheddar. "In case you gentlemen are hungry," she said.

"Thank you, my dear," said Parker. "Erica, you remember Mr. Klein, don't you?"

"Yes, of course. I have read of your exploits in the newspapers, Mr. Klein. I do hope you are able to assist Mr. Powers. He's a fine man. It's all quite shocking. I was very fond of Emily. She visited us often during the past year. I just can't understand what is happening in the world today. Now talk of war and more death."

"Now, now Erica," said Dr. Parker. "Please don't become upset. See to our other guests upstairs. Inform them Mr. Klein and I will be along shortly."

Once Erica left the parlour, Klein lit a cigarette.

"I suppose you are wondering why I've summoned you here in the middle of the night."

"The thought has occurred to me."

"Tell me," said Parker, squinting at a piece of paper in his hands, "does the phrase, '*Nay-en, Abe, Nay-en. Loz Meer*,' mean anything to you? Someone suggested it might be a form of German. I haven't had an opportunity yet to consult a linguistics expert at Wesley College."

"It might be something I recognize — I'm not certain."

"Very well, think further about it. Now, I want you to see something." He reached for a brown office file folder. "Here look at these pictures," said Parker, handing the folder to Klein. "They were taken last night upstairs in my house."

Klein opened the folder and studied the photos of the white cloud drifting in front of Mrs. Flood's mouth.

"You recognize the image?" asked Parker.

"It looks familiar."

"You sound skeptical, Mr. Klein. Is that not Emily Powers?"

"With all due respect, Doctor, I've read newspaper stories about psychic claims — a month later they're proven to be fake."

"Like the case of Mia Beth Knight, the London girl recently exposed by Professor Summers in Oxford?"

Klein had indeed read a lengthy article in the *Free Press* a few months back about the woman who, with help from a medium named Megan Morrissette, staged an elaborate hoax in which she had pretended to be spirits from the other world. The revelations had embarrassed the staunch members of the British Psychic Society. In the past, the press had recounted similar frauds perpetuated by the likes of Florence Cook, Mary Rosina Showers, and Annie Eva Fay, tricksters one and all.

"Yes, I was thinking of Miss Knight," replied Klein, looking more closely at the pictures. "Let me ask you — will you verify the integrity of the photographer? Who knows what fakery they're capable of?"

"John Duffin? I would vouch for his integrity at any time. I was in the dark room with him, Mr. Klein. The photographs are real. Please trust me."

"I don't doubt you, Doctor, but I would still like to reserve judgement. It seems to me that your experiments with ghosts attract a certain kind of person — the desperate, the lost, always searching for life's hidden meanings."

"I didn't know you were such a philosopher, Mr. Klein."

"Only when I have to be."

"We live in an uncertain age where the Church's teachings have been challenged by science and progress. Spiritualism does offer hope that there is life in the hereafter. It's a comforting thought, wouldn't you agree?"

"Comforting? Perhaps. I think blind faith can also be dangerous."

"If you ever have the time, Mr. Klein, you should read the work of W.T. Stead. The poor chap drowned when the Titanic went down two years ago. But he was a wonderful writer and influential journalist. When he left the *Pall Mall Gazette* many years ago, he turned to spiritualism and found some much-needed peace. I suspect that he was one of the few passengers on the great ocean liner who didn't fear death in the cold Atlantic, for he already understood that it wasn't the end of his life, merely a new beginning. But enough talk. I've brought you here to see for yourself, so please follow me."

Parker led Klein up the wide staircase to the second floor of the house, down the hallway and into his "spirit chamber," as he liked to call it. The small room at the back of house was locked and off-limits, except during evening gatherings. It took a moment for Klein's eyes to adjust. A single flickering candle provided the only light and gave an eerie illumination to the faces around the table.

"Please, Mr. Klein, allow me to make a few introductions before we begin."

Parker went around the room and introduced Klein to Mrs. Edith Flood, again dressed in black, photographer John Duffin, and the other participants. In all, there were a dozen people, two grain brokers, an accountant, a hardware salesman from Ashdown's, one lawyer Klein ecognized, several housewives, Parker's wife Erica, and Rosie Chudley, Alfred Power's young and pretty stenographer.

"Rosie, I didn't expect to find you here," said Klein.

Rosie blushed. "Emily, I mean Mrs. Powers, brought me here several months ago. I've been returning ever since. It's quite remarkable. I believe she was here with us last night, Sam. She's the witness who can save Mr. Powers."

"You think so?" Klein smiled weakly as he envisioned Rosie in the witness stand testifying that the ghost of Emily Powers had stopped by to reveal who had murdered her and Rossi.

"Mr. Klein has yet to be convinced," said Parker. "Let us show him there is truth to what goes on here." He guided Klein to the one empty chair at the table, directly opposite Mrs. Flood. As the grandfather clock in the parlour struck two, Dr. Parker instructed his wife to blow out the candle and signalled Duffin, standing beside his tripod, to ready his camera.

Klein was more than a little uncomfortable when the man and woman on either side of him grasped his hands. But he had come all this way, so he might as well play along. He had indeed recognized the foreign words Parker related to him earlier. "*Nay-en*, Abe, *Nay-en. Loz Meer.*" It was Yiddish: "No, Abe, No. Leave me."

For a few moments, the darkened room was silent. Klein began to wonder if they had all stopped breathing. Then, as happened the previous night, the table shifted and seemed to rise off the floor. "What the hell," whispered Klein. "What's going on Parker?"

"Steady, Mr. Klein."

Klein freed his hands and touched the table. It wouldn't move. He pushed harder on it, but still nothing happened. Then, just as suddenly, it returned to the ground as Mrs. Flood began to moan. At first, the sounds emanating from behind her were garbled.

"Oh my God," whispered Rosie, her voice tight.

"Be quiet," ordered Parker.

The others around the table didn't say anything. With the windows sealed, the air in the room grew stuffy and stale. For a moment, all that could be heard was a strange gabble of meaningless sounds.

Then the throaty voice behind Mrs. Flood spoke the same words as it had the evening before: "*Nay-en*, Abe, *Nay-en. Loz Meer,*" she repeated over and over again.

"It's her," said Rosie. "It's Emily."

"Rosie, please be quiet," said Parker. "What do you think, Mr. Klein?"

Klein decided to try something. "*Vos veel stoo?*" he asked in Yiddish. There was no immediate response. "*Ver bistoo?*"

"What are you saying?" whispered Parker.

"I'm asking what she wants and who she is."

"Try again."

"*Vos veel stoo?*" Klein repeated. "*Ver bistoo?*"

"*Papeer,*" replied the voice. "*Papeer, papeer.*" The voice sounded desperate.

"She wants a piece of paper."

"Erica, quickly."

In seconds, Erica Parker placed a piece of paper and pencil before Mrs. Flood. Her eyes were closed, yet she raised her right hand and seized the pencil. Slowly she began to scribble a series of lines.

"Now, Duffin," said Parker, as the photographer snapped more pictures.

Mrs. Flood collapsed on the table and the women in the room screamed. Parker stood up, struck a match, and re-lit the candle. He reached for the piece of paper and examined it. "Nothing but a bunch of incoherent lines."

"May I see that?" asked Klein.

Parker handed Sam the paper. He stared at it for a few moments.

"Tell me, is Mrs. Flood a Jew?"

"Edith Flood?" laughed Parker. "Born in Scotland and raised as a good Presbyterian. Why do you ask?"

"These lines on the paper — "

"Yes."

"They're Hebrew letters."

"What are you talking about?"

"This is the Hebrew letter '*Aleph,*' like the letter 'A,'" said Klein pointing to the first squiggle. "Yes, *Aleph, Samech, Tuff,* and *Raishe.*" Suddenly, there was a look of recognition on Klein's face.

"What is it, Mr. Klein, please tell us?"

"It's a name, a woman's name. The letters spell 'Esther.'"

Taber detested this part of the city. The tenement houses were decrepit and the squalor impossible to ignore. To his mind, the unfamiliar odours emanating from the shops on King Street made this area worse than so-called "New Jerusalem" where the Jews lived.

It was only ten o'clock in the morning and already the neighbourhood was crowded. Women scurried in and out of the shops carrying bundles and bags, while men with pigtails stood reading Chinese posters plastered on fences and walls. Every so often, a slew of angry words were exchanged, generating a great debate which Taber neither understand nor wanted to. And, of course, there was the one distinguishing characteristic of this neighbourhood, as in every Chinatown across the Dominion: clouds of thick steam rising from the laundries. As he made his way down Pacific Avenue, Taber figured that dropping off your clothes at a laundry was the only real reason ever to visit Chinatown — that, and opium.

Taber had tried the drug several times while he was still living in New York. He had been investigating a robbery on Mott Street and had stumbled almost by accident into a Chinese opium den operated by a Chinaman who had, as Taber recalled, an exquisite seventeen-year-old daughter. Following an afternoon of smoking with her, he had enjoyed hours of satisfying oral sex with the young girl. The opium heightened his senses and she had already been trained in the art of pleasure. Needless to say, he returned many more times to the Chinaman's house, never smoking enough to become addicted to the drug—he was too wary to let that happen — but he did learn to appreciate its mysterious powers.

Taber prided himself on being in control of any situation he encountered. Antonio Rossi's untimely death and its aftermath, however, had complicated matters. Klein's meddlesome investigations were also starting to get beyond annoying. But Kwong had assured him he could take care of the Hebrew troublemaker.

Taber had met Rossi through his connections with Kwong and his women. At first, the Italian's devious scheming and his sense of purpose had impressed him. Money was what drove him. His greed gave him focus, and he seemed intelligent enough.

Two matters demonstrated that Taber's usually reliable judgement had been wrong. First, Rossi became consumed with the Powers woman. She was all he ever talked about. Then she began to infringe on their business affairs. "Never trust a woman with business," he had instructed Rossi. "They are only good for one thing." But Rossi hadn't listened. He had a big mouth and it was threatening to get them all in trouble, serious trouble.

On top of that, Rossi had failed to deliver on a promise. Taber had put up the $5,000 to pay off the customs inspector in Montreal. The opium tins had been shipped from Hong Kong via Germany hidden in large sacks of rice and addressed to the fruit and confectionery store owned by Rossi's uncle. It was a foolproof plan — at least that was what Rossi had assured both Taber and Kwong. From Winnipeg, Kwong had already arranged for Chinese and Negro peddlers to sell the dope at a sizeable mark-up as well as to market some of it in rural areas where even more profits could be made. During the fall harvest season, demand for high quality opium was great from the threshermen and travelling farm workers who toiled their way across the Prairies.

The precious cargo was supposed to have arrived on a train two and a half weeks ago. When it failed to show up, Rossi had cabled his man in Montreal and received an unfriendly reply: an additional $5,000 had to be sent before the opium would clear customs. Taber had become livid when he learned of this new development, and angrier still when Rossi had the gall to ask him to cover this further bribe. A physical confrontation had nearly broken out between Rossi and Taber — only Kwong's soothing had prevented it. As it was, Taber almost took Rossi's head off with a billy club. A deal was eventually brokered, which Rossi had reluctantly agreed to. He was to come up with $2,500 and Kwong the balance. But before the money could be gathered together, Rossi and his woman were found dead.

Taber knocked on the door of the dilapidated house on Pacific Avenue. He knew someone was home — the smell of burning opium filled his nostrils.

"Kwong, open up," he shouted.

About a minute passed before someone answered the door. In front of Taber stood young Tina, a black-haired oriental beauty, who despite her unfortunate addiction to opium, still managed to retain a youthful appearance. On most nights, she could earn upwards of fifty dollars, which she split with Kwong. Tina stood in front of Taber wearing nothing but a flimsy black gown.

"What do you want?" she asked, so drugged she didn't recognize him.

"I want to speak with Kwong, you stupid whore."

"Not here, come back later," she muttered. As she tried to close the door, Taber stuck his boot in the way and flung the door open. He pushed himself, and with his right arm grabbed Tina around the waist, drawing her body closer to his. He tried to kiss her, but she pushed his face out of the way with her hands.

"You not handsome," she said, squirming in his strong arms.

"Go on, struggle," he laughed.

Two Chinese men appeared from the back room and Kam Kwong was right behind them. The detective pretended not to notice.

"Taber, I'm here, let's talk," said Kwong. "Let her go…if you wouldn't mind."

"Well as long as you're asking politely. Certainly." He released his grip and Tina immediately ran to one of Kwong's men. Taber tipped his hat. "Perhaps we can get acquainted this evening."

Tina said nothing. Instead, she spat on the floor in front of him. She left with the bodyguards and returned to the main parlour, collapsing on a mattress already occupied by two other white women. They passed her an opium pipe while Kwong's men watched.

"Always the grand entrance, Taber. No wonder the ladies like you so much."

Taber lit a cigarette, dropping the wooden match on the floor. "Enough small talk. Do you have the money yet?"

"Almost. I managed to scrape together about two thousand dollars. I was hoping you'd put up the last five hundred."

Taber laughed and then without warning slapped Kwong hard on the side of his head. The blow was so strong he nearly lost his balance. "Listen you pain-in-the-ass chink, I thought we'd already been through this. Look what kind of luck Rossi had when he disappointed me. Who knows what could happen to you? One night, someone could torch this whorehouse and then how would you make a living?"

"Okay, relax Taber. Want a smoke? A glass of whisky?"

"I want nothing right now, but for you to finish this deal. We have more than twenty-five thousand dollars of opium sitting in a warehouse in Montreal. I want all delays cleared up and I want those drugs on a train bound for this prairie rat hole. For my inconvenience, I've decided that I'm entitled to a seventy percent cut of the profits. Any objections?"

"Yeah, I do have…"

Once more, Taber struck Kwong hard on the side of his head, this time sending him reeling into a wall. Hearing the commotion, Kwong's two men came running, but Taber was waiting for them. "Stop right there," he shouted. He held a pistol in his hand and was aiming it at Kwong's head. "Either you leave now or your boss's brains will be splattered all over the wall."

Kwong stood up and issued an order in Chinese. The two men left the room.

"Nice to see men who obey."

"Put the gun away, Taber, or you'll never see that opium. I promise you."

"Have it your way." The detective returned the pistol to his pocket. "Now can we do business or not?"

Kwong rubbed his head and nodded.

"Excellent. Did I ever tell you what a rotten childhood I had growing up in the slums of New York City? Why the tenement I lived in was worse than this hole. Every night, my poor, stupid old man used to come home with the few dollars he earned carting furniture around for some big time Jew. Made me sick. Other days, he'd drink away our dinner money. Come home, beat me and my mother."

"Is there a point to this miserable story?"

"There is. I just want to let you know that I've been dirt poor before and I don't aim to be again. After this deal, and a couple more like it, I can retire in style."

"I aim to accommodate you, I promise."

The detective smiled. "I believe you, Kwong." He clasped his hands together. "So we're agreed, then. You'll find the rest of the money by the end of this week and then we'll send it to Montreal. Two weeks from today, I want to smell that opium."

A bead of sweat ran down Kwong's face. "By the end of this week, yes, the money will be in place."

"Now, we have one more matter to discuss."

"Klein?"

"Precisely. I've had second thoughts about him. At first, I thought he could be scared off. But now I figure he won't stop till he's discovered the truth about Rossi and the two of us."

"And what is the truth?"

"Who knows, you tell me."

Kwong shrugged. "So what about Klein?"

"Yes, our Hebrew detective. He'll have to suffer a fate like that of his lawyer friend now sensibly locked up in jail. Powers is a murderer — can you imagine that? They say he killed his wife and her boyfriend."

"So they say."

"Isn't it marvellous how things always turn out for the best? Anyway, Klein has to be taken care of. Maybe an accident. He could fall off a building on Princess Street — say the Chamber of Commerce. What do you think?"

"I have a better idea. Why not get Tina to lure him here with a promise of some revealing information — the identity of the killer who murdered Antonio and the woman. And the next morning, Sam Klein will be found in the street dead from an excessive dose of opium."

Taber laughed. "Wonderful, Kwong. And here I doubted my partnership with you. I'll leave the arrangements to you. But please keep me informed."

After taunting Tina once more, Taber finally departed. Kwong slumped in a chair, his head spinning. When he first became involved with Taber, he thought it was a good move. After all, how could you go wrong with a detective on your side? Yet he hadn't been prepared for Taber's nasty unpredictability. He had learned fast that he could never turn his head when Taber was in the room. My God, he thought, look what had happened to Rossi. Had Taber killed both Rossi and Emily Powers and then framed her husband? Why not? The man was seemingly capable of any act of violence. And he was certainly cunning enough to plot such a scheme.

All right, he had bought some much-needed time. He didn't have the rest of money. He wasn't even close. He had lied from the beginning to protect himself. If he had his choice he would rather say goodbye to the profits from this opium deal and end his association with Taber. From where he sat, the future of their partnership didn't look promising. Kwong butted his cigarette on the floor and reached for another one. There was a way, he thought, in which he could rid himself of Taber and maybe even keep the opium from Montreal. It would be dangerous. He was certain that few people had double-crossed Taber and lived to talk about it. But in these circumstance, he had little choice.

Klein felt awful. Hungover from drinking too much whisky and still spooked by what had transpired at Dr. Parker's, he covered his head with a pillow, trying to fall back to sleep. Where was Sarah? How could she have walked out on him? He was starting to have second thoughts. Maybe it was possible for her to manage a brothel and keep her clothes on. But that had to be the whisky affecting his brain. His head was spinning. He had thought he was on the right track in thinking that the double murder had some connection to Antonio Rossi's relationship with Kam Kwong and maybe, just maybe, with Detective Alex Taber. How sweet that would be. But then, he had gone to Parker's.

As much as he didn't want to admit it, that woman in Parker's photographs was Emily. Twice now, she had appeared in what the doctor referred to as "teleplasmic phenomena." Whatever it was called, it was damn peculiar. If he hadn't heard the Yiddish with his own ears, he never would have believed it. And what was he to make of the Hebrew writing. Esther? Who in the hell was Esther?

The ringing of the phone interrupted his concentration. He pulled himself out of the bed and slowly made his way into the kitchen.

"Hello, Klein here."

"Sam, it's me."

For a moment, he heard Sarah's voice swimming in his head. "Who is this?" he asked.

"Sam, it's Melinda. What's wrong with you? You sound terrible."

"I had a late night. What happened?"

"Katie committed suicide at the hospital."

"What?"

"They found her this morning. She left a note and then slit her wrists."

"A bit strange, don't you think?"

"I do. Sam, that girl was strong. She had lots of will power. She was hungry for money. Why would she kill herself?"

"What was in the note?"

"That she killed herself because of her opium addiction. It's a lie, Sam. That girl was no dope fiend."

"Okay, I'll ask around."

Melinda paused. "Any luck with the murder investigation?"

"Hard to say. I had a hunch, but I'm not sure anymore."

"Why, what changed your mind?"

"Melinda, you wouldn't believe me if I told you. You heard from her yet?"

"Sarah? No. I guess you haven't either. Don't worry, honey, she'll show up eventually. She just needs time to think things through. If she does call, I'll telephone whether she wants me to or not."

"Thanks Melinda, I appreciate it."

Klein placed the receiver back on the hook. He grabbed another piece of wood in a dwindling pile in a corner of the kitchen, threw it into the stove and placed a full pot of coffee on top of the burner. Peering out the window, he could see the wind was picking up and the snow beginning to blow. Shit, he thought, not another storm. How was he going to get work done if the streetcars shut down?

Unlike in other parts of the country incapacitated by a few inches of snow, Winnipeg persevered through winter weather that brought most cities in the Dominion to a standstill. It took a lot of snow and a vicious wind to keep Winnipeggers inside. They prided themselves on their indefatigable ability to stand up to the worst nature could throw at them. In few other parts of the civilized world did the weather shape a city's collective character as it did in this prairie outpost.

Sufficiently awake after a few cups of coffee, Klein made several more telephone calls. McCreary didn't know much more than Klein about Katie Johnson's suicide. "Pretty routine to me," the detective told him. "Opium is a menace. Blame the Orientals." Still, he assured Klein that if he heard anything different, he'd pass the information on to Eddie at the Brunswick. He also checked in with Graham Powers at his office downtown, busily preparing his legal argument to have his father's confession thrown out. As for Alfred Powers himself, Graham said that his father was doing well under the circumstances. Klein promised to keep digging.

"I'm close to something," he tried to assure Graham. "If I have it my way, you'll be able to go to court on Monday to have the murder charges dismissed." That Klein had little to go on was beside the point. Something was bound to break in this case — it always did.

Graham informed Klein as well that the police had finally released the bodies of the murder victims. The Rossi family had already arranged for Antonio's body to be delivered to St. Mary's Cathedral downtown. Graham himself, acting on his father's orders, had Emily's body sent to nearby Holy Trinity Church, the same church where Alfred and Emily had been married. Officials there had been instructed to bury Emily on Sunday morning whether Alfred Powers was present or not. Graham had pleaded with Chief MacPherson about allowing his father to attend the private ceremony. The Chief was still thinking about it.

Klein hung up the phone and it rang again. His heart raced. Please make it be Sarah.

"Hello. Klein speaking." When he heard the deep, strong voice, his face turned red. "Kwong, you've got a lot of nerve calling me at my home. What do you want? And talk fast, I haven't got time for games."

"No games," said Kwong. "Meet me at midnight on Monday at 520 McFarlane. Upstairs. You know where that is?"

"Yeah, I know. I used to live a block away. But why should I trust you?"

"Listen Klein, I have all the answers you've been looking for. There's only one other thing. There's a price for this information, so bring cash and lots of it."

"You've got to be kidding?"

"After you hear some details we'll negotiate a price. Monday midnight."

Mighty peculiar, thought Klein as he hung up the phone. Maybe this was the break he was waiting for. On the other hand, he wasn't about to put himself in danger. He'd be a fool to think Kwong was being straight with him. He needed someone to watch his back. And besides, he had already learned that plenty could happen in two days.

"You look much better this morning, my dear," said Madame Gauthier.

"I do feel a little better," confirmed Sarah. "I don't know what my stomach will take."

"Come into the kitchen. There's coffee or tea. I have porridge and pancakes. Anything you wish."

"You're much too good to me. I think coffee and a piece of bread with jam is about all I can manage."

"I could arrange for you to see Dr. Lavigne. He's very discreet."

"Maybe. Let me think about it further. For now I have these stomach pills." She held up a bottle of Owbridge's tonic. "It doesn't taste so good, but it does ease the pain a little."

In fact, the last thing she wanted was a doctor poking around her private parts. She had good idea what was wrong with her — she just wasn't ready to admit it. On top of everything else, she couldn't stop thinking about Emily's diary. She had read in the newspaper that Alfred Powers was scheduled to appear in court on Monday. She would wait until then and see what happened. Then, if it seemed absolutely necessary, she would give Sam the diary. She was also going to make a concerted effort to finish reading it. But it was slow going. Emily's small handwriting was difficult to read. Nevertheless, she was determined to persevere.

"I don't mean to pry, my dear," remarked Madame Gauthier, "but don't you think you should let him know where you are?"

Sarah laughed. She'd had this conversation with Madame Gauthier before, several years ago when she was also running from her troubles. It seemed she still hadn't learned anything. On that occasion Sam had understood just as Madame Gauthier had predicted. But now? Who knew what he was thinking.

"There's someone I do need to contact. May I use your telephone?"

"You go ahead. It's in the front parlour. I'll shut the door to let you have your privacy."

"That's not necessary."

Sarah found the telephone standing beside Madame Gauthier's phonograph cabinet. Last evening she had entertained Sarah with a new recording of opera star Mary Garden singing her acclaimed role of Melisande in Debussy's *Pelleas et Melisande*. It was delightful and the sound as crisp and as clear as if you were sitting in the opera in Paris — at least that's what Madame Gauthier claimed. "Only three dollars down and three dollars a month," she had mentioned. "From the Winnipeg Piano Company. A very honest business, and run by a nice English couple, too."

"Operator, please give me Justice 6900."

"One moment, Ma'am," said the polite female voice.

"Hello. How can we pleasure you today?"

Sarah instantly recognized the seductive voice. "Darlene, it's Sarah. I need to speak with Melinda."

"I hear you might be coming back into the business."

"I'm thinking about it, but not as a working girl."

"No, of course not," said Darlene.

"I didn't mean anything by that. Oh for goodness sakes, let me speak with Melinda."

"I'm here, honey," said Melinda taking the receiver. "Where are you? Do you have any idea how upset Sam is? I promised him I'd call him if I heard from you and I aim to follow through on that promise."

"I just need a little more time to sort out a few matters. I think I'm going to take you up on your offer. If it's still available."

"You sure about this? I'd hate to see you and Sam break up. You're a good match. I always thought so."

"Yeah, a match made in heaven. When you talk with him, tell him I'm sorry but I've got to have time to think."

"Anything else?"

Sarah paused for a moment. "Tell him…tell him I love him."

"I think he knows that, honey."

"Well, tell him anyway."

Sarah hung up the phone and keeled over in pain. The cramping was unbearable. "Madame Gauthier," she yelled as loud as she could. "Please help…" As Sarah fell onto the parlour floor, her arm hit a framed photograph of the late Mr. Gauthier sitting on a table. The photograph tumbled to the floor, its glass shattering in a dozen pieces.

Across the city, the telephone rang in the detective's office. "For you, Taber," announced Pete Norton, a younger detective who had been recently promoted. He had put in five years toiling as a beat officer and had surprisingly managed to stay out of any serious trouble. His worst failing had occurred several months ago, when he had accepted a "gift" from a brothel a few doors down from Melinda's. Chief MacPherson fortunately didn't find out about it.

"Thanks Norton," said Taber, grabbing the receiver. "Taber speaking."

"Monday at midnight at 520 McFarlane."

Taber's eyes widened. "Yeah, thanks very much for that. I'll see what I can do."

"I thought you'd want to be there to make sure the job gets done properly."

"I certainly do appreciate this call, sir." Taber placed the receiver back down. His face was flushed.

Not far away, Kwong hung up the receiver of his telephone as well. Excellent, he thought, everything was set for Monday evening. He would make sure the brothel was cleared out by eleven thirty. And then neither Taber nor Klein would be a problem again.

The snowstorm the *Tribune* had promised turned out to be a gusty wind that blew throughout the afternoon. Still, it was strong enough to keep most people indoors. In need of some air and time to think, Klein wandered down to Selkirk Avenue and stopped by Sam Magid's small sandwich shop. No one made a better pastrami on rye in the city, naturally served with a dash of Mrs. Magid's homemade sweet hot mustard.

Selkirk, too, was unusually quiet, even for the winter — not like in the spring and summer months, when merchants displayed their wares on rows of tables, and the crowds were thick and boisterous. Then, Selkirk Avenue, the commercial street of the North End, with its mix of Jews, Galicians, Slavs and Poles was like any other Eastern European marketplace. On Saturdays, some of the more observant Jews, like Frank

Shinbaum who ran a shoe store, still closed their shops for the Sabbath. The less devout accepted the fact that in the New World things were done differently. Sam Magid didn't work on *Shabbas*. He did, however, keep his restaurant open by handing it over to his nephew for that day.

From the perspective of the *goyim*, such Jewish behaviour was more than a little strange and hypocritical — either you were a practising Jew or not a practising Jew. But in fact it wasn't that simple. Klein's sister, Rivka, for example, regarded herself and her Bundist friends as committed Jews, though they rarely stepped inside a synagogue. "It was what is in the heart that counts," Rivka used to say. "Not what the Rabbi tells you to think." To Jews such as Freda Klein, such talk was blasphemous. But for the new generation in Canada and the United States, there was no choice but to change and assimilate, while at the same time maintaining their ancient roots.

"I thought I'd find you here," said the person hovering beside Klein.

"Maloney, hell, I haven't seen you in months."

"Been busy. I got a new job, been dating a new girl. Life is wonderful," he laughed. A short man with a trimmed moustache and thin brown hair, John Maloney was a diligent news reporter who, thanks to his association with Klein several years before, had regained his reputation and integrity. True, he would have exposed his own mother if needed, but only if the story was accurate.

"I heard you crossed the street to the *Free Press*."

"I know, I know. I'm as surprised as you are. Dafoe offered me a hundred dollars more a month. How could I turn that down?"

"What about Dafoe's 'Liberal' politics? Christ, I've heard you refer to that newspaper a hundred times as the 'Hun' and the 'snake.' It was the great defender of the CPR and the Exchange. Richardson must have gone crazy when you told him. He hates the *Free Press* more than the Devil."

"He wasn't happy. On the other hand, I've changed my mind about things. I got a right to do that, don't I? A man has to make a decent living, doesn't he?"

Klein shook his head in disbelief.

"Besides," continued Maloney, "Leila and I are planning to be married in the summer."

"Married? Good for you, Maloney."

"Believe it or not, she's one of you," whispered the reporter.

Klein bellowed. "Leila is Jewish? That's priceless, Maloney."

"Leila Chisvansky. She's twenty-five, from Cleveland, long brown hair, very lovely. Her father is an accountant, for Christ sakes."

"How did a *schmuck* like you meet her?"

"She's a professional dancer. She was performing in a show at the Empress about a year ago. I was able to meet her through the stage manager, an acquaintance of mine, and we've been together ever since. What can I say?"

"And she's willing to stay in Winnipeg and quit her career?"

"Right now, she's got a job choreographing a local production that'll be opening at the Orpheum in a few weeks."

"Well, if you want my advice, keep an eye on her. Women change faster than the prairie weather. You can't put a lot of faith in them…"

"You sound as if you're having some problems."

Klein grimaced. "That's putting it mildly. I haven't seen or heard from my wife since Friday. And I'm not sure if I even care."

"I'm sorry to hear that. I always liked Sarah."

"Yeah, I know you did."

"Listen, I heard you're investigating the Powers-Rossi murders and trying to clear Alfred Powers. That might be difficult. Word on the street is that they got a signed confession from him."

"I know all about it."

"Anyway it's kind of the reason I came looking for you. I got some good news and some bad news. Which do you want to hear first?"

"If you got something, Maloney, then let's hear it."

The reporter paused for a moment, while a young girl placed a pastrami sandwich in front of Klein. "I'll have the same as him," said Maloney, "and a cup of coffee."

"Okay, here it is," continued the reporter, "Dafoe wanted me to tell you that he received a telegram from his contact at the *New York Times* this morning and there was nothing in their files about Alex Taber. The few tidbits of information he could gather suggested that Taber was a pretty good cop. The worst trouble he got himself into while he was a constable on the New York force was being caught in a Lower East Side whorehouse. He was reprimanded. Other than that, he seems to have been a model police officer. I guess that's why MacPherson hired him."

"I hope that's the bad news."

"This'll make you happier. It took me only one day and a visit to Melinda's to verify your allegations about Jordan. He's been a regular there for months. And wait, it gets better. Not only did the girl of his dreams commit suicide last night, but according to the nurse on duty, Jordan was the last person to visit her."

"I already knew about the suicide, or maybe we should call it the alleged suicide."

"What are you getting at?"

"Maybe, Jordan got scared. Maybe Katie threatened to expose him. I don't know. Have you spoken to Doc Macdonald yet about the cause of death?"

"Oh, she slit her wrists…"

"You mean her wrists were slit. There's a difference."

"Give me some credit, Klein. I asked the doctor about that. He says the angle of the cut confirms it was self-inflicted."

"So, what are you going to do about Jordan?"

"I got an appointment later with MacPherson. Dafoe wants me to have something ready for Tuesday or Wednesday's paper. If you ask me, the Morality Inspector's days on the force are numbered."

"It couldn't happen to a bigger *schmuck*, sticking his nose where it doesn't belong. Telling people how to behave. You'd think we were back in Russia."

Maloney's sandwich arrived and he took a large bite. "Whew, that mustard is hot," he said reaching for his coffee.

"Puts hair on your chest."

"On my head would be fine."

Klein finished his own sandwich and lit a cigarette. "Tell me Maloney, what do you know about Oliver Parker?"

"The doctor and crystal ball gazer?"

"That's right. You ever attend one of his meetings?"

"No. I don't go in for that hocus-pocus. A bunch of nonsense, if you ask me. On the other hand, I do know lots of rich folks who swear by it. He's supposed to be an excellent doctor. And you do know that Arthur Conan Doyle himself, the great Sherlock Holmes creator, is a personal friend of Parker's. He paid him a visit a while back. Why do you ask?"

"I was there last night."

"At Parker's?"

"Yeah. If I hadn't seen it with my own eyes I never would've believed it."

"What happened?" asked Maloney taking out his note pad and a pencil.

"No, put that away. There's no story here. Forget it, it's not important."

"That's it? You're going to leave me hanging?"

"Afraid so, Maloney," said Klein standing up. "We'll talk more about it another time."

Thirty minutes later, Maloney was back at the *Free Press* newsroom on Carlton Street. Even though the paper had moved to a brand-new building, after a few short months the newsroom was as filthy and drafty as the *Tribune* and *Telegram* buildings back on Newspaper Row. Maloney's personal habits hadn't changed either: His desk was still as messy as ever, piled high with old papers, books and half-eaten sandwiches.

Maloney noticed that Dafoe's office door down the hall was closed, as it usually was this time of the day. The great man was piecing together "The Page," as it was so reverentially called — editorials and opinion pieces that informed the country's politicians and citizens about what Dafoe had decided was important for the day. What will it be this morning, wondered Maloney — another editorial about the failings of Manitoba schools, the seemingly unsolvable dilemma in the Balkans, more on Serbian nationalism, or perhaps another skewering of the Tories and Sir Rodmond Roblin. If you asked Dafoe about the Tories, he'd lambaste them as "the wealthy, the plutocrats, the privileged who yap about loyalty to the mother country to divert attention from the pressing needs of Canada." How he hated these "liars and political brigands," as he had often labelled them.

"Maloney," yelled Tim Franks, a young reporter. "Where have you been? Some woman has been telephoning you non-stop for the past hour."

"What woman? Who is she?"

"Says her name is Noreen Devers. Here, I wrote down the information," said Franks, handing Maloney a small message pad.

Maloney quickly scanned the piece of paper. "Interesting. Yes, I think this could be very interesting."

Franks was a cub reporter, but he'd been around the newsroom long enough to smell a good story. "Come on Maloney. Tell me what's going on."

"Honestly, I'm not sure, kid."

"Who's Noreen Devers?"

"The nurse at the hospital. The one I interviewed about the whore's suicide. She wants to talk some more."

10

Manitoba Free Press, Saturday, January 31, 1914

ON THE BOOK TABLE

Our Paris correspondent writes:

"The Psychoneuroses and Their Treatment by Psychotherapy" by Dr. Joseph Dejerine and E. Gaukler, Philadelphia and London: J.B. Lippincott Company. An accomplished professor of psychiatry at the Salpetriere, Dr. Dejerine, with the help of his assistant Mr. Gaukler, has written a controversial and important medical work. This book is intended for physicians and serious readers only. It attempts to explain the inner working of the human "subconscious," to use their term, and the way it can affect physical illness. The authors present a series of case studies and ably demonstrate how "emotional shock" and "trauma" cause not only hysteria but also visible physical reaction.

In one case a woman had a contracture of the right arm each time she tried to attack her husband. In another, a young girl, the victim of an assault, suffered from a contracted leg.

"It is evident that in these two cases," Dr. Dejerine writes, "it was the very nature of the emotional traumatism which determined the seat of the symptoms, and the patient became immobilized, in the latter case in a position of defence and in the former in a position of attack. The very nature of the shock which was experienced determined the seat of the hysterical symptom."

This is an important book that will shape and advance our understanding of human behaviour."

IT WASN'T DIFFICULT for Klein to find the right house on Wolseley Avenue. Even if he hadn't remembered the address, number 223, it was plain to see by the number of horses and sleds lined up in front that there was some sort of gathering taking place.

This part of Wolseley was a relatively new neighbourhood, populated by middle-class Anglo-Saxons. The homes were more affordable than in upscale Crescentwood or nearby Armstrong's Point. In those neighbourhoods a man had to be of a certain means to be admitted. Wolseley, on the other hand, with its young elm trees, offered an accountant, a teacher, or a salesman a little bit of the good life. The homes had four and five bedrooms, finely crafted brick fireplaces and white picket fences. In some there were even third floors in case homeowners chose to rent a room to a boarder. A single female teacher or nurse was generally preferable.

Klein walked up the frozen path and peered in the front window. The parlour was crowded with about twenty women sitting prim and proper in a circle. Their hands were folded on their laps and no one, of course, was smoking. Some of the ladies he already knew. Grace Ellis, looking very serious, was seated near the fireplace and beside her was Lila Mackenzie, the hostess for the evening's gathering. Klein instantly recognized Nellie McClung, who stood in the middle of the circle holding a Bible. Another woman stood before her with right hand flat on the book. In the stillness of the night, he could hear them.

"Repeat after me Cynthia," said McClung. "I hereby promise, God helping me, to abstain from all distilled, fermented and malt liquors, including beer, wine and cider, as a beverage, and to employ all proper means to discourage the use of and traffic in the same."

The woman carefully pronounced each word of the vow. When she had finished, McClung pinned a white ribbon with a knot onto her flowered dress.

"Always remember our motto, my dear — 'For God and Home and Every Land.'"

She said it out loud as the other women in the room rose and repeated the words with her.

"Welcome, Cynthia, you are now a full-fledged member of the Women's Christian Temperance Union. Congratulations."

A brief spurt of clapping followed as McClung and the W.C.T.U.'s newest member of the South West Union, Winnipeg District, took their seats.

Klein knocked on the door and a young girl, about twelve, opened it. "Yes, sir, can I help you?" she asked as politely as she could.

"Who is it, Annie?" Lila Mackenzie called out in a louder tone. "Remember what I told you about talking to strangers."

"I believe it's Sam Klein, the Jew detective."

Young Annie stepped aside as her mother approached. "It's more polite to say Jewish detective, dear. Mr. Klein, how nice of you to come. Mrs. McClung and Miss Ellis mentioned you might be stopping by. Please come in out of the cold. A nasty wind tonight, isn't it?"

"Not too bad." Klein stamped his boots on the floor so that he wouldn't track in any snow.

"Ladies," Lila Mackenzie announced, "Mr. Klein has arrived."

Immediately, twenty female heads turned. They stared for what seemed a long moment, sizing him up and down. Despite his years working in a brothel with at least as many women, Klein felt more than a little uncomfortable under their well-bred but inscrutable gaze.

"Welcome, Mr. Klein," said Nellie McClung, walking forward towards him. "Here, please have a seat. We just have a short agenda and then I would like a word with you."

Klein sat down, nodded at Grace Ellis, and accepted the cup of tea handed to him by Lila Mackenzie. From the other side of the room, Elizabeth Powers, looking somewhat despondent and sitting by herself, whispered hello.

A short Bible reading was first on the agenda, a passage from Romans 13:8 recited by Mrs. Helen Kelly, the Union's District president: "The night is far spent, the day is at hand; let us therefore cast off the works of darkness, and let us put on the armour of light. Let us walk honestly as in the day; not in rioting and drunkenness, not in chambering and wantonness, not in strife and envying. But put ye on the Lord Jesus Christ, and make not provision for the flesh, to fulfil the lusts thereof."

Klein glanced in Grace Ellis's direction. If she found the reading ironic — in light of their earlier conversation about Emily Powers — she didn't show it.

"And we all pray for our dear sister Elizabeth and her family," continued Mrs. Kelly, "May they only be blessed with happiness and good health."

"Amen," declared the women in unison when Mrs. Kelly was finished. She closed the Bible as Elizabeth rose from her chair and extended her hand. Helen clasped it and then hugged Elizabeth. "You've been very brave, my dear," Mrs. Kelly said softly.

Klein watched the women carefully. He didn't doubt that Elizabeth's pain was genuine. Yet there was something about her that didn't sit right with him. It was nothing she had said or done — merely a nagging feeling he had that she wasn't being entirely honest. Who knew for sure? These days he trusted few people, man or woman. Melinda had lied to him and his wife had deceived him. Perhaps the opponents of woman's suffrage were correct — women were too damn impulsive and illogical to be given the vote.

As Elizabeth resumed her seat, Helen Kelly rose to deliver her general report. She noted some successes being won across the country in the war against liquor. "The community has awakened to the economic fact that the industry of producing poison from wholesome grain is worse than turning the grain into ashes."

This was followed by a catalogue of the various evils attributed to alcohol abuse. The latest Canadian statistics revealed that 75 percent of crime, 75 percent of the pauperism, and 42 percent of the lunacy were caused by liquor. "No country, has a right to sanction, much less protect, an institution that cruelly and wantonly takes the happiness and brightness out of a child's life as it sends its victims down to untimely and dishonoured graves," she said.

Another round of clapping greeted her concluding remarks. As Klein fidgeted in his chair, the gathering heard from the heads of various committees about charity drives, presentations organized for the Y.W.C.A., a temperance rally set for a week from Sunday at the Grace Methodist Church, and financial matters. Finally, it was Mrs. McClung's turn to speak about political issues.

"As you all know," she began slowly, "a provincial election is imminent. Thus far, Mr. Roblin has show no indication that he is prepared to hold banish-the-bar referendums, never mind institute prohibition."

"He's in league with the devil," one of the women said.

"Indeed, he might be," continued McClung. "On both liquor and the vote for women, Mr. Roblin has been stubborn, obstinate, and condescending."

"Just like any man," muttered another woman.

"Now, now ladies, let us be civil," Helen Kelly admonished. "After all, we don't want Mr. Klein here to think that we hate men."

"No, just most of them," said Grace Ellis, prompting laughter.

"In any event, if I may finish," resumed McClung, "Each woman here should make it her solemn duty to convince her husband, father, brothers and any other male acquaintance to vote against Mr. Roblin's party. I have had several meetings with Mr. Norris and he and the Liberals are much more open to liquor referendums and women suffrage."

"Hear, hear," several of the women said.

"Once the snow melts," added McClung, "we should organize a woman's parade. Nothing militant of course, no demonstrating. With all due respect, we are not Mrs. Pankhurst and her daughters. In Winnipeg, unlike in Britain, there will be no damaged property, hunger strikes and unnecessary deaths."

Every woman in attendance understood McClung's message. The bitter fight waged by the British suffragettes led by Emmeline Pankhurst and her two daughters — Christabel and Sylvia — had been marked by violence and confrontation. The more the British women pressed for their rights, the more the male politicians and legal authorities resisted. Who didn't remember reading about how the suffragettes were thrown in punishment cells, stripped naked and handcuffed? And then, when they refused to eat, British prison doctors ordered that liquid be forcibly poured down their throats. When that didn't have the desired effect, long tubes were inserted into their nasal passages and the nutrients squeezed into their bodies that way.

"I just cringe to think of Nellie," said Lila Mackenzie. "Especially after what happened last June."

"So dreadful," added several women, "and so desperate."

Klein knew what they were alluding to. It had been the talk of the city for weeks — how on June 4, 1913, Emily Wilding Davison, an uncompromising suffragette, had rushed onto the horse racing course on Derby Day. She had grabbed the bridle of Anmer, King George's horse, and was killed when the horse fell onto her. She had committed this act, she had told her friends earlier, to awaken "the conscience of the people." But, in fact, little had changed.

"But you have to give our suffragette sisters credit for perseverance," stated Grace Ellis.

"Perseverance, yes," said McClung, "but still very foolish. What have these violent tactics accomplished but heartache? Our conciliatory approach will eventually have its desired effect and produce the necessary changes. Certainly it's the Christian way to do things."

Several women nodded their approval.

"Anything else to add, Nellie?" asked Helen Kelly.

McClung glanced at her notes for a moment. "No, only that I'd like to remind the ladies that our dear, departed sister Emily, God rest her soul, will be interred tomorrow morning. At Mr. Powers's request, I will be attending and any of you are welcome."

"No amount of praying will save that woman from damnation," murmured Lila Mackenzie, louder than she intended.

"Amen to that," whispered Elizabeth Powers.

"I'll go with you, Nellie," said Grace Ellis.

McClung stood up to address the gathering. "Thank you, Grace. Let me repeat this to the rest of you, especially you, dear Elizabeth. This is for your benefit as well, Mr. Klein. Emily Powers was far from perfect but we are not here to judge her. That is for our Lord to do. And remember none of us is above reproach. Are you Elizabeth? Are you Grace?"

Neither woman responded.

"None of us is truly innocent," she continued. "Please heed the words of St. John, 'He that is without sin among you, let him first cast a stone.' Can any of you stand before us and say that you are innocent of all sin?"

No one said a word.

"We will accompany you, Nellie," several women finally stated.

McClung bowed her head and sat back down on her chair.

"On that note, ladies," said Helen Kelly, "the meeting is adjourned. Lila has prepared more tea and cakes for us."

The women stood up and moved toward the dining room table.

"I hope you weren't put off by any aspect of our meeting, Mr. Klein," said McClung, suddenly beside him. As she smiled she seemed to radiate both kindness and authority. Klein sensed that before him stood a woman of consequence.

"I found the meeting quite...eye-opening."

McClung nodded. "I truly meant what I said about Emily. I imagine you must find my position a little peculiar considering my public pronouncements on other issues."

"No, not at all."

"You're too kind. Let me try to explain. I believe that our environment shapes us and at the moment our environment needs much reform. Witness the slums, poverty and excessive numbers of foreigners arriving each day. Sooner or later, this city, like others, will topple under the pressure of it all. My view is that women can make a difference. That is the reason I'm fighting so hard for our rights.

"As for Emily, dear Emily. She lost the battle that all of us struggle with each day: the battle against temptation and lust. She had a good heart, Mr. Klein. I'm afraid she strayed a little too far, however."

Strayed a little too far, Klein thought. McClung was being naive. Emily had cheated on her husband and did God knows what else. Then again, maybe his judgement was too harsh. Others had scorned Sarah for flaws that he himself had come to forgive.

"In any event," said McClung. "I'm at your disposal. My husband and I have known Alfred Powers for a number of years. We both believe him to be innocent of the crime which the police allege he has committed."

"And confessed to," added Klein.

"Yes, and confessed to. But people do odd things under pressure. Would you not agree?"

"I would, yes."

"Now is there anything I can do at the present time to assist your investigation?"

"Yes, there is. I haven't had much luck tracking down any of Emily's relatives in Chicago. Do you think you might be able to find someone who knows their whereabouts?"

"I think I could do that," said McClung. "First thing Monday morning, I will try my best. It is the least I can do for both Emily and Alfred."

"If you have any information, please telephone me at my home number, Justice 5942." Klein pulled out his cigarette case. "Now, if you'll excuse me for a moment, I must step outside."

"Yes, of course. It really is a terrible habit, Mr. Klein, if you don't mind me saying so."

Klein nodded politely as he headed to the front door. Once outside, he lit a cigarette and inhaled deeply.

"I thought I'd find you out here."

Grace Ellis stepped out of the shadows.

"Grace. It's nice to see you again. Would you like one?"

"Truthfully, yes. But tobacco is almost as bad as liquor around here. I try not to smoke while I attend these meetings."

"Sounds reasonable."

"Had you ever heard Mrs. McClung speak before?"

"No, I can't say I've had that pleasure."

"Impressive, isn't she?"

"She is. I suspect Roblin is underestimating her."

"Yes, she's a formidable opponent. He'll learn that soon enough. If not for her support, I don't think I would've made it through these last few days. I miss Emily terribly. It is as if a part of my life has been snatched away. Have you ever had a good friend die on you, Mr. Klein?"

"As a matter a fact, I have."

"It's only been a few days, but I almost feel as if Emily never existed at all."

"Would you mind if I ask you something about her?"

"Please, go ahead."

"You recall the other day when we were speaking about Emily's most intimate details."

Grace blushed. "Yes, I recall."

"I asked you if you knew anything about Emily and Antonio going to the Leland Hotel and later the Royal Albert."

"Yes."

"The odd thing is this. I've spoken with Sid Rochon. Do you know who he is?

"No."

"The owner of the Leland. Sid, whom I trust completely, assures me that a woman matching your description often reserved and paid for hotel rooms for Emily's use."

""I…I don't know what to say, Mr. Klein."

"The truth would be a start."

"I do apologize. I didn't mean to lie to you. It was just that I didn't want you think any less of me. The simple truth is that Emily was my friend and I would have done anything for her. She had to trust someone with the details and with paying for the rooms. I mean, Antonio usually had no money."

"Why doesn't that surprise me."

"Emily was weary of making the arrangements herself. I did it for her. That's it, the whole truth…honestly."

"Thank you. I appreciate your candour."

"It's too cold out here for me, Mr. Klein. If you'll excuse me, I must return indoors."

"Of course. I was wondering, and please forgive me if I'm being impolite, but would it be rude of me to ask you to lunch sometime next week?"

"Mr. Klein, you're a married man."

"I am. What of it?"

"If it is to discuss Emily's murder, I see no impropriety in that. How about next Wednesday at Dolly's?"

"Twelve-thirty?"

"Perfect. I'll see you then."

Klein smiled at her as she opened the door and went back in the house. He threw his cigarette onto the snow outside the porch and watched it flicker and fizzle into blackness. He liked Grace, liked the way she smiled. And, more important, he felt she was being honest with him about her involvement with Emily and Antonio. Yes, it all seemed to make sense.

"Hello my dear, would you like something?"

Still groggy, Sarah slowly opened her eyes and was greeted by the kind face of Madame Gauthier. As she slowly sat up, she could see the large gold crucifix hanging prominently on the wall in front of her bed. "Where am I? What happened to me?"

"Not so fast, my dear. The doctor said someone in your condition must rest."

"What happened? Please tell me."

"You fainted. You're in a private room at St. Boniface Hospital. It's Sunday morning. Dr. Lavigne gave you a sedative last night to help ease your pain and allow you to sleep."

"Yes, I feel much better. I'm sorry to have put you through so much. I don't know what I would have done without you."

Two nuns entered the room. "We are glad to see you are awake, Miss," one of them said in a thick French accent. Sarah could barely understand them. Madame Gauthier said something to them in French. They smiled, patted Sarah on the hand and left the room.

"What's wrong with me? Do I have consumption?"

"No, no, my dear," said Madame Gauthier with a warm smile. "You are going to live a long and happy life."

"Then what is it? Why is everyone being so kind?"

"Because, my dear, you're pregnant. Sarah, you're going to be a mother."

Sarah's eyes widened and her mouth went dry. "Oh my God," she whispered. "How can that be?"

"Grace is that you?"

"It's me, father."

Frank Ellis emerged from the back room of the small apartment he shared with his daughter. Nearly sixty years old and bald except for a few strands of grey hair, Ellis still had the strong physique of a man half his age. He was proud of that fact.

"Why, it's nearly midnight, Grace. The meeting run late?"

One look at her father and she knew that he had been drinking whisky all evening. His one vice — in fact, his only vice — was that he sometimes drank too much. When his wife Mary was still alive, it wasn't so much of an issue. She had managed him and the problem well.

Mary's solution would have been several strong cups of coffee. She always made it the way he liked it — black and strong. He used to brag to his friends that she was like a vaudeville magician in the kitchen. Whatever he wanted — coffee, cake, chicken potpie, or roast ham — Mary knew how to prepare it as well as any hotel chef in the city. Grace certainly resembled her mother, and possessed Mary's common sense, but unfortunately didn't inherit her mother's culinary skill. Every day since Mary had died from a terrible bout of influenza, Frank Ellis had thanked the Lord for giving him a daughter like Grace. It was only too bad, he used to joke, that she didn't know how to make a better cup of coffee.

Grace was upset to find her father drunk, but she had a lot on her mind at the moment and it was too late for an argument.

"The meeting didn't go late. I decided to walk home. I needed some time to think. Don't you think you should get some sleep, father?"

"It hasn't been the easiest few months, has it? First, your dear mother, then Emily. What you need is a change of scenery. You should take a holiday, Grace. Maybe go visit Aunt Ruth in Victoria."

The last thing Grace needed was to spend time with her father's sister Ruth, a more meddlesome woman she did not know. "Don't worry about me, father, I'll be fine. Don't you have a lot of work to do tomorrow? The Stevens need their stove fixed and there was a leak in the Bramptons' apartment."

"You take good care of me, Grace — just like your dear mother. Bless her soul. But you do need to have your own life. You can't be staying here with me for the rest of your life. What about that idea of Mrs. McClung for you to become a lawyer?"

"A pipe dream, father. That's all."

"Well, what about finding a decent man and settling down? I won't stand in your way."

"No, I know you won't," she said, giving her father a kiss on his cheek. "Now why don't you go to sleep. I'll clean things up in the kitchen. I imagine there are a few empty bottles lying around the apartment."

Frank Ellis knew that when his daughter made up her mind, she wasn't about to change it. Her stubborn streak was inherited from him.

"I miss your mother, Grace. That's all."

"I know you do."

As soon as her father had retired to his bedroom, Grace reached for a pack of cigarettes she kept hidden on the top shelf in the kitchen. That was her vice. She walked quietly down the narrow hallway to the parlour and sat down beside a large red brick fireplace that dominated the room.

Even in his inebriated state, her father was correct. She missed her mother and Emily very much. Both women had given meaning as well as a semblance of order to her life. Now everything seemed far too confusing. She found it difficult to relax. Images of her mother, Emily, Nellie McClung, and Sam Klein ran through her head like a runaway train. The ease at which Klein discovered her lie about the hotel was ample proof of his expertise as an investigator. He wasn't a man to be underestimated.

As one cigarette burned down, she used it to light another. Why, she thought, did Emily have to get herself in so much trouble? She had warned her countless times that her relationship with Antonio would lead to nothing but trouble. Emily wouldn't listen. That was her fatal flaw: too often she let her emotional side get the better of her.

Of the two of them, Grace was by far the more rational and reasonable — at least most of the time. Occasionally, she got carried away and it was

Emily who had rescued her. Only a few weeks ago, Grace had lost her temper with a clerk at Carsley's and it had been Emily who had calmed her down. Now who would do that for her? There weren't many times in your life that you forged a bond with another person the way she had with Emily. Whether it was discussing the latest fashions or talking about women's rights, each friend knew what the other was thinking. That was what Grace truly loved about Emily and why she knew it would be impossible to find someone to replace her.

Grace took a deep drag on her cigarette. It was odd how life worked out, she thought. She had planned on finding her own place to live, perhaps in an apartment off of Broadway Avenue. She had had discussions with Emily about the two of them opening a hat shop. Emily had seemed to think that Alfred might finance such a venture. Nothing would come of that now. For the moment, she was destined to be the daughter of an apartment manager. Watching the smoke rise from her cigarette and vanish into the darkness of the room, she bit her lip and contemplated what might have been.

Graham Powers threw another log on the fire and sipped a glass of port. He had been working almost non-stop for the past forty-eight hours, digging his way through legal files and poring over law reports. He had only taken a brief break to attend Emily's funeral earlier in the day. Elizabeth had refused to accompany him, but he had honoured his father's wishes and gone. It was an intensely sad affair. A small collection of people gathered to bid farewell to this beautiful woman who had affected so many lives. Few of his father's friends had bothered to show up. There was only Graham, and a group of women led by Mrs. McClung who read a prayer.

"Our Father, which art in heaven, hallowed be thy name. Thy kingdom come. Thy will be done on earth as it is in heaven. Give us this day our daily bread. And forgive us our trespasses…."

Could Emily's trespasses ever be forgiven, wondered Graham? For some reason, another passage he had learned many years ago in Sunday school flitted through his head. It was from St. Luke: "Her sins, which are many, are forgiven; for she loved much." It seemed to him that that was the real message of Emily's life. To resent Emily as his sister did was a waste of energy. He had decided to remember her for what she was, flaws and all. It was, as Nellie McClung pointed out, the Christian thing to do.

Later that Sunday afternoon, once the sombre mood of the funeral had dissipated, he felt ready to conquer the world — or if not that, at least to marshal a strong argument the next morning as to why his father's confession should be rejected. His prodigious research, guided by some valuable hints of where to look from Alfred Powers, had turned up two precedents that he planned to introduce at the *voir dire*.

The first, Martin v. Tyler, was an Ontario case from 1882 in which the defendant Wilmer Martin brought an action against Robert Tyler, a Toronto constable, for brutality. The judge of the Ontario court ruled that Martin's confession to a robbery had been obtained through a beating he had received at the hands of Constable Tyler. The confession wasn't allowed as evidence, and the robbery charge against Martin was dismissed.

The second and more recent case from the Nova Scotia court, Rex v. Holmes, was even more compelling since it had a relevant psychological aspect. In February 1913, the body of eight-year old Joseph Holmes was discovered mutilated in a field outside of Shelburne. Following a brief investigation, the boy's father, Theodore Holmes, was arrested. Almost immediately the distraught man confessed to the killing. However, within days he recanted and his lawyer challenged the admissibility of the confession at a *voir dire*.

The judge ruled in favour of Holmes, having been persuaded by a defence submission from Dr. Louis Simone, a local graduate from the Salpetriere Institution in Paris. Dr. Simone, who had trained with the eminent professor of psychiatry, Joseph Dejerine, argued that a false confession could have been provoked by the "emotional traumatism" of the son's death. The father, said Dr. Simone, had felt so guilty for having allowed the boy to wander off by himself, that he was impelled to claim full responsibility.

Graham wasn't certain he believed such radical ideas about the workings of the human mind, but if it helped his father, he figured he might as well use whatever he could. However, he knew that his one real obstacle was Magistrate George Findly. An elderly and conservative judge, Findly wasn't going to be won over by psychiatric studies of the mind or speculations about hysteria.

Graham himself had read the 1909 English translation of a controversial book first published in 1895 called *Studies in Hysteria* by two European doctors, Josef Breuer and a Viennese Jew named Sigmund Freud. They wrote of the benefits of hypnotism and how they had used it to unlock the "repressed memories" of their "hysterical" patients, suffering as they were from a variety of traumatic memories.

Perhaps hypnotism, Powers thought, could discover the truth about what had really happened that night in the alley behind the Walker Theatre. Who knew for certain what his father had seen or heard, or what he had "repressed," in the language of Breuer and Freud.

The more he contemplated such an outlandish approach, the more his mood turned sour: he realized he was grasping at straws. He downed the glass of port, took the Swedish glass decanter, his late mother's favourite, and poured himself another. How their lives had been turned upside down since her death. He didn't blame his father or even Emily particularly. Graham wasn't one to dwell on the past. Most often, he felt there were no reasons why things happened in the manner they did. It was just life unfolding as it had to.

He reached for a pencil and pad of paper to jot down more notes but as he began to scribble, he pressed too hard, snapping the lead. He reached into his pocket for his penknife and then remembered he had left it at his office. He got up to search for another writing utensil in the parlour and then in the kitchen cupboards, but none was to be found. Elizabeth must have one, he thought.

Graham trudged up the wide staircase, turned down the upstairs hall with its gleaming hardwood floors, and entered his sister's bedroom. It was as austere as she was. A simple bed, a dresser, and a desk. A framed photograph of their mother, long before her illness, was the only accoutrement in sight. Powers knew that his sister, given her penchant for privacy, wouldn't have appreciated his snooping through her dresser. However, he needed a pen or pencil. He opened the top drawer first where she kept her various undergarments. Quickly he shut that. Several blouses, a black skirt, and a new wool sweater still in its Hudson's Bay box were in the next drawer. He opened the bottom part of the chest, and there under a program from the Winnipeg Oratorio's last concert at the Walker Theatre was a slightly nibbled pencil.

He was about to close the drawer when something tucked away at the back caught his eye. He pushed aside some papers, a bottle of two-dollar cough syrup, and an advertisement for Dingwall Jewellers and Silversmiths on Portage Avenue (the store was having a sale on combs and brushes), and pulled out a gold chain with a locket attached to it. Funny, he thought, he didn't ever recall seeing Elizabeth wearing jewellery. He grasped the locket in his fingers and flicked it open. Inside was a picture of two young women, neither of whom he recognized. Still, the more he stared at the photograph, the more one of the girls looked familiar. On the inside of the cover was engraved the following: "E.M. & H.M. N.Y. 5 May 1904." What the hell was this he wondered and why was it in Elizabeth's dresser drawer?

He sat down on the edge of his sister's bed just as Elizabeth Powers burst into the room.

"Graham, what are you doing here?" she asked. "Haven't I asked you to respect my privacy?"

"I was looking for a pencil," he said. "And I don't appreciate your tone."

"I don't really care what you appreciate. Please leave at once."

"What is this?" He held up the locket in front of her face.

"Where did you get this," she shouted. "Have you been through my dresser? Graham how could you?"

"What is this?" he repeated. "Who are these girls?" Then it hit him. "This one girl," he said, pointing to the photograph. "It's Emily, isn't it? The letters engraved here, 'E.M.,' must stand for Emily Munro. Yes, that's it isn't it? But where did you get this? You're the last person Emily would have given it to."

"She was wearing it the night she was killed," Elizabeth blurted out.

"How do you know that? Tell me quickly. Were you there?"

"No I wasn't there, you fool. What, do you think I murdered her? I hated her, but it wasn't me who did the deed. The locket was given to me by Father."

"Father?"

"You heard me. It was the other day when I visited him. He had hidden it inside the lining of his jacket. The police didn't find it when they searched him."

"What did he say about it? Why didn't he turn it over to them as evidence? My God, why would he hide this but give them the murder weapon?"

"I don't know, Graham. All he said was to hide the locket in the house somewhere and…"

"And what?"

"And not to tell you about it."

"He said that?"

Elizabeth nodded.

Graham was dumbfounded. Then a thought suddenly occurred to him. Elizabeth immediately noticed the change of expression on her brother's face.

"Yes, Graham, that's occurred to me as well. Father may have done it just like he said. Or, worse, his confusion, his confession, his remorse — may have all been part of some scheme to confuse you and the police. He counted on you doing everything you could to have the confession repudiated thus casting more doubt on his guilt. And, of course, tomorrow morning in court that's exactly what is going to happen."

"That's impossible. Father concoct this whole charade. Why? Why would he do that?"

"To get away with murder."

"That's preposterous."

"Well, there's only one person who knows, isn't there?"

"Yes. I'm going to the police station."

A hundred different scenarios went through Graham Powers's head as he drove the team of horses himself towards the station. With Elspeth still not well, yet expected back on the job within a week, it didn't seem worthwhile to find a temporary replacement. Besides, Powers might have been a member of the esteemed elite, but he still knew how to drive a sleigh through Winnipeg's snowy streets.

A serenity descended on the city each Sunday. Banks and businesses were closed. The Grain Exchange trading floor, during the week the most frantic place on the Prairies, was as quiet as a hospital ward. Timothy Eaton, the department store magnate, certainly understood the importance of a day of rest. To thwart temptation, he ordered that the drapes on his stores' windows be drawn on the Lord's Day. Sunday was for Church and family, not shopping.

As Graham urged the horses down Main Street, he wished he'd been able to find Klein. He wanted him there when he questioned his father. He had telephoned Klein's home as well as the brothel, but he was nowhere to be found. His father genuinely liked the Hebrew detective and regarded him with a respect he rarely accorded someone of his background.

Graham left his rig on Rupert Avenue and marched into the station. Now that he was there, his feelings of betrayal had turned to apprehension. To be honest, he thought as he entered the building, he wasn't certain if he really wanted to discover the truth. In his eyes, there was no greater man walking the earth than Alfred Powers, K.C. Graham fancied himself a decent lawyer. But he knew that his legal knowledge would never match that of his father's, nor would his eloquence in a court room.

"Powers, what are you doing here on a Sunday?" the jailer asked.

"Take a guess," said Graham. The intellect of the average Winnipeg constable had never impressed him. But what could be expected for a salary of less than $90 a month and seventy-two hour work week? There were easier and more profitable ways to make a living. A fast-talking salesman could make more and certainly didn't have to work as hard.

The constable ignored the sarcastic tone in Graham's voice and opened the door to the cell area. "Follow me, but watch the mess on the floor. The Saturday night drunks are still sleeping it off."

Graham found the odour of sweat and vomit that permeated the congested cell area revolting. They stopped in front of Alfred Powers's new home and Graham patiently waited until the police officer opened the cell door.

"Don't worry, you get used to it," said the elder Powers, noticing his son's discomfort. "That's Charlie over there, and I'm also friends with Hank down the hall. If you listen you can hear them both snoring."

"Just yell, when you want me to let you out," the constable said, locking them in.

"You went to the funeral?" asked Alfred Powers.

Graham nodded, carefully taking a seat on the lone wooden chair. He knew from previous visits that its back was prone to falling off. "She's been laid to rest, just as you requested. Mrs. McClung read a prayer."

"Good. Emily deserved that. Damn MacPherson, how could he not permit me to attend? If I ever get out of here, I'm going to do everything I can to have him fired. Deacon, Gray, Bond, Rigg, Munroe and every other member of council are going to hear about this shabby treatment."

"Father, we have to talk."

"Yes, of course. You're ready for tomorrow, I assume. You've found the case, Martin v. Tyler, I told you about. Remember the extent of the beating isn't so much the issue, but rather the intimidation."

"I found it, along with another one from 1913, a case from Nova Scotia. But I should warn you, if I decide to introduce it, questions will be raised about your mental state. It deals with hysteria and the effects of traumatic shock. It may be too advanced for Magistrate Findly."

"I don't understand. What do you mean 'if you decide to introduce it'? Why wouldn't you? If it will help explain my memory loss at the time I discovered the bodies and my confession after being assaulted by Taber. I thought I had taught you better than this. Don't you remember? Never dismiss a possible precedent and never underestimate the intellectual capacity of any judge, even an old coot like Findly. What's wrong with you, Graham? My God, I've placed my life in your hands."

"Let me ask you, father, is there anything about that night which you haven't told me?"

"Nothing."

"Is that so?"

"What's on your mind, Graham? Out with it. I'm not one of your ignorant commercial clients."

Graham reached into his inside coat pocket and pulled out the locket and gold chain.

"Emily's locket. Where did you find that?"

"Please, Father, don't play dumb with me. You're much too clever for that. Where did I find this? I found it in Elizabeth's dresser drawer, where she hid it after you secretly gave it to her. And, I might add, after you instructed her not to tell me." Graham stepped back as if he had finished a closing argument.

Alfred Powers slumped in his bunk. He couldn't look his son in the eye. "I apologize Graham, I truly do. I wasn't trying to keep any secrets from you."

"And yet you did."

"Don't use that tone with me — I'm still your father. I deserve respect."

"Yes, you do. But right now you're also my client and I'm sorry to say that I don't completely trust you. I'm going into court tomorrow morning to defend you and I don't want to have any doubts."

"What is it you want to know?"

"Start with the locket."

Powers shook his head. "I only found it in my pocket after I'd been arrested. I honestly don't recall how it got there. Please, Graham, believe me. I don't know why I did what I did. Since the beginning of this whole sorry episode, I haven't been myself."

"That's somewhat of an understatement."

"I gave the locket to Elizabeth because I didn't want to lose that last piece of Emily. She didn't wear it much, but I do know that she cherished it greatly. I feared that if you learned of it, the locket would wind up in an evidence bag, and I'd never see it again. And that's it. In retrospect, I realize I was being foolish."

Graham flipped open the locket. "That's Emily?" he asked pointing to one of the photographs.

"Yes. I think she was about fifteen then, possibly younger."

"And the other girl?"

"Her sister. Henny, I believe she said, that was what her name was. I don't know anything about her or even if she's still alive. Emily didn't speak much of her family."

Graham Powers stared at his father for a moment. "I'd better get this over to Klein. He might find it useful. Now, is there anything else?"

"No. That's the whole truth. Trust me, son. But maybe you should go ahead with introducing that case about traumatic shock. I don't how else you could explain what's come over me."

"Let me pose another question. Would you consent to being hypnotized?"

"Hypnotized? You mean mesmerism?"

"Yes."

"Whatever for?"

"As much as I understand it, I believe you have repressed the memory of the night of the murder. You say that you recall some of it, but I think there is more hidden inside your brain. A hypnotist might be able to bring it out."

"I don't know, Graham. I'll have to think about it."

"What is there to think about? As your lawyer, I believe it would be very helpful. Nothing will happen to you. I've read that it's very safe."

"Well, if you think it's necessary."

"I do. I'm going to arrange something as soon as I can."

"Do you have a doctor in mind?"

"Yes, someone who knows you, or at least knew Emily, Dr. Oliver Parker. Not only is he a renowned surgeon, but I understand from Klein that he has an interest in hypnotism."

"He also believes in talking to the dead. He holds seances, Graham. Do you really think he would be a credible witness?"

"Time is short, father. There is, to my knowledge, no one else in Winnipeg capable of performing this. What if he can assist you in recalling what happened when you stumbled across Emily? Do you not want to know?"

"Of course, I do."

"Good. I must leave now. They'll bring you to Police Court tomorrow morning at ten o'clock."

Alfred Powers watched Graham leave the cell area, led down the hall by the constable.

"That your son?" one of the drunks in the other cells asked. "Do you think he could help me get out of here?"

Powers ignored his neighbour and lay down on the thin mattress on his bunk. He was concerned. There was, in fact, more that he wasn't telling Graham. It wasn't important — at least that's what he told himself. But what if this hypnosis actually worked? What if he was forced to reveal what he really knew of Emily's past? That he had fallen in love with and married a woman who was nothing like she pretended to be. What would Graham and Elizabeth think then?

He had learned only weeks before her death that Emily Munro didn't really exist. There was no Emily Munro, never had been. In reality his dear wife was Esther Mandelbaum, a poor Hebrew immigrant from New York. A Jewess! He grew momentarily angry as he thought about the ruse she had perpetrated upon him, upon everyone in the city. He wondered how Nellie McClung and other ladies of the W.C.T.U. would feel?

The worst part was that Powers had discovered something about himself that he didn't particularly like: he wasn't as open-minded and liberal as he believed. Part of him was ashamed that he had unknowingly exchanged wedding vows with a Jewish fraud. Now he had allowed her to be interred in a Christian cemetery as well. What choice did he have? He knew that at some point he would pay for allowing this sacrilege to occur.

And to complicate matters further, more secrets had been revealed that terrible day last year. Secrets — Emily, dear sweet Emily, had far too many. Some, he knew, had to be buried forever. He had hoped he had solved one problem by enlisting the help of Sarah Klein. No sorcerer was going to make him divulge anything else. That much he was certain of.

11

Winnipeg Telegram, Monday, February 2, 1914

MURDER VICTIMS BURIED

In two separate funerals held yesterday, Mrs. Emily Powers, the wife of Mr. Alfred Powers, and Mr. Antonio Rossi, nephew of Mr. and Mrs. E. Rossi, were laid to rest. Both were killed last Wednesday in a brutal crime. Police discovered the bodies behind the Walker Theatre.

The service for Mr. Rossi, attended by more than a hundred people of the city's Italian community, was held at St. Mary's Cathedral. Mrs. Powers had a much smaller service at Holy Trinity Church. A delegation of ten led by Mrs. Nellie McClung from the Women's Christian Temperance Union, of which Mrs. Powers had been a member, attended.

Despite the requests from Mr. Graham Powers as well as Archdeacon Fortin, police officials refused to permit Mr. Alfred Powers to attend the funeral of his wife. The elder Powers has been in custody after confessing to the murder.

A hearing will be held today in Police Court to determine the validity of the confession.

"IS THAT ALL you have, Mr. Powers?" asked Magistrate George Findly. Wrapped in his black gown, he methodically stroked his white beard. "These two supposed precedents? I don't see how they are relevant to the case before us today." He looked for approval from the numerous spectators and reporters seated in front of him.

There was a small delegation from the police department, of course. Chief MacPherson had taken time from his busy schedule to see what would transpire, especially with the allegations that an officer had coerced a confession from the accused. Detectives McCreary and Taber joined him after they had testified. Many of Alfred Powers's friends — lawyers and politicians mostly — had decided to attend their esteemed friend's preliminary hearing and *voir dire*. The *Free Press* had sent two reporters and the *Tribune* and *Telegram* several more.

The good Christian citizens of this prairie metropolis might pretend they were horrified by the tragic deaths of Emily Powers and Antonio Rossi. But most reporters worth their salt knew better. The truth was that most Winnipeggers, the ladies included, couldn't wait to read about the salacious details of this sordid case.

"Former Boy Mayor Goes On Trial Today," the *Trib's* front-page headline had blared in the morning edition. Alfred Powers, as everyone knew, had been elected mayor of Winnipeg when he was only thirty-two-years-old.

Among the crowd as well was Sam Klein. His plans for his evening's meeting with Kwong were set. Perhaps that would lead to the break he was waiting for. His fingers reached into his pocket and he pulled out the locket Graham Powers had delivered to him. He examined the two hazy black and white photographs. One was Emily, that much was certain, and the other her sister, Powers had told him. But what significance it had, if any, was the real question, one that stumped Klein — at least for the moment.

He sat at the back of the Police Court watching Graham Powers's confrontation with Magistrate Findly and Special Crown Prosecutor Timothy Jarvis, an old rival of Alfred Powers, who had been reluctantly conscripted by the attorney-general into taking on this case.

"Let me reiterate then, Your Honour," said Graham Powers, his voice straining and sounding more and more desperate. He stared at his father seated in the defendant's box for moral support. Alfred Powers responded with a nod and sad smile. "In Martin v. Tyler, the presiding Magistrate ruled that a confession obtained through a physical assault isn't admissible. While in Rex v. Holmes, the Nova Scotia court decided that emotional shock had played a part…"

"Let me stop you right there, Mr. Powers. Obviously you haven't had the legal training I assumed you have." He stared in Alfred Powers's direction. "In the first place, you haven't demonstrated at all that the defendant was treated with anything but respect by the police. Both Detectives Taber and McCreary have, I think, convincingly testified to that fact. Moreover, you yourself have concurred with the Crown's supposition that your client freely signed the confession."

"Your honour — "

"Please, Mr. Powers, permit me to finish. As to the second case you have cited, in all my many years as a Magistrate, I have never heard such nonsense. I don't know what goes on in Nova Scotia, but in this court the mental state of the defendant isn't at issue. Dr. Henry Kliener, a professor and physician from the University of Toronto, brought to the city at the province's request, has examined your client and found him to be quite fit, physically and mentally. Trying to determine what he was feeling or thinking at the time in question is pure speculation."

"There's a way to find out," replied Graham.

"And what kind of magic would that be?" asked the Magistrate, playing to the courtroom audience like a seasoned vaudevillian.

"Are you familiar with the medical work of Dr. Jean-Martin Charcot or one of his distinguished students, Sigmund Freud?"

"Yes, I have heard of Dr. Freud's work. In fact, I happened to be on a visit to Toronto several years ago when Dr. Ernest Jones, a Welsh psychiatrist, first discussed Freud's theories in public. As I recollect, neither the physicians in attendance nor the commentaries in the press after, were especially favourable."

"I was not referring to Freud's notions about the sex lives of children."

"Mr. Powers, there are ladies present."

"Excuse me, Your Honour. I would like to allude to Freud's work with hypnotism."

There was a murmur among the crowd, and more than a little snickering. Even Klein wondered if young Powers didn't need some medical attention himself.

"I must object, Your Honour," said Timothy Jarvis. "Mr. Powers is going on a fishing expedition."

"I agree. Mr. Powers, if you have a point to make, then do so. If not, please sit down."

"As I was saying, Dr. Freud, following in the footsteps of Charcot, has shown that hypnotism can not only help cure hysteria but equally enable physicians to explore memories of traumatic events which have been deliberately repressed." Try as he might to be convincing, even as Graham himself doubted his words as they fell from his lips.

Magistrate Findly stared at the lawyer for several moments without uttering a word. A few restless spectators chuckled.

"What exactly are you proposing Mr. Powers and please speak English."

"That before you make your final ruling on allowing a jury to hear my client's confession, that the court permit Dr. Oliver Parker, a well-known surgeon in the city and a recognized expert in hypnotism, to place my client in a trance. This trance will provide testimony which will be offered to this court no later than two weeks hence."

"Your Honour," pleaded Jarvis, "do you not think this has gone on long enough? My word, trances! What will be next, witnesses from the hereafter?"

"That's right, Jarvis, I also plan to call on the deceased Dr. Franz Mesmer to testify about animal magnetism and he's been dead since 1815."

"Alfred, please restrain your son."

The elder Powers shrugged.

"Gentlemen, enough of this. Both of you sit down at once." The two lawyers reluctantly did as Findly ordered. "Rest easy Mr. Jarvis, I'm not about to let Mr. Powers turn my court into a circus. I'm ready now to make my ruling. I find there is more than sufficient evidence to put the defendant on trial in provincial court." Graham Powers placed his right hand on his father's shoulder. "As for the issue of the confession," continued Findly, "there is nothing in Mr. Powers's argument that convinces me of any wrong doing by the police or of any medical problems which affected the defendant's judgement. That said, however, I believe that any further evidence pertaining to the defendant's mental state be dealt with as it arises — including the question of hypnosis."

As soon as Findly had left the court, Klein moved through the crowd towards Graham and Alfred Powers. Journalists hovered around both of them like ravens.

"Get the hell out of the way," said Klein. He had no use for newspapermen. He didn't trust any of them, not even Maloney. For a story, they'd do just about anything. How can you deal with such desperate recklessness? Klein would never forget that it had been Maloney's "blood libel" stories in the *Tribune* that had caused the riot in the North End a few years back.

"Will you submit to hypnosis?" shouted one reporter.

"What's your strategy now, Mr. Powers?"

"Gentlemen, my father has nothing to say at the moment," said Graham. A constable grabbed Alfred Powers by the arm, handcuffed him and led him back to the cell area. "Be careful," demanded Graham.

"He'll be transferred to the jail on Vaughan Street tomorrow morning," said the officer.

"Is that really necessary? That place is a dungeon."

"You know that's the way we do things, Powers. Speak to the Chief if you have problems."

Klein squeezed Graham's arm. "Sorry things didn't work out," he said.

"It was a long shot. I guess I'll have to get ready for the trial, unless you've found something that'll prove my father is innocent."

"Not yet, but let's talk tomorrow. You really going to let Parker hypnotize your father?"

"Why? Don't tell me you think it's sorcery too."

"No, but I've met Parker. I've seen the strange things that go on at his house. My advice would be to be careful."

"Well, when it happens, I'll make certain you're present."

Klein wished Graham well and turned to leave the courtroom. Running towards him from the opposite end of the hall was John Maloney.

"Klein, I thought you'd still be here."

"Yeah, I'm here. Powers is going to trial."

"I already heard. Saw a couple of the boys outside. But that's not why I was looking for you."

Klein lit a cigarette, anticipating Maloney's news with mild interest.

"I've just come from Doc MacDonald's. I don't even think MacPherson knows about this yet," Maloney said, looking around.

"Out with it, Maloney. What do you think you know?"

"Okay, here it is. Doc Macdonald has had another look at that young prostitute who supposedly committed suicide in the hospital."

"What do you mean supposedly?"

"He's changed his mind. Seems the little lady was smothered, and then her wrists were sliced open."

"You mean — "

"That's right, my friend — Katie Johnson was murdered."

"You think Jordan was involved?"

"I don't know, but hell in this town anything is possible."

Madame Gauthier had advised her to return home and really what choice did she have? For a moment, Sarah contemplated ending her pregnancy. She knew about the "doctor," or at least that's what he called himself, who lived in a small shack on Pritchard near McPhillips. For $20, he'd do the job for you. But it was dangerous. Sarah remembered one girl from a brothel on Anabella Street who nearly bled to death after a visit. Melinda had advised all of her employees to stay away from the man.

"He'll cut you up and let you bleed," were her exact words. When pregnancy was a problem for a working girl, Melinda suggested that it was better and safer to send the baby to an orphanage after it was born. But that, too, was no option. Even if Sarah ran away and never told Sam about her condition, she couldn't live with the guilt. How could she possibly give up a baby boy or girl? Her child and Sam's. It was beyond comprehension.

And so, after a night of tossing and turning, she had finally arrived at a decision. Whatever health problems had ailed her seemed to have passed. She bid Madame Gauthier farewell, packed her bags, and hopped a street-car bound for North Main Street.

Sarah took a seat at the back of the crowded car and stared out the window, reflecting on how she was going to present her case to Sam. Naturally, she would have the baby. But she would also insist on becoming Melinda's partner. The money was too good to pass up, especially with a little one to provide for. He would appreciate that fact. Sam's mother would be more than willing to care for her grandchild while Sarah was at work. If not her, perhaps they could hire a nanny like the rich ladies who lived in Crescentwood. But who was she trying to kid? Shaking her head, she knew that her conversation with Sam wasn't going to be easy. He could be so stubborn.

An abrupt stop by the streetcar operator pushed her forward. "Sorry folks, a horse and cutter got stuck in the snow, it'll only be a moment," announced the driver. "Any strong gentlemen care to help?" Immediately several tall and husky men leapt to their feet and left the car. In quick order, they dragged the sled off the tracks and the streetcar continued on its way.

Needing a distraction from her own problems, Sarah reached into her bag and pulled out Emily's diary. Though she had read the last half of the book, she was still confused about the last two years of Emily's life. All she knew for certain was that Emily was cheating on Alfred, having a liaison with Antonio, and worried about some photographs. Several times there were also elliptical references to another person, but no names were used.

Sarah flipped to the last entry and read it again. It was dated January 25, 1914, three days before she and Rossi were murdered.

Have made decision to stop seeing Antonio. He has been tense for weeks. Will not tell me what he is involved in, but I sense he is in trouble. Keeps promising big money in the future. Why don't I believe him? Definitely do not need more complications. Leaving him will solve at least one major problem. Photographs, too, are nearly safe. Must be destroyed. What would I do without Alfred?

As she reached the end of the diary, the streetcar suddenly lurched forward once again. The diary flew from her hands and Sarah nearly fell from her seat.

"Here let me help you up Miss," said an elderly man. He was dressed in a fine overcoat lined with a fur collar and an expensive looking black bowler hat.

"Haven't we met somewhere before?"

Sarah brushed herself off and looked up at him. "No, I don't think so." In fact, she had seen him at Melinda's several years earlier. Such meetings with former clients happened all the time. Thankfully, most of them didn't recognize her without her clinging, transparent nightgown. If the man's memory was slipping, so much the better.

"Here is your book," he said handing her the diary. "It's very odd. I'm sure we've met."

Sarah took the book from him and placed it back in her bag.

"Oh, Miss," the man called out.

Here it comes, Sarah thought, preparing herself for the moment when it would suddenly dawn on him who she was — or rather, had been.

"This paper fell out of your book." He passed it to her.

The streetcar stopped at Bannatyne Avenue across from Ashdown's Hardware Store, and the elderly man exited, tipping his hat to Sarah as he descended. As the car pulled away, she glanced out the window and saw a large grin cross his face. He looked up and waved to her. He had finally remembered.

As the car continued north, she examined the piece of paper that had fallen out from the diary. Funny, she hadn't seen it earlier. She unfolded it and was immediately startled by what she saw. There in front of her was a full page of writing, but in Yiddish. What in the world, she thought. Why would Emily have had this? She began to read it.

New York, July 5, 1906.
My life as I know it has ended. I have tried to tell Henny that I must leave at once. It is difficult. I have made arrangements to go to Chicago and then maybe to Canada. I could barely tell her what happened at Abe's. She was very upset...

As Sarah continued reading, her face went white. Oh my God, she thought. Yes, that's it. That was it all along. And then she understood her uneasiness about Emily. She flipped back in the diary to June 1906 and reread several entries. Yes, she was right, there was an earlier reference to an "Abe."

New York, June 10, 1906
...Am very excited, Abe is offering me $50 for something special. That's all he'll tell me...

Sarah turned the page, but it suddenly skipped to the end of July. Emily had already arrived in Chicago by then. She examined the diary more closely, and noted the ragged edges — two pages had been torn from the book.

Sipping a hot mug of coffee and smoking the next cigarette in a chain which had begun hours before, Klein puzzled over the past few days' events. The seance at Dr. Parker's and the Yiddish message from a supposedly departed soul had caused him more than a little uneasiness. Now, Alfred Powers's life appeared to be literally hanging on the results of a hypnotic trance. Had Graham lost his mind? Or, was there really something to this medical hocus-pocus? Hypnotists who made people dance like fools or sing like canaries were a standard act in vaudeville productions. But Klein knew those performances were likely rigged and that the wondrous acts of "suggestion" were as phoney as the man who caught a bullet in his teeth. He had better come up with something on the murders, and fast, or Alfred was as good as convicted. Now that the jury would be allowed to read his confession, there was just too much physical evidence pointing to him as the perpetrator.

As he butted a cigarette in a metal bowl, Klein checked his pocket watch. It was already ten o'clock in the evening — not long till his meeting with Kwong. It would be good to get this over with. Not that he was nervous — he was much too confident to be worried about a two-bit hood like Kwong. Still, only a fool wouldn't be a little concerned. At least, he mused, the vagaries of this case had proved a welcome distraction from the real issue at hand: Sarah.

Earlier in the day, he had received a message from One-Arm Eddie at the Brunswick that she was doing well. All she had told Eddie in a brief telephone conversation was that Klein shouldn't fret about her whereabouts. She wasn't in any danger and she'd contact him when the time was right.

"When the time is right!" He slammed down his half-empty coffee mug. The sound of the apartment doorknob turning got him to his feet.

"Who is it?"

The door opened and there stood Sarah.

Sam felt a rush of conflicting emotions. Seeing the tentative expression on her pale face, he wanted to seize her and hold her tight. At the same time, two days of anger and resentment pushed to the surface. His face settled into a cold mask.

"So now the time is right?"

"May I come in?" She ignored his sarcastic tone.

"This is your place as well as mine." He lit yet another cigarette.

"We have to talk," she said hanging up her coat. "I've missed you, *Shailek*."

He ignored her comment. "Are you here to stay or is this just a visit?"

"That depends."

"On what?"

"On whether we can come to an agreement."

"Christ, Sarah, this isn't a business negotiation. I'm not one of your goddamn clients."

"Don't you think I know that," she said, her voice breaking. "Please, come sit down. I have to tell you something."

Reluctantly, Klein sat down on a wooden chair across from her.

"I heard about Alfred. I'm sorry."

"It's far from over."

"Actually, I might be able to help out."

"How?"

"Later about that. First, my news."

"I'm listening."

"I guess there's no easy way to say this. I don't know what you'll think."

"Let me guess, you want me to move back into a house on Anabella Street. You can be the Madam, and I'll be the errand boy."

"No, nothing like that. *Shailek*, I'm…We're going to have a baby. I'm pregnant."

For a moment, Klein was speechless. He showed no emotion and then slowly a wide grin crossed his face. "A baby? A son?"

"Or a daughter," added Sarah with a smile.

"When…when will it happen?"

"In about six months."

He moved closer, took her in his arms and held her.

"I'm sorry," she said. "I've been so foolish. I do love you. I do want to spend the rest of my life with you. I don't know…"

"You don't make it easy but I love you too. The only thing is, what about your deal with Melinda?" he asked pulling back. "You still plan on going back to work?"

"Do we have to talk about his now?"

"Yeah, I think we do. I don't know about you, but I don't want my kid growing up with a Madam for a mother."

"There's a lot of money involved."

"You can't be serious."

"What if I helped get things started and then became a silent partner once the baby is born."

"Graham Powers knows a doctor you should really see. He can do things for your head."

"You don't have to be insulting."

Klein stood up. Women. Maybe he should get his own head examined. He checked his watch. "I have to go out, but it shouldn't take too long. It has to do with Alfred's case. Please stay here tonight. We need to work this out, Sarah."

"You mean, I have to see things your way."

He shook his head. "Please just stay here."

"Tell me you'll at least consider what I want."

"I will," he said putting on his coat and hat. He opened the small dresser drawer near the door and pulled out two items — a switch-blade knife and a small billy club, a gift from McCreary. He put both of them in a pocket inside his coat that he had his mother sew for him.

"Where exactly are you going?"

"To sort out a problem"

"*Shailek*, be careful."

"I always am."

"When you come back," she said kissing him on the cheek, "I have something to show you. It might be useful in your investigations.

"What's it about?"

"When you come back."

The wind and snow had begun to blow again, but at least the temperature had risen slightly. By the end of February, Klein really started to detest winter.

It took no time at all for Klein to reach the Point Douglas neighbourhood. He knew he was getting close when he started passing men with satisfied looks on their faces. Only a visit with the girls on Anabella and McFarlane Streets produced that kind of gratification.

As he turned the corner onto McFarlane, he quickened his pace. His mind raced with a dozen thoughts. He was clearly excited by Sarah's wonderful news — a baby, wait until his mother heard she was going to be a "Boba." At the same time, he knew he would have to convince her that managing a whorehouse was no job for a Jewish mother. Klein had been around Melinda's enough to know that even so-called "managers" occasionally did favours for their wealthy clients. If she wanted to work, fine. But go to work in a garment factory, work as a sales lady, or become a stenographer. Granted, the odds of Eaton's department store or the Hudson's Bay Company hiring a Jew to sell floor merchandise were next to nil. There had to be something else Sarah could do to earn a few dollars.

As he reached his destination, Klein tried to clear his head for the task at hand. Number 520. The ramshackle house was quiet and dark, except for a dim light shining through an upstairs windows. Klein stood for a moment and examined the surroundings. There were several sets of footprints in the snow and they appeared to be fresh. He wasn't alone.

"Hey buddy, you got a spare nickel," yelled a drunk from the other side of the street.

The noise startled Klein. He shook his head and the man moved along, stumbling his way through the snow. Klein proceeded cautiously up the path to the front door. He peered into the window, but couldn't see much. There was a mattress on the floor and some discarded opium pipes. He turned to the door and saw that it was slightly ajar. He pushed, and it swung open. He checked to see that the billy club and knife were still in his jacket pocket and then pushed the door completely open with his foot. Still, there was silence.

"Kwong, I'm here. Where are you?"

After a long moment, he got a reply. "Up here," came the familiar voice. "Top of the stairs, first room on your right."

"You alone?"

No answer.

Klein moved into the house and towards the stairs directly in front of him. He stepped over a mattress and nearly bumped into a chair that was tipped over on the floor. "You should hire a maid, Kwong," he shouted, his voice echoing through the house. He began to walk up the stairs, conscious of the wooden steps creaking beneath his boots.

As he peered down the second-floor hallway, two of Kwong's men stepped out of the shadows, and a third appeared behind him at the base of the staircase, armed with two small black batons joined by a small link chain.

"I thought this was going to be a friendly visit?"

The door to one of the bedrooms opened, revealing Kam Kwong in a large leather chair puffing on a cigarette and looking like a Chinese emperor. Beside him on the floor was twenty-year-old Lily Steeves. By the glazed look in her eyes, Klein figured she had just smoked some opium.

"Sam, nice to see you again. You don't mind if I call you Sam?" asked Kwong.

"For now, you can call me anything you want."

"Let's get business done with, shall we? Did you bring the money?"

"First you tell me what you got, then we'll talk about money."

"Care for a cigarette? Maybe a glass of whisky?"

"Nothing, thanks. But perhaps you could tell your boys here to give me some breathing room." One gesture from Kwong and the three men backed up into the hallway. "That's better. Now, what information am I going to pay for? It has something to do with your deal with Rossi? Was Taber involved as well?"

Kwong looked directly at him. He was trying to be calm, though it was clear to Klein he was trembling slightly. "It was Taber's idea from the beginning. He linked up with that dago Rossi and then the two of them came looking for me."

"What do you know about Rossi's death?"

"Nothing, I swear to you. But if you ask me, I think Taber did it. He was angry that Rossi couldn't find the extra cash needed to pay off the customs officer."

"Agreed. But what evidence can you give me? Am I supposed to deliver you to the police with a promise that you're telling the truth about one of their prized detectives? They'll lock me up with you."

"Do you think I'm an idiot, Klein?"

"Well — "

"In fact, I got a piece of paper with Taber's signature on it. A three-way contract between Rossi, Taber, and me. It was the only way that I was prepared to do business with them."

"And Taber signed it?"

"You don't believe me?"

"No, it doesn't sound like something he'd do. I thought he was smarter than that."

"Well, I guess not. Anyway, now you know what I got. The letter will put Taber away."

"Tell me Kwong, why not go to the police yourself? They might make you a deal."

"Not for the kind of money I want from you. And don't worry, I'll testify against him in court. I don't want him loose after he realizes I've double-crossed him. Then, I'll disappear. Believe me, there are a lot more profitable places to live than this shit-hole of a city." Kwong noticed his men were becoming anxious. "Okay, enough of this chit-chat. Here's what I want. I'll give you the goods on Taber but it'll cost you $5,000. You give me whatever you got now as a down payment and bring the rest by tomorrow evening."

Klein laughed. "You must have been dipping into your opium tonight. Where do you think I'm going to lay my hands on that kind of money?"

"Ask your lawyer friend Powers. I expect he isn't going to need any cash before long."

"Sorry, Kwong. You're missing the point of this little get together. I could care less about the opium deal that you and Taber and Rossi put together. The only thing I want know is who killed Rossi and Emily. Now, if you have proof that Taber did it, then we can talk more. If you don't, then I'm gone."

Kwong grimaced. "You're not gone yet, Klein, but soon."

He clapped his hands twice and shouted in Chinese. Immediately, the man with the sticks and chain began twirling it around his shoulders. Not having seen this kind of weapon before, Klein wasn't sure what to do. Then, before he could react, the man whipped one of the sticks against Klein's left knee. The force sent him reeling to the floor. In an instant the other two thugs were on top of him, pummelling his ribs and face. Klein retaliated wildly, flailing his arms, managing to punch one of them in the groin. The man keeled over. Klein struggled to get to his feet, but another flick of the sticks to his head kept him down.

From the other side of the room, Kwong pulled out a jewelled dagger. Again he yelled in Chinese and two of the men grabbed Klein's arms and held them tight. He couldn't move.

"You should've agreed to my terms, you stupid kike." He moved closer, waving the knife dangerously close to Klein's nose. "You see, Sam, this is my dilemma. Taber ordered me to deal with you. That wasn't really what I wanted, but since you're not going to play by my rules, I have no choice."

From behind Kwong's men, a deafening shot rang out.

Everyone froze while Bill McCreary, a huge Smith & Wesson revolver in his upraised hand, stepped out of the shadow.

"All of you put down your weapons. Kwong, my gun is aimed directly at your head. Drop the knife and tell your men to put down their weapons. Now."

"It's about time," said Klein, frowning, as he brushed off his jacket. "Don't you have a watch? I said midnight. A few more minutes and God knows what would have happened."

McCreary stepped further into the room. "Move over there," he ordered the three men. "Now get down on your stomachs." They didn't move.

"Your Mandarin a bit rusty, McCreary?" said Klein.

"Kwong, tell them what to do and quickly."

Kwong did so and the three thugs lay down on the floor beside Lilly, who hadn't moved during the entire altercation.

"Kick that knife over here," demanded McCreary.

With his right foot, Kwong slid the dagger across the floor. Klein picked it up. "Very nice quality, wouldn't you say?" McCreary nodded in agreement. "Okay, now what's your plan?" asked Klein.

"The plan," said a familiar voice from behind McCreary, "is for you and Bill to drop the knife and gun onto the floor." The tone was firm, direct and in control.

A large grin spread across Kwong's face. "You don't play chess do you, Klein? — anticipate your opponent's move, then do one better."

From the darkness emerged Alex Taber. He was holding a black revolver. "Kwong, take the gun."

"Still think I'm an idiot, Sam?" said Kwong as he grabbed McCreary's pistol. Kwong's men sprang to their feet and found their weapons on the floor.

"I knew you were rotten to the core, Taber," said Klein. "But teaming up with the likes of Kwong and Rossi — even for you that's low."

"Trying to bait me, Klein? It won't work."

"Easy, Sam," warned McCreary. "What are you going to do, Taber?"

"This has gotten far too complicated. It was supposed to be a simple opium deal. But Rossi screwed everything up. His contacts in Montreal got greedy."

"So you killed him and Emily?" asked Klein.

Taber shook his head. "Not me. If you want to know what happened, talk to Kwong."

"How many times do I have to tell you, Taber, I didn't do it. I've thought all along it was you who knifed the two of them."

"What's the point of lying about it now?" said Taber. "Klein and McCreary won't be around to tell anyone. Go ahead, share your secrets, then we'll finish this business with a couple of bullets."

Now Kwong was angry. "Are you deaf? I said I didn't do it." He turned to one of his men and gave an order. At that moment, and before Taber or Kwong could react, Klein, moving like a cat, drove Taber against the wall. Taber elbowed Klein in the side of the head, dropping him to his knees. At the same time, McCreary rushed forward pushing Kwong into his men, punching one of them on the jaw. Kwong scrambled back to his feet and pointed the Smith & Wesson at McCreary.

Standing only a few feet away, Taber slowly raised his weapon and pointed it at Kwong. "Drop it, Kwong," ordered Taber, "or you'll die right here."

"Taber, what the hell are you doing?" Kwong asked in disbelief.

"That's what I'd like to know," added Klein, looking even more perplexed than Kwong.

"All of you," Taber said, waving his gun at the three thugs, "Back down on the floor. McCreary, show them what I mean." The detective walked toward one of the men and pushed him hard to the floor. The other two immediately followed. McCreary then cuffed them together with a pair of handcuffs.

"Here's another pair." Taber threw some cuffs to his partner. McCreary caught them and secured Kwong.

"McCreary, talk to me," said Klein, rubbing the side of his head.

Before McCreary could reply, Kwong spoke up, his voice tight with anger. "It's simple, Klein. Taber has been acting all along. The whole thing, the deal, the talk. It was all a charade. Right, Taber?"

"Is that it?" Klein demanded. "This was a set up? McCreary say something, damn it."

McCreary glanced at Taber. "Tell them, Alex."

Taber nodded. "The chink's got it right."

"I'm sorry I couldn't tell you, Sam," said McCreary. "We had to keep it between us. Not even MacPherson knew."

"You see, Klein," continued Taber, "we had to break-up the opium trade in the city. I got to know Rossi and convinced him I was ready to make a big deal. He introduced me to Kwong and everything unfolded from there. The only thing we didn't count on was Rossi getting murdered."

"So Kwong killed them both?" asked Klein.

"I didn't kill anyone," insisted Kwong.

"I thought so at first," said Taber. "But now, I'm not so sure."

"But what about how you treated Alfred Powers — the confession, the hold-up of Graham Powers?"

Taber shrugged. "I'm no saint. But if it'll make you happier, I'll apologize to the old man and to his kid. This was a bit of a hair-brained scheme, I'll admit that. After the murders happened, I suspected Kwong right away. I asked him about it, but he said he didn't know anything about it. I didn't believe him. He was acting nervous."

"I didn't do it," said Kwong.

"McCreary, shut him up. MacPherson ordered us to bring in Powers for questioning," continued Taber. "That's when McCreary and I hatched this idea. We had to figure out a way to have Powers charged with the murder, in order to get Kwong to think he was home free — then he might start shooting his mouth off. At least, that was the original idea. But things changed quickly and, sure, we lost control of the plan. What we didn't expect was that Powers would confess. Christ, who'd have thought that? And I did get a little carried away, punching Powers in the face — once. As for the hold-up, I told Kwong to buy me some time alone with the old Powers by stopping his son from getting to the station. But it soon became clear — to me anyways — that Powers probably did it. As I've already said, his confession merely confirmed that. Things were already set in motion and I couldn't stop them."

Klein lit a cigarette. "You're still a son-of-a-bitch, Taber. This doesn't change anything."

"Doesn't change anything? For a Jew, you don't have the brains your tribe is famous for."

Klein took a menacing step forward but McCreary grabbed him impatiently and spun him around.

"Have both you lost hold of your senses? Calm down. Now, let's clean this stinking mess up and go share a bottle of whisky." Klein didn't move. "Sam, you hear what I said?"

"I heard you, McCreary. I'm glad you and Taber are pleased with yourselves. Hell, you've shut down Kwong's drug operation. That's great news. But I'm not sitting down for a drink with that damned Russian," he said, jabbing a finger at Taber. "And I don't mean to spoil your day, but you're forgetting one thing. If Kwong didn't kill Rossi and Emily Powers, and I don't think he did, then who in the hell did?"

"If it wasn't Kwong, then it had to be Powers, obviously," said Taber. "He found out about his wife's affair, killed them, and confessed. He had the murder weapon. It's an open and shut case."

"I think he's right, Sam," added McCreary. "You better face it."

They were wrong, thought Klein, dead wrong. Alfred Powers wasn't a killer — he didn't care how much evidence pointed at him. He was missing something, but what? At that moment, he took comfort in only one thing: one part of this puzzle was now solved — Antonio Rossi wasn't the intended target of the murder, Emily was.

12

Manitoba Free Press, Tuesday, February 3, 1914

Dear Editor: As a mother of five children ages 3 to 12, I believe that Mrs. McClung and her ilk are misguided women. They are nothing but destroyers of the family. Sometime ago, I read a pamphlet that was published in Toronto. It is called "Motherhood" and its message rings even truer today. Every woman in Winnipeg should take notice.

"The relations of mother and child are the highest, holiest, most important in existence. The duties and responsibilities of motherhood are of most vital consideration. 'The hand that rocks the cradle, is the hand that rules the world.' Considering the duties and responsibilities devolving upon the mother, as the moulder of nations, how vastly important it becomes that she be able to govern and develop her own progeny, that they grow in physical, moral, and intellectual strength, and become fitted to bear the duties and burdens of life, as well as share in its pleasures." Amen.
S.B. "A Concerned Mother and Wife."

"THIS IS QUITE extraordinary, Mr. Powers," said Magistrate Findly. "Extraordinary indeed. Police detectives plotting behind the scenes with criminals?"

Findly turned to face Chief MacPherson. "Is Mr. Powers's account of the events accurate, Chief."

"They are."

"It's beyond my purview to tell you how to run your department, but I trust you realize that a man's life is at stake here, not to mention the court's time." The magistrate was seated behind his desk in his small office in the back room of the Police Court on Rupert Avenue. Three men sat on chairs on the other side of the desk opposite him.

"I'm quite aware of these factors," replied Chief MacPherson. "However, as I explained, such wrinkles couldn't have been avoided without jeopardizing Detectives Taber and McCreary's operation. I myself didn't learn about it until most recently. But as you know I encourage such independence within my force." MacPherson hardly sounded convincing.

"Anything to add, Mr. Jarvis?" asked Findly.

The veteran prosecutor, dressed in his trademark black suit with a high-collared shirt and black tie, wasn't happy. "As you know, Your Honour, the police chief didn't see fit to inform me of these schemes," he said glaring at MacPherson.

The Chief shifted uncomfortably in his chair. "I believe I have already said, Mr. Jarvis that…"

"Yes, I know all about your independent-minded detectives." He turned his attention back to the magistrate. "Nonetheless, I believe there is more than enough evidence to put Mr. Powers on trial. I think you would agree that despite Detective Taber's unorthodox treatment of Mr. Powers, he did confess to the crime of his own free will."

"A lie," said Graham.

"Okay, Mr. Powers, your turn."

"To repeat my earlier objections, I am quite mortified by this turn of events. I don't care how important it was for the police to put a dent in the city's opium problems. If I understand the whole story, Detective Taber initially suspected that Mr. Kam Kwong had murdered Mr. Rossi and Mrs. Powers because their business over an opium contract had soured. And then, in order to not alarm Mr. Kwong and to persuade him that he could trust Detective Taber, my client was made to confess to a crime that he didn't commit."

"Not true," interrupted Jarvis.

"Furthermore, the detective," asserted Graham more loudly, "allowed me to be robbed and my driver to be nearly killed. This was all done as part of an elaborate scheme to force Kwong into admitting his role in the double murders. And this, the police chief would have us believe, is how justice is dispensed in Winnipeg. In my life, I have never heard…" He paused for a moment, regaining his composure. "Therefore, I ask the court that the charges against my client be dismissed at once," concluded Graham, "and charges be brought against Detective Taber for assault."

"For God's sake, Powers," bellowed MacPherson, "the man was merely doing his job. Have you any idea what narcotics are doing to our city? Last week, one of my constables stumbled into a den in Chinatown where he found two Christian girls under the spell of a Negro dope fiend. We must stop such calamities by any means possible."

"Including breaking the law?" asked Powers.

"Temporarily, yes, as long as no serious harm is done. There may be a war soon, Mr. Powers. What do you think will happen if we send soldiers over to defend the mother country addicted to opium and cocaine?"

"Gentlemen, I've heard enough," said Findly. "Granted, Mr. Powers, the police department's methods in this regard leave much to be desired. But I am forced to concur with Mr. Jarvis. Detective Taber's actions were secondary to the confession. Moreover, there is more than enough physical evidence to warrant a trial."

"Nice, try, Graham," whispered Jarvis.

"I'll see you in court. And Chief, don't be surprised if my driver Elspeth files a lawsuit against Detective Taber and the Police Department."

MacPherson waved his hand in Graham's face. "Do what you have to. You won't get far." He stood up, bid Magistrate Findly and Jarvis goodbye, and left the office, indignant. He was convinced his position was the right one. He felt that it was a question of community standards versus individual freedom and at this particular moment, the former outweighed the latter. In truth, however, he was angry at Taber and McCreary. Even if they did get the job done as they had promised, their unorthodox plan had contravened his orders about taking independent action. For now, he would have to play along with the charade that he had approved of their decision. There was no point in him looking like a fool in front of Findly or Jarvis. Later, he would discipline both of his detectives.

They had had the right idea, but their strategy was flawed from the beginning. He would have told them so, had they bothered to confide in him. From MacPherson's perspective, believing that Kwong would confess to the Rossi-Powers murders in a moment of conceit was ill-considered. Why Bill McCreary had gone along with such a poorly conceived plan, he wasn't certain. Still, it was too bad that the Chinaman Kwong hadn't confessed. It would have made life much simpler. Despite what young Powers thought, he had no desire to see Alfred Powers hang from a rope at the Vaughan Street Jail.

The Chief's office was one flight of stairs down from the courtroom. As he rounded the corner in hallway, he saw an unwelcome visitor.

"Maloney, not now. I'm too busy."

"Hey, you stood me up yesterday, too, Chief. I got a job to do just like you."

"That's too bad. You tell Mr. Dafoe that you couldn't get any details for your story today. I'm sure he'll understand."

"Not likely. Besides, I thought we could chat about the fact that John Jordan was the last person to see Katie Johnson alive."

"So what? No doubt he was questioning her about her addiction. That night she killed herself — probably the cravings drove her to it."

"Except," interrupted Maloney, "she didn't kill herself. I spoke with Doc Macdonald. I've read his report."

MacPherson stared at the reporter for a moment. "That damn fool Macdonald," he muttered under his breath. "How many times have I told him to keep his mouth shut."

"What's that Chief?" Maloney removed his bowler hat to reveal a thin head of hair.

"I said, Mr. Maloney, the doctor shouldn't have shown you that. But since you've seen it, yes, it does appear that Miss Johnson may not have committed suicide after all."

"You mean she was murdered?"

"Possibly. My detectives have to investigate further. Nonetheless, I don't see how Inspector Jordan is involved."

"With all due respect, you must be joking."

"No, I'm quite serious."

"You must be the only person in your own department, perhaps in the entire city other than Mrs. Jordan, who doesn't know that John Jordan had more than a professional interest in Katie Johnson, much more."

"I have no idea what you are referring to, Mr. Maloney and as I said I have a lot of paper work to catch up on."

"You can dismiss me now, Chief, but you can't suppress the truth. My advice would be get rid of Jordan, fast, before he costs you your job as well."

"The day the police department starts taking advice from a *Free Press* reporter is the day I'll retire, Mr. Maloney. I warn you again: tread carefully. You are playing a dangerous game here. Whatever his faults, Inspector Jordan is the kind of man who holds this community together."

"Thanks, but no thanks," said Maloney. "Frankly, I don't need the likes of Jordan telling me what to believe and how to live my life."

"Enough debate, Mr. Maloney, please leave."

"As you wish, but I'd keep an eye on the newspaper if I were you."

Maloney turned and walked towards the stairs. MacPherson was sweating but the building wasn't particularly hot. Of course he knew all about

Jordan's visits to the red light district and about his interest in the young whore. He had repeatedly warned Jordan to stop seeing her and had been assured that he would. Obviously, he hadn't. The Chief had already decided to reassign his Morality Inspector, but such an administrative shuffle couldn't appear to be a response to public pressure. My God, he thought, last year Jordan had received the force's meritorious service medals, and now he was possibly linked to the murder of a prostitute. MacPherson would be the laughing stock of the country.

"Selma," he shouted to his stenographer in an adjoining office. "Get Taber and McCreary up here at once."

"Yes, sir," replied the young woman, a niece of one of MacPherson's Crescentwood neighbours.

Though the Powers case was far from being closed, and though McCreary and Taber's judgement in this manner was open to question, they were still the most capable detectives in the department. He felt he had no choice but to assign them to the Katie Johnson murder. If Jordan was involved, he had better find out soon, certainly before Maloney and the *Free Press* did.

"How are you feeling? You need another glass of water or something?" asked Klein.

"*Shailek*, what's got into you? I'm feeling quite well. Now will you please sit down? I don't need any water. You've been fussing over me all morning."

Neither of them had yet raised the issue of Sarah's business venture or her desire to return to work in Point Douglas.

"I guess I'm excited. You should have seen my mother's face when I told her. She was beaming with pride. She can't wait to help out. I know she can be a little meddlesome, but she means well. And you know she hasn't been feeling well lately. So this news really cheered her up. Trust me there's nothing she won't do for my son."

"Or daughter."

"Okay, or daughter," said Klein with a smile.

Sarah moved closer to him and kissed him.

"What was that for?"

"A wife can't kiss her husband?" she remarked with a twinkle in her eye. "You have to go out yet?"

Klein knew what that gaze meant. "In your condition? You're kidding, right?"

"Nothing will happen to the baby, *Shailek*."

"How do you know?"

"You remember Gertie?"

"How could I forget her? That black laced gown she used to prance around Melinda's in…"

"Well, she gave birth to a daughter last year."

"So what of it?"

"*Shailek*, she didn't stop working at Melinda's until about August and the baby was born the following February. She was pregnant for a good two months and working and nothing happened to her baby. So I think it'll be okay if you and I go into the bedroom right now."

"I don't know. Maybe you ought to speak with the doctor about this."

Sarah laughed. "I'm not speaking to any doctor about this," she said, unbuttoning the top button of his shirt.

Before Klein could argue further, she had removed his clothes as well as her own and climbed on top of him — right on the parlour floor. With other things — like refusing a bribe — he showed some willpower, some restraint, but with Sarah he had a difficult time saying no. Within moments, sounds of pleasure echoed through the apartment and down the hall.

"You think you'll be up for more of this for the next couple months?" Klein asked an hour later in their bed, turning onto his side and pushing a pillow under his arm.

"You never know," she said, snuggling next to him under the Hudson's Bay blanket. "*Shailek*, now that you're feeling good. I think we have to talk more."

Klein sat up. "You're not still thinking of going into business with Melinda, because…"

She reached up and placed a finger over his lips. "It's not that. But if it'll make you feel any better, I did speak with Melinda last night and told her that I couldn't make up my mind yet. She tried to convince me — said she could find another partner easy enough."

"She'll have to."

"Will you let me think about it more?"

"Yeah, I guess. So what's got you so nervous?"

She stood up and walked naked across the parlour to a shelf by the window. Klein smiled, admiring the sensuous curves of her body.

"What the hell are you looking for?" he murmured. "There's nothing but old papers up there."

"And this," said Sarah, holding a black leather-bound book in her right hand.

"What is that?"

She sat down beside him, her head slightly lowered. "Before you get angry, please remember that I was only doing what I promised. Here," she said handing him the book, "this is Emily's diary."

"My God." For several moments, he stared at the book in his hand. "How? You had this and you didn't tell me? Christ, why? Sarah, tell me why."

"I swore to Alfred."

"Alfred? You must be joking. Why didn't he tell me?"

"That morning before he turned himself in, he gave me the diary. He had it with him. I think he had taken it from Emily's handbag. I'm not sure. He made me swear that I wouldn't tell anyone about it, including you. But now, because of everything that's happened — and especially if what you told me is true, that it was Emily not Antonio who was being targeted — well, my conscience won't let me rest."

"Have you read it? What did she write?"

"You have to read it yourself. But I think you're going to have to travel to New York to find out the truth about our friend Esther."

Klein's shivered as he heard the name. "Esther? You mean Emily?"

"No, I mean Esther. Emily Powers's real name was Esther Mandelbaum."

"Emily was a Jew!"

"That's right. You'll find a page of Yiddish tucked in near the middle."

"That's impossible. How could I have not known?"

"Think about it *Shailek*, the way she talked sometimes, her mannerisms. There was always something *haimshe* about her, as if she really didn't belong in the world of Nellie McClung and Alfred Powers. Still, she did a good job of hiding it, I have to admit that. And I think there's more to the story. I just don't know what. Two pages are missing from around June 12, 1906."

Klein stood up, picked up his clothes and dressed. He thought about the mysterious writing at Parker's house. If Emily was Jewish, then perhaps he had truly witnessed something real and miraculous. He poured himself a cup of coffee, sat down at the kitchen table, lit a cigarette, and placed the diary before him. He took a deep drag, staring at the engraved initials on the cover. Then he opened it and began to read.

13

New York City
June 1906

I WAS LATE. Abe Fineman had ordered me to be at his studio in the back room of his music hall at four o'clock sharp. It was already five minutes past the hour. His clients were important businessmen who didn't like to be kept waiting, I'd been told with an air of authority only someone as arrogant as Abe Fineman could muster. I wasn't sure what was expected of me once I reached my destination. Some modelling, that was all Abe had said. Two hours work for fifty dollars. It was a treasure beyond my wildest dreams.

Still, I was nervous. I had heard the rumours about the back room of Abe's Allen Street music hall. Liza Epstein, a girl I knew from the factory, had also taken an evening job as a dance hostess. Last May, she disappeared. When she stumbled back home three days later, Liza was a different person. The gossip among the girls at the dance hall was that a Chinaman from Mott Street had corrupted her, forced her to smoke opium. She lost her job at the garment factory and aimlessly shuffled along the street in a stupor. The last I had heard, Liza had become an Allen Street prostitute to feed her insatiable drug habit.

Who knew the truth about anyone in the East Side? Abe dismissed the rumours and stories as nonsense.

"Nothing happened here with opium. I don't even let Chinamen in my place," he had announced to me as if he were a lawyer addressing a jury. The editor of the Yiddish Daily, the Forward, knew better. The "flesh mongers," as he called them, owned this street.

I had seen women selling themselves in the neighbourhood, sprawled on chairs in revealing frilly dresses, legs swinging, patiently waiting for their next customer. From all appearances, they seemed to be enjoying themselves, chewing on sunflower seeds and gossiping about nothing in particular. I suspected that I would have been popular, if I ever were to join them. I have red hair that hangs over my shoulders and I am proud of my figure made smooth, I should add, by the "Gibson Girl" corset that I like to wear under my blouse and skirt. The tailors in the factory used to joke with me that I was a real *sheyne meydel* — a "knockout." But for the moment, I was content with my new job as a dance hostess.

As I moved down Delancey Street towards Allen, I searched the crowd. The congestion on Delancey was unbearable, as usual. Men, women, and children scurried in a thousand different directions. Gangs of young boys crouched shooting marbles. Others just lingered, waiting for something out of the ordinary. Like always I held tightly on to my locket that dangled from a gold chain around my neck. It was one of the few possessions I valued. Henny had the exact same one. Inside both was a small photograph of us taken when we first had arrived in New York. I knew I had to be careful. Pickpocketing and grifting were as rampant in the East Side as tuberculosis.

Dominating the streets were peddlers hawking their goods from pushcarts. Their cries — Yiddish with a sprinkling of broken English — could be heard for blocks. For sale were rags, bottles, pots, pans and utensils of every shape and variety. It was as if the marketplaces of the old country had been transported here in their entirety.

Some of the bearded men stood dressed in torn black suits, their heads covered with caps, sweating under the hot June sun, their tiny, unkempt tables and kiosks before them. The smell was as bad as the congestion. Customers gathered around the tables, jabbering and arguing for a better price, while horse-drawn wagons ambled by seeking a place to park so more goods could be displayed. From dawn until dusk, the parade of merchandise was endless. There was nothing you couldn't buy, barter or trade in the East Side.

Above, through narrow windows of the wooden tenements, I could hear the familiar clicking of foot-powered sewing machines. They never stopped, not even for the Sabbath any longer. That was how desperate life had become in America. It wasn't a question of becoming rich — it was a matter of survival. I didn't have to glance at the wretched men and women hunched over the cloth and garments, ten, twelve hours a day, to know their pain. Thank God that I had left that life behind. Sweatshop slaves was what I called them, "greeners" searching for their goldeneh medina, their golden land. Or so they thought when they had disembarked from the ships among the crowded hordes at Ellis Island. They believed they were the lucky ones. They had left the Old World behind, with its prejudices and hardships, for America. They were going to be rich is what they had told their parents, siblings, neighbours, and anyone else *in the shtetl who would listen. They were going to be a "somebody." But no gold is to be found in America, only misery.*

I knew that well. At sixteen I had left my parents in Vilna and followed my sister Henny and her foolish husband, Jacob Greenspon of Lida, to New York.

"Go with them, Esther," my mother Gitel had told me. "You'll find a husband, start a family. And then papa and I will join you. Besides, if you don't go, who will watch over Henny? Jacob is a good boy. He means well, but I still worry."

My mother's concerns were well founded. Jacob was going to open a dress shop, "Greenspon's Fine Garments." He would buy a store and all three of us were to live above the shop. Henny and me were going to be sales ladies. After a few years we'd be rich and then we'd send money for our parents. They would journey to the New World as well. That was the great plan. Nothing could go wrong.

Jacob had five hundred American dollars in his pocket when the ship landed — precious money he was given by his father and half the town of Lida — and promptly lost most of it to a gang of swindlers in a card game. Henny had screamed at him.

"Where will we sleep? How will we eat?"

But Jacob wasn't worried. So he had made a mistake. He assured us that all would be fine. He found a small room for us in a dark, dilapidated tenement on Delancey. He took the first job he was offered at a garment factory on Hester Street owned by a German Jew named Wertheim. Then he arranged jobs for Henny and me, mainly sewing women's gloves and boys' knee pants. The hours were long and the pay was pitiful. If Jacob worked ten hours a day, six days a week — which he rarely did — he could take home about $12, just enough to cover the rent of the room. I usually made less than $10, enough for bread, herring, tea, a few potatoes, and a little meat. It took me two months to scrimp together the five dollars a Hester Street peddler wanted for a black silk dress with lace edgings. I had to hide the dress from Jacob, for I knew he'd try to hawk it on the street.

Wertheim's wife was Frima, a rather bitter woman, who looked after the office, and her ten-year old brat of a daughter called Molly. The young girl constantly ran up and down the crowded aisles bumping into the machines and demanding this and that. Still, Wertheim seemed like a pleasant enough man.

"Ignore them all," was the advice I received from an older woman named Rachel who worked beside me. "And never be caught alone with Wertheim."

"And why not?" I had inquired.

"Trust me, dear," replied Rachel, "just trust me. He likes them young."

I was hardly worried. I could take care of myself. Occasionally, I would catch Wertheim staring at me. Who could blame him? I had to admit that I was a difficult woman to ignore. When I entered a room, most men noticed. More to the point, Wertheim's wife Frima was nothing to look at and I doubted that their sex life amounted to much. I pretended not to notice Wertheim's leering at me and acknowledged his stares with a coy smile and that was that. He did nothing more. Besides, I had more serious concerns than the stares of a lecherous forty-year old garment factory owner.

For two years, I toiled as a seamstress — cutting, sewing, and ironing. In the summers, Wertheim's shop was so hot you couldn't breathe. During the winter, the wood stove, if it was burning at all, was inadequate and we froze. Then at night I had to listen to Jacob and Henny's incessant arguing or, worse, Jacob's slobbering lovemaking. Thankfully for Henny, it was usually over quickly. In truth, I had no life, no privacy, nothing I could call my own, except that black silk dress. Like a thousand other Jewish immigrants, I was a nobody, going nowhere. I didn't have the heart to write the truth to my parents back in Vilna. So I lied.

"Dear Mama and Papa, Everything is wonderful in America. I have a good job sewing dresses and Henny and Jacob are doing well. They are happy. I think Henny would like to have a baby. I have met a lot of nice Jewish people in the East Side. I know you will love it when you finally come here. Love, your daughter, Esther."

Who was I fooling? My mother, Gitel Mandelbaum, was a clever woman and I could tell from her letters that she sensed the falseness of my words. It was during that second winter in New York, the cold winter of 1904, that the letters from Vilna abruptly stopped. Until then, my mother had written at least once a month.

I persevered and accepted my lot in life. My one refuge was reading. I was a voracious reader. It wasn't only the Forward with its ruminations about immigrant life that captured my attention, but English publications as well. Month by month my language skills improved so that by the spring of 1906 I could read as well as a 'real' American, perhaps better. Even my thick Yiddish accent gradually disappeared.

I was a regular reader of the Sunday World that I bought for a nickel each week. I loved the articles about the vaudeville theatre stars and all the money they made. When I was in a more serious frame of mind, I dipped into the stuffier New York Times, scanning the headlines for stories about Susan B. Anthony and Lucy Stone. I realized that I had nothing in common with these American suffragette pioneers, but something about their fight for women's rights gnawed at my heart. In my mind, their fight made more sense than the one being waged for better working conditions and bargaining rights by the Jews of the East Side. I had no desire to take orders from any trade union. But obtaining the right to vote, that made sense.

If I had a free moment, I also enjoyed visiting Mr. Rabinovitch at the Astor Place library a few blocks away near Lafayette Street. A renowned Yiddish and Russian lecturer (at least among patrons of the East Side cafes), Chaim Rabinovitch could speak for hours on a wide-range of diverse topics, everything from Darwin to Shakespeare, from Ancient Rome to Karl Marx. A widower, he was a well-respected member of the neighbourhood intelligentsia and commanded a speaking fee of five dollars — although he would also lecture for free if that was the only way he could be heard on any particular evening.

His "office" was in a back corner of the Astor Library, where I could always find him immersed in research for his next talk. With no children of his own, he took a keen interest in my education. I knew that some of the neighbourhood women who frequented the library, on the other hand, took a different and more cynical view of our relationship. "It's a shundah," they would murmur in Yiddish, but loud enough for me to hear. "A man of his years with such a young girl. There's only one thing on his mind and it is not books."

But the women were wrong. Rabinovitch gently guided me into a previously unknown and wonderful world of literature where I immersed myself in the fiction of Jack London, Charles Dickens, F. Marion Crawford (I loved his book Katherine Lauderdale). Yet my real passion — as well as Rabinovitch's — remained the Russian works of Dostoevsky. My Russian was still better than my English. Who couldn't identify with the passionate Dmitri or the mystical Alyosha, the brothers Karamazov? I liked to pretend that I was as beautiful as Grushenka, with men killing each other so that they could be by my side. Predictably, Jacob had a different view of the hours I spent at the library.

"Why do you waste your time on that?" he would ask me with disdain in his voice. "You should be worrying about how you can find a husband. Can your Dostoevsky do that?"

I always remained silent, confident that in such writings were the secrets of life that I was searching for. Only then it was still beyond my grasp. Someday, I was certain, I'd find it. Someday.

The letter had arrived on August 20, 1904. That date was forever etched in my mind. It was a blistering hot day, a Monday. My mother had always said she would die on a Monday. Henny and Jacob were working late, but I had told Wertheim that I was too ill to sew that day.

"Excuse me, sir," I had said to him. I knew that he liked it when I referred to him as a "sir." It made him feel like an American boss. "My bones ache and my head hurts. I won't be any good to you today," I'd told him. "Couldn't I have the day off? I promise, I'll make it up another time," I had pleaded, mustering all of the girlish charm I was capable of — and it was considerable.

"A day off," Wertheim muttered. "I ought to..."

Quickly I moved my face closer to him. I know that the lilac scent of my hair stirred him. I made sure that my lips were only inches from his hairy face.

"Esther," he flustered, "you know the rules."

"Please, sir," I said with a phoney politeness that I was certain Wertheim wasn't clever enough to detect. And then I let my right hand brush the side of his leg. I kept it there for only a moment. It was long enough.

"Fine. You can take the day off. But not a word about this to the other girls or they'll all want a day off and then where will I be?"

"Not a word," I said. "Not a word to anyone." I smiled at him and left.

I had spent the day doing nothing in particular — reading a magazine, munching on a penny's scoop of vanilla ice cream served by Jashke, the hokeypokey man, on a piece of brown paper (you had to eat it quickly when the weather was hot). In the morning, I had sat on the stoop watching the people go by: peddlers, young boys playing stickball and their sisters nearby immersed in a game of "potsy." There were anxious shopkeepers trying to keep the area in front of their store clear of children, and Jewish women rushing to their jobs as typists. To be a typist, I understood, was something special. You worked in the English world and were called "Miss" by your employer. I could only dream of being accorded such respect.

In the early afternoon, I had wandered down to the Grand Theatre to see if I could catch a glimpse of the Yiddish drama world's royal couple, Jacob Adler and his beautiful wife, Sarah. I had recently seen Jacob perform in The Jewish King Lear, a birthday gift from Henny. Adler in all his glory was magnificent.

I had arrived home at about four o'clock, feeling happy for a change. The letter was waiting in my mail box.

It was from my mother's brother, Harry, and written in Yiddish. "Dear Esther and Henny," it began (Uncle Harry never cared for Jacob much). I am

*sorry I have to be the one to tell you this, but there was a fire at your parents'
home several months ago. I know I should have written sooner. I didn't know
how to tell you this. The police believe the fire was started by a gang of hoodlums. I don't know anything more. Girls, both your papa and mama, my dear,
dear sister Gitel, died in the fire. There was nothing anyone could do for them.
May their souls be bound up in everlasting peace. Please write if you need any
help. Uncle Harry."*

*With tears in my eyes, I read that letter over and over again. I couldn't
believe it. I told Henny that I was going back on the first ship. I had to see for
myself. Surely Mama and Papa would be there to greet me. Henny merely
cried.*

*"It was an accident. These things happen," said Jacob with his typical indif-
ferent attitude. "We are in America now. Look ahead to the future."*

*The future, I thought, what kind of future did I have in this hellhole? After
news of the terrible tragedy, there was a decided change in me. I grew more
remote and withdrawn. Nothing Henny said or did made the least bit of difference. I stopped communicating, stopped caring about anything. Henny
started to worry that I would become another immigrant suicide story recorded on the front page of the Forward: "Esther Mandelbaum genumen di gez."
That would be the headline, she said.*

*Then one day I awoke from this state of depression. It was triggered by
Wertheim of all people. It was late on a Friday, an hour before the Sabbath
was to begin. I was diligently finishing the stack of two hundred knee pants I
had been given at dawn. Wertheim had uncharacteristically allowed the rest
of his employees to leave early to prepare for Shabbas. I had refused to stop
working until I had completed my quota.*

*"Suit yourself, my dear," Wertheim had remarked. "I'll be in the office until
you are done."*

*And with that he had left me alone in the factory room. I worked in silence.
The only thing that could be heard was the clicking of the foot pedal on my
machine. But as always the sweatshop's human stench, the smell of toil and
grime, hung in the air like an invisible cloud. It was funny, the odour had
bothered me when I had first started working. Now I just accepted it.*

*Thirty minutes passed before Wertheim reappeared. He had changed his suit
jacket and attempted, without much success, to comb his hair and beard. He
stood behind me for a moment but said nothing.*

*Sensing his presence, my foot abruptly stopped pumping the machine. I
swung my head around just as he grabbed me.*

"Get off me," I screamed. "What are you doing?"

"Esther, my dear Esther, I must do this," he whispered. His breath was repugnant.

"No, you're an animal," I said continuing to struggle.

"An animal! I'm animal, is that what you think, you slut? I have seen you looking at me. I know what you want. I'll bet you aren't even a virgin," he yelled.

And with that his right hand came down across my face. My head flung back toward the sewing machine desk. With my left hand I found a pair of metal shears. Now he had his arms around my shoulders and he was desperately trying to force his right hand under my blouse. As his other hand tried to tear off my skirt, I plunged the scissors into his left leg.

"My God, what have you done?" he said as he stumbled backward. Blood poured from the wound I had given him. He fell to the floor.

Without another word, I ran from the factory, down the stairs and out in to the street. My state of depression was over.

I found Abe Fineman pacing on the street not far from the corner of Allen and Delancey. He was about six feet tall, wearing a black pin stripe vest and matching pants. A black bowler hat, slightly tilted to the left, was on his head. His white shirtsleeves were rolled up and he was smoking a cigar. Abe was an immigrant from Minsk. He had arrived in New York about ten years earlier with only pennies in his pocket. Now he owned a dance hall on the East Side. It was very exciting inside. There was always a brass band playing — a drummer, one trumpeter, a clarinet and a piano player. They enticed young Jewish singles to come in for a bit of fun. Men had to pay ten cents for admission, the cost to women was only a nickel.

I loved to dance. It always made me feel better. In the weeks after Wertheim had attacked me, I had found myself more and more at Fineman's Fun Palace. For a variety of reasons, I had decided not to tell anyone about the incident. Not even Henny knew. But I never returned to the floor of the garment factory, no matter how much Jacob demanded it. As for Wertheim, the employees were told that their boss had had an accident and was required to stay in bed for a few months. His wife Frima ran the factory and working conditions slightly improved. Before long, Abe Fineman took a liking to me and offered me a job as a regular dance hostess at $15 a week.

"I'm sorry I'm late," I said with a smile.

"I thought I told you to be here at four sharp," Abe said. He was not in a good mood. "If you want to be a somebody in this world, Esther, you had better be punctual. Machers don't like to be kept waiting. You know what I mean."

"I promise," I said, "it'll never happen again."

"Right," mumbled Abe. "Now you do as you're told today. You want to make this fifty bucks, correct?"

I nodded.

"You trust me, don't you?"

"I suppose. This is a modelling job. That's what you said."

"Yeah, modelling. Honey, I'm going to make you famous."

I followed Abe through the dimly lit and as yet empty music hall to his private backroom studio. The curtains were drawn. I squinted as I entered. To one side sat three men, all smoking cigars and drinking whisky. They ignored me. On the far side of the room was a petite blonde woman in a black silky dress and a man in grey suit standing in front of a box mounted on a tripod. A large black cloth covered the top of the box.

"Come Esther," said Abe grabbing my arm. "I'm about to make you a star."

14

New York Times, Saturday, January 29, 1914

BOOK REVIEW OF SEX ANTAGONISM
(NEW YORK, PUTNAM'S) By Walter Heape

The bulk of those who take an active part in the [women's] movement are undoubtedly spinsters, a dissatisfied and we may assume an unsatisfied class of women...Should extended political power be granted to women, it seems certain that those who will exercise that power most freely are women of this class — and they will exercise it chiefly for their own advantage. This extended power given to women threatens to result in legislation for the advantage of that relatively small class of spinsters who are in reality but a superfluous portion of the population..."

KLEIN RUBBED HIS eyes and glanced out the kitchen window. The sun was already going down. The dusky light narrowly beamed into the apartment, casting small shadows on the walls of the pots and pans scattered on the counter tops.

He had been unable to put the diary down. Page after page recorded in fascinating detail Esther's move to Chicago, her interest and subsequent involvement in the women's suffrage movement, her decision to relocate to Winnipeg and, of course, her amazing transformation into Emily Munro. In a matter of only a few years, Esther Mandelbaum, that young and naive Jewish immigrant, had ceased to exist. Instead, she was replaced by Emily Munro: confident, intelligent, in control of her life. Everything was there except the reason why it had happened in the first place. Klein stared at the spot in the diary where the two pages had been torn.

He also held a small piece of paper in his hand. It had been pasted onto the cover at the back and scribbled on it was a name and an address: "Henny Greenspon, #5-185 Delancey St., New York, N.Y." He reached into a container beside him on the table and pulled out the locket and gold chain Graham Powers had given him. He pried it open and gazed at the two photographs inside. There they were: Esther Mandelbaum and Henny Greenspon, two happy sisters. What had so upset their lives that one of them had to flee and alter her identity? That was what Klein was determined to find out. He was convinced that in uncovering the dark secrets of Emily or Esther's life he would also discover the truth about that night behind the Walker.

He checked the time. It was nearly 7:30 p.m. There was a train leaving for New York at eleven o'clock. For $60, he could be there in forty hours. He knew he could stay with one of his mother's cousins, Max Rosen, who owned a small delicatessen on East Houston. But Alfred Power's retainer would cover his hotel expenses, and he preferred the quiet comforts of a cheap hotel room to the noisy hospitality of the Rosen house.

"Sarah," called out Klein, "I'm leaving for New York in three hours."

She emerged from the bedroom dressed in a night-gown. "I'm not surprised. Come, I'll help you pack your bag."

"You're certain you'll be able to manage by yourself for a few days? My mother and Rivka aren't too far away…"

"*Shailek*, really, who are you asking?" she said kissing his cheek. "When haven't I been able to manage by myself?"

"True." He'd ask his mother to check in on Sarah anyway.

"Enough talk, go get your razor and brush. I'll fold your pants and you'll need a few shirts. Aren't you a little excited, *Shailek*? New York, I'd love to go with you."

Any other time, Klein would have been more enthusiastic about this trip — after all, this was his first visit to New York since he was a young child. And that earlier visit he could barely remember. The one image that stood out vividly was of mobs of people, yelling, shouting, running here and there. For that matter, he would have willingly taken Sarah along. Perhaps the time away from the city help them to solve a few of their problems. Yet he had work to do and that came first. He sensed the momentum was building at the police station, and among the Winnipeg legal establishment, to be done with the Alfred Powers case as quickly as possible.

"I'll send you a telegram and let you know where I'll be staying. But in case of an emergency of some sort, you can always contact the Rosens. My mother has their address."

"*Shailek*, stop worrying," she said, handing him a beaten-up brown valise. "Maybe someday we'll be able to afford something a little fancier."

"I like this one," he said, grabbing the handle and kissing her good-bye. "Be careful and don't do anything foolish. And look after my son."

"Daughter," said Sarah, pushing her husband out the door of the apartment.

Sarah watched him descend the stairs and returned to the kitchen for a cup of tea. She was now more torn than ever about her future plans. She loved Sam more than he knew. Hurting him was the last thing she wanted. And yet this strong spirit of independence gnawed at her insides. She sipped her tea and gently patted her stomach. A broad smile slowly crossed her face. The baby's needs. How could she have been so selfish? Yes, she thought, the baby must come first. Before her and before Sam.

At that moment, she came to a decision. Her business venture would have to be temporarily delayed. Perhaps she could scrape together some money for a small investment in some other commercial activity. She knew Melinda had many contacts at city hall. Anything was possible. But whatever she ended up doing, she knew for sure was that she would decide, not Sam. He would just have to live with such realities. For now, however, she would content herself with being a mother. Strange, she thought — she had never envisioned herself in that role. She could barely remember her own mother.

She would call Melinda in the morning and inform her friend that her plans had changed. For the foreseeable future, her life was now with Sam and their child. As she poured herself another cup of tea, she felt positive for the first time in a long time. To a certain extent, she was shutting the door on her past life. Sarah Bloomberg, the most expensive whore in the city, was truly retired — and this time for good.

It was the crowds, the masses of people on the streets, that made the biggest impression on Klein. That, and the tall buildings forming the Manhattan skyline in the near distant. Yiddish signs everywhere offered soda water, suits, dresses, cigars, and hats. Still tired from his long journey, Klein wandered down the milling streets among the pushcart peddlers hawking their goods and the children playing games in the middle of Delancey and in nearby narrow alley ways.

He passed the Grand Street Theatre and noticed its large advertisement for a forthcoming performance by the distinguished Yiddish actor Jacob Adler. There were synagogues and *cheders*, cafes for *minskers* and another for *landsleit* from Vilna, and rows upon rows of dilapidated tenement houses. He ventured as far west as Washington Square, standing for a moment in front of the Triangle Shirtwaist Company factory where, as Rivka had once told him, two hundred Jewish and Italian labourers had perished a few years before in a raging fire.

Later, standing at the corner of Delancey and Allen, Klein revelled in the warm weather as well as the late afternoon excitement. The sheer variety of activity, people coming and going in every direction, made Winnipeg's Selkirk Avenue seem very small indeed. Yet Klein also noticed the Jews on the streets appeared more weary and ragged than those back in Canada.

His first stop was his relatives' delicatessen on East Houston near Orchard Street. After the introductions were made, his mother's cousin Max Rosen and his wife Seema couldn't stop doting on him.

"Here, Sam, first eat," said Max, a round and robust looking man in his early fifties. "Then we'll talk." He sat Klein down at a front table in the medium-sized restaurant and Seema, just as round as her husband but with slightly more hair, served him a plate of herring, potatoes and a large chunk of pumpernickel with a tall glass of seltzer. After subsisting on the bread, cheese, and few vegetables he had had taken on the train, the Rosens' food was much appreciated. The first-class dining car, with its entrees of beef, chicken, and roast duck, was off-limits to those travelling by berth.

"So tell us about your mother and Rivka," asked Max. "It's been far too many years."

"They are both well and send their regards," mumbled Klein between mouthfuls.

There seemed to be no point in relating to them Freda Klein's recent health problems. The night Klein had departed from Winnipeg, he had noticed his mother wincing from a pain in her chest.

Typically, she had dismissed her son's worries. "A son shouldn't worry about a mother," Freda Klein was fond of saying. "It's a mother's right to worry about a son, no matter how old he becomes." When he had inquired further about her health, she had changed the subject. "I'm going to start sewing baby clothes tomorrow morning," she had said beaming with pride. "With something like this, I might even start to become fond of your wife."

Klein had shaken his head. "Ma, I'll make you a deal," he had said, rather exasperated. "I'll go visit the Rosens, if you call Rivka or Sarah when you're not feeling well."

"So, of course, you'll stay with us, Sam," declared Max Rosen. "We have an extra room in the back we have rented out to boarders from time to time, but its empty right now. The last one was such a *schlemiel*. He drank too much liquor and we had to chase him each week for the rent. Eventually, Seema made me throw him out. However, the room is comfortable and you can stay as long as you wish. We are only a shout away upstairs, if you need anything."

Despite Klein's attempt to refuse his cousins' gracious offer, they insisted and he relented.

"So tell us," asked Max, "we hear you are a private investigator. You can make a living like this?"

"It pays the rent, usually."

"I don't know," said Seema, "a salesman or a businessman I can understand, but this sounds like trouble. Besides, who ever heard of a Jewish detective." She paused. "I suppose you have to be pretty rough with the criminals…"

"Seema, please," said Max, "leave Sam out of this."

"No, go ahead," smiled Klein. "You'd be surprised how, um, capable I can be."

Max hesitated. "It's nothing, really. About a month ago, some young neighbourhood toughs came in, demanding that I pay them to protect my store. Of course, I tried to push them out the door, but they're persistent."

"They punched Max in the face is what those gangsters did," interrupted Seema. "And Jewish boys. It's hard to believe."

"Do they have a leader?" asked Klein.

"Benny Fein, 'Dopey Benny' is what they call him. He's the big shot."

Klein patted his lips with a napkin. "I'd be glad to help you out if I can. I'm only in the city for a few days, but if they come in when I'm here, I'll have a talk with them."

Seema seemed relieved. "Here, Sam, more herring. Maybe you'd like a *shtickel* salami?"

"No, my stomach is full," said Klein, pulling out a piece of paper from his pocket. "Tell me, 185 Delancey, it's not far from here?"

"A ten minute walk," said Max. "Not a very nice tenement, even for the East Side. You got business there?"

"Yeah, I have to speak with a Henny Greenspon. Have you heard of her?"

Max laughed. "Sam, you know how many Jews live on the East Side? I'll tell you, more than all the gentiles in Winnipeg. You expect us to know one poor woman."

"Why don't you rest," said Seema, "and tomorrow morning you can find this Henny."

Though time was of the essence, Klein couldn't do much for Alfred Powers that evening. He followed Seema's advice and retired early with a glass of *schnaps* and a cigar offered by Max. Alone in the cozy back room of the delicatessen, he reread parts of Emily's diary that he had marked with scraps of paper during the train journey. It was the entry for January 4, 1913 that had intrigued him.

"...Met the caller again. Strangely, money is not the issue. I cannot allow the photographs to be published, though my effort seems half-hearted at best. God damn, Abe. Why did he make me do that?..."

What photographs was she referring to? He hoped that once he found her sister Henny, he would also find some answers. Still, the diary had made this much clear to him: someone Emily knew was blackmailing her, but not for money. With such thoughts on his mind, he closed his eyes.

Number 185 Delancey, mid-way between Forsyth and Allen, was no different than hundreds of other tenement houses in the East Side. Four stories high with a cheap brownstone facade, its small rooms housed at least twenty families in a space meant for half as many.

Klein stopped for a moment to light a cigarette. "Hey mister, want a paper?" asked a young boy hawking newspapers. He was wearing a flat brown cap, black baggy pants, and a matching suit jacket too large for his small body. Klein figured the kid was twelve years old at most. The stack of newspapers barely fit under his arm.

"Maybe later. I got some business to attend to."

"How about a smoke, then?"

"You old enough to smoke?"

"Been old enough for three years."

Klein threw the boy a cigarette. "How come you aren't in school, kid?"

"Schools are for sissies. I got to earn a living or else me and my little brother don't eat. My ma sews dresses, but that don't put enough food on the table."

"Here, kid," said Klein throwing the boy a quarter. "Give me a paper and keep the change."

The boy's eyes widened. "Thanks a lot mister. If you need any help, you just find me. I know everybody around here."

"I'll keep that in mind."

Klein marched up to the entrance of the tenement, side-stepping several boxes of garbage. The stench reminded him of the putrid smells along Dufferin Avenue on a hot July day. From what he'd seen of the East Side thus far, he expected that such odours were hard to escape. The activity on the streets might have been more exciting than back home, but the poverty was much worse as well. Klein could see it in the weary eyes and gaunt bodies of youngsters like the newsboy and all the other children aimlessly roaming the streets.

Inside, the tenement was even more dilapidated. The hallway was dimly lit, damp, and musty. Whatever paint there had been on the walls had peeled away long ago. He knocked on the door to apartment five. A few moments passed before it opened and a short woman, her dark hair tied back under a *babushka*, stood before Klein. She wore a white, long-sleeved blouse and an ankle-length grey skirt covered by a dirty white apron. Though she appeared haggard and tired, Klein instantly recognized her face from the photograph in the locket. It was Emily's sister Henny.

"What do you want?" she asked in Yiddish. "I'm busy. Got work to do."

"Are you Henny Greenspon?" he asked in Yiddish as well.

She eyed Klein suspiciously. One learned in the East Side to be wary of strangers asking questions. "What if I am?"

He tugged on the gold chain inside his jacket pocket and out popped the locket.

Henny covered her mouth. "Where…where did you get that? Oh my God, what's happened to Esther?"

"My name is Sam Klein. I'm from Winnipeg, Canada. May I come in please?"

She opened the door wider and Klein stepped in. She led him through a narrow hallway past three rooms into a small kitchen. A sewing machine sat in the middle of the room beside a wooden table piled high with different coloured cloths. In the far corner was a black coal stove.

"Can we sit down somewhere?" asked Klein.

Henny found two chairs. "We can talk English if you want. My English is very good."

Klein nodded, then waited until she had settled into her chair before leaning forward to hand her the locket. With trembling fingers she took it from him.

"I remember the day I gave her this. So many years ago." She pried it open and stared at the grainy photographs. "Esther was such a pretty girl. And look at me. The years haven't been kind, have they?"

Klein smiled. What was he supposed to say? She was right. Henny was probably no more than twenty-eight, but she looked forty. "Is your husband here? He might want to hear what I have to say as well," he said.

"Jacob? Ha! That bastard. What a *shnorer*. I say, good riddance. I haven't seen him in years. I hope he's dead. After…after the baby died, he left me. At first, I tried to find him everywhere. I even put an advertisement in the *Forward*. That turned up nothing. Eventually, you accept the pain. Just like when Esther disappeared."

"Tell me about that."

Henny paused. "It was back in 1906. Summer. She was in some…you have to understand, Esther was different from me. She had lots of ambition. She didn't want to live here forever, she used to say. And I believed her. She was so bright. She'd go to the library and after tell me about what she had read." A warm smile crossed Henny's face. "Anyway, one day she told me she was going to visit our cousins in Chicago. I never saw her again. I got one postcard maybe three years ago but nothing since. All she said was that she was starting over."

Henny straightened her shoulders. "What's happened to her? She's dead, isn't she?"

Klein hesitated. "I'm afraid there's no easy way to tell you this. She was murdered. Stabbed in the streets. I'm here trying to find out who did it. The police believe her husband did it, but I don't. He's a friend of mine."

"She was married," said Henny, almost smiling. "Good for her. But why do they think her husband killed her? And why don't you?"

"The husband turned himself in with a bloody knife. And there was a boyfriend — he was killed too."

"Sounds like the kind of thing Esther would get mixed up in. My God, why did she never learn?" A tear trickled down her cheek.

"I'm certain her husband didn't do it. He's a good man. Not even in a jealous rage would he have committed murder."

Henny nodded absently. For several minutes she and Klein sat in silence.

"So how can I help you?" Henny finally said. She stood and moved to the table where she began to sort through the pile of cloths.

"Tell me, did your sister ever know a man named Abe Fineman?"

Henny's eyes opened wider. "As filthy a man as they come. Makes my Jacob look like an angel. He treated Esther like a dog. It makes me ill just thinking about it. He used to own a music hall on Allen Street, a block from here. But I don't know where he is now. Last I heard, he owned a bar somewhere on the Bowery. I don't know. I never go near those places. I sew. I look after my *boarderkes*. That's all."

Klein wasn't sure what she was talking about. "Well, if I have his name, it shouldn't be too difficult to find him. Do you know what happened between him and Esther?" He reached into his coat pocket and pulled out the diary.

"You have that!"

Klein nodded.

"Have you read it? Please, tell me about her, about her life," urged Henny.

"As far as I can gather from it, she left New York for Chicago. For about a year or so she lived on Maxwell Street and managed to save some money."

"I won't ask how."

"But she wasn't happy," continued Klein. "She changed her name to Emily Munro and arrived in Winnipeg in late 1911.

"A *shiksa!*" Henny gasped.

Klein covered a grin. "About a year later, she married my friend, Alfred Powers, a lawyer. She became active in the suffragist movement, fought for prohibition. And, well you know the rest."

"You know more than I do."

"There are two pages torn from the diary around June of 1906. Something happened to her involving Abe. I'm not sure, but I think it's somehow connected to her murder. There are also references to photographs. Seems like someone was blackmailing her."

Henny stared at Klein. "You seem like a good man, Sam Klein. You have children?"

"My wife is pregnant."

"That's wonderful. Once I had a beautiful little boy, Moishe. Just after his fourth birthday he came down with the 'Jewish disease' — that's what they call it here."

"Consumption?"

"He died six months later." For about a minute, she said nothing further. Klein could tell by her distant gaze that she was far away, in some other time. Then, suddenly, she walked over to the shelves above the kitchen counter. She opened a jar and pulled out two yellowed scraps of paper.

"Esther told me to burn these, but I never did. I'm not sure why," she said handing the roll to Klein. "I believe you'll find some of the answers you're looking for in those two pages. But don't judge her harshly. Esther loved new experiences, pleasure, excess — that's all."

"I've been told that."

He carefully unfolded the papers and held them against the torn edges in the diary. The ragged seams matched perfectly.

"You stay here and read, Mr. Klein. I'm going to fetch some bread and herring from the store."

Klein heard the door of the apartment close. He lit a cigarette and examined the missing pages.

15

New York City
June 1906

I LOST track of time. I sat on the hard stoop. I didn't even know where I was and I didn't care. A swirl of emotions churned inside me — anger, shame, embarrassment — and yes, even excitement, though I tried desperately to tell myself that I hadn't really found the experience pleasurable.

Smoking one cigarette after another, I replayed the events in my head as if I was watching a show at a Grand Street nickelodeon.

Abe started by insisting that I have a shot of whisky. After I gulped it down, he finally told me what he wanted me to do: pose for some photographs with the blonde woman in the studio — Cynthia, he said her name was, from somewhere uptown. After he said this, he offered me another shot of whisky. To be honest, I felt kind of anxious so I took it from him. The photographer was a hefty man in a sweat-stained suit. He grinned at me as he adjusted his camera.

The three gentlemen behind him didn't speak with me, though they did chat amongst themselves and periodically called out to Abe in English. I could tell that they were rich because of their fine suits and bowler hats, a cut above the ones for sale on nearby Hester Street.

My head was spinning from the whisky. At that moment, I started thinking that it would be fun to be photographed, even by someone as unpleasant looking as that photographer. Suddenly Cynthia started touching my hair. And then she rubbed my arms.

"Why don't you put this on?" she whispered in my ear, handing me a black negligee like the one she was wearing. When I didn't immediately respond, Abe came toward us grabbed me by my wrist and told me, with his teeth clenched, that he wanted me to change.

"I'll help you," Cynthia said, unbuttoning my blouse and then my skirt.
"What are you doing?" I said. I pushed at Cynthia's hands. "Stop it."
At this point, the photographer began taking picture after picture, the flashes of powder momentarily blinded me.
"Take everything off," Abe ordered, "and then put on the gown."
"I won't do it. I'm sorry Abe, but I didn't bargain for this," I said.
"No bargaining now — just do it." With that he struck me hard across the face.
"Please, honey," Cynthia told me, "do as he says. I won't hurt you."
Reluctantly I obeyed. I removed my undergarments. As soon as the three businessmen saw me naked, they stopped talking.
"Very good, Abe," one of them remarked, lighting another cigar.
"I figured you'd think so," Abe said with a twisted smile, "but there's more to come."

I let Cynthia slip the black garment over top of me and then — still not sure why — I allowed her to do to me what she wanted to. Kisses, touches — Cynthia's tongue roamed over my throat, shoulders, belly. The sensation was overwhelming, like nothing I had felt before. My mind was saying stop, but my body was listening to some secret part of myself. I even rubbed my hands over her breasts, as the men quietly cheered me on.

After the photographer had taken a dozen or more photographs, Abe turned and sauntered out of the studio. "You can go," he shouted to me when he reached the door. "But I'll need you to come back from time to time. If you don't, I'll start sending a few of these photos to your sister. And maybe even tack a few around your neighbourhood."

He left, the door scraping the floor as it closed. As I gathered my clothes, I began to tremble with fear. By the time I was dressed, my fear had turned to revulsion about what had just taken place. Worse though, was that I started feeling sick to my stomach because the truth was that deep inside me I could not stop thinking that I had found Cynthia's touching pleasurable.

Now, as I shiver on the dark stoop and recall these events of a few hours ago, I feel humiliated. I remember a book I read at the library a while back, the author's warning about women becoming too close: "Girls are apt at certain periods of their lives to be rather gushing creatures. They form most sentimental attachments for each other…When girls are so fond of each other that they are like silly lovers, and weep over each other's absence in uncontrollable agony, the conditions are serious enough for the consultation of a physician. It is an abnormal state of affairs, and if probed thoroughly might be found to be a sort of perversion, a sex mania, needing immediate remedy."

I wonder if that is what I have become, a "sex maniac," a pervert. I am not going back to Abe's — not ever. I am going to leave New York.

I have been writing for more than an hour now. The pain and embarrassment have subsided a little. And yet as dreadful as these events may be, one thought presses through my shame — I yearn, oh how I yearn, to touch Cynthia again. Oh dear Lord, save me.

16

Chicago Medical Recorder, January 1914

"NOTES ON PEDERASTIC PRACTICES IN PRISON"
by Dr. Douglas C. McMurtrie

"Sing Sing Prison, New York — Various acts of incredible atrocity were found to have been committed. The keepers had full knowledge of conditions and yet did nothing to improve them. There was one instance of the assault of a young new prisoner by seventeen men, the method employed being immissio membri virilis per anum. *As a result of the mistreatment the boy went insane and had to be transferred to one of the state asylums."*

"RATHER SHOCKING, ISN'T it Mr. Klein?" asked Henny Greenspon. "I've lost many hours of sleep thinking of the indignities described in those torn pages."

"Indignity yes, but Emily — I mean Esther — was very intelligent. She must have gone there knowing that Abe was up to no good."

"You mean she got herself into that mess."

Klein shrugged.

"Perhaps that is partly true, Mr. Klein. But that doesn't explain why she seems to have enjoyed such unnatural acts, being with a woman as she would be with a man. It's difficult for me to comprehend. I once broached this subject with Dr. Beckerman, the husband of a friend who used to live down the street. He confirmed that what Esther had done was against the laws of nature. Yet he also told me that what he called 'sexual inversion' was more common than people realized. He said that even here in New York, there are places — steam bath houses, literary societies, actors' clubs — where men and women meet their own kind in secret, for the purposes of pleasure." As she said this last word, she blushed and turned away.

Klein nodded, thinking of Melinda's. "It makes you wonder."

There always had been clients frequenting Melinda's who had peculiar tastes — the banker who wanted Darlene to tie his hands behind his back came to mind, or the wealthy city aldermen who paid for "mouth sucking" only. He had heard stories about "inverts" and jokes about men, "fairies," who liked to act like women, and women who liked to act like men. There had been only one occasion when a male customer, a businessman from Toronto, had visited Melinda's requesting that two girls touch each other while he watched. But Melinda refused to permit on her premises such "perversion," as she had called it, no matter how much money the man offered. That's what made the revelations in Esther's diary so shocking.

"So do you think what happened to Esther here is connected to why she was killed?" asked Henny.

"Maybe," nodded Klein. "From what I can gather, someone was blackmailing her and those photographs played a big part."

"Are you going back to Canada right away?"

"Not quite yet. I'd like to have a chat with Abe Fineman, if I can find him. And I'd also like the address of the Dr. Beckerman you spoke with. There's something I'd like to ask him."

Klein felt right at home. The Bowery with its derelicts, bars and dance halls might have passed for Winnipeg's Main Street — there was just more of everything: more drunks, more thugs, and more white slavers seeking ways to take advantage of poor immigrant girls.

His first stop was a place called "Big Joe's," a bar and pool room near the corner of the Bowery and East Houston. Henny had told him that Abe Fineman might be part owner or at least that he had been seen there during the past year. Stepping over a ragged drunk in the middle of the sidewalk, Klein walked into the smoke-filled and musty establishment. A few men were sitting at round wooden tables drinking and smoking cigars. Another dozen or so stood by the bar. On the other side of the room, several younger men were shooting a game of pool.

"What can I get you, mister," the elderly bartender asked Klein.

"A glass of beer."

A moment later, the bartender returned with a tall glass of frothy lager.

"Listen, maybe you can help me, I'm looking for a friend of mine, Abe Fineman. You seen him around?"

"You a friend of Abe's?"

"That's right. I'm visiting all the way from Canada. Thought I'd say hello."

"Well, sorry stranger, Mr. Fineman don't like no unannounced visitors."

"I'd think he'd change his mind if he knew I was here."

"This guy bothering you, Joe?" asked a young man standing at the other end of the bar. He was wearing a shiny belted jacket and flat hat. A jagged slash under his left eye was healing.

"It's nothing, Benny. He's looking for Abe," replied the bartender. "Says he's an old friend from Canada. You ever hear Abe talk about any friends in Canada?"

"Not me." The man turned to face Klein. "I think you'd better finish your beer. Your business here is done." A few more young men wandered up behind their friend.

Klein took out his cigarette case. "Your name's Benny?" he asked the man as he lit a cigarette.

"That's right. You got a problem with that?"

"You wouldn't happen to be Benny Fein, would you? Dopey Benny?"

"Yeah, you heard of me?"

"I heard of you."

"Well, here, let me introduce you to some of my friends," he said pointing at the men standing to his left. "That's Louis Buchalter, but you can call him 'Lepke.' That's Charlie Kaufman, and that youngster is Meyer Lansky."

The men stared at Klein, but no one smiled. They were young and tough. Klein figured Lansky couldn't have been more than sixteen years old, though among all of them he had a look of fierce intelligence that the others didn't.

"Now that we made the introductions, you can get the hell out of here."

Klein blew smoke into Benny's face. "Introductions? How rude of me. The name is Klein, Sam Klein," he said, extending his right hand.

Fein laughed and glanced at his friends. Then with a smirk, he grabbed Klein's hand and tried to twist it behind the detective's back. With one fluid movement, Klein pivotted on his heel, dropped his shoulder and threw Benny through the air onto the sawdust floor. Then he pulled the gangster's arm up into a wristlock and twisted. "Take one step more," Klein said to the other men, "and I'll snap his arm like a twig."

"Back off," shouted Fein, grimacing in pain. "I don't think he's kidding."

The men stepped back, though Kaufman brandished a flat throwing knife in his hand.

"Tell him to put that on the bar and slide it over here," said Klein, putting more pressure on Fein's arm.

"Charlie, for God's sakes, do as he says."

Reluctantly, Kaufman placed the knife on the bar and slid it over to Klein. He picked it up and placed the knife directly under Dopey Benny's chin. "Now, all of you," he said to the men, "ease over to the other side of the room." In unison, the hoodlums backed away.

"Okay, tough guy, now what are you going to do?" Fein asked.

"You and I are going to have a little talk, except it's going to be the one-way kind."

"One-way?"

"Yeah, you're going to listen and I'm going to talk. You got that?"

"Yeah, I got it. Hey, you're breaking my arm."

Klein pressed the knife ever so gently into Fein's Adam's apple. "You want me say this in Yiddish or do you understand English?"

"I prefer English."

"English it'll be. Okay, Dopey Benny or whatever the hell your name is. I hear you've been bothering some relatives of mine over at a delicatessen near East Houston and Orchard. The Rosens. You know who I'm talking about?"

"Yeah, I know them. They got to pay their protection money like everyone else."

"Well, this is the point, Benny," whispered Klein. "They aren't like everyone else. Go near them again and I'll kill you like a dog, *farshtey*? Do you understand?" For emphasis, he drew a thin line of blood with the knife.

"Okay, okay. I'll leave them alone."

"Good. I'm glad we could work this out. Now, where can I find Abe Fineman?"

Fein remained silent.

"I thought you and I had an understanding." Klein pushed harder on Fein's arm.

"I'm right here, bud. What do you want?" Klein turned to his right and saw a man in a pin stripe suit standing near the end of the bar. He had a thick black mustache, speckled with grey, and wore a smart-looking bowler.

"You Fineman?"

The man nodded. "Why don't you let Benny go so you and I can talk. I got an office in the back."

Klein weighed Fineman's offer for a moment. "Okay, but keep this trash away from me." He dropped Fein's arm to the floor and straightened up. Immediately Kaufman, Lansky, and Lepke began to move toward Klein.

"Leave him," ordered Fineman. "Go have a drink on me."

Young Lansky helped Dopey Benny to his feet. Klein tipped his hat toward him and followed Fineman to the back of the bar.

"Okay, start talking, tough guy," said Fineman, lighting a fat cigar. "First your name." He sat down behind a cluttered wooden desk and leaned back in his chair.

"Sam Klein. I'm from Winnipeg in Canada. Ever hear of it?" Klein couldn't help but notice the assortment of opium pipes and paraphernalia tucked into the corner of a shelf behind Fineman.

"North of Chicago, right? Yeah, I heard of it, done some business there I think. So, what do you do for a living, Klein?"

"I'm a private investigator."

Fineman took a deep drag on his cigar and blew a large cloud of smoke. "Sounds important."

"It's a job. Can we cut the small talk? I'm in a bit of rush."

"What's on your mind?"

"Does the name Esther Mandelbaum mean anything to you?"

A wide sneering smile spread across Fineman's face. "Now there's a name I haven't heard in a long time. Esther was a real beauty. Probably a virgin when I found her in some stinking factory. I opened her eyes to some new experiences. Made a fair bit of money off of her as well. Too bad she left the city."

"Tell me more."

"Why should I? What's in it for me?"

"Nothing. Just the satisfaction that you're helping me out."

Fineman laughed. "You're a real pistol, Klein. Do you know that?"

"I've been told. But anyway, tell me about Esther. We both know you want to." Klein had met many pompous fools like Fineman. They were all small-time hoods who dreamed of being kings. Nothing made them happier than sounding off.

"Yeah, I guess I do. Okay, what the hell. I owned a dance hall in those days, not far away over on Allen Street. I used to do a favour now and again for a friend of mine getting into the photography business, Eddie Giles. He liked taking photographs of women and was glad to pay me for arranging it. Anyway, one day he introduces me to three high rollers from Fifth Avenue, fancy suits, you know the type. They offered me and my friend two thousand each, no less, if we could arrange a session for them with two women. And pictures weren't the only thing they had in mind, if you know what I mean." Fineman grinned crookedly.

"I can imagine," Klein said, nodding.

"Well, I knew this good looking whore named Cynthia. She preferred women to men." Fineman stopped for a moment to gauge Klein's reaction, but he showed none. "I liked Esther and I had this good feeling about her. I was right," he said laughing. "If I hadn't seen it with my own eyes, I wouldn't have believed it."

"And Esther did this willingly?"

"She needed a little encouragement, but I think she enjoyed herself, if that's what you're asking."

"What happened after that?"

"The photographs were very popular with the gentlemen. They paid us what we had agreed to. In fact, I used my money for a down payment on this place."

"And the pictures?"

"For a while, we sold dozens, hundreds, of them, then interest died away. Eddie and I tried a few more sessions with Cynthia, then she got arrested and Eddie moved to San Francisco. I haven't seen him since the fall of 1910."

"So you're out of that business now?"

"Mostly, I manage the affairs of a few girls and run this bar. I get help from some of the more ambitious boys in the neighbourhood. But you already met them. They're eager. I'm sure they'll be making lots of money in no time."

"From dealing opium, you mean?" Klein asked, glancing at the pipes.

"Sure, we make a few dollars with that," said Fineman with a shrug. "It's the Negroes — if they can afford it, they like opium. The rich white folk favour cocaine and morphine. It's all a lot easier to move than booze. But enough business talk — tell me how you know Esther."

"She was a friend."

"Was?"

"She was murdered about ten days ago. I'm looking into it."

"Murdered. Now, that's a real shame."

Klein had just about enough from Fineman. The man was as sleazy a character as he had ever met. He was now certain the photographs Fineman gloated about were the same ones Emily mentioned in her diary. Sitting in Fineman's filthy office, he thought about levelling him with one punch as he got up to leave. But the thought of touching Fineman's grinning face repulsed him.

Klein's work in New York was nearly complete. Only one last bit of information was needed to confirm his suspicions about what had happened behind the Walker Theatre.

From the moment Klein had uncovered the truth about Emily, or Esther, his curiosity had been aroused by the revelations of her sexual preferences. On those rare occasions when it was mentioned in the newspapers — almost always in the context of a crime — sexual inversion was regarded by physicians, clergymen, lawyers, and other guardians of morality, as an "abnormal" perversion, one whose only treatment was a life-sentence in a lunatic asylum. Journalists still alluded to the downfall of playwright Oscar Wilde, "the sodomite," jailed in London in 1895 for his scandalous behaviour with younger men. Still, Klein wasn't entirely convinced. Were Emily's actions really the result of a diseased mind? He was hoping Dr. Julius Beckerman, Henny Greenspon's friend, could enlighten him.

As Henny had explained it to Klein, Dr. Beckerman, the son of Russian immigrants, was a rarity among Lower East Side Jews: he had managed to get out. Now he had a Fifth Avenue address, lived in a magnificent palazzo-style mansion with a view of Central Park, summered in the Catskills, and treated patients with last names like Astor, Carnegie, Belmont, and Ryan. He attended the Metropolitan Opera instead of the Yiddish theatre and, if he made an appearance at synagogue at all, it was only on *Rosh Hashana* or *Yom Kippur*.

While he was by all accounts a brilliant physician who treated both the mind and the body, his wealth had arisen from a few bold investments in railways and Long Island property. Now his new financial advisors, the German Jews who ran Kuhn, Loeb and Company, ensured that his fortune would continue to grow.

Marching up Fifth Avenue towards Central Park, Klein was struck by the gentility of the street. The crowds of gentlemen and ladies outfitted in the finest suits, dresses, and hats money could buy affirmed he had entered another world. The poverty of the East Side was now nowhere to be seen. Instead, the houses he passed were more like castles and the horse-drawn rigs, hansom cabs, and automobiles testified to the immense wealth of the avenue's patrons.

Near the corner of 79th Street, Klein saw the discreet sign on the black steel gates: "Dr. Julius Beckerman, M.D." He walked up the path through a garden of flowers and sculptures until he reached the steps leading to large oak double doors. He banged once with the lion-headed knocker, and one of the doors opened. An elderly gentleman in a black suit stood before him.

"I have an appointment to see Dr. Beckerman," said Klein.

The man looked Klein over for a moment and then invited him into the entrance hall. The floor was white marble and a wide twisting staircase was directly in front of him.

"If you wait here, sir," said the man, "I will summon the doctor."

Klein nodded and pulled out his cigarette case.

"Excuse me, sir, the doctor only permits smoking in his study."

Klein returned his cigarette case to his inside jacket pocket and waited. He ventured farther into the house and caught sight of a painting hung on a wall in the adjacent parlour. It was a carefully rendered depiction of a group of men, all with seventeenth century moustaches and pointed beards, gathered around a cadaver. A distinguished-looking man in a black suit and wide-brimmed hat leaned over the body with a medical utensil in hand.

"You appreciate art, Mr. Klein."

Klein turned to face Dr. Beckerman. With his suit and beard, he might have passed for one of the men in the painting.

"That piece," he said, pointing, "is entitled 'The Anatomy Lesson of Dr. Nicolaas Tulp' done by Rembrandt. I picked it up several months ago at an auction held at the Waldorf. It's quite impressive, don't you think?"

"I don't know much about painting," said Klein, "but it does look quite real."

"Precisely. The style is referred to in Italian as *chiaroscuro*. Notice the way in which he has manipulated the light and the shadows. Brilliant."

Klein was curious about how much such a painting might cost, but thought better of asking.

"Now," continued the doctor, "I know you didn't come hear to discuss art. I received a telephone call from Henny last night, who provided me with some details. I understand, a terrible tragedy has transpired with her sister, but it is not entirely unprecedented. Please follow me so we can discuss this more privately."

Beckerman led Klein up the stairs to the second floor. "My wife and children are away visiting relatives so the house is rather quiet."

He led Klein into a large office. The floor was covered with an Oriental rug and the walls were lined with books. A beautiful roll-top desk sat against one wall surrounded by cloth-covered chairs.

"Please sit down, Mr. Klein," said Beckerman, producing a cedar humidor. "Care for a cigar? This is the only room where I can smoke. My wife is bothered by dust, pollen, just about anything in fact. But she permits me to smoke in my study if the doors are closed."

"Yeah, I found that out," Klein said, taking a cigar.

"You mean Benjamin? Yes, he is quite protective of Mrs. Beckerman."

For a moment, both men puffed in silence. "Shall we get down to business?" asked Beckerman.

Klein nodded, and eyed the doctor. "I've been around, but I've never dealt with anything like this before."

"You mean inversion? Homosexuality?"

"Yes. The more I dig into the life of Esther Mandelbaum, or Emily Munro as I knew her, the more questions I have. Maybe I should tell you about the case I've been working on."

For a few minutes, Klein took Beckerman through the story of Emily and Antonio's murder, the arrest of Alfred Powers, and his subsequent investigation, including the information he found in Emily's diary. "And so yesterday I spoke with Fineman," Klein concluded. "I'm now certain that Emily was being blackmailed over the photographs but by who I don't know."

"And you are convinced your friend Powers is innocent, that he didn't find Emily with this Italian and murder them both?"

"Seems unlikely to me. Call it intuition. But usually I've been right about these things."

"I see. In any event, sexual behaviour of the type you have described in Esther Mandelbaum has been one my interests for some time. My reading of the earlier medical literature, the work of Irving Rosse, C.H. Hughes, Krafft-Ebing, James Keirnan and of course, Dr. Havelock Ellis, has led me to conclude the following — that many inverted relationships are characterized by an obsessiveness not found in normal male-female relations. Thus the resulting suicides and crimes of passion. Do you understand what I mean?"

"I think so. These people can't control themselves."

"Precisely. In fact, I knew of one young fellow, a lawyer who practised just a few blocks from here, who I had treated for an ulcer. One day, out of the blue, he confessed to me his homosexual urges. Yet his sense of propriety prevented him from indulging them. A terrible conflict arose in him. Six months ago, he hanged himself. A terrible shame."

Dr. Beckerman paused and rested his cigar in a glass tray on his desk. "Let me now add something very important. My position on this issue has shifted over the past few years. I used to believe, like many medical practitioners, that inversion — homosexuality between men, or sapphoism or tibadism between women — was immoral and perverted. Certainly not a normal sexual love as between husband and wife. To a degree, this remains my opinion. However, Dr. Ellis has convinced me that not all inverts are criminals, nor are they all insane. In some cases, male and female inverts are by all appearances normal, though many do lead double lives to protect their true sexual desires."

Klein remained silent and expressionless as he listened to the doctor's words.

"In short, I agree with Dr. Ellis's view that sexual inversion is neither a disease nor a type of degeneration, but a congenital abnormality that is biological in character. It may stay hidden or latent during a person's entire life or it may be awakened by a number of social factors. Place of residence, for example. Obviously living in New York and frequenting bars and clubs in the Bowery is much different from spending one's days tending cows in South Dakota. In the case of Esther, the photograph session appears to be have been the pivotal factor. I should point out, of course, that most medical articles on this subject regard Dr. Ellis's work as being rather liberal and overly sympathetic."

Dr. Beckerman's breadth of knowledge and compassion impressed Klein. He didn't quite understand everything the man said, but enough. "You mentioned crimes of passion, precedents. Could you tell me more?"

"There was an extortion case a few years back when a lawyer by the name of Fischer-Hansen attempted to blackmail a homosexual from Philadelphia. It was a very messy trial. There was a nineteen-year old involved. However, a jury acquitted Fischer-Hansen, despite the preponderance of evidence against him. Before that there was an incident in Chicago when a woman invert, one Nettie Miller, attempted to kill a man named Charles Seibert. Why? Because Seibert was engaged to Hattie Leonard, a woman who had lived with Mrs. Miller for a number of years. They were 'in love' as the newspapers put it. And, of course, there is the infamous Mitchell-Ward case of 1892. It might be just the example you've been searching for. Now where is that?" said Beckerman, searching through his bookshelves.

It took him only a few minutes to find the publication he was looking for. He pulled out a thin book with a photograph of a curly-haired woman on the cover. "You should read this if you have the opportunity. It's based on the Mitchell-Ward case, though it has a happier ending. It is called *Norma Trist: A Story of the Inversion of the Sexes* by Dr. John Wesley Carhart. He published it back in 1895."

Klein flipped through the fifty-cent book, as an uncomfortable idea began to form in his mind.

"But I'm getting ahead of myself," continued Beckerman. "Let me go back. The story began in Memphis in 1892. Alice Mitchell was nineteen and Freda Ward, a beautiful girl, two years younger. Both were daughters of rich merchants and very close friends. In fact, they loved each other like man and wife, so much so that when Alice asked Freda to marry her, Freda agreed. However, a short time later, Freda returned Alice's engagement ring."

"On January 25, 1892, Alice attacked Freda in the street and slit her throat, killing her. She claimed that if she couldn't be with Freda, then it would be better if Freda were dead. At her subsequent murder trial, the jury decided that Alice was insane. The judge ordered her to be placed in an asylum, where she resides still. Naturally, the case was much discussed in the newspapers and the medical literature. Most physicians then and now considered Alice Mitchell to be a sexual pervert."

"You believe that as well?"

"I've never met Mitchell or examined her. But I'd probably subscribe to the view held by a Dr. J.H. Callender, an expert in mental infirmity. He interviewed Alice and concluded that she suffered from a morbid passionate attachment."

"In English, please, doctor."

"Yes, of course," Beckerman said with a smile. "Simply that Alice Mitchell's love for Freda transformed into passionate jealousy when she was faced with the prospect of living without her. Her concomitant delusions prevented her from understanding the absurdity of her marriage plans. There's no question that a deep and passionate jealousy, characteristic of female inverts, played an important role in this terrible crime. Interestingly, in Carhart's novel, the character based on Mitchell also kills her female lover. However, she recovers in the asylum, is hypnotized to never love a member of her sex again, and happily marries a man named Frank Artman. Such are the differences between fiction and reality."

As Klein tried to fit the new pieces of the puzzle together, the doctor turned his head to glance at a large clock ticking languidly on the mantel.

"You will have to excuse me Mr. Klein," he said. "I have an appointment with my banker."

Klein stood up and extended his hand. "Thanks very much. I appreciate your time."

"Not at all. I hope this helps your investigation."

"I believe it might."

Once he was back outside on Fifth Avenue, Klein's mind began to race. The pieces were finally falling into place. Thanks to Dr. Beckerman, he had a strong hunch what had happened to Emily. He would have to return to Winnipeg to flush the real murderer of Emily Powers and Antonio Rossi out into the open. That might prove to be difficult, he thought, but he had a long train journey ahead to work out the details.

It took Klein about an hour to arrive back at the Rosens' delicatessen on East Houston. It was late in the afternoon and the restaurant was quiet except for a few old men chatting over a cup of tea and a piece of Seema's honey cake. Immediately, Klein noticed a sombre look on Max Rosen's face. Then he heard Seema crying in the back room.

"Max, what's wrong? What happened?"

"Sam, come sit down. I have some bad news for you."

"Please, Max, tell me, now."

"I received a telegram from your sister a few hours ago."

Klein looked at him blankly.

"I'm terribly sorry, Sam, but your mother has suffered a heart attack. She died early this morning."

17

Winnipeg, Canada
February 13, 1914

" [My feeling for Mrs. LaMoreaux] is as pure as the deepest, purest, most God-given passion between two of the opposite sexes can possibly be, and I may modestly say, as intelligent… The stronger the passion the happier I was; it was and is a stimulus to my ambition, prompting me to highest intellectual effort, inspiring me with delightful, unflinching courage…"
Norma Trist in Dr. John Wesley Carhart, *Norma Trist: A Story of the Inversion of the Sexes* (Austin, Texas: Eugene von Boeckmann, 1895)

"TO BE HONEST, Mr. Powers," said Dr. Oliver Parker, glumly surveying the small confines of the jail cell. "I would much rather have done this at my home."

"I tried, Doctor," said Graham Powers. "The police refused to budge, as did Magistrate Findly. So this will have to do."

"The doctor is quite right," remarked Alfred Powers reclining on the narrow bed. "This cell is hardly acceptable. I'd much rather be in my study smoking a cigar."

"You're certain that this won't hurt him, Dr. Parker?" asked Elizabeth.

"We've been over this," snapped Graham.

"I assure you Miss Powers, nothing will happen to your father. In fact, he will feel much more relaxed when I have finished. I have been practising hypnosis for many years. I have studied the work of the finest French medical hypnotists, Hippolyte-Marie Bernheim and the late Ambrose-August Lebeault. There is nothing to be concerned about."

"I'm sorry, Dr. Parker, but I remain skeptical."

"I understand your fears. If you don't want me to proceed…"

"We want nothing of the sort," interjected Graham. "Elizabeth, do you want father to rot in jail or worse?"

"Of course not."

"Then sit down and be silent. If the doctor is able to help prove father's innocence then we should do everything we can to support him."

"Graham, Elizabeth, stop the bickering please," the elder Powers said. "Dr. Parker, please get started."

Elizabeth took a seat on a chair near the door of the cell. Graham sat on a stool beside her.

"Alfred," said Parker more softly. "I want you to lie back and do two things: concentrate on my voice and focus on the light on the ceiling." He paused for a moment while Powers did as he was instructed. "Now, Alfred, take four deep breaths, but continue to stare at the light. You feel yourself becoming sleepy, don't you? Your eyelids are becoming heavier. You want to sleep. Shut your eyes, Alfred."

At first, Powers resisted. "This isn't working."

"No, Alfred," insisted Parker, "you must listen to my voice and concentrate on it. Nothing else."

Powers nodded. The lines that creased his face began to vanish as he relaxed. He closed his mind to everything but the sound of Dr. Parker's voice as he continued to speak soothingly. Five minutes passed. Finally, his eyelids began to flutter and then slowly close. He lay perfectly still, and then seemed to tense as a look of frustration and anxiety suddenly appeared on his face. It was apparent to everyone in the room that these feelings were emerging from deep within this troubled man.

"Is he asleep?" whispered Elizabeth.

"No," said Parker quietly. "He is in what is called an hypnotic trance." He returned his attention to Powers. "Alfred, can you hear me?"

"Yes," said Powers, his voice barely audible.

"Good. Listen carefully. We are going back to the night of January 28. Can you tell us about that day?"

"Yes. I can see it clearly. I'm leaving the house early for the office because I have to prepare for a complex case. It involves a questionable land transaction. I kiss Emily good-bye. She looks radiant. I love her dearly. We arrange to meet at the Walker Theatre. She is to be in the mock Parliament that Mrs. McClung has organized. We talk about her role as Leader of the Opposition. I am looking forward to the show. The ladies are going to give Roblin a dose of his own medicine. And then — " He suddenly stopped.

"Go on, Alfred. Tell us what happened."

"I'm leaving my office. It's about six o'clock in the evening. I'm hoping to stop and chat with Emily before the performance begins. The wind is cold and the snow miserable. It's not a pleasant walk over to the theatre. I cross Ellice Avenue. Then I hear a scream. The voice. I recognize the voice. Emily. I run down Smith Street toward the alley way behind the theatre. Oh my God, she's lying there in a pool of blood. He is beside her…

"Look up, Alfred, what else do you see in the alley? Is anyone else there?"

Tears were running down Powers's face.

"I want this to stop now," demanded Elizabeth. "He is suffering."

"No, let's finish it," ordered Graham. "Doctor, please continue."

"Very well. Alfred, what do you see in the alley apart from the two bodies?"

"The alley is barren. Full of mud and snow. There are fresh horse tracks as if a small cutter has recently gone through."

"Is there anything else, Alfred?"

"Yes. Near the end of the alley towards Donald Street, there are two trashcans. Someone is watching me. I can see. I can see her."

"Her?"

"Yes. It's a woman. I'm quite sure. She's wearing a long coat."

"Do you recognize her? Can you see her face?"

The lawyer's voice trembled. "I don't know. It's dark, I can't see very well. I get to my feet but as I do the woman turns and runs. I don't know who it is. I collapse on top of Emily. I'm holding her in my arms. Why? Why did she do this to me? The knife is still inside her. I pull it out. Blood everywhere…" Powers's body was now wracked with sobs.

"I can't bear anymore, Graham," said Elizabeth. "Please tell him to stop."

"Do you think he knows any more, Doctor?"

"I believe he has told us everything his memory has retained. He truly doesn't know who the woman was."

"Can you bring him back now?"

"Of course. Alfred, can you hear me?"

"Yes. Where is Emily? I miss her so."

"Alfred. Pay attention to my voice. When I clap my hands, you will open your eyes. You will feel as if you have slept all night long. You will feel very relaxed. You will recall our conversation. Do you understand?"

"I do."

Parker clapped his hands twice and immediately Powers opened his eyes.

"How do you feel father?" asked Graham.

"Much better. But…

"But what?"

Powers's eyes teared. "I remember…I remember everything now," he said, covering his face with his hands.

"Father, please," said Graham.

"There was a woman."

"Yes, we heard, father. You were telling the truth. Emily and Rossi were already dead when you arrived at the scene. They were killed by someone else. That woman?"

"I…I don't know. It's possible I suppose."

"Not possible. It happened. I have to contact Klein. What's wrong father?"

Powers took a deep breath. "Graham, you know as well as I do that even if Dr. Parker testifies as to what we have heard today, no jury will believe it. Jarvis will say that I'm concocting the whole thing. What woman? She has no name, no face. He'll tell the jury that the entire story is a fabrication. It will be his word against mine. Why should they believe me? It's hopeless."

"No, not hopeless," said Graham, tightening his jaw. "We're going to find this woman. I promise you that."

"Yes, father," added Elizabeth, though with less enthusiasm. "We will find her."

"Sam, finally. I'm so glad you've returned." Rivka Klein walked swiftly to greet her brother. She was wearing a black dress with a dark kerchief around her head. Her eyes were red and puffy.

"What happened?" asked Klein. He was unshaven and haggard. The journey back to Chicago and through the wide expanse of Wisconsin and Minnesota hadn't been easy. Terribly distressed about his mother's passing, he had had to force himself to sort through the details of his New York investigations. The result was that he had hardly slept for the past two days. Worse, by the time the train pulled into the station in Winnipeg, he still hadn't worked out a plan. He only knew for certain that Alfred Powers was innocent. He also suspected that Powers knew more about his wife's secret life than he had told him. How could he not? And now, on top of the murder, and Sarah, now this.

"I found her at her sewing machine. The doctor says it was her heart. Sam, I don't know what I'm going to do without her…" She collapsed in his arms.

Freda Klein was buried the next day at the Shaarey Shamim cemetery far down North Main Street. Rabbi Aaron Davidovitch delivered a stirring eulogy about Freda's dedication to her two children and her many virtues. Afterwards, the Klein house on Flora Avenue grew crowded with friends and well wishers. A death in the North End Jewish community always meant two things: heartfelt condolences and a lot of food.

Led by Klein, the male visitors prayed for Freda's soul, while their wives ensured there was an abundance of herring, rye bread, whisky and honey cake. Rivka sat on a hard chair beside her mother's dearest friend, Clara Hirsch, accepting sympathy and reassurance. Her boyfriend, Solomon Volkon, and her friends from the garment factory sat nearby.

Amidst the Yiddish and English conversation, no one felt more out of place than Graham Powers. As the son of a wealthy lawyer and civic leader, he had led a rather sheltered life removed from the city's burgeoning immigrant groups. Sam Klein was the only Jew he knew well. And certainly, he had never stepped foot in a synagogue prior to that afternoon. Still, he had found the Hebrew chanting quite moving.

"Thanks for coming, Graham," said Klein shaking the lawyer's hand. "I appreciate it, especially given the circumstances."

"I'm sorry for your loss. Now both our mothers are gone."

"Come let's talk in the back room where it's quieter." Klein led Graham through the crowded kitchen to a storage area. Graham greeted Sarah, busy making coffee, and noticed that the mirror in the hallway was covered with a black cloth.

"During the *shiva* or seven days of mourning," explained Klein, noticing Graham's puzzled expression, "you aren't supposed to look at yourself. It doesn't matter if your hair is combed or your clothes look right."

The small room adjacent to the kitchen was chilly. Both men crossed their arms, unsure how to begin. Klein shut the door and lit a cigarette.

"There was a woman in the alley," Graham blurted.

To Graham's surprise, Klein simply nodded. "How did you find out?"

"Parker hypnotized my father yesterday. It was fascinating to watch. He took him through the day of the murder. He says that he arrived in the alley when Emily and Antonio were already dead. But there was a woman hiding. He's certain of that. Unfortunately, he didn't get a good look at her. He doesn't know who she is. Obviously it'll be almost impossible to convince a jury he's not making up the whole story. Sam, what I need is hard evidence. Did you have any luck in New York?"

"I did and I believe that we're closer to solving this case than you might think."

"What do you mean? What did you find out about Emily?"

"Graham, you wouldn't believe me if I told you. I have to say that this is the most damn peculiar case I've ever worked on. I thought that having worked at Melinda's, that I knew what went on in the world. But to be honest, after all of this, I'm not sure about anything."

"Klein, you're not making any sense. Do you have something I can use or not? I have to go into court tomorrow and all I have is the word of my father and a surgeon who's more famous as a spiritualist than a physician."

"Graham, you'll have to trust me. I do have a plan. Where's your sister? I need to speak with her."

"Elizabeth? She's at work in the North End. Why? She'll tell you the same thing as me, except for some reason she's more suspicious of our father's story."

"Is that so?"

"I don't know what has gotten into her lately. But she'll be home by six o'clock if you want to reach her. But don't you have to stay here?"

"I'll stay for the afternoon prayers and then arrange things for tomorrow. If all goes according to plan, I suspect that tomorrow will be your first and last day in court."

"How are you holding up, *Shailek?*" asked Sarah, nuzzling closer to him. "With your poor mother's funeral, we haven't had a chance to talk about your trip to New York."

"I'm feeling as well as can be expected. I'm only sorry my mother won't be here to see her first grandchild," he said rubbing his hand over Sarah's stomach. "She would have liked that. I know the two of you never did get along that well. But she always loved her family."

"I know she did."

Klein remained silent for a moment, then opened his eyes and turned toward her.

"As for New York, you would've loved the excitement. The houses and shops on Fifth Avenue — I've never seen anything like it."

"And?"

"And I found Emily's sister Henny. She was very accommodating. The missing pages in the diary were there and you wouldn't believe what I learned about your friend." Out of the corner of his eye, Klein noticed Sarah furrow her brow. "You knew about Emily? Didn't you?"

"I knew what?" she asked, turning her face to examine the ceiling.

He sat up in the bed. "You knew about her…about her interest in other women."

A frown, then a flicker of a smile, passed over Sarah's face. "Perhaps. I don't know, Sam. I suppose I suspected. It was way Emily touched my hair or casually brushed my arms. I had seen it before at Melinda's with Frances O'Mally."

"Frances is an invert, a lesbian?"

"She enjoyed the companionship of both women and men."

"Like Emily?"

"Yes."

Klein was shocked. He had known Frances for many years. She was one of Melinda's most popular girls. Last year she had taken an extended vacation to Chicago and never returned. She telegraphed Melinda that she had found a job at a brothel and would be staying. "I had no idea."

"Don't be so hard on yourself. It's not the kind of thing a man would ever notice."

"I suppose."

"There's nothing wrong with it, *Shailek*. It's not a disease or illness. It's just being different."

"Maybe. I did have an interesting conversation with a doctor who seemed to know a lot about it."

Sarah stared at Klein for a moment, watching his mind at work. "My God, *Shailek*, you think it was a woman who murdered Emily and Antonio, don't you? But who? Why?"

Klein lay back down, kissing his wife's shoulder. "Not now, let's speak in the morning about this." His hand slipped beneath her nightgown. Sarah nodded.

"You're certain the baby won't be hurt?"

She giggled. "Yes, I promise, nothing will happen to her."

He smiled as he slid the straps of Sarah's night gown off her shoulder. "I just want to be reminded that sometimes a woman prefers the touch of a man."

The remorse was unrelenting. As much as she tried, sleep wouldn't come. She tried reading, but that didn't work. Desperate, she even took a sip of whisky. It tasted terrible. How Emily had ever drank this stuff was beyond her. She was glad that the trial would start tomorrow. Truly, she wished him no harm. The evidence against him was strong, she was aware of that, yet something inside her hoped beyond hope that he would be declared innocent — as he indeed was.

If she could turn back the clock, she would. Why had Emily deceived her so?

She lay back down and shut her eyes again. Tomorrow, things would be clearer. There was the lunch meeting that would be enjoyable. Still, why did she suspect something was amiss? Perhaps she really was going mad. Suddenly, she leaped out of her bed and opened her handbag. The small pistol was still there, just where she had left it. She checked for bullets — there were three. More than enough to solve any problem, if there was trouble.

For late February in Winnipeg, you couldn't have asked for milder weather. The snow was sticky and wet, perfect for children to use in making a snowman. After weeks of freezing temperatures, a warm breeze always brought people out of their homes and onto the streets.

Klein had a busy day planned. By dinnertime, he was confident that Alfred Powers would be out of jail and declared innocent. He had spoken to Elizabeth Powers and the lunch meeting at Eaton's Grill Room was set for noon. Klein figured there was less likely to be any serious problems if the meeting took place at such an elegant establishment.

First, however, he needed to speak with Powers in private.

"You're here awful early, Klein," remarked the young desk sergeant.

"Yeah, I never sleep. Always working."

The police officer chuckled. "You're not such a bad guy, Klein. I don't know why they make such a fuss over you around here."

"It's my good looks. They're always getting me in trouble."

"I guess so. Okay, you know the routine, sign here and you can go down to the cellblock. Powers is alone today. It was quiet last night for a change."

Klein made his way down the stairs and into the jail cell area. The constable on duty nodded and allowed him to proceed. He found Powers in his cell reading the newspaper.

"Sam, what are you doing here?"

"You nervous about today?"

"No. Graham is a good lawyer and my memory has returned."

"I heard."

"I just wish I could see that woman's face. I've been racking my brains over it."

Klein leaned up against the cell. "You know I was in New York. I met Emily's sister."

Powers put down the newspaper and peered at his friend.

"You know about her past, don't you Alfred? And I'm not just talking about her being Jewish. You know everything there is to know about the late Esther Mandelbaum, don't you?" He didn't wait for Powers to respond. "Why didn't you tell me earlier, when we talked about Emily's unusual interest in pleasure. Didn't you think I should've known? For Christ's sakes, Alfred, you could hang if we don't find out who really killed them."

"Don't you think I know that. I just couldn't tell you. It was bad enough she was…"

"A Jew."

"Yes. I apologize. I realize now how foolish I've been about that. She told me about six months after we were married. She swore that she had become fully dedicated to living a Christian life and that no one would ever know. It troubled me greatly, I won't lie to you. But I learned to live with it. The other matter, however," he said shaking his head. "That I could never accept."

"How did you find out?"

"She was being blackmailed over some photographs. I found a threatening note. At first, Emily denied it, but then she told me more than I wanted to know. I was shocked and embarrassed. An invert, my God! She said that often she preferred to be with a woman instead of a man. I couldn't at first comprehend it. Of course, in time, I forgave her. She was too dear to me. And we never spoke about it again. She told me her problem with the photographs had been taken care of. And to be honest, I didn't want to know any more than I already did."

"Do you know who was blackmailing her?"

"Yes. A woman who worked at Melinda's."

"What are you talking about?"

"Katie, Emily called her. Yes, Katie Johnson, the prostitute who committed suicide the other day."

"Katie was blackmailing Emily," Klein repeated. It makes sense. Katie was always looking for some scheme to make more cash. She somehow got hold of the photographs, figured out that it was Emily and threatened to expose her if she didn't pay up. That was what the reference in the diary was all about. Damn, it had been staring him in the face the whole time.

"You get ready for your day in court, Alfred. I have some work to do. Don't worry — this will all be over by lunch time."

"Sam, what do you mean? Tell me what is going on?"

"I'll explain later, I promise. It's better that you don't know yet. Trust me." Klein walked toward the cellblock door, turned and smiled at his old friend. "Just trust me."

Typically by mid-morning, Eaton's department store was buzzing with customers. In fact, the moment the store opened at 8:30 a.m. until it shut its doors at five in the afternoon, the sales clerks didn't have a minute to rest. Dresses, hats, pots and pans, there was little that couldn't be found in Timothy Eaton's grand emporium. Moreover, unlike on Selkirk Avenue, the prices marked were the prices that were paid — no bartering allowed. At first, back in '05 when the store opened at the corner of Donald and Portage, it took Winnipeggers a little while to get used to that strict policy. But now, it seemed to make perfect sense.

"Fifth floor, please," Klein told the elderly elevator attendant. He was resplendent in his navy Eaton's uniform, complemented nicely by gold brocades and tassels on each shoulder. Klein was the only passenger.

"Meeting someone for lunch at the Grill Room, sir? I hear the beef pot pie is excellent today."

"I'll remember that." Klein checked his inside pocket once more. He didn't expect trouble, but you could never tell what might transpire in such situations.

The elevator stopped just below the fifth floor door, but it took the attendant only a moment to adjust the circular handle and reach the correct spot. Like all Eaton's employees, the old man bid Klein a nice day.

Quickly and cautiously, Klein made his way through the aisles of women clothing and hats toward the restaurant. A small line-up of mainly women shoppers, dressed in their best, stood in the Grill Room's grand oak-panelled entrance way. Klein took his place in the line and tipped his hat to the group of ladies in front of him. They smiled and resumed their hushed conversations. It took about ten minutes for Klein to reach the front.

"May I help you, sir?" asked the maitre d'. He was the epitome of a Canadian gentleman: A black suit with tails, a crisp white shirt with a high collar and a silk black tie. His moustache was pencil-thin and immaculately trimmed. He stared at Klein up and down, paying particular attention to his few days of growth on his beard. During the period of mourning, Jewish men did not normally shave.

"I'm here for a lunch meeting. I think if you'll check your book, you'll find a reservation under the name of Powers."

The man stared at Klein again and then looked in the large book on an upright wooden stand beside him. "Yes, here it is. You are little early but I believe your table is ready. Follow me, please."

Klein proceeded behind the maitre d' into the Grill Room. The ceiling was high and the light from the iron chandeliers dim. In the far corner, Klein caught sight of the string quartet quietly entertaining lunchtime diners. The maitre d' stopped by a table near the back and Klein took a chair so that he had a good view of the room. The table was covered with a white lace cloth and set with Minton china and an array of silverware. Immediately, a waiter approached Klein with a pitcher of ice water. Now, he thought, the real fun will begin. He checked his watch. It was 11:40 a.m. Elizabeth had promised to meet him by 11:45 a.m.

The five minutes passed by unbearably slowly. He sipped his water and anxiously kept a watch on the front entrance. Then, he saw her. Elizabeth was dressed plainly and her hair was up in a bun. She nodded to Klein as she approached. Klein looked behind Elizabeth and saw the person he was really waiting for. He stood up to greet the two women.

"Elizabeth, Grace, I'm so glad you could come."

Grace Ellis was slightly taken aback when she saw Klein standing before her. "I thought…I thought, this was to be a lunch with Elizabeth only," she stammered.

"Well, actually, this was my idea," said Klein. "Please sit down, we have much to discuss."

"Elizabeth, really," said Grace, tightly holding on to her handbag as she sat down. "I thought you said we were meeting to discuss a women's rights parade. What is he doing here?"

Elizabeth sat beside Grace and smiled coldly. "He is here, Grace, to find the truth."

Grace's face flushed. The waiter arrived with more water and she immediately took a long sip. She put the glass down and raised her chin. "I have a right mind to walk out of here."

"You could do that," said Klein, "but you probably wouldn't get very far."

"And why's that?"

"Well, if you look over by the front entrance, you'll see a tall, husky rather disagreeable man. That's Detective Bill McCreary." McCreary waved. Behind him were a group of three or four constables. "Now cast, your eyes over to the table by the kitchen door," continued Klein. "Do you see that gentleman with the bowler hat. He is Detective Alex Taber and he is even more of a problem." On cue, Taber tipped his hat. "I think they would like to talk with you, once I'm done."

Grace laughed. "You think you have this all figured out. Don't you Mr. Klein?"

"Some of it perhaps, yes. But I would like to hear from you first."

"So would I," added Elizabeth.

"What do you want me to tell you?" asked Grace, her voice loud amongst the clatter of dishes and the buzz of conversation.

"The truth," said Klein. "Are you capable of that?"

Suddenly, Grace's expression changed. "Mr. Klein, do you understand what it is to love another person? Truly love her? We were going to spend the rest of our lives together. Emily had promised me. Once we had enough money, we were going to run away to New York or Chicago and start over. Just the two of us. But then, she changed her mind. No matter how much I argued with her, she wouldn't consent. She promised that she would leave Alfred and stop seeing Antonio. It sickened me. Her with that Italian. She said, he gave her pleasure. Didn't I satisfy her?"

Grace was speaking loud enough that a trio of shocked women at the next table began to take notice. The waiter approached Klein's table but he waved him away.

"Tell us what happened, Grace."

"It began at the wedding, if you can believe it."

"At my father's wedding?" asked Elizabeth.

"Not only did Emily meet Antonio there, it was a fateful meeting as it turned out. Their afternoon liaisons began soon after that. And I was forced to make the arrangements at the hotel. My God, it made me ill. It was also then…." She paused for a moment. "It was also then, I first approached Emily. I let her know that I knew the truth about her. That I had seen the photographs."

"What photographs?" asked Elizabeth.

"Please, Elizabeth, let me do this," said Klein. "You obtained the photographs from Katie Johnson, didn't you Grace?"

She nodded. "Katie knew about my likes and dislikes. I sometimes visited another girl that she was a friend with. When Katie got a hold of the photographs from a travelling American salesman, she immediately recognized Emily. She sold me the photographs and I thought that was the end of it. But she had in fact acquired two copies and started threatening Emily with exposure. She was blackmailing her. Emily paid her once, but she wouldn't stop, she would not stop."

"So you killed her, didn't you Grace?"

"She was an evil woman, a greedy prostitute. She had to be stopped. I hired two men to beat her, hoping she would be scared, but when I went to see her in the hospital, she was just as adamant. I couldn't let her tarnish Emily's memory."

"And the fact that she probably threatened to expose you as the murderer of Emily and Antonio had nothing to do with it?"

Grace put her hands over her face. "I loved her so much. I saw her with him, before the show at the Walker. I don't know what happened. I couldn't bear it. I told them to stop their fornication. Outside in an alley way like two wild dogs. He laughed at me. I became so angry, I don't know what came over me. I carried a knife with me for protection. I stabbed him first and Emily struggled with me…I don't know. Then the knife was inside of her. There was blood everywhere. I heard someone coming."

"Father," whispered Elizabeth.

"Yes, your father. I hid behind some trash cans and then ran."

"You would have let him hang for your crimes, wouldn't you Grace?" asked Elizabeth. "How could you do that? I think you are insane. You disgust me. To love another woman like that…"

She wasn't insane, thought Klein, just a jealous and deeply troubled person. He was certain that Elizabeth's judgement would have been quite different had the perpetrator been a man. Then the jealousy and rage would also have been considered terrible, but somehow more understandable.

Grace uncovered her face and stared at both Elizabeth and Klein. Deftly, she unbuttoned her handbag and before Klein could move, she pulled her pistol out, stood up from her chair and aimed the gun at Elizabeth's head.

The women at the nearby table screamed as the entire restaurant erupted in shouts of terror. "She has a gun," someone yelled. People dropped to the floor and hid under the tables. From both sides of the room, McCreary and his constables moved forward. McCreary pulled out his revolver as did Taber near the kitchen doorway.

"Why do you want to do that?" asked Klein. He slowly moved his right hand up towards his vest pocket.

"Stop or I'll shoot," she said. Her voice was steady. There was no doubt in Klein's mind that she was quite capable of more killing.

"Put down the gun, Miss," yelled McCreary. "Right now."

"I did it all because I loved her," whispered Grace. "She was so beautiful and full of life."

"Yes, she was," said Klein. "What do you think she would say if she could see you now?"

"I...I don't know," Grace said, her hand beginning to tremble. "I do so miss her."

Suddenly, before Klein could move, Grace turned the pistol and pointed it at her own chest.

"No don't," shouted Klein. He knocked Grace's arm just as she pulled the trigger. The bullet hit her in the shoulder. She dropped slowly to the carpet as the sound of the shot echoed through the grand ballroom.

Klein rushed over and checked the wound, and — despite the flow of blood — decided it might not be fatal. He cradled Grace's head in his hands.

"You'll be all right, Grace."

She smiled back at him. "I'm not insane, you know, Sam. Really, I'm not."

"I know you're not," said Klein, and he meant it.

18

Winnipeg, Canada
August 5, 1914

Winnipeg Free Press, August 5, 1914

TODAY'S MESSAGE

"War is a crime committed by men and therefore, when enough people say it shall not be, it cannot be. This will not happen until women are allowed to say what they think of war."

Mrs. Flora Macdonald Denison, President of the Canadian Suffrage Association in *War and Women (Toronto, 1914).*

NATURALLY ENOUGH, THEY called her Freda. She was a bright, beautiful baby girl with a head full of brown curly hair born in the wee hours of August 3, 1914. Less than twelve hours later, on the first full day of baby Freda Klein's life, Canada joined Britain in declaring war on Germany and the Axis powers.

She had Sarah's features, but anyone looking at her could also tell that she was Sam Klein's daughter. There weren't prouder parents in the entire city. Despite the ominous threat overseas, Klein still handed out cigars to anyone who would take one.

The past few months hadn't been easy. On advice from the doctor, Sarah had been forced to remain bed ridden or risk losing the baby. That was enough for her to curtail her activities and put any further thoughts about going back to work out of her mind for a little while. But she had spoken to Melinda about the possibility of opening a small cosmetics shop, a trend and fashion among women that was quickly gaining in popularity. "Soon no woman will be seen in public without lipstick and face powder," she had predicted when Melinda had come to visit her. Though somewhat skeptical, Melinda had promised her that she would investigate a business opportunity that had become available at a property not too far from Carsley's.

Klein, himself, had been occupied with Grace Ellis's trial. For reasons he couldn't quite explain, he felt sorry for Grace. He knew she was a murderer. Nonetheless, he had pressured Graham Powers to find Grace a decent lawyer, which he had reluctantly agreed to. One of his partners, George Whyte, who specialized in criminal cases, was convinced to take the case. Whyte heeded Klein's recommendation and at his own expense, paid for Dr. Julius Beckerman to visit Winnipeg and give an expert testimony on Grace's behalf.

The proceedings of the trial at the provincial law courts — the revelations of Lesbian love lost — proved far too scandalous and shocking for a majority of the city's citizens. Still, most of them didn't miss one word in the newspapers about this sensational and sordid case. Many days, it pushed stories about the political tensions in Europe and the Manitoba election right off the top of the front page.

Alfred Powers — who had been immediately released from jail with all charges dropped following the events at the Grill Room — didn't miss a day of Grace's trial. He tried to understand Grace's actions, but it was difficult — as difficult as it was for him to comprehend the actions of Emily. At Klein's suggestion, he did send Emily's sister Henny in New York some money and promised more would be forthcoming in the future. It was the least he could do for her under the circumstances.

In the end, neither the members of the jury nor the judge were prepared to hang a woman for murder, particularly since they considered her to be insane. Moreover, in Judge Winston Graves's charge to the jury it was clear that he refused to accept Dr. Beckerman's learned opinion that Grace understood the difference between right and wrong and had killed Emily and Antonio in an uncontrolled jealous rage. In the Judge's view, by the standards established in the M'Naghten Rules, Grace "was suffering from a severe defect of the mind." This also explained, he believed, the subsequent murder of prostitute Katie Johnson.

Uncertain what to do with her, Graves finally decided to incarcerate Grace at the Rockwood Asylum in Kingston, Ontario. She was to be held there for six months, observed and treated. Then doctors were to make a recommendation to the courts.

By mid-July, right around the time of the provincial election that saw Roblin and the Conservatives hold on to power, despite the best efforts of Nellie McClung and the suffragists, Klein heard through Graham Powers that Grace was being co-operative. Nonetheless, she wouldn't accept the opinions of Rockwood's psychiatrists that as an inverted woman she was suffering from a mental illness that in time was curable.

Klein, too, was skeptical of such medical diagnosis. He agreed that sexual inversion might be rightly regarded as abnormal behaviour, maybe even perverse as reporters and others suggested, but he couldn't accept that Grace should be locked in an asylum for the rest of her natural life. That seemed to him more perverse. She needed to be punished—she had murdered three people after all, no one was disputing that fact. But the question was, could she be rehabilitated like the fictional character Norma Trist?

For that matter what was the real significance of her being an invert? Did it make her a more passionate and violent person as the experts maintained? Klein doubted that bit of wisdom — he had seen far too many so-called "normal" people commit acts just as vicious. More to the point, he suspected that Grace's extreme jealous reaction would have been triggered had she fallen in love with a married man who had vowed to leave his wife for her, and then reneged on his promise.

Besides, the world was changing faster than anyone could have dared imagine. Earlier in April, Maloney's stories about Morality Inspector John Jordan's infatuation with Katie Johnson, led to his dismissal from the Winnipeg Police Department. For once, Chief MacPherson was speechless. He could only apologize on behalf of his men and promised to work more diligently at instituting proper moral behaviour among his constables and detectives.

But in Sam Klein's opinion that was the real problem. Not that he condoned John Jordan's actions any more than he did Grace Ellis's. It was only that he felt the time had come for the moralists—even the good-hearted ones like Nellie McClung who fought so valiantly against Roblin and the liquor lobby during the election campaign—to take a step back and examine precisely what they were trying to accomplish. Klein would have agreed with McClung that liquor and drugs like opium threatened to unravel the fabric of Canadian life, and that hoodlums like Kam Kwong got what they deserved. But at the same time there was room for greater latitude of understanding and an appreciation of individual choice. Rules made Klein anxious, especially when they were established with little or no input from the very people for whom they were intended to control and whose lives they meant to regulate.

It was funny, thought Klein, as he stared into the large round eyes of his new baby daughter, Esther Mandelbaum probably understood such sentiments. She had lived her life according to her values and no one else's. Perhaps that was what had drawn someone such as McClung to Esther or Emily in the first place. It was her lively spirit and her love of life.

"Emily was born at the wrong time, that's all," Sarah Klein remarked one day, her arms around her husband, their baby asleep by the fire. "Maybe it'll be different when we're old and grey."

Maybe things would really change, thought Klein, admiring his family. Maybe the world Freda and her children would one day be a part of would be different and more accepting of individual differences. How Sam Klein would like to live long enough to see that.